BONE CROSSED

Titles by Patricia Briggs

The Mercy Thompson Novels
MOON CALLED
BLOOD BOUND
IRON KISSED
BONE CROSSED

The Alpha and Omega Novels
ON THE PROWL
(with Eileen Wilks, Karen Chance, and Sunny)
CRY WOLF

MASQUES
STEAL THE DRAGON
WHEN DEMONS WALK

THE HOB'S BARGAIN

DRAGON BONES
DRAGON BLOOD

RAVEN'S SHADOW
RAVEN'S STRIKE

BONE CROSSED

PATRICIA BRIGGS

ACE BOOKS, NEW YORK

THE BERKLEY PUBLISHING GROUP
Published by the Penguin Group
Penguin Group (USA) Inc.
375 Hudson Street, New York, New York 10014, USA
Penguin Group (Canada), 90 Eglinton Avenue East, Suite 700, Toronto, Ontario M4P 2Y3, Canada
(a division of Pearson Penguin Canada Inc.)
Penguin Books Ltd., 80 Strand, London WC2R 0RL, England
Penguin Group Ireland, 25 St. Stephen's Green, Dublin 2, Ireland (a division of Penguin Books Ltd.)
Penguin Group (Australia), 250 Camberwell Road, Camberwell, Victoria 3124, Australia
(a division of Pearson Australia Group Pty. Ltd.)
Penguin Books India Pvt. Ltd., 11 Community Centre, Panchsheel Park, New Delhi—110 017, India
Penguin Group (NZ), 67 Apollo Drive, Rosedale, North Shore 0632, New Zealand
(a division of Pearson New Zealand Ltd.)
Penguin Books (South Africa) (Pty.) Ltd., 24 Sturdee Avenue, Rosebank, Johannesburg 2196,
South Africa

Penguin Books Ltd., Registered Offices: 80 Strand, London WC2R 0RL, England

This is an original publication of The Berkley Publishing Group.

This is a work of fiction. Names, characters, places, and incidents either are the product of the author's imagination or are used fictitiously, and any resemblance to actual persons, living or dead, business establishments, events, or locales is entirely coincidental. The publisher does not have any control over and does not assume any responsibility for author or third-party websites or their content.

Copyright © 2009 by Hurog, Inc.
Map illustration by Michael Enzweiler.

PRINTING HISTORY
Ace hardcover edition / February 2009

Library of Congress Cataloging-in-Publication Data

Briggs, Patricia.
   Bone crossed / Patricia Briggs.—1st ed.
      p. cm.
   ISBN 978-0-441-01676-1
   1. Thompson, Mercy (Fictitious character)—Fiction. 2. Automobile mechanics—Fiction.
3. Metamorphosis—Fiction. 4. Vampires—Fiction. 5. Werewolves—Fiction. I. Title.

   PS3602.R53165B66 2009
   813'.6—dc22

                                                                               2008046403

PRINTED IN THE UNITED STATES OF AMERICA

10 9 8 7 6 5 4 3 2 1

For Jordan, whimsical, musical friend of critters furred, scaled, and feathered

ACKNOWLEDGMENTS

There are dozens of people who have helped in this endeavor, but I am especially grateful to those who, on a moment's notice, went through the manuscript with a fine-tooth comb—Mike Briggs, Dave and Katharine Carson, Laurie Martin, Jean Matteaucci, Anne Peters, Kaye Roberson, and Anne Sowards. I also would like to take a moment to thank the people who've worked so hard to determine that, yes, you can indeed cast a silver bullet—Mike Briggs, Dr. Kevin Jaansalu, Dr. Kyle Roberson, and Tom Lenz.

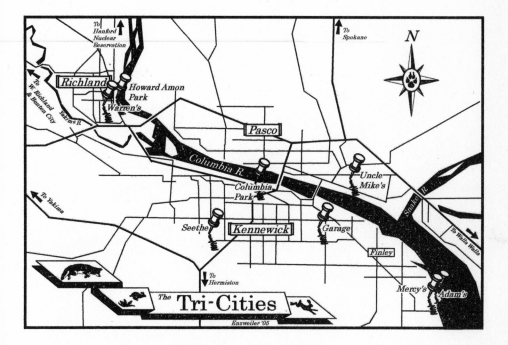

1

I STARED AT MY REFLECTION IN THE MIRROR. I WASN'T pretty, but my hair was thick and brushed my shoulders. My skin was darker on my arms and face than it was on the rest of my body, but at least, thanks to my Blackfoot father, I'd never be pasty pale.

There were two stitches Samuel had put in the cut on my chin, and the bruise on my shoulder (not extensive damage considering I'd been fighting something that liked to eat children and had knocked out a werewolf). The dark thread looked from some angles like the legs of a shiny black spider. Aside from that slight damage, there was nothing wrong with my body. Karate and mechanicking kept me in good shape.

My soul was a lot more battered than my body, but I couldn't see it in the mirror. Hopefully no one else could either. It was that invisible damage that left me afraid to leave the bathroom and face Adam, who waited in my bedroom. Though I knew with absolute certainty that Adam wouldn't do anything I didn't want him to do—and had wanted him to do for a long time.

I could ask him to leave. To give me more time. I stared at the woman in the mirror, but all she did was stare back.

I'd killed the man who'd raped me. Was I going to let him have this last victory? Let him destroy me as he'd intended?

"Mercy?" Adam didn't have to raise his voice. He knew I could hear him.

"Careful," I told him as I left off mirror-gazing and began pulling on clean underwear and an old T-shirt. "I have an ancient walking stick, and I know how to use it."

"The walking stick is lying across your bed," he said.

When I came out of the bathroom, Adam was lying across my bed, too.

He wasn't tall, but he didn't need height to add to the impression he made. Wide cheekbones and a full, soft mouth topping a stubborn jaw combined to give him movie-star beauty. When his eyes were open, they were a dark chocolate only a shade lighter than mine. His body was almost as pretty as his face—though I knew he didn't think of himself that way. He kept himself in shape because he was Alpha and his body was a tool he used to keep his pack safe. He'd been a soldier before he was Changed, and the military training was still there in the way he moved and the way he took charge.

"When Samuel gets back from the hospital, he's going to spend the rest of the night at my house," Adam said without opening his eyes. Samuel was my roommate, a doctor, and a lone wolf. Adam's house was behind mine, with about ten acres between them—three were mine and the rest were Adam's. "We have time to talk."

"You look horrible," I said, not quite truthfully. He did look tired, with dark circles under his eyes, but nothing short of mutilation could make him look terrible. "Don't they have beds in D.C.?"

He'd had to go to Washington (the capital—we were in the state) this weekend to clean up a little mess that was sort of my fault. Of course if he hadn't ripped Tim's corpse into bits on camera, and if the resultant DVD hadn't landed on a senator's desk, there wouldn't have been a problem. So it was partially his fault, too.

Mostly it was Tim's fault, and whoever had made a copy of the DVD and mailed it off. I'd taken care of Tim. Bran, the head-honcho werewolf above all of the other head-honcho werewolves, was apparently taking care of the other person. Last year, I would have expected to hear about a funeral. This year, with the werewolves barely having admitted their existence to the world, Bran would probably be more circumspect. Whatever that would mean.

Adam opened his eyes and looked at me. In the dimness of the room (he'd only turned on the small light on the little table by my bed), his eyes looked black. There was a bleakness in his face that hadn't been there before, and I knew it was because of me. Because he hadn't been able to keep me safe—and people like Adam take that pretty seriously.

Personally, I figured it was up to me to keep me safe. Sometimes it might mean calling in friends, but it was *my* responsibility. Still, he saw it as a failure.

"So have you made up your mind?" he asked.

Would I accept him as my mate, he meant. The question had been up in the air too long, and it was affecting his ability to keep his pack under control. Ironically, what happened with Tim had resolved the issue that had kept me from accepting Adam for months. I figured if I could fight back against the fairy magic potion Tim had fed me, a little Alpha mojo wasn't going to turn me into a docile slave either.

Maybe I should have thanked him before I hit him with the tire iron.

Adam isn't Tim, I told myself. I thought of Adam's rage when he'd broken down the door to my garage, of his despair when he persuaded me to drink out of that damned fae goblet again. In addition to robbing me of my will, the goblet also had the power to heal—and I'd needed a lot of healing by that point. It had worked, but Adam had felt like he was betraying me, believed I'd hate him for it. But he'd done it anyway. I figured it was because he wasn't lying when he said he loved me. When I'd hidden in shame—I put that down to the fairy brew, because I knew . . . I *knew* I had nothing to be ashamed about—he'd pulled my coyote self out from under his bed, bitten my nose for being foolish, and held me all night long. Then he'd surrounded me with his pack and safety whether I needed it or not.

Tim was dead. And he'd always been a loser. I'd be damned if I was going to be the victim of a loser—or anyone else.

"Mercy?" Adam stayed on his back on my bed, taking the position of vulnerability.

In answer, I pulled the T-shirt over my head and dropped it on the floor.

Adam was off the bed faster than I'd ever seen him move, bringing the comforter with him. He had it wrapped around me before I could blink . . . and then I was pressed tightly against him, my bare breasts resting against his chest. He'd tipped his head to the side so my face was pressed against his jaw and cheek.

"I meant to get the blanket between us," he said tightly. His heart pounded against mine, and his arms were shaking and rock hard.

"I didn't mean you had to sleep with me right now—a simple 'yes' would have done."

I knew he was aroused—even a regular person without a coyote nose would have known it. I slid my hands up from his hips to his hard belly and up his ribs and listened to his heart rate pick up even further and a light sweat broke out on his jaw under my slow caress. I could feel the muscles in his cheek move as he clenched his teeth, felt the heat that flushed his skin. I blew in his ear, and he jumped away from me as though I'd stuck him with a cattle prod.

Streaks of amber lit his eyes, and his lips were fuller, redder. I dropped the comforter on top of my shirt.

"Damn it, Mercy." He didn't like to swear in front of women. I always counted it a personal triumph when I could make him do it. "It hasn't even been a week since you were raped. I'm not sleeping with you until you've talked to someone, a counselor, a psychologist."

"I'm fine," I said, though in fact, once distance had released me from the safety he brought with him, I was aware of a sick churning in my stomach.

Adam turned so he was facing the window, his back to me. "No, you're not. Remember, you can't lie to a wolf, love." He let out a breath of air too forcefully to be a sigh. He rubbed his hair briskly, trying to get rid of excess energy. Obligingly, it stuck up in small curls that he usually kept too short to look anything but neat and well-groomed. "Who am I talking about?" he asked, though I didn't think the question was directed at me. "This is Mercy. Getting you to talk about anything personal is like pulling teeth at the best of times. Getting you to talk to a stranger . . ."

I hadn't thought myself particularly closemouthed. Actually, I'd been accused of having a smart mouth. Samuel had told me more than once that I'd probably live longer if I learned to bite my tongue occasionally.

So I waited, without saying a word, for Adam to decide what he wanted to do.

The room wasn't cold, but I was shivering a little anyway—it must be nerves. If Adam didn't hurry up and do something, though, I was going to be throwing up in the bathroom. I'd spent too much time worshipping the porcelain goddess since Tim had made me overdose on fairy juice to view the thought with any equanimity.

He wasn't watching me, but he didn't need to be. Emotions have a scent. He swung back to look at me with a frown. He took in my state with one comprehensive look.

He swore and strode back to me, wrapping me in his arms. He pulled me tight against him, making low, soothing sounds in the back of his throat. He rocked me gently.

I took a deep breath of Adam-scented air and tried to think. Normally, this wouldn't be difficult for me. But normally I wasn't all but naked in the arms of the hottest man I knew.

I'd misunderstood what he'd wanted.

To double-check, I cleared my throat. "When you said you needed my answer to your claim today—you weren't actually asking for sex?"

His body jerked involuntarily as he laughed, rubbing his jaw against my face. "So, you think I'm the kind of person who'd do something like that? After what happened just last week?"

"I thought that's what it took," I mumbled, feeling my cheeks heat up.

"*How* long did you spend in the Marrok's pack?"

He knew how long. He was just making me feel stupid. "Mating wasn't something everyone talked to me about," I told him defensively. "Just Samuel . . ."

Adam laughed again, one of his hands on my shoulder, the other moving in a light caress on my butt, which should have tickled but didn't. "I just bet *he* was telling you the truth, the whole truth, and nothing but the truth right then."

I tightened my grip on him—somehow my hands had landed on his lower back. "Probably not. So all you needed was my agreement?"

He grunted. "It won't help with the pack, not until it's for real. But with Samuel out of the way, I thought you'd be able to decide if you were interested or not. If you weren't interested, I could regroup. If you agreed to be mine, I can wait until Hell freezes over for you."

His words sounded reasonable, but his scent told me something else. It told me that my reasonable tones had soothed his worries, and his mind was now on something other than our discussion.

Fair enough. Being this close to him, feeling his heat against me, feeling his heartbeat race because he wanted me . . . someone told me that knowing someone desires you is the greatest aphrodisiac. It was certainly true for me.

"Of course," he said, still in that curiously calm voice, "waiting is much easier in abstract than reality. I need you to tell me to back off, all right?"

"Mmm," I said. He brought a cleanness with him that washed the feel of Tim off my skin far better than the shower did—but only when he touched me.

"Mercy."

I lowered my hands, sliding them beneath the waistline of his jeans and digging my nails lightly into his skin.

He growled something more, but neither of us was listening. He turned his head and tilted it. I expected serious and got playful as he nipped at my lower lip. The roughness of his teeth sent tingles to my fingertips, zings past my knees and down to my toes. Potent things, Adam's teeth.

I brought my suddenly shaking hands around to worry at the button on his jeans, and Adam jerked his head up and put a staying hand on mine.

Then I heard it, too.

"German car," he said.

I sighed, slumping against him. "Swedish," I corrected him. "Four-year-old Volvo station wagon. Gray."

He looked at me in surprise that quickly turned to comprehension. "You know the car."

I moaned and tried to hide in his shoulder. "Damn, damn. It was the newspapers."

"Who is it, Mercy?"

Gravel shooshed, and headlights flashed on my window as the car turned into the driveway. "My mom," I told him. "Her sense of timing is unreal. I should have realized she would read about . . . about *it*." I didn't want to name what had happened to me, what I'd done to Tim, out loud. Not while I was mostly naked with Adam, anyway.

"You didn't call her."

I shook my head. I should have, I knew it. But it had been one of those things I just couldn't face.

He was smiling now. "You get dressed. I'll go stall her until you're ready to come out."

"There is *no way* I'll ever be ready for this," I told him.

He sobered, put his face next to mine, and rested his forehead against me. "Mercy. It will be all right."

Then he left, shutting the door to my bedroom as my doorbell rang the first time. It rang twice more before he opened the outside door, and he wasn't being slow.

I grabbed clothes and desperately tried to remember if we'd done the dishes from dinner. It was my turn. If it had been Samuel's turn, I wouldn't have had to worry. It was stupid. I knew that she could care less about the dishes—but it gave me something to do other than panic.

I'd never even considered calling her. Maybe in ten years I might feel ready.

I pulled on my pants and left my feet bare while I searched frantically for a bra.

"She knows you're here," Adam said on the other side of the door—as if he were leaning against it. "She'll be out in a minute."

"I don't know who you think you are"—my mother's voice was low and dangerous—"but if you don't get out of my way right this instant, it won't matter."

Adam was the Alpha werewolf in charge of the local pack. He was tough. He could be mean when he had to—and he wouldn't stand a chance against my mom.

"Bra, bra, bra," I chanted as I pulled one out of the dirty-clothes basket and hooked it. I pulled the thing around so fast I wouldn't be surprised to discover I'd given myself a rug burn. "Shirt. Shirt." I ransacked my drawers and found and discarded two shirts. "Clean shirt, clean shirt."

"Mercy?" called Adam, sounding a little desperate—how well I knew that feeling.

"Mom, leave him alone!" I said. "I'll be right out."

Frustrated, I stared at my room. I had to have a clean shirt somewhere. I had just been wearing one—but it had disappeared in my search for a bra. Finally, I pulled on a shirt that said *1984*: GOVERN-MENT FOR DUMMIES on the back. It was clean, or at least it didn't stink too badly. The oil smudge on the shoulder looked permanent.

I took a deep breath and opened the door. I had to duck around Adam, who was leaning against the door frame.

"Hey, Mom," I said breezily. "I see you've met my—" What? Mate? I didn't think that was something my mother needed to hear. "I see you've met Adam."

"Mercedes Athena Thompson," snapped my mother. "Explain to me why I had to learn about what happened to you from a newspaper?"

I'd been avoiding meeting her gaze, but once she three-named me, I had no choice.

My mother is five-foot-nothing. She's only seventeen years older than me, which means she's not yet fifty and looks thirty. She can still wear the belt buckles she won barrel racing on their original belts. She's usually blond—I'm pretty sure it's her natural color—but the shade changes from year to year. This year it was strawberry gold. Her eyes are big and blue and innocent-looking, her nose slightly tip-tilted, and her mouth full and round.

With strangers, she sometimes plays a dumb blonde, batting her eyelashes and speaking in a breathy voice that anyone who watched old movies would recognize from *Some Like It Hot* or *Bus Stop*. My mother has never, to my knowledge, changed her own flat tire.

If the sharp anger in her voice hadn't been a cover for the bruised look in her eyes, I could have responded in kind. Instead, I shrugged.

"I don't know, Mom. After it happened . . . I stayed coyote for a couple of days." I had a half-hysterical vision of calling her, and saying, *"By the way, Mom, guess what happened to me today . . ."*

She looked me in the eyes, and I thought she saw more than I wanted her to. "Are you all right?"

I started to say yes, but a lifetime of living with creatures who could smell a lie had left me with a habit of honesty. "Mostly," I said, compromising. "It helps that he's dead." It was humiliating that my chest was getting tight. I'd given myself all the self-pity time I would allow.

Mom could cuddle her children like any of the best of parents, but I should have trusted her more. She knew all about the importance of standing on your own two feet. Her right hand was balled into a white-knuckled fist, but when she spoke, her voice was brisk.

"All right," she said, as if we'd covered everything she was going to ask. I knew better, but I also knew it would be later and private.

She turned her angelic blue eyes on Adam. "Who are you, and what are you doing in my daughter's house at eleven at night?"

"I'm not sixteen," I said in a voice even I could tell was sulky. "I can even have a man stay all night if I want to."

Mom and Adam both ignored me.

Adam had remained in position against my bedroom door frame, his body held a little more casually than usual. I thought he was trying to give my mother the impression that he was at home here: someone who had authority to keep her out of my room. He lifted an eyebrow and showed not even a touch of the panic I'd heard in his voice earlier. "I'm Adam Hauptman, I live on the other side of her back fence."

She scowled at him. "The Alpha? The divorced man with the teenage daughter?"

He gave her one of his sudden smiles, and I knew my mom had made yet another conquest: she's pretty cute when she scowls, and

Adam didn't know many people gutsy enough to scowl at him. I had a sudden revelation. I'd been making a tactical error for the past few years if I'd really wanted him to quit flirting with me. I should have smiled and smirked and batted my eyelashes at him. Obviously, a woman snarling at him was something he enjoyed. He was too busy looking at my mom's scowl to see mine.

"That's right, ma'am." Adam quit leaning against the door and took a couple of steps into the room. "Good to meet you at last, Margi. Mercy speaks of you often."

I didn't know what my mother would have said to that, doubtless something polite. But with a popping sound like eggs cracking on a cement floor, something appeared between Mom and Adam, a foot or so above the carpet. It was a human-sized something, black and crunchy. It dropped to the floor, reeking of char, old blood, and rotten corpses.

I stared at it for too long, my eyes failing to find a pattern that agreed with what my nose told me. Even knowing that only a few things could just appear in my living room without using the door couldn't make me acknowledge what it was. It was the green shirt, torn and stained, with the hindquarters of a familiar Great Dane still visible, that forced me to admit that this black and shrunken thing was Stefan.

I dropped to my knees beside him and reached out before snatching my hand back, afraid to damage him more. He was obviously dead, but since he was a vampire, that wasn't as hopeless a thing as it might have been.

"Stefan?" I said.

I wasn't the only one who jumped when he grabbed my wrist. The skin on his hand was dry and crackled disconcertingly against my skin.

Stefan has been my friend since the first day I moved here to the Tri-Cities. He is charming, funny, and generous—if given to miscalculations on how forgiving I might be about innocent people he killed trying to protect me.

It was still all I could do not to jerk away and rub off the feel of his brittle skin on my arm. Ick. Ick. Ick. And I had the horrible feeling that it was hurting him to hold on to me, that at any moment his skin would crack and fall off.

His eyes opened to slits, his irises crimson instead of brown. His mouth opened and shut twice without making any sound. Then his hand tightened on mine until I couldn't have pulled free if I had wanted to. He sucked in a breath of air so he could talk, but he couldn't do it quite right, and I heard air hissing out of the side of his ribs, where it had no business escaping from.

"She knows." His voice didn't sound like his at all. It was rough and dry. As he pulled my hand slowly toward his face, with the last of the air from that breath, he said intently, *"Run."* And with those words, the person who was my friend disappeared under the fierce hunger in his face.

Looking into his mad eyes, I thought his advice was worth taking—too bad I wasn't going to be able to break free to follow it. He was slow, but he had me, and I wasn't a werewolf or vampire with supernatural strength to help myself out.

I heard the distinctive *clack* of a bullet chambering, and a quick glance showed me my mother with a wicked-looking Glock out and pointed at Stefan. It was pink and black—trust my mom to have a Barbie gun, cute but deadly.

"It's all right," I told her hastily—my mother wouldn't hesitate to fire if she thought he was going to hurt me. Normally I wouldn't worry about someone shooting at Stefan, vampires not being that vulnerable to guns, but he was in bad shape. "He's on our side." Hard to sound convincing when he was pulling me toward him, but I did my best.

Adam grabbed Stefan's wrist and held it, so instead of Stefan pulling me toward him, the vampire was slowly raising his own head off the floor. As he came closer to my arm, Stefan opened his mouth and scraps of burnt skin fell on my tan carpet. His fangs were white and lethal-looking, and also a lot bigger than I remembered them being.

My breathing picked up, but I didn't jerk back and whine, "Get it off! Get it off!"—full points to me. Instead, I leaned over Stefan and put my head into Adam's shoulder. It put my neck at risk, but the smell of werewolf and Adam helped mask the stench of what had been done to Stefan. If Stefan needed blood to survive, I'd donate to him.

"It's all right, Adam," I said. "Let him go."

"Don't put down the gun," Adam told my mother. "Mercy, if this doesn't work, you call my house and tell Darryl to collect whoever is there and bring them here."

And, in an act of bravery that was completely in character, Adam put his wrist in front of Stefan's face. The vampire didn't appear to notice, still pulling himself up by his grip on my arm. He wasn't breathing, so he couldn't scent Adam, and I didn't think he was focusing any too well either.

I should have tried to stop Adam—I'd fed Stefan before without any ill effects that I knew of, and I was *pretty* sure that Stefan cared whether I lived or died. I wasn't so sure how he felt about Adam. But I was remembering Stefan telling me that there "shouldn't" be any problems because it had only been the once, and I'd met a few of Stefan's band of sheep—the people who served as his breakfast, dinner, and lunch. They were all completely devoted to him. Don't get me wrong, he's a great guy for a vampire—but I somehow doubted that those people, mostly women, could live together devoted to one man without some sort of vampire mesmerism at work. And I'd sort of had my fill of magical compulsion for the year.

Any protest I made to Adam would be an exercise in futility anyway. He was feeling especially protective of me at that moment—and all I would do was stir up tempers, his, mine, and my mother's.

Adam pressed his wrist against Stefan's mouth, and the vampire paused his incremental closing of the distance between my arm and his fangs. He seemed confused for a moment—then he drew air in through his nose.

Stefan's teeth sank into Adam's wrist, his free hand shot up to grab Adam's arm, and his eyes closed—all so fast it looked like the motion of a cheaply drawn cartoon.

Adam sucked in his breath, but I couldn't tell if it was because it hurt him or because it felt good. When Stefan had fed from me, I'd been in pretty rough shape. I didn't remember much about it.

It was strangely intimate, Stefan holding me as he drank from Adam's wrist, and Adam leaning harder into me as Stefan fed. Intimate with an audience. I turned my head to see that my mother still held her gun in a steady two-handed grip, pointed at Stefan's head. Her face as calm as if she saw burnt bodies appear out of nowhere, then rise from the dead to sink fangs into whoever was closest to them all the time, though I knew that wasn't true. I wasn't sure she'd ever even seen one of the werewolves in wolf form.

"Mom," I said, "the vampire is Stefan, he's a friend of mine."

"I should put the gun away? Are you sure? He doesn't look like a friend."

I looked at Stefan, who was looking better, though I still wouldn't have recognized him without my nose. "Truthfully, I'm not sure how much good it would do anyway. Bullets, if they are silver, may work on werewolves, but I don't think any bullets do much to vampires."

She tucked the Glock, hot, into the holster inside the waistline of the back of her jeans. "So what *do* you do to vampires?"

Someone knocked on the door. I hadn't heard anyone drive up, but I'd been a little distracted.

"Don't let them in your home in the first place," suggested Adam.

Mom, who'd been on the way to the door, stopped. "Is this likely to be a vampire?"

"Better let me get it," I said. I wiggled my arm, and Stefan released me and took a better grip on Adam. "Are you all right, Adam?"

"He's too weak to feed fast," Adam commented. "I'm good for a while yet. If you'll get my phone out for me and hit the speed dial, I'll call for some more wolves, though. I doubt one feeding will be enough."

With Mom watching, I behaved myself while I dug his phone out of the holder on his belt. Instead of taking the time to sort through his contacts, I just punched in his house number and handed him the ringing phone. Whoever was outside was growing impatient.

I straightened my shirt and took a quick look at myself to make sure there wasn't anything that said, "Hey, I have a vampire in my house."

I was going to have a bruise on my forearm, but it wasn't too noticeable yet. I slipped past Mom and opened the door about six inches.

The woman standing on the porch didn't look familiar. She was about my height and age. Her dark hair had been highlighted with a lighter shade (or her light brown hair had been striped with a darker color). She wore so much foundation that I could smell it over the perfume that a purely human nose might find light and attractive. Her grooming was immaculate, like a purebred dog ready to be shown—or a very expensive call girl.

Not a person you'd expect to find on the porch of an old mobile home out in the boonies of Eastern Washington at night.

"Mercy?"

If she hadn't spoken, I'd never have recognized her because my nose was full of perfume and she didn't look anything like the girl I'd gone to college with. "Amber?"

Amber had been my college roommate Charla's best friend. She'd been studying to be a veterinarian, but I'd heard she'd dropped out her first year in vet school. I hadn't heard from her since I'd graduated.

When I'd last seen Amber she'd been wearing a Mohawk and had had a ring in her nose (which had been bigger) and a small tattooed hummingbird at the corner of her eye. She and Charla had been best friends in high school. Though it had been Charla who had decided they shouldn't room together, Amber had always blamed me for it. We had been acquaintances rather than friends.

Amber laughed, doubtless at the bewildered look on my face. There was something brittle in the sound, not that I was in any position to be picky. My manner was stiffer than usual, too. I had a vampire feeding from a werewolf behind me; I wondered what *she* was hiding.

"It's been a long time," she said, after a short, awkward silence.

I joined her out on the porch and shut the door behind me, trying not to look like I was keeping her out. "What brings you here?"

She folded her arms over her chest and turned to gaze at my

scraggly-looking field where a rusty VW Rabbit rested on three tires. From where we stood, the graffiti, the missing door, and the cracked windshield weren't visible, but it looked junky anyway. The old wreck was a joke between Adam and me, and I wasn't going to apologize for it.

"I read about you in the paper," she said.

"You live in the Tri-Cities?"

She shook her head. "Spokane. It made CNN, too, didn't you know? The fae, werewolves, death . . . how could they resist?" For a moment there was a flash of humor in her voice, though her face stayed disconcertingly blank.

Lovely. The whole world knew I'd been raped. Yeah, that might have struck me as funny, too—if I'd been Lucrezia Borgia. There were a lot of reasons I'd never bothered to keep in contact with Amber.

She hadn't driven over from Spokane to hunt me down after ten years and tell me she'd read about the attack, either. "So you read about me and decided it might be fun to tell me that the story about how I killed my rapist was all over the country? You drove a hundred and fifty miles for that?"

"Obviously not." She turned back to face me, and the awkward stranger had been replaced by the polished pro who was even more a stranger to me. "Look. Do you remember when we took a day trip to Portland to see that play? We went to the bar afterward, and you told us about the ghost in the ladies' room."

"I was drunk," I told her—which was true enough. "I think I told you I was raised by werewolves, too."

"Yes," she said with sudden intentness. "I thought you were just telling stories, but now we all know that werewolves are real, just like the fae. And you're dating one."

That would have come out in the newspaper story, I thought. Double yippee. There was a time when I tried to stay out of the spotlight because it was safer. It was still safer, but I hadn't been doing so good at stealthy living the past year.

Unaffected by my inner dialogue, Amber kept talking. "So I thought if you were dating one now, you had probably been telling the truth then. And if you told the truth about the werewolves, then you were probably telling the truth about seeing ghosts, too."

Anyone else would have forgotten about that, but Amber had a mind like a steel trap. She remembered everything. It was after that trip that I quit drinking alcohol. People who know other people's secrets can't afford to do things that impair their ability to control their mouths.

"My house is haunted," she said.

I saw something move out of the corner of my eye. I took a step toward Amber and turned a little. I still couldn't see anything out there, but with Amber a little downwind so her perfume didn't ruin my nose, I could smell it: vampire.

"And you want *me* to do something about it?" I asked. "You need to call a priest." Amber was Catholic.

"No one believes me," she said starkly. "My husband thinks I'm crazy." The porch light caught her eyes, just for a minute, and I could see that her pupils were dilated. I wondered if it was just the darkness of the night or if she was on something.

She was making me uneasy, but I was pretty sure it was just the weirdness of seeing Amber, queen of the unconventional, dressed up like a rich man's mistress. There was something soft and helpless about her now that made me think *prey*, while the Amber I'd known would have taken a baseball bat to anyone who annoyed her. She wouldn't have been afraid of a ghost.

Of course, my unease could have been caused by the vampire lurking in the shadows or by the one in my home.

"Look," I said. Stefan and what had been done to him were more important to me than what had happened to Amber, or anything she might want from me. "I can't get away right now—I have company. Why don't you give me your phone number, and I'll call you as soon as things calm down."

She fumbled her purse open and handed me a card. It was printed on expensive high-cotton paper, but all that was on it was her first name and a phone number.

"Thank you." She sounded relieved, the tension flowing from her shoulders. She gave me a small smile. "I'm sorry that you were attacked—but I'm not surprised you got your own back. You were always rather good at that." Without waiting for me to answer, she walked down the steps and got into her car, a newer Miata convertible with the soft top up. She backed out of the driveway without looking at me again and sped off into the night.

I wished she hadn't been wearing perfume. She'd been upset about something—she'd always been a terrible liar. But the timing was just a little too convenient: Stefan arrives, tells me to run, and Amber arrives with a place for me to run to.

I knew what Stefan had been telling me to run from, and it wasn't him. "She knows," he'd said.

"She" was Marsilia, the Mistress of the Tri-Cities' vampires. She'd sent me out hunting a vampire who'd been on a killing spree that risked her seethe. She'd figured I was her best chance to find him because I can sense ghosts that other people don't see, and vampire lairs tend to attract ghosts.

She hadn't thought I would really be able to kill him. When I did, it made her very unhappy. The vamp I'd killed had been special, more powerful than the others because he'd been demon-ridden. That the demon had made him crazy and he'd been killing humans left and right hadn't bothered her except that it might have exposed the vampires to the human world. He'd gone out of control when he'd grown more powerful than his maker, but Marsilia believed that she could have fixed that, taken control of him. She used me to find him—she'd been sure he'd kill me.

And she'd have been right if I hadn't had friends.

Since she'd sent me after him, she couldn't seek retribution without risking losing control of her seethe. Vampires take things like that very seriously.

I'd have been safe if it hadn't been for the second vampire.

Andre had been Marsilia's left hand where Stefan was her right. He'd also been responsible for creating the demon-possessing vampire who'd killed more people than I could count on both hands. And Andre and Marsilia had intended to make more. One had been more than enough for me. So I'd killed Andre, knowing that it meant my death.

But Stefan had hidden my crime. Hidden it with the deaths of two innocent people whose only crimes had been that they were Andre's victims. He'd saved me, but the cost had been too high. Their deaths had bought me two months.

Marsilia knew. She'd have never hurt Stefan so badly for anything else.

She'd tortured and starved him and let him free to come to me. I looked down at the red marks Stefan had put on my arm—if he'd killed me, no blame would have fallen on her.

There was a noise, and I looked up. Darryl and Peter were walking past the battered hulk of the Rabbit.

Darryl was tall, athletic, and Adam's second. He got his dark skin from his African father and his eyes from his Chinese mother. His perfect features came from the happy combination of very different genes, but the grace of his stride came from the accident that had turned him into a werewolf. He liked nice clothes, and the crisp cotton shirt he wore probably cost more than I made in a week.

I didn't know how old he was, but I was pretty sure he wasn't much older than he looked. There's something about the older wolves, an air they carry of being not quite of this age of cars, cell phones, and TVs, that Darryl didn't have.

Peter was old enough to have been in the cavalry, but here and now he worked as a plumber. He was good at his job, and he had a half dozen people (human) on his payroll. But he walked to the right and behind Darryl because Darryl was very dominant and Peter was one of the few submissives in Adam's pack.

Darryl stopped at the foot of the porch. He didn't like me much most of the time. I'd finally decided it was snobbery—he was a wolf and I a coyote. He was a Ph.D. working in a high-priced think tank, and I was a mechanic with dirt under my fingernails.

And worst of all, if I was Adam's mate, he had to follow my orders. Sometimes the chauvinism that permeates the rules by which the werewolves operate works backward. No matter how submissive the mate of the Alpha is, her commands are second only to his.

When he didn't say anything, I just opened the door and led Adam's two wolves into my home.

2

STEFAN WASN'T AMENABLE TO CHANGING DONORS, SO
Peter and Darryl knelt, one on either side, and began to pry his grip
loose. When I approached to help, Adam snarled at me.

If he hadn't snarled, I'd probably have let the wolves take care
of it. After all, they all have awesome werewolf superstrength. But if
Adam and I were going to have a relationship, something that was
giving me butterflies already, it was going to be on an equal footing.
I couldn't afford to back down when Adam growled.

Besides, I despised the cowardly part of me that flinched at his
anger. Even if I was pretty sure it was the smart part.

Peter and Darryl were working on Stefan's hands, so I went to
his head. I slipped my fingers into one side of his mouth, hoping
that vampires had the same reaction to pressure points as the rest

of us. But I didn't need to use any nerve pinches, because as soon as my fingers touched his mouth, he shuddered and released Adam, his arms going limp at the same time as he pulled his fangs out.

"Won't," Stefan said as I pulled my fingers out of his mouth. "Won't." It came out a whisper and faded eerily as he ran out of air.

His head moved until he rested against my shoulder, his eyes closed. His face almost looked like his now, filled out and healing. The broken places on his skin, hands, and lips looked like wounds now. It said something about how bad he'd been that oozing wounds were an improvement.

If his body hadn't shook against me as if he were having an epileptic fit, I'd have been happier.

"Do you know what's wrong with him?" I asked Adam helplessly.

"I do," Peter said. He casually pulled a huge pocketknife out of its belt sheath and made a small cut in his wrist.

He moved me out from under Stefan and moved him around until Stefan was lying down with his head on Peter's lap, held steady by the werewolf's unwounded hand. Peter held his bloody wrist in front of the vampire, who clamped his lips together and turned his head away.

Adam, who had wrapped his hand around his own wrist to staunch the bleeding, leaned forward. "Stefan. It's all right. It's not Mercy. It's not Mercy."

Red eyes slitted open, and the vampire made a sound I'd never heard before . . . and wished I could still say that. It raised every hair on the back of my neck, high-pitched and thin like a dog whistle but harsher somehow. He struck and Peter jerked, gritting his teeth and hissing.

I didn't notice when my mother left us, but she must have at some point because she had Samuel's big first-aid kit from the main bathroom open on the couch. She knelt by Adam, but he surged to his feet.

Alpha werewolves don't admit to any pain in public, and seldom in private. His wrist might look like it had been savaged, but he'd never let my mother do anything about it. I stood up, too.

"Here," I said, before he could say something to offend her or vice versa. "Let me see."

I tugged and pulled until I could see the wounds. "He'll be all right," I told Mom with satisfaction. "It's scabbed over already. A half hour from now it'll just be a few red marks."

That was good.

My mother raised her eyebrow, and murmured, "And to think I was always worried that you didn't have any friends. I suppose I should have been counting my blessings."

I gave her a sharp look, and she smiled past the worry in her eyes. "Vampires, Mercy? I thought they were made-up."

She had always been good at making me feel guilty, which was more than Bran had ever managed. "I couldn't tell you," I said. "They don't like it when humans know about them. It would have put you in danger." She narrowed her eyes at me. "Besides, Mom, I've never actually seen any in Portland." And had been very careful not to look when I smelled them. Vampires like Portland—lots of rainy days.

"Can all of them just pop in wherever they want to?"

I shook my head, then reconsidered. "I only know of two, and Stefan's one of them."

Adam was watching Stefan feed; he looked worried. I hadn't realized he and Stefan were more than casual acquaintances.

"Is he going to be all right?" Mom asked.

Adam was pale but healing just fine. Other wolves would have taken longer, but Adam was an Alpha, and his pack gave him more power than other wolves had. But if Stefan gnawed on Peter the way he'd chewed up Adam, it would take Peter a while longer to heal.

She looked at me, and her dimples peeped out. "I was speaking of the vampire. You do have it bad, don't you?"

I'd been trying not to dwell on Stefan's condition and why it was so bad—and how it was my fault. "I don't know, Mom," I leaned against her, just a little, before straightening to stand on my own. "I don't know that much about vampires. They're hard to kill, but I've never seen one as bad as this who survived." Daniel, Stefan's . . . what? Friend hadn't quite covered it. Maybe just *Stefan's*. Daniel had quit feeding because he believed he had run crazy and killed a whole bunch of people. He'd looked bad, but not as bad as Stefan.

"You care about him, too."

She didn't sound surprised, but she would have been if she knew as much as I did about vampires.

I knew Stefan kept a bunch of people virtual prisoners to feed from—though none of them had seemed to mind. I'd had my rose-colored glasses ripped off when he'd killed two helpless people, people I'd *rescued*, in order to protect me. It might have been the enigmatic vampire Wulfe who'd twisted their necks, but Stefan had been the director of that macabre little conspiracy.

But it hurt to see him like this.

"Yes," I told Mom.

"You can let him go now," Adam told Darryl. "He's feeding."

Darryl dropped Stefan's arm and stepped back as if fearing contamination. There wasn't a lot of room left in my living room, but he bumped his back up to the counter that separated the larger room from the kitchen and curled his lip. Adam gave him a considering look before turning his attention to the other wolf.

"Are you all right, Peter?" Adam asked.

I looked at the werewolf and saw that there was sweat gathering on his forehead and he'd closed his eyes and turned them away from the vampire, who was sprawled across his lap and fastened to his arm. Judging from the difference between his reaction and Adam's, it might have been better to find a more dominant wolf to feed to Stefan.

Peter didn't answer, and Adam walked behind him so he could put a hand on the skin of his neck. Almost immediately I could see the impact of that touch as Peter relaxed against his Alpha with a sigh of relief.

"I'm sorry," Adam said. "If there'd been someone else . . . Ben should be here soon."

There had been Darryl, who was staring at his shoes. Adam's remark hadn't been pointed, but Darryl looked like he'd been slapped.

Peter shook his head. "No problem. It was bad for a minute, though. I thought it was supposed to be a myth that vampires could trap your mind."

That was one of the problems with the vamps. Like the fae, there was so much misinformation out there it was hard to sift truth from fact.

"He's not himself," I found myself saying. "He wouldn't do it on purpose." I wasn't entirely sure that was truthful, but it sounded good. He'd taken me over once. It had all worked out just fine, but I'd rather it never happened again.

My mother looked at me. "Do you have orange juice or something else with sugar in it for the blood donors?"

I should have thought of that. I hopped over Stefan's legs so I could go to the kitchen and look. Once my roommate had declared me completely unadventurous in my food choices, he'd taken over shopping. I had no idea what he'd managed to stuff into the fridge.

I found a half-full bottle of low-pulp orange juice and poured two glasses. I handed the first to Adam and held the second in front of Peter.

"Do you need help?"

Peter gave me a half smile, shook his head, and took the glass, downing it in quick time and handing me back the glass.

"More?"

"Not now," he said. "Maybe when it's over."

MOM AND I SAT ON THE COUCH, ADAM TOOK A CHAIR, and Darryl stayed where he was, pointedly not looking at the vampire.

There was a sharp knock on the door, and Darryl said, "Ben."

He made no move to answer it, but it popped open anyway and Ben stuck his head in. His blond hair looked almost white illuminated by the porch light. He glanced at Stefan and said in his nifty British accent, "Bloody hell. He's in bad shape."

But his attention was all for my mother.

"She's married," I warned him. "And if you call her a rude name, she'll shoot you with her pretty pink gun and I'll spit on your grave."

He considered me a moment and started to open his mouth.

Adam said, "Ben. Meet Mercy's mother, Margi."

Ben paled, closed his mouth, and opened it again. But nothing came out. I didn't think Ben was used to meeting mothers.

"I know." I sighed. "She looks like my younger, better-looking sister. Mom, this is Ben. Ben is a werewolf from England, and he has a foul mouth when Adam's not around to ride herd on him. He's saved my life a couple of times. Against the wall is Darryl, werewolf, genius, Ph.D., and Adam's second. Peter, also a werewolf, is the nice man feeding Stefan."

And after that, the awkwardness set in. Darryl wasn't talking. Ben, after one more bemused look at Mom, kept his head down and his mouth shut. Peter was obviously distracted by the feeding vampire. Adam was staring at Stefan with a worried frown.

He knew what Stefan's first words had meant, too. But he couldn't talk to me about it in front of my mom until I did. And I wasn't going to let her know that Marsilia and her vampires were after me. Not unless I had to.

Mom wanted to ask me about . . . about the incident last week. About Tim and how he died. But she wouldn't ask me about anything until everyone *else* was gone.

Me? I'd just as soon not talk about any of it. I wondered how long I could keep everyone together, awkwardness being better than the stomach-churning panic that conversation with Adam or my mother was going to cause.

"I'm done in," Peter said.

Stefan wasn't any happier about changing donors this time. But having an additional wolf did the trick and, with only minor damage done to my end table, he was soon feeding off Ben. But only a few minutes later, Stefan went limp, his mouth falling away.

"Is he dead?" Peter asked and took a sip of his second glass of orange juice.

"Him?" asked Ben, extracting his wrist. "He's been dead for years."

Peter grunted. "You know what I mean."

Truthfully, it was difficult to tell. He wasn't breathing, but vampires didn't, not unless they needed to talk or pass for human. His heart wasn't beating, but again, that didn't mean much.

"We'll take him to my house," Adam said. "The . . ." He glanced at Mom. "My basement has a room without windows, where he'll be safer." He meant the cage where they locked up werewolves when they had control issues. He frowned. "Not that that will stop *whoever* dumped him in the middle of your living room, Mercy." He knew "whoever" all right.

Marsilia, I thought, though maybe it had been Stefan himself. Or maybe some other vampire. The one who'd explained that Marsilia and Stefan were the only ones who could teleport like that was Andre, the one I'd had to kill. Hard to trust his information too far.

"I'll be careful," I told Adam. "But you have to be careful, too. There was a vampire watching the back of the house when I was out talking to Amber."

"Who's Amber?" Adam's question was just a hair faster than my mother's "Amber? Charla's friend Amber from college?"

I nodded at Mom. "She read about . . . I've apparently made national news. She decided that she should look me up to check into her haunted house."

"That sounds like Amber," Mom said. Char and Amber had spent a number of weekends at my parents' house in Portland while I was in college. "She always was self-centered, and I don't suppose that would change. Though why would she think that you could help her with a haunted house?"

I had never told Mom about seeing ghosts. I hadn't really thought it was anything unusual until recently. I mean, people see ghosts all the time, right? They just don't talk about it much. Having a daughter who turned into a coyote was bad enough, so anything else I could keep quiet about, I had.

This didn't seem like the time to tell her about it either. I hadn't told her about last week. I hadn't told her about vampires. I had no intention of informing her of any other secrets I'd been keeping.

So I shrugged. "Maybe because I associate with werewolves and the fae."

"What did she expect you to do about it?" Adam asked. He'd have listened in on the whole conversation with Amber; werewolves have very good hearing.

"Beats me," I told him. "Do I look like an expert at laying ghosts?" Seeing them was a long way from sending them away. I wasn't even sure it was possible. I thought about what Amber had said. "Maybe she just wanted me to go tell her that her house really is haunted. Maybe she just needs someone to believe her."

Adam knelt on the floor and picked up Stefan. "I'll take him home now." Though Stefan was obviously taller than he was, Adam's supernatural strength wasn't apparent—he just *looked* like someone who could carry a great deal of weight without effort.

It should have been Darryl who picked up Stefan, not Adam. The Alpha just didn't do the heavy lifting when there were capable minions about. Ben and Peter had both fed the vampire, but Darryl didn't have that excuse. He must have a real thing about vampires.

Adam didn't seem to notice anything wrong with Darryl. "I'll send someone back to watch your house, tonight." He looked at my mom. "Do you need a place to stay? Mercy's"—he glanced around—"a little short on space."

"I'm staying at the Red Lion in Pasco," Mom said to Adam. To me she said, "We left in a hurry and I couldn't find anyone to watch

Hotep. He's in the car." Hotep was her Doberman pinscher, who liked me even less than I liked him.

Adam nodded solemnly though I didn't remember telling him that my mom's dog hated me.

"Adam," I said. "Thank you. For saving Stefan."

"No thanks necessary. We didn't save him for you."

Ben gave me an expression that might have been a smile if his face hadn't been so tight. "You weren't there in the basement with that *thing*." Andre's demon-possessed vampire, he meant, the first vampire I'd killed. He had captured several of the wolves and Stefan and . . . played with them. Demons like causing pain.

"If it hadn't been for Stefan . . ." Ben shrugged, as if letting a memory die away unspoken. "We owe him."

Adam glanced at Darryl, who opened the door. I thought of something.

"Wait."

Adam stopped.

"If I talk to Mom . . . does that count?" He'd told me I had to talk to someone, and my mother wouldn't go away until I told her everything. It seemed like I should be able to kill two birds with one stone.

He handed Stefan to Ben and walked to me. He touched my jaw, just below my ear, and, as if our fascinated audience wasn't watching, he kissed me, touching me with nothing more than his fingertips and his mouth.

At first the heat flushed through me . . . followed by a horrible choking fear. I couldn't breathe, couldn't move . . .

When I came back to myself, I was sitting on the couch with my head between my knees, Adam crooning to me. But he wasn't touching me, and neither was anyone else.

I sat up and came face-to-face with Adam. His face was still, but I could see the wolf in his eyes and smell the wild on his skin.

"Panic attack," I said needlessly. "I haven't been having them as often." I lied and saw from the expression on his face that he knew it. This one made four today. Yesterday, I'd done better.

"Talking to your mother counts," he said. "We'll take things slowly . . . see how it goes. You talk to your mother or anyone else you'd like. But it'll all keep until kissing me doesn't cause a panic attack, all right?"

He didn't wait for an answer, just strode out of the house followed by his entourage. Darryl waited until both Ben and Peter were out the door before closing it gently behind them all.

"Mercy," said my mother thoughtfully, "you never told me your werewolf neighbor was quite that hot."

"Mmm," I said. I appreciated her effort, but now that the time was at hand, I just wanted to get it over with. "And you didn't get to see him rip Tim's corpse to pieces."

I heard Mom suck in a hard breath. "I wish I had. Tell me about Tim."

So I did. And she didn't say a word until I was finished. I hadn't meant to tell her everything. But she didn't say anything, didn't move, didn't look at me. So I talked. Just barely, I managed to keep Ben's name out of it—his secrets were his to reveal—but everything else roared in jagged bits or choked roughly out of someplace dark and vile. It took a while to get it all out.

"Tim reminded you of Samuel," she said when I was through.

I jerked my head off her lap.

"No, I'm not crazy." She handed me a wad of tissues from the box that sat on an arm of the couch. "That's why you didn't see it coming. That's why you didn't see what he was. Samuel was always a bit of an outcast, and it left you with a soft spot for outcasts."

Samuel? Cheery, sweet-tempered (for a werewolf) Samuel an *outcast*?

"He was not." I grabbed a handful of tissues and wiped snot and salt water from my face. My nose runs when I cry.

She nodded. "Sure he was. He likes humans, Mercy—and most werewolves don't." She shivered at some memory or other. "He listened to heavy metal and watched *Star Trek* reruns."

"He was the Marrok's *second* before he came here to lone wolf it for a while. He wasn't an outcast."

She just looked at me.

"Lone wolf doesn't mean outcast." I set my jaw.

The door popped open, and Samuel, who'd been sitting out on the porch for a while, came in. "Yes, it does. Hey, Margi—why'd you bring that dog with you? He's creepy-looking."

Hotep was black with reddish brown eyes. He looked like Anubis. Samuel was right, he was creepy-looking.

"I couldn't find a sitter for him," she said, standing up to get hugged. "How have you been?"

He started to say fine . . . then looked at me. "We've been taking our knocks, Mercy and I. But, so far, we've gotten back into the ring."

"That's all you can do," said Mom. "I need to go. Hotep will be fit to burst by now, and I need to get some sleep." She looked at me. "I can stay for a few days—and Curt wanted me to tell you that you're welcome to come home for a while." Curt was my stepfather, the dentist.

"Thank you, Mom," I told her, and meant it. Horrible as it had been, I thought spilling it all might have helped. But I had to get her out of town before Marsilia made her next move. "That was exactly what I needed." I took a deep breath. "Mom, I need you to go back to Portland. I worked today. It was better, doing what I always do. I think if I just stick to my normal routine, I'll put it behind me."

My mother narrowed her eyes at me and started to say something, but Samuel had reached into his pocket and handed her a card.

"Here," he said. "Call me. I'll tell you how she's doing."

Mom raised her chin. "How is she doing?"

"Fair to middling," he told her. "Some of it's an act, but not all of it. She's tough—good genes. She'll make it fine, but I think she's right. She'll make it better after folks quit running around with sympathy and pity and staring at her. And the best way to do that is to get back to work, back to normal until other people forget about it."

Bless Samuel.

"All right," Mom said. She gave Samuel a stern look. "Now, I don't know what's going on between you and my daughter and Adam Hauptman—"

"Neither do we," I muttered.

Samuel grinned. "We have it pretty well worked out as far as the sex goes—Adam gets it—someday—and I don't. But the rest is still up for negotiation."

"Samuel Cornick," I sputtered in disbelief. "That is my *mother*."

Mom grinned back at him and pulled him down so she could kiss his cheek. "That's how I was reading it as well. But I just wanted to check." She sobered, and, after a glance at me, said to Samuel, "You take care of her for me."

He nodded solemnly. "I will. And Adam has his whole pack on it. Let me walk you to your car."

He came back in the house, and I heard my mother's car drive off. He looked as tired as I felt.

"Adam has a couple of wolves on stakeout at the Red Lion, just waiting for your mother to get there. She'll be all right."

"How was the emergency?" I asked.

He lit up. "Some poor fool took his pregnant wife across the country to visit her mother two weeks from her delivery date. I got there just in time to play catcher."

Samuel loved babies. "Girl or boy?"

"Boy. Jacob Daniel Arlington, six pounds four ounces."

"Did you go to Adam's and see Stefan?" I asked.

He nodded. "I stopped by his house before I came home. Much good as I did. Mostly I help people before they die. I'm not so helpful afterward."

"So what do you think?"

He shrugged. "He's doing whatever it is that vampires do during the day. Not sleeping, but something close to it. I expect he'll rest tonight and through tomorrow day. Which is what anyone of common sense would tell you—and so Adam said. He declared me tired and useless, then sent me back over here to keep an eye on you in case Marsilia decides to try something else."

"'Tired and useless,'" I said in mock sympathy. "And even that didn't get you out of a job."

He grinned. "Adam seems to think you've declared yourself his. But, given his record of doing that without consulting you, I thought I'd ask you myself."

I raised my hands in helpless surrender. "What can I say. My mother thinks he's hot. I have no choice but to take him. Besides, it's a terrible thing to see a man crawling . . . begging."

He laughed. "I bet. Go to bed, Mercy. Morning comes early."

He started down the hallway to his bedroom, then turned, walking backward. "I'm going to tell Adam that you said he begged you."

I raised an eyebrow. "Then I'll tell him that you accused him of lying."

He laughed. "Good night, Mercy."

I'd taken Adam for mine, chosen with my eyes and heart open. But Samuel's laugh still made me smile. I loved Samuel, too.

He worried me. Sometimes he seemed just like the old Samuel, funny and lighthearted. But I was pretty sure that a lot of the time he was just going through the motions, like an actor given a cue— "Enter downstage left and smile happily."

He'd come here, to stay with me, to try to get better—which was a good sign, like an alcoholic who goes to his first A.A. meeting. But I wasn't sure if being here was helping him or not. He was old. Older than I'd known when I'd grown up in his father's pack. And though werewolves don't die of old age the way humans do, it can kill them just as effectively.

Maybe if I could have loved Samuel differently. Maybe if Adam hadn't been there. If I had taken Samuel as my mate as he'd wanted me to when he'd moved himself into my home, maybe it would have fixed him.

He frowned at me. "What's wrong?"

But you can't marry someone to fix him, even if you love them. And I didn't love Samuel the way a woman should love her mate, the way I loved Adam. Samuel didn't love me that way either. Close, but not quite. And except in horseshoes and hand grenades, *close* doesn't count.

"I love you, you know," I told him.

His face went blank for a moment. He said, "Yes. I do know." His pupils contracted, and his gray eyes lightened to icy winter. Then he smiled, a sweet, warm thing. "I love you, too."

I went to bed with the distinct feeling that, this time, *close* might really be just enough to do the trick.

———

SAMUEL WAS RIGHT—MORNING DID COME TOO EARLY. I yawned as I turned my van onto the street where my shop was—and stopped dead in the middle of the road, all thoughts of sleep gone.

Someone had taken spray paint and had fun last night all over my place of business.

I took it all in, then drove slowly into the parking lot and parked next to Zee's old truck. He came out of the office and walked up to me as I got out and shut the van's door, a tallish, thinnish, graying man. He looked like he was in his late fifties or early sixties, but he was a lot older than that: never judge one of the fae by their outward appearance.

"Wow," I said. "You've got to admire their dedication. They must have been here for hours."

"And no one drove by?" Zee snapped. "No one called the *polizei?*"

"Umm, probably not. There's not a lot of traffic here at night." Reading the graffiti made me realize that there were themes and insights to be gained from the canvas that someone had made of my garage.

Green Paint, I was almost sure, was a young man whose thought patterns paralleled Ben's if the words he used were any indication.

"Look, he misspelled *whore*. I wonder if he did it on purpose? He spelled it right on the front window. I wonder which one he did first?"

"I have called your police friend Tony," Zee said, so angry his teeth clicked together as he spoke. "He was sleeping, but he will be here in a half hour." He might have been upset on my account, but mostly, I thought, it was the state of the garage. It had been his business long before I bought it from him. Last week I'd have been angry, too. But so much had happened since then that this ranked pretty low on my list of worries.

Red Paint had a more pressing agenda than Green Paint. Red had painted only two words: *liar* and *murderer*, over and over. Adam had installed security cameras so we'd know for sure, but I was betting Red Paint was Tim's cousin Courtney. Tim had killed his best friend before he attacked me, and there just weren't all that many people left who'd have gotten this worked up over his death.

I could hear a car approaching. An hour later, when traffic started to build up with people headed to work, I wouldn't have noticed. But it was quiet this early in the morning, so I heard my mother's approach.

"Zee," I said urgently. "Is there any way you could hide this"—I waved my hands at the shop—"for a few minutes?"

I didn't know much about what he could and couldn't do—outside of fixing cars and playing with metal, he didn't use magic much in front of me. But I'd seen his real face once, so I knew his personal glamour was good. If he could mask his face, surely he could hide a bunch of green and red paint.

He frowned at me in deep displeasure. You didn't ask for favors from the fae—not only was it dangerous, but they tended to take offense. Zee might love me, might owe me for freeing him from a tight spot, but that would only take me so far.

"My mother is coming," I told him. "The vampires are after me, and I have to get her to leave. She won't do it if she knows I'm in danger." Then, because I was desperate, I played dirty. "Not after what happened with Tim."

His face stilled. Then he grabbed my wrist and pulled me with him so we were both standing closer to the garage.

He put his hand on the wall next to the door. "If it works, I won't be able to remove my hand without breaking the spell."

When Mom turned the corner, the graffiti was gone.

"You're the best," I told him.

"Make her leave soon," he said with a grimace. "This is not my sort of magic."

I nodded and had started to walk to where Mom was parking her car when I saw the door clearly. Covered by red and green paint, it hadn't been as noticeable. Someone with some artistic skill had painted an X on the door. In case I didn't get the right idea, instead of two mere lines, the shape was formed by two bones. They were ivory with grayish shadows and just a faint blush of pink—not painted by a couple of self-righteous and irate kids with spray paint. All it was missing to keep it from Jolly Rogerhood was a skull.

"You'd better hide that," Zee said. "Magic won't."

I put my back against the door and folded my arms.

"So why don't you think it's running right?" I asked him as my mother walked over from her car, with Hotep on a leash.

"Because it is old," Zee told me, taking the cue I had given him. "Because it was not well designed in the first place. Because air-cooled engines need constant tinkering."

"I was— Hey, Mom."

"Margaret," Zee said coolly.

"Mr. Adelbertsmiter." My mom didn't like Zee. She blamed him for my decision to stay in the Tri-Cities and fix cars instead of finding a teaching job, something much more in line with the kind of work she thought I should be doing. Politeness done, she turned back to me. "I thought I'd stop by before heading home." She couldn't get too close though, because as soon as he caught my scent, Hotep growled and lowered his head aggressively: protecting my mom from the bad coyote.

"I'll be fine," I told her, curling my lip at the Doberman. I actually like dogs, but not this one. "Give my love to Curt and the girls."

"Don't forget to work things out so you can come to Nan's wedding." Nan was my younger half sister, and she was getting married in six weeks. Luckily, I wasn't part of the wedding party, so all I had to do was sit and watch.

"I have it on the calendar," I promised. "Zee's going to take care of the shop for me."

She glanced at him, then back at me. "Fine, then." She started to give me a hug, then gave Hotep a rueful look. "You need to teach him to behave like you did Ringo."

"Ringo was a poodle, Mom. A fight between Hotep and me wouldn't end well for either of us. It's all right. Not his fault."

She sighed. "All right. You take care of yourself."

"Love you. Drive carefully," I told her.

"I always do. Love you."

Zee was sweating by the time the car was out of sight. He took his hand off the building and the paint returned. "I didn't do it for you," he grouched. "I just didn't want her hanging around longer than necessary."

We both stepped away from the door to look at the painting that was now mostly covered by a big, fat-lettered red "LIAR." The paint of the crossed bones was thicker than the spray paint, so even though I couldn't see most of the color, I could see the outline of it.

"The vampires dropped Stefan in my living room last night," I told him. "He was in pretty rough shape. Peter . . . one of Adam's wolves, thinks whoever did it was hoping Stefan would attack me and we'd both be out of the way. Stefan wasn't in any shape to talk much, but what he did manage to convey was that Marsilia found out I killed Andre."

Zee traced his fingers over the bones and shook his head. "This *might* be vampire work. But, Mercy, you've been putting your little nose so many places it doesn't belong; it could almost be anyone. I'll talk to Uncle Mike—but I expect your best bet for information about it is Stefan, because it doesn't feel like fae magic. How badly is Stefan hurt?"

"If he were a werewolf, I think he'd be dead. You think this is magic?" It felt like that to me, but I was hoping I was wrong.

Zee frowned. "For an evil bloodsucker, he's not a bad sort." High praise from Zee. "And yes, there is magic here, but nothing I'm familiar with."

"Samuel thinks Stefan will be all right."

Tony turned the corner in his unmarked car, which was discreetly police modified with extra mirrors, a few extra antennae, and a bar of lights along the back window, hidden from the casual eye by extra-dark glass. He slowed when he caught sight of the damage. He pulled up next to us and opened the door.

"You decorating for Christmas early, Mercy?" Tony could blend in even better than I did. Today he looked like a Hispanic cop . . . like the poster child for Hispanic cops, handsome and clean-cut. When he was playing drug dealer, he did it better than the real thing. I'd first met him playing a homeless man. There was nothing magic or supernatural about him, but the man was a chameleon.

I glanced at the building again. He was right. If you didn't pay any attention to the words, it had a sort of Christmasy look to it. The green paint tended to be short top to bottom but long front side to side. The red paint was fat and closed up. It looked sort of like garlands with red balls hanging down.

There was even "Ho, ho, ho," if you skipped around a little and deleted an "e" on the last "ho." Our green painter had a limited vocabulary and occasionally mixed up a professional working woman with a garden implement.

"Not really Christmasy thoughts," I told Tony. "But the colors are right. Actually, if the white wasn't so dingy, it would almost look festive—like that little Mexican restaurant in Pasco—the one with the really *hot* salsa." The fresh colors made the original paint job look tired.

"Your boyfriend still got surveillance video going?"

"Yes, but I don't know how to run it."

"I do," said Zee. "Let's go take a look."

I glanced at him. *Vampires, remember? We don't want the nice human cops to see the vampires.*

He gave me a bland look that clearly said, *If the vampires were clumsy enough to get caught by the cameras, that was their problem.* I couldn't object out loud, but if the vampires made themselves obvious, it would be *Tony* who was in danger.

Well, I thought as I led the way into the office, at least vampires looked like everyone else. As long as they didn't display their fangs for the camera—or throw a car around—it was unlikely they'd be spotted for what they were. And if it was obvious . . . Tony wasn't stupid. He knew a lot about how the fae and the werewolves worked, and I knew he suspected that there were a lot more nasties still keeping quiet about themselves.

While Zee played with the electronics, Tony looked at me.

"How are you?" He smelled of worry, with a little of the metallic scent of protective anger.

"Really tired of answering that question," I replied blandly. "How about you?"

He flashed his pearly whites at me. "Good for you. Do you think Bright Future did this?"

If our minds kept working this much in sync, I'd pity poor Tony.

"Sort of. I think this is Tim's cousin's work," I told him. "She's a member of Bright Future, but she didn't do this under their banner. Everything was directed at me—not the fae."

"You want to press charges?"

I sighed. "I'll call my insurance company. I'm afraid they might force me to press charges in order to be reimbursed. I can't afford to hire someone to repaint it unless I use my insurance, and I can't take the time off work to repaint it myself." I still had other things to pay for—the damage a fae who wanted to eat me had done to Adam's house and car, for instance. And Zee had told me he was collecting the rest of what I owed him on the business. Fae cannot lie, and we hadn't had time to work that out.

"How about Gabriel's family," Tony suggested. "There are enough of them, and they could work after school. It would be cheaper than hiring professionals and . . . I think they need the money."

Gabriel Sandoval was my man Friday, a high school student who came in weekends and late afternoons to do paperwork, answer phones, and do whatever else needed doing.

I had a sudden vision of the shop being overrun with little Sandovals hanging from ladders and ropes. I'd let them loose in the office for cleaning, and it was almost hard to recognize the place—for a bunch of kids they were amazingly industrious.

"That's a good idea. I'll have Gabriel call his mom as soon as he gets here."

"Here," said Zee. He turned on the little security monitor and flipped a switch. The system that Adam had installed was slick and expensive. It ran on motion sensors, so we only had to watch it when there was something moving. Something first moved at 10:15; we watched a half-grown rabbit bop unhurriedly across the pavement out of sight. At midnight someone appeared at the door of the garage. It wasn't two people with spray paint, so I was pretty sure it was whoever painted a pair of crossed bones on my door.

His image was oddly shadowed, unrecognizable. The miscreant kept his face out of camera range—impressive since there was a camera placed just in front of the door to catch the face of anyone breaking in.

The only thing the camera got a clear shot of was the gloves he wore—the old-fashioned kind: white with little buttons on the wrist. There were odd glitches in the pictures, jumps where the camera turned off because there was no movement for it to follow. By the timers, it took him forty-five minutes to paint the bones on my door—of which the cameras caught about ten minutes. Part of the missing time covered how the painter got there and how he left.

I didn't think he knew the cameras were there, and he still avoided them. Some supernatural creatures just don't film well: by tradition, vampires are among them. The height was right for Wulfe, who would be my first choice in any vampire magicking. Since Wulfe was the vampire who knew for certain that I'd killed Andre, he was also my top suspect for the informer who had told Marsilia about my crimes.

The camera caught movement again.

"Stop it," Tony said.

Two figures, still indistinct, froze on the edge of the lights of my parking lot, and the little numbers on the lower right of the screen read 2:08 A.M. Time had jumped almost a half hour from when the bone painter had last been there.

"What was that all about?" he asked. "The person at your door?"

"I don't know," I told him. I almost said that his guess was as good as mine, but it wasn't. "Maybe someone was trying to break in, but didn't make it." Impossible to tell what he'd been doing from the camera shot. "It doesn't matter, though, because he obviously wasn't the one who graffitied all over."

Tony stared at me. Cops were almost as good as werewolves at sensing lies. He turned abruptly and opened the door to examine it. Like Zee, he traced the crossed bones with a light finger.

"Who have you been ticking off besides Bright Future? This looks almost like something the old Mob might do—classy, but designed to frighten the hell out of whoever received it."

I sighed, shrugged. "No one wanted me to get Zee out of the murder rap. But it's not the kind of thing a fae would do—too visible. And a werewolf who was ticked off that badly would just attack. I've got some people who'll look into it for me better than the police can."

Frowning, Tony made an irritated noise. "Is this another one of your 'It's too dangerous for you mere human cops?'"

I rubbed my arms, but I wasn't cold, just chilled. I was under no illusions. Marsilia could have just killed me, but she was playing. But no matter how playful the cat is, the mouse is just as dead in the end.

And the end would be whenever she decided. The only question was how many people—how many of my friends—she decided to take down with me.

Maybe I was panicking prematurely. Maybe she would settle for a punishment. Stefan was hers, there was no reason for the gut-deep feeling that he wouldn't be the last to suffer for my sins. I didn't know Marsilia well enough to make that kind of prediction.

"Mercy?"

"I don't know what the crossed bones mean." *Other than bad news.* "Zee tells me it is magical but probably not fae magic." Zee was out, anyone who cared to would know that he was fae, which was the reason that the garage was mine now, instead of his. There was a lot of prejudice against the fae. "He has a few contacts who'll take a look at it for me. I know a few other people I can ask, too." Adam had a witch on the pack's payroll for cleanup. She was good, but it would cost me a lot to hire her if Uncle Mike and Stefan didn't know what it was. This was shaping up into a real macaroni-and-cheese month. "However, none of them will come within a hundred miles of a police investigation. Do you have anyone on the KPD who is an expert in magic?"

Tony held my gaze for a minute before giving up with a sigh. "Hell no, Mercy. You should have seen the brass's faces when they watched that video—" He stopped and gave me a guilty look. It was a video of me killing Tim . . . and all the stuff before that. He shrugged nervously and looked away. "There are a few who know something about fae or werewolves, but . . . if they know anything more, they keep it quiet for fear of losing their jobs."

He sighed and came back into the shop. "Go ahead," he told Zee. "Let's watch Tim's cousin paint the shop."

Once the two shadowy people moved fully onto the parking lot, Courtney was unmistakable. Instead of watching the whole process, Zee fast-forwarded it until the pair walked off with bags of empty spray-paint cans almost two hours later. He stopped the images when Courtney was close to the camera and impossible to mistake, her pretty, rounded face hard and angry. Zee flipped back and forth a little until we got a clear view of her companion's face, too.

The security system hadn't been in place long, but Zee loved gadgets. He must have spent some time playing with this one.

"It's Courtney all right . . . I don't remember her last name," I told Tony. "I don't recognize the man at all. If it were Bright Future, there'd have been more people."

"It's personal," Tony agreed grimly. "You are going to want to give me those disks and file charges so we can give her some time to cool off. She's not going to stop harassing you anytime soon unless someone heads her off at the pass. It's safer for everyone if it's the police and not the werewolves or the fae."

Zee ejected the disk and handed it to Tony.

Tony frowned at it a moment. "I'm not worried about the kids, Mercy. But there's something about those bones and that guy that is sending my old radar into fits. If that's not a death threat, I'll be a monkey's uncle. You stick close to that werewolf boyfriend of yours for a while."

I gave him a martyred sigh. "Why do you think Zee is still here? I suspect I'm not going to get a moment to myself for the next year, at least."

"Yeah," he said, a smile lighting his eyes. "It's tough when people care about you."

Zee made a sound that might have been a laugh. He covered it by saying sourly, "Not that she makes it easy on them to watch over her. You just wait. All she's going to do for the next few weeks is complain, complain, complain."

3

~~~

WORD HAD GOTTEN OUT THAT I WAS BACK IN THE SHOP
and my regular customers started stopping in to express their sympathy and support. The graffiti only made things worse. By nine I
was hiding in the garage, with the big overhead doors shut, even
though that meant that the garage was hot and stuffy, and my electric bill was going to suffer.

I left Zee to handle the customers, poor customers. Zee is not
a people person. Years ago, when I first came to work here, his
nine-year-old son was in charge of the front desk and everyone was
properly grateful.

I spent most of the morning trying to figure out the troubles of
a twenty-year-old Jetta. Nothing more fun than sorting through in-
termittent electrical problems, as long as you have a year or two to

waste. The owner got off her job at three in the morning and twice had gone to start her car and found the battery drained though the lights were off.

There was nothing wrong with the battery. Or the alternator. I was upside-down in the driver's seat, with my head up the Jetta's dash, when a sudden thought came to me. I rolled over and looked at the shiny new CD player in the ancient car, which had held only a cassette player when it had last visited here.

When Zee came in, I was using Power Words to describe service techs who didn't know how to tie their own shoes but felt free and easy meddling in one of my cars. I'd been taking care of this Jetta for as long as I'd been working on cars, and felt a special affection for it.

Zee blinked at me a couple of times to hide his amusement. "We could give your bill to the place that put her stereo in."

"Would they pay for it?" I asked.

Zee smiled. "They would if *I* took it in." Zee took a personal interest in our customers' cars, too.

We locked up for lunch and went to our favorite taco wagon for authentic Mexican tacos. That meant no cheese or iceberg lettuce, but cilantro, lime, and radishes instead—a more-than-fair trade in my view.

The wagon was parked in a lot next to a Mexican bakery just across the cable bridge over the Columbia River, putting it in Pasco, but just barely. Some wagons are step vans, but this one was a small trailer laden with whiteboards that listed the menu with prices.

The sweet-faced woman who worked there spoke barely enough English to take orders—which probably didn't matter because there were very few English-only speakers among her patrons. She said something and patted my hand when I paid—and when I checked the bag to make sure the little plastic cups of salsa were there, I saw she'd added a couple of extra of my favorite tacos in our bag. Which proved that everyone, even people who couldn't read the newspaper, knew about me.

Zee drove us to the park on the Kennewick side of the river, where there were waterfront picnic tables for us to eat at. I sighed as we walked along the river's edge between the parking lot and the tables. "I wish it hadn't made the papers. How long before everyone forgets, and I don't get any more pitying looks?"

Zee grinned wolfishly at me. "I've told you before; you need to learn Spanish. She congratulated you on killing him. And she knows a few other men who could benefit from your efforts." He picked a table and sat down.

I sat down across from him and set the bag between us. "She did not." I don't speak Spanish, but everyone who lives in the Tri-Cities for long picks up a few words—besides she hadn't said very much, even in Spanish.

"Maybe not the last part of it," agreed Zee, pulling out a chicken taco and squeezing one of the lime segments over it. "Though I saw it in her face. But she did say, *'Bien hecho.'*"

I knew the first word, but he made me ask for the last, waiting until curiosity forced the words out of my mouth. "Which means? Good—"

"Good job." His white teeth sank into the tortilla.

Stupid. It was stupid to let other people's opinions matter, but having someone else who didn't view me as a victim cheered me up immensely. After pouring green hot sauce over my goat taco, I ate with a renewed appetite.

"I think," I told Zee, "that I'll go to the dojo tonight after I get done with work." I'd already missed Saturday's early-morning session.

"It should be interesting to watch," Zee said, which was as close as he could come to lying. He had no desire to watch a bunch of people working themselves up into a noxious puddle of sweat and fatigue (his words). He must have been elected to be my bodyguard for a little longer than just the workday.

SOMEONE HAD TALKED TO THEM ALL. I COULD SEE IT IN the casual way they greeted me as I walked into the dojo. Muscles in Sensei Johanson's jaw twitched when he first saw me, but he led us through the opening exercises and stretches with his usual sadistic thoroughness.

By the time we started sparring, the muscles in my lower back, which had been tense for the last week, were loose and moving well. After the first two bouts, I was relaxed and settled into my usual love-hate relationship with my third opponent, the devastatingly powerful brown belt who was the bully of the dojo. He was careful, oh so careful that Sensei never saw him do it, but he liked to hurt people . . . women. In addition to the full-contact part of Sensei's chosen form, Lee Holland was the other reason I was the only woman in the advanced class. Lee wasn't married, for which I was glad. No woman deserved to have to live with him.

I actually liked to spar with him because I never felt guilty about leaving bruises behind. I also enjoyed the frustrated look in his eyes as his skilled moves (his brown belt justly outranked my own purple) constantly failed to connect as well as they should.

Today there was something else in his eyes when he looked at the stitches on my chin, a hot edge of desire that seriously creeped me out. He was turned on that I had been raped. Either that or that I'd killed someone. I preferred the latter but, knowing Lee, it was probably the former.

"You are weak," he told me, whispering so no one else could hear.

I'd been right about what had excited his interest.

"I killed the last person who thought that," I said, and front kicked him hard in the chest. Usually, I tempered my speed to something more humanly possible. But his eyes made me quit playing human. I'm not supernaturally strong, but in the martial arts, speed counts, too.

I was moving at full tilt when I stepped around him while he was still off balance. Tournament martial arts have two opponents facing each other, but our style encourages us to strike from the back or the side—keeping the enemies' weapons facing the wrong way. I stepped hard on the back of his knee, forcing him to drop to the floor. Before he could respond, I hopped back three feet to give him a chance to get up, this being only sparring and not a death match.

Our dojo did some grappling, but not much. Shi Sei Kai Kan is all about putting your opponent down fast and moving on to the next guy. It was developed for warfare, when a soldier might be facing multiple opponents. Grappling left you vulnerable to attack from another opponent. And I had no desire to get up close and personal with Lee.

He roared with humiliation-charged rage and came for me. Block and block, twist and dodge, I kept him from contacting me.

Someone called out sharply, "Sensei! Check out Lee's fight."

"Enough, Lee," Sensei called from the far side of the dojo, where he'd been working with someone. "That's enough."

Lee didn't appear to hear him. If I hadn't been so much faster than him, I'd have been hurt already. As it was, I made sure he couldn't connect any of his hits. For a while, at least, until I got cocky and overconfident.

I fell for a sham move with his right hand, while he slammed me in the diaphragm and laid me out on the floor with his left. Ignoring my lack of breath as much as I could, I rolled and stumbled to my feet. And as I rolled, I saw that Adam was standing in the doorway in a business suit. He had his arms folded on his chest as he waited for me to deal with Lee.

So I did. I thought it was Adam's presence that gave me the idea. I'd spent some time at his dojo—in his garage—practicing a jumping, spinning roundhouse kick. It was developed as a way to knock an opponent off his horse, a sacrificial move that the foot soldier would not expect to survive. Mounted warriors had more value as a weapon than foot soldiers, so the sacrifice would be worth it. In modern days, the kick is mostly for demos, used in combat with another skilled person on the ground it is generally too slow, too flashy, to be useful. Too slow unless you happened to be a part-time coyote and supernaturally fast.

Lee would never expect me to try it.

My heel hit Lee's jaw, and he collapsed on the floor almost before I'd decided to use the move. I collapsed right next to him, still fighting for breath from his hit to my diaphragm.

Sensei was beside Lee, checking him out almost before I landed. Adam put his hand on my abdomen and pulled my legs straight to facilitate breathing.

"Pretty," he said. "Too bad you pulled it; if anyone deserved to lose his head . . ." He didn't mean it as a joke. If he'd said it with a hair more heat, I'd have been worried.

"Is he all right?" I tried to ask—and he must have understood.

"Knocked out cold, but he'll be fine. Not even a sore neck for his trouble."

"I think you're right," Sensei said. "She pulled it, and angled her foot perfectly for a tournament hit." He held Lee still as the big man moaned and started to stir.

Sensei looked at me and frowned. "You were stupid, Mercy. What is the first rule of combat?"

By this time I could talk. "The best defense is fast tennis shoes," I said.

He nodded. "Right. When you noticed he was out of control—which I'm sure was about two full minutes at least before I did, because I was helping Gibbs with his axe kick—you should have called for help, then gotten away from him. There was no point in letting this continue until someone got hurt."

From the sidelines, Gibbs, the other brown belt, said, "She's sorry, Sensei. She just got her directions confused. She kept running the wrong way."

There was a general laugh as tension dispersed.

Sensei guided Lee though a general check to make sure nothing was permanently damaged. "Sit out for the rest of the lesson," he told Lee. "Then we'll have a little talk."

When Lee got up, he didn't look at me or anyone else, just took up a low-horse stance with a wall at his back.

Sensei stood up, and I followed suit. He looked at Adam.

Who bowed, fist to hand and eyes hidden behind dark sunglasses he hadn't been wearing when I'd first glimpsed him in the doorway. Most of the werewolves I know carry dark glasses or wear hats that can shadow their eyes.

"Adam Hauptman," he said. "A friend of Mercy's. Just here to observe unless you object."

Sensei was an accountant in real life. His day job was working for an insurance firm, but here he was king. His eyes were cool and confident as he looked at Adam.

"The werewolf," he said. Adam was one of five or six of his pack who had chosen to come out to the public.

"*Hai,*" agreed Adam.

"So why didn't you help Mercy?"

"It is your dojo, Sensei Johanson." Sensei raised an eyebrow, and Adam's sudden smile blazed out. "Besides, I've seen her fight. She's tough, and she's smart. If she had thought she was in trouble, she'd have asked for help."

I glanced around as I rolled over and stood up, as good as new except for the pretty bruises I was going to have on my belly. Zee was gone. He wouldn't have lingered, with Adam to take over guard duty. His nose had wrinkled at the smell of sweaty bodies when we'd come in—he'd been lucky it was relatively cool this fall. In full summer, the dojo smelled from a block away, at least it did to my nose. To me the scent was strong but not unpleasant, but I knew from the comments of my fellow karate students that most humans disliked it almost as much as Zee did.

Drama over, Adam went back to the sidelines, loosening his tie and pulling his suit jacket off as a concession to the heat. Sensei had us do three hundred side kicks (Lee was called from his position of disgrace to participate) first to the left, then to the right. We all counted them off in Japanese—though I suspected if a native speaker had dropped in, they might've had difficulty understanding what we were saying.

The first hundred were easy, muscles warm and limber from earlier calisthenics; the second . . . not so much. Somewhere about 220, I lost myself in the burning ache until it was almost a shock when we stopped and switched sides. Wandering through the ranks of students (there were twelve of us tonight) Sensei adjusted people's form as he saw necessary.

You could tell those of us who were more serious because our two hundredth kicks looked just like our first. Students less diligent lost height and form as exhaustion took its toll. There were still some students in good form on the three hundredth kick—but not me.

AFTER CLASS, PEOPLE WERE TOO BUSY TRYING NOT TO stare at the werewolf—all the while getting in a good look—to pay any attention to me. I changed in the bathroom and took my time, out of courtesy, so that they would all have time to change in the anteroom in front of the dojo before I came out.

Sensei was waiting for me when I emerged.

"Good job, Mercy," he told me with an emphasis that told me he wasn't talking about Lee. It was odd that the words he had for me were the same ones, in a different language, that the woman in the taco wagon had used, meant the same way.

"If it hadn't been for this"—I tilted my head to indicate the dojo—"I would have died that night instead of my attacker." I gave him a formal bow, two fists down. "Thank you for your teaching, Sensei."

He returned my bow, and we both ignored the suspicious watering of eyes.

Adam was waiting near the front door carefully examining his fingernails. He had chosen to be amused by all the people staring at him, which was a good thing. He had a temper. Sweat darkened his Egyptian-cotton shirt, so it clung to the round lines of his shoulders and arms, announcing to anyone that he was a hard body.

I took a deep breath to cool my jets and introduced him around. Only Lee met his eyes for longer than a moment, and at first I thought Adam was going to lose it. He gave Lee a scary smile. I was afraid of what he—either he—was going to say, so I grabbed Adam's arm and tugged him out the door.

If he'd wanted to, Adam could have shaken me off, but he went along with it. I hadn't brought my car because the dojo was just a short hike across cheatgrass and down the railroad tracks from my shop. Adam's SUV wasn't there either.

"Did you drive a different car?" I asked in the parking lot.

"No, I had Carlos drop me off after work so I could walk back with you to your shop." Carlos was one of his wolves, one of three or four who worked for him at his security business, but not one I knew well. "I remember you told me you liked to cool down on the walk back."

I'd told him that several years earlier. He'd been waiting for me at my shop with a warning . . . I looked down at the asphalt and turned my head so he wouldn't see my smile.

It had been after I first hauled the old parts car out of my pole barn and stuck it in the middle of the field so Adam couldn't help but see it out of his window. He'd been dispensing orders left and right and, knowing werewolves as I had, I hadn't dared to defy him outright. Instead, knowing how organized and neat Adam was, I'd tortured him with the battered old Rabbit.

He'd stopped by the garage and found my car but not me. He'd never said, but I thought he must have trailed me to the dojo—and instead of complaining about the junkmobile, he'd dressed me down about wandering around the Tri-Cities by myself at night. Exasperated, I'd snarled right back at him. I'd told him I used the not-very-long walk back to my shop as an after-workout cool off. It had been after his divorce, but not by much. Years ago.

He'd remembered all this time.

"What are you so smug about?" he asked me.

He'd remembered what I'd told him, as if I'd been important to him even then . . . but I could have described the exact shade of the tie that he had worn that day, the tone that worry had given his voice.

I hadn't wanted to admit I was attracted to him. Not when he'd been married, and not when he'd been single. I'd been raised by werewolves, had left them, and didn't want to find myself back in that claustrophobic, violent environment. I especially had no desire to date an Alpha werewolf.

And yet here I was, walking with Adam, who was as Alpha as could be.

"Why didn't you jump into the fight with Lee?" I asked, changing the subject. He'd wanted to—that's why the glasses had come on, so that everyone wouldn't see that his eyes had lightened to the wolf's gold.

He didn't answer right away. The man-made bank up to the railroad track, which was the shortest route to my shop, was steep, and the small gravel made it a bit treacherous. I was sore, so I ran up it. My quads, tired from three hundred kicks, protested the additional effort I was asking of them, but running meant the climb was over faster.

Adam ran easily up the slope behind me, even in slick dress shoes. Something about the way he was following me made me feel nervous, like I was a deer being stalked. So I stopped at the top and stretched out my tired legs. I'd be damned if I would run from Adam.

"You had him," Adam said, watching me. "He's better than you in form, but he has never fought for his life. I wouldn't want you tied up and alone with him for very long, but he never had a chance in the dojo." Then his voice deepened with a slightly rougher tone. "If you hadn't been stupid, you wouldn't have even gotten hit. Don't do that again."

"Nossir," I told him.

I'd been trying not to think about Adam all day—since the crossed bones on my door made it clear that Marsilia wasn't finished with me. I knew, even though Zee would check out other things, I *knew* that it had been the vampires marking my business. And, like Tony had said, it felt like a death threat. I was a dead woman, it was only a matter of time. All I could do was figure out a way to keep other people from dying with me.

Adam would die for his mate. He wouldn't let me just leave, either. Christy, his first wife, hadn't been his mate or they'd still be married. I had to figure out some way to undo what I had done last night.

But it was hard to believe in death with him here beside me, the rich autumn sunlight glinting in his dark hair and lightening his eyes, making him squint and highlighting faint laugh lines.

He took my hand in a casual move I had no way of evading without making a big deal of it. Especially when I didn't want to evade him. He tilted his head as if trying to figure me out—had he caught what I was thinking? His hand was broad-palmed and warm. The calluses on it made it no softer than my own work-roughened skin.

I turned away from him, but kept his hand as I started down the track to my shop. It was awkward for about four steps, then he made an adjustment to his gait, and suddenly the rhythm of our bodies synced.

I closed my eyes, trusting my balance and Adam to keep me headed in the right direction. If I cried, he'd ask me why, and you can't lie to a werewolf. I needed to distract him.

"You're wearing a new cologne," I told him, and my voice was husky. "I like it."

He laughed, a warm rumbly sound that settled in my stomach like a warm piece of apple pie. "Shampoo most likely—" Then he laughed again and tugged me off balance until I bumped against him. He let go of my hand and took a light grip on my far shoulder, his arm warm across my back. "No. You're right, I'd forgotten. Jesse sprayed something at me as I left the house tonight."

"Jesse has excellent taste," I told him. "You smell good enough to eat."

The arm across my shoulders stiffened. I thought back over what I'd said and felt my cheeks warm right up. Part of it was embarrassment . . . but part of it wasn't. But it hadn't been the Freudian slip that had caught his attention.

Adam stopped. Since he was holding me, I stopped, too. I looked at him, then followed his gaze to my shop.

Whoops. Oh well, I'd been looking for a way to distract him so he wouldn't wonder why I was upset. This wasn't the ideal way to do it.

"I guess Zee didn't tell you?"

"Who did it?" There was a growl in his voice. "The vampires?"

How to answer that without telling a lie, which he would smell, or starting a war?

If I had known that Marsilia knew I'd killed Andre, I never would have told Adam I was willing to be his mate. Another wolf might understand that a war with the vampires wasn't going to save me, just get more people killed. A war with the vampires here in the Tri-Cities might spread like the plague throughout all the Marrok's dominion.

But Adam wouldn't let it go. And Samuel would be at his side. I would never be the great love of Samuel's life, nor he of mine. But that didn't mean he didn't love me, just as I loved him. And Samuel would bring his father, the Marrok, into it.

Don't panic, keep it casual, I told myself. "The vamps added some decoration to my door, but most of it was Tim's cousin and a friend. You can watch it on the video if you want. Gabriel's mother and siblings are coming out Saturday to help paint it. The police are taking care of it, Adam." The last was because he was still stiff. "Tony thinks it's Christmasy. Maybe I'll leave it for a few months."

He turned his hot gaze on me.

"She still believes in her cousin, Adam. She thinks I made it all up to get out of a murder charge." I let him hear the sympathy for Courtney's plight in my voice, knowing Adam wouldn't approve. About wrong and right, Adam was pretty black-and-white. He'd be irritated with my attitude, and it would distract him. Keep the focus on Courtney and off the vampires.

Adam didn't relax, but he did start walking again.

USUALLY I SHOWER AT THE SHOP AFTER PRACTICE, BUT I didn't want Adam to get a good look at the crossed bones on the door. I wanted to keep him thinking about things other than the vampires until I knew what my options were. So we jumped in my Vanagon (my poor Rabbit was still in repairs from the damage a fae had done to it last week).

Maybe I'd move. If I traveled to another vampire's territory, it might slow Marsilia down, especially if it was a vampire who didn't like her. Running away would chafe, but if I stayed, she'd kill me— and Adam wouldn't take it well and a lot of people would probably die besides me.

I could try to take out Marsilia.

I actually gave that serious consideration, which was a sign of just how desperate I was. Sure, I'd killed two vampires. The first one I'd killed with a lot of help and a boatload of luck. The second one I'd taken while he slept.

I had about as much chance of taking out Marsilia as my cat Medea did of taking on a mountain lion. Maybe less.

While I thought, I chattered to Adam all the way home. My home. Gas was expensive, and he wouldn't mind walking the short distance back to his.

If he wanted to wait while I showered, I figured I could walk with him. I glanced at the sky and decided I had time to take a shower without risking Adam's being the first one to talk to Stefan.

I needed to find out what the artwork on my door meant—and to make sure that running would work. Stefan might know, but neither question was something I wanted to ask in public. I'd figure out how I was going to get him alone when the time came.

"Mercy," Adam said, breaking into my monologue about Karmann Ghias and air-cooled versus water-cooled engines as I turned into my drive. He sounded both amused and resigned. It was a tone I heard from him a lot.

"Hmm?"

"Why did the vampires paint a pair of bones on your door?"

"I don't know," I told him in a deliberately relaxed voice. "I don't even know that it was the vampires. The camera didn't catch who it was exactly. Zee and I just figured it was the vampires because of Stefan. He's going to check with Uncle Mike to be sure it wasn't a fae, though."

"I won't let Marsilia hurt you," he told me in the quiet tones he used when making a vow of honor.

The wolves do that, some of the older ones, anyhow. I wouldn't have thought Adam was one of them. He was a 1950s model, stuck forever looking like he was in his midtwenties. When I say older wolves, I mean a lot older than 1950, a couple of hundred years at least.

It's not that modern men don't have honor, just most of them don't think of it that way. It gives them a flexibility that the previous generations didn't have. Some of the old lobos take their vows very, very seriously.

What I wouldn't have given to be stupid enough to believe that Adam could promise that Marsilia wouldn't kill me—and even more to believe that he wouldn't kill himself trying to keep his word.

I wasn't resigned to my fate or anything like it, but if I had learned one thing being raised by werewolves, it was to keep a clear eye on probable outcomes and how to mitigate damage. And if Marsilia wanted me dead . . . well that was just the most probable outcome. Really probable. Enough so that I could feel another stupid panic attack hovering. My first today, if I didn't count a little shortness of breath once or twice.

"She's not dumb enough to attack me," I told him, opening my door. "Especially once she hears I've officially accepted you as my mate. That puts me under your pack's protection. She won't be able to do much to me." It should have been true . . . but I didn't think it would be that easy. "Stefan's the one in trouble."

He got out and waited for me to round the front of the van, then he asked, "Would you go out with me tomorrow . . . to someplace nice? Dinner and a little dancing."

It hadn't been what I expected him to say, not when he was watching me with those cool, assessing eyes. It took me a moment to change subjects, my impending death at Marsilia's hands being a little preoccupying.

Adam wanted to take me on a date.

He touched my face—he liked to do that and had been doing it more and more lately. I could feel the warmth of his fingers all the way to my toes. Suddenly, my approaching demise wasn't so engrossing.

"All right. That would be good." I put my hand on my stomach to settle the butterflies, unsure as to whether it was the notion of going on another date with Adam or the knowledge that I was going to have to break it off with him before I brought death to him and his pack. Maybe I'd have to go on the run tonight—would it hurt him more that I'd agreed to a date? Should I find a reason that tomorrow wouldn't work?

A sudden thought came to me. If I hurt him enough, drove him from me in anger . . . would he care when Marsilia killed me, or would he let it go? A newly familiar breathlessness started to shiver up from my stomach—that panic attack that had been hovering.

"I need to take a shower," I told him, my voice very steady. "But then I'd like to talk to Stefan."

"No problem," he said agreeably, going up my front steps ahead of me. He opened the door and held it for me. "I'll wait while you shower—Samuel's not home."

There was no reason to feel like Adam's prey, I told myself firmly as I walked past him into my own house. No reason to feel Adam's intent eyes on my back. He couldn't read my mind to know that I was planning on running. But I didn't turn back as I said, "Make yourself at home. I'll be right out." And I closed my bedroom door on him and leaned against it.

I SCRUBBED MY HANDS FIRST, USING A STIFF-BRISTLED brush and Fast Orange to get the last of the day's grime off. It never managed to get it all, but if it bothered Adam to run around with someone who had dirt ingrained in the skin of her hands, he'd never said anything. When they were as good as they were going to get, I stepped into the shower.

Could I change my mind about being Adam's mate?

I'm not as sensitive to pack magic as the werewolves are. They don't talk much about it. Secretive bunch, those werewolves. I've been finding out that there's a lot more to it than I'd believed. I knew it was possible for a mated pair to dissolve their union, though I'd never met any who had.

Had my agreement been just words, or had it started some process in the pack magic? Consent, I knew, was necessary for a lot of magic to take place. I am immune to some magic. Maybe mating would turn out to be one of those things. I also knew pack magic worked subtly differently for the Alpha than it did for the rest of the pack. Adam had bound himself to me by declaring me his mate before his pack—and it had had an effect on the pack's magic, and on Adam. I was pretty sure it didn't work quite that way for most wolves, that both had to agree, and that their mating was a more private matter.

I frowned. There was a ceremony. I was almost certain of it. Something happened to make a couple into a mated pair—and then there was some sort of werewolf-only ceremony. Maybe Adam had done it backward? Maybe mating an Alpha was no different than mating with any other wolf.

Maybe I was going to drive myself crazy. I needed real information, and I had no idea who to ask.

It couldn't be any of Adam's pack—it would undermine his authority. Besides, they'd just go tell him I was asking. Samuel didn't seem like a good choice either, not after we'd only just agreed not to try it as a couple. Or Bran, for the same reason. I knew he had sent Samuel to the Tri-Cities in a misguided attempt at matchmaking. I wasn't sure Samuel had told him it hadn't worked. I wished, not for the first time, that my foster father, Bryan, was still around. But he'd killed himself a good long time ago.

I turned my face in to the hot spray of my shower. Okay. So assume the mating thing wasn't permanent. How would I make Adam hate me?

Well, I certainly wasn't sleeping with Samuel. Or hurting Jesse.

Water hit the healing wound on my chin, and I tipped my head down. Making him leave me had seemed logical, but Adam wasn't the kind of person to leave when things got rough. And even if I managed it, wouldn't he still care if Marsilia killed me? Maybe if I had a few months or a year to work on it, I might manage.

Could I run? With my bank balance, I might make it as far as Seattle.

The threatening panic attack faded as relief swamped me. First time being broke had ever made me happy.

I might be a dead woman, but I was going to get to keep Adam for however long I had left.

———————

THOUGH ADAM'S HAND WAS COURTEOUSLY UNDER MY arm as we walked across my field to the barbed-wire fence between our properties, there was a proprietary feeling to the charged air that always seemed to accompany him. *Mine,* it said.

If it weren't for Marsilia, doubtless I'd have been grumpy about the possessiveness stuff. As it was, I was unhappy because I couldn't just relax into the safety he represented . . . not without risking his getting hurt because of me.

Maybe I needed to leave, money or not.

My stomach was back in knots, and if I didn't bottle everything up, I was going to have that stupid panic attack, and not safely behind the sound of water and the closed bathroom door. Right here where anyone could see. Next to the poor beat-up Rabbit, with Adam's phone number painted on the roof. *For a good time call . . .*

He stopped. "Mercy? What are you so angry about?"

He would know. Even I could smell it: anger and fear and . . . I had it all, and I had *nothing*.

It was too much. I closed my eyes and felt my body shake helplessly and my throat close, refusing to let air through . . .

Adam caught me as I fell and pulled me against him, in the shadow of the old car. He was so warm, and I was so cold. He put his nose against my neck. I couldn't see him, lack of air left me with black dots impairing my vision.

I heard the growl shake Adam's chest, and his mouth closed on mine—and I sucked a deep breath though my nose. I could breathe again, and the weight on my stomach lifted, and I was left shaking, with blood . . . no, snot running down my face.

Embarrassed beyond anything, I jerked free of Adam's hold—knowing with humiliating certainty that he *let* me go. I wiped my face with the bottom of my shirt. And settled in the shelter of the Rabbit, my cheek against the cooling metal.

Weak. Broken. God damn it. God damn *me*. I felt the wave of it hovering, ready to descend upon me again. Despair and helpless anger . . . They were all dead. *All dead, and it was my fault.*

But no one was dead. Not yet.

All dead. All of my children, my loves, and it was my fault. I put them at risk and failed. They died because of my failure.

I smelled Stefan.

Adam's golden eyes met mine, the color proving the wolf ascendant. He kissed me again, pressed something against my lips, forcing it between my teeth with a forefinger and thumb without removing his mouth from mine.

It was such a small scrap of bloody meat to burn down my throat as it had. It meant something.

"Mine," he told me. "You aren't Stefan's."

The dry grass crackled under my head, and the coarse dirt made a noise like sandpaper that echoed behind my eyes. I licked my lips and tasted blood. Adam's blood.

The Alpha's blood and flesh . . . pack.

"From this day forward," said Adam, his voice pulling me out of wherever I had been. "Mine to me and mine. Pack and only lover." There was blood on his face, too, and on the hands he touched my face with.

"Yours to you, mine to me," I answered, though it was a dry croaking voice that made the noise. I didn't know why I answered, other than the old "shave and a hair cut" involuntary response. I'd heard this ceremony so many times, even if he'd added the "only lover" part.

By the time I remembered why I shouldn't do it, what it meant, it was already too late.

Magic burned through me, following the path of that bit of flesh—and I cried out as it tried to make me other than I was, less or more. *Pack.*

I felt them all through Adam's touch and Adam's blood. His to protect to govern. All of them were mine now, too—and I theirs.

Panting, I licked my lips and stared at Adam. He let me go, coming to his feet and taking two steps away from me where I lay against the side of the old car. He'd bitten his forearm savagely.

"He can't have you," he told me, his gold eyes telling me the wolf was still speaking. "Not now. Not ever. I don't owe him that."

Belatedly, I realized what had happened. I wiped my mouth with my wrist to give myself time to think. My wrist was pink with Adam's blood.

Stefan was awake . . . and somehow he'd invaded my mind. It had been his panic attack I'd felt.

All dead . . . I had a sick, sick feeling that I knew who he meant. I'd met some of the people, human people who fed Stefan. Had learned how horribly vulnerable they were if something happened to the vampire who fed off them and protected them.

I glanced at the setting sun. "It's a little early for a vampire to be up, isn't it?" I asked.

Time for everyone to calm down. Me, included.

My sense of the pack was fading, but it would never completely go away. Not now that Adam had made me pack. It was more usual to do it in a full pack meeting, but the pack wasn't required. Just a bit of the Alpha's flesh and blood and an exchange of vows.

I hadn't thought it possible to induct someone who wasn't a werewolf. I certainly hadn't thought that he could make me pack. Magic works oddly on me sometimes, and at others I'm pretty much immune to it. But from the results I could feel, it had worked just fine this time.

Adam had turned and stood with his back to me, his shoulders hunched, his hands fisted at his side. He didn't answer my question, but said stiffly, "I'm sorry for that. I panicked."

I put my forehead down on my knees. "There's been a lot of that going around recently."

I heard the dry grass crunch as he walked back to me. "Are you laughing?" he sounded incredulous.

I looked up at him. The last rays of the sun silhouetted him in golden rays and obscured the expression on his face. But I could see shame in the set of his shoulders. He'd made me pack without asking me—without asking the pack either, though that wasn't strictly necessary, just traditional. He was waiting for me to yell at him as he felt he deserved.

Adam was used to paying for the consequences of his choices—and sometimes the choices were hard ones. He'd been making a lot of hard choices for me lately.

Stefan had been so far in my head that I had smelled like him. And Adam had made me pack to save me. He was prepared to pay the price—and I was pretty sure there would be a price extracted. But not by me.

"Thank you, Adam," I told him. "Thank you for tearing Tim into small Tim bits. Thank you for forcing me to drink one last cup of fairy bug-juice so I could have use of both of my arms. Thank you for being there, for putting up with me." By that point I wasn't laughing anymore. "Thank you for keeping me from being another of Stefan's sheep—I'll take pack over that any day. Thank you for making the tough calls, for giving me time." I stood up and walked to him, leaning against him and pressing my face against his shoulder. "Thank you for loving me."

His arms closed around me, pressing flesh painfully hard against bone. Love hurts like that sometimes.

4

~~~

I'D HAVE LOVED TO STAY THERE FOREVER, BUT AFTER A few minutes, I felt the cold sweat break out on my forehead and my throat started to close down. I stepped back before I had to do something more forceful in reaction to the aversion to touch that Tim had left me with.

Only when I was no longer pressed against Adam did I notice we were surrounded by pack.

Okay, four wolves doesn't a pack make. But I hadn't heard them come, and, believe me, when there are five werewolves (including Adam) about, you feel surrounded and overmatched.

Ben was there, a cheerful expression that looked just wrong on his fine-featured face, which was more often angry or bitter than happy. Warren, Adam's third, looked like a cat in the cream. Aurielle,

Darryl's mate, appeared neutral, but there was something in her stance that told me she was pretty shaken up. The fourth wolf was Paul, whom I didn't know very well—but I didn't like what I did know.

Paul, the leader of the "I hate Warren because he's gay" faction of Adam's pack, looked like he'd been sucker punched. I thought I'd just given him a new most-hated person in the pack.

Behind me, Adam laid his hands on my shoulders. "My children," he said formally, "I give you Mercedes Athena Thompson, our newest member."

Much awkwardness ensued.

IF I HADN'T FELT HIM EARLIER, I WOULD HAVE THOUGHT Stefan was still unconscious or dead or whatever from the sun. He lay stiffly on the bed in the cage, like a corpse on a bier.

I turned the light on so I could see him better. Feeding had healed most of the visible damage, though there were still red marks on his cheeks. He looked fifty pounds lighter than he'd been the last time I'd seen him—too much like a concentration camp victim for my peace of mind. He'd been given new clothes to replace his filthy, torn, and stained ones, the ubiquitous replacement clothing every wolf den had lying around—sweats. The ones he wore were gray and hung off his bones.

Adam was conducting what was rapidly developing into a full pack meeting in his living room upstairs. He'd looked relieved when I'd excused myself to see Stefan—I thought he was worried someone would say something that might hurt my feelings. In that he underestimated the thickness of my hide. People I cared about could hurt my feelings, but almost complete strangers? I could care less about what they thought.

Wolf packs were dictatorships, but when you're dealing with a bunch of Americans brought up on the Bill of Rights, you still had to step a little carefully. New members were generally announced as prospective rather than as faits accomplis. A little care would have been especially appropriate when he was doing something as outrageous as bringing a nonwerewolf into the pack.

I'd never heard of anyone doing that. Nonwerewolf mates weren't part of the pack, not really. They had status, as the mates of wolves, but they weren't pack. Couldn't be made into pack with fifty flesh-and-blood ceremonies—the magic just wouldn't let a human in. Apparently my coyoteness was close enough to wolf that the pack magic was willing to let me in.

Probably Adam should have discussed bringing me in with the Marrok, too.

Cars were pulling up in front of the house, more of the pack. I could feel the weight of them, their unease and confusion. Anger.

I rubbed my arms nervously.

"What's wrong?" asked Stefan in a quiet, sane voice that would have reassured me more if he'd moved or opened his eyes.

"Besides Marsilia?" I asked him.

He looked at me then, his lips curving faintly. "That's enough, I suppose. But Marsilia isn't the reason this house is filling with werewolves."

I sat on the thickly carpeted basement floor and leaned my head against the bars of the cage. The door was shut and locked, the key that sometimes hung on the wall across the hallway gone. Adam would have it. It didn't matter though. I was pretty sure Stefan could leave anytime he chose—the same way he'd appeared in my living room.

"Right." I sighed. "Well that's your fault, too, I expect."

He sat up and leaned forward. "What happened?"

"When you jumped inside my head," I told him, "Adam took offense." I didn't tell him exactly how everything had played out. Prudence suggested Adam wouldn't be pleased with me if I shared pack business with a vampire. "What he did—and you'll have to ask him, I think—brought the pack down on his head."

He frowned in obvious puzzlement, then slow comprehension dawned. "I am sorry, Mercy. You weren't meant to . . . I didn't mean to." He turned his head away. "I'm not used to being so alone. I was dreaming, and there you were, the only one left with a tie of blood to me. I thought I dreamed that, too."

"She really had them all killed?" I whispered it, remembering some of what he'd given me while he'd been in my head. "All of your . . ." Sheep wasn't really PC, and I didn't want to tick him off, even if sheep is what all the vampires called the mundane humans they kept to feed off. "All of your people?"

I knew some of them, and liked one or two. For some reason, though, rather than the faces of the people I'd met living, it was the young vampire Danny I remembered, his ghost rocking in the corner of Stefan's kitchen. Stefan hadn't been able to protect him either.

Stefan gave me a sick look. "Disciplining me, she said. But I think it was revenge as much as anything. And I can feed off them from a distance. She wanted me starving when I landed at your feet."

"She wanted you to kill me."

He nodded jerkily. "That's right. And if you hadn't had half of Adam's pack at your house, I would have."

I thought of the obstinate look on his face. "I think she underestimated you," I told him.

"Did she?" He smiled, just a little, and shook his head.

I leaned my head back against the wall. "I'm . . ." *Still angry with you* didn't cover it. He was a murderer of innocents, and here I was talking to him, worried about him. I didn't know how to complete that thought, much less the sentence, so I went on to something else.

"So Marsilia knows I killed Andre, and you and Wulfe covered it up?"

He shook his head. "She knows something—she didn't talk much to me. It was only me she punished, so I don't think she knows about Wulfe. And maybe not me . . ." He looked at me from under the cover of his bangs, which had grown in the last day—I'd heard a heavy feeding could cause that. "I got the feeling I was being punished by association. I was the seethe's contact with you. I was the reason she went to you for help and gave you permission to kill Andre's pet. I was the reason you succeeded. You are my fault."

"She's crazy."

He shook his head. "You don't know her. She's trying to do what is best for her people."

The Tri-City seethe of vampires had mostly been in the area before the towns were established. Marsilia had been sent here as punishment for sleeping around with someone else's favorite. She'd been a person of influence, so had come here with attendants—mostly, as far as I knew, Stefan, Andre—the second vampire I'd killed—and a really creepy character named Wulfe.

Wulfe, who looked like a sixteen-year-old boy, had been a witch or wizard as a human, and sometimes dressed like a medieval peasant. I supposed he could be faking it, but I suspected that he was older than Marsilia, who dated from the Renaissance, so the clothes fit.

Marsilia had been sent here to die, but she hadn't. Instead, she'd seen to it that her people survived. As civilization began to grow, life in the seethe became easier. The fight for survival mostly a thing of the past, Marsilia had settled into a decades-long period of apathy—I'd call it sulking. She had only just begun to take an interest in things going on about her, and as a result, the hierarchy of the seethe was restless. Stefan and Andre had been loyal followers, but there were a couple of other vamps who hadn't been so happy to see Marsilia up and taking charge. I'd met them: Estelle and Bernard, but I didn't know enough about vampires to figure out how much of a threat they were.

The first time I met Marsilia, I'd kind of admired her . . . at least until she'd enthralled Samuel. That had scared me. Samuel's the second-most-dominant wolf in North America, and she and her vampires took him . . . easily. That fear had grown with every meeting.

"Not to be argumentative, Stefan," I said. "But she's bug-nuts. She wanted to create another of those . . . those *things* that Andre made."

His face closed down. "You don't know what you are talking about. You have no idea what she gave up when she came here, or what she has done for us."

"Maybe not, but I met that creature, and so did you. Nothing good could ever come of making another one." Demonic possession isn't a pretty thing. I inhaled and tried to control my temper. I didn't succeed. "But you are right. I don't know what makes her tick. I don't know you, either."

He just looked at me, expressionlessly.

"You play human very well, driving around like Shaggy in your Mystery Machine. But the man I thought you were could never have killed Andre's victims like that."

"Wulfe killed them." He was making a point, not defending himself. It made me angry; he *should* feel the need to defend himself.

"You *agreed* to it. Two people who had already been victimized enough, and you two snapped their necks as if they were nothing more than chickens."

About that time he got angry, too. "I did it for *you*. Don't you understand? She would have destroyed you if she'd known. They were nothing, less than nothing. Street people who would have died on their own anyway. And *she* would have killed *you*!" He was on his feet when he finished.

"They were nothing? How do you know? It wasn't like you had a conversation with them." I stood up, too.

"They would have had to die anyway. They knew about us."

"There we disagree," I told him. "What about your vaunted power over human minds?"

"It only works if the contact with us is very short—a feeding, no more than that."

"They were living, breathing people who were murdered. By *you*."

"How did you know that Mercy was at Andre's?" Warren's calm voice broke between us like a wave of ice water as he came down the stairs. He walked past me and used the key to open the cage door. "I've been wondering about that for a while."

"What do you mean?" asked Stefan.

"I mean that *we* knew she'd found Andre because she told Ben, thinking he couldn't tell anyone else because he'd not changed back from his wolf in all the time since the demon-possessed died. Ben changed so he could tell us, but we still couldn't go after her because we didn't know where Andre was. You had no way to know what she was doing. How did you know she was off killing Andre, just in time to cover up the crime?"

Stefan made no move to come out of the cage. He folded his

arms and leaned a shoulder against the bars instead as he considered Warren's question.

"It was Wulfe, wasn't it?" I said. "He knew what I was doing because one of the homes I found was his."

"Wulfe," said Warren slowly, after Stefan didn't answer. "Is he the kind of man who would be outraged that Marsilia would call down a demon to infest a vampire? Would he want it stopped at the cost of Andre's destruction? Go to you for help doing it?"

Stefan closed his eyes. "He came to me. Told me Mercy was in trouble and needed help. It was only later that I wondered why he'd done it."

"You've had these thoughts already," Warren said. "So what did you decide?"

"Does it matter?"

"It's always a good thing to know your enemies," answered Warren in his lazy Texas drawl. "Who are yours?"

Stefan gave him the look of a baited bear, all frustration and ferocity. "I don't know." He gritted out.

Warren smiled coolly, his eyes sharp. "Oh, I think you do. You aren't stupid; you aren't a child. You know how these things work."

"Wulfe used me to get to you," I said. "Then he told Marsilia what you'd done."

Stefan just looked at me.

"With you and Andre out of the way, there is Wulfe, Bernard, and Estelle." I rubbed my hands together and wondered if knowing what had happened would do Stefan any good. It wouldn't change things, and knowing that he'd fallen into Wulfe's trap wasn't going to help Stefan now. Still, as Warren had said, it is a good thing to know your enemies. "And Bernard and Estelle, Marsilia already doesn't trust them, right?"

Stefan nodded. "They work against her where they can, and she knows it. They are of another's making, given as gifts by a vampire not easily refused. She must take care of them, as she would any such gifts—but that doesn't mean she has to trust them. Wulfe . . . Wulfe is a mystery even to himself, I think. You believe Wulfe engineered this as a rise to power?" He looked away and didn't speak for a minute, obviously thinking about what I'd said.

Finally, he wrapped his hands around the bars of the open cage. "Wulfe already has power . . . if he wanted more, it was his for the asking. But it looks like he had a part in my downfall for whatever reason suited him."

"If Marsilia knows that you helped when Mercy killed Andre, why isn't Mercy dead?" Warren asked.

"She was supposed to be," Stefan said savagely. "Why do you think Marsilia starved me until I was no more than a ravening beast, then dropped me into Mercy's living room? You didn't think I did it myself, did you?"

I nodded. "So she thought she'd get it all without cost to her or the seethe? If you'd killed me, she could have claimed you'd escaped while she was punishing you. Too bad you showed up in my house and killed me. But she underestimated you."

"She did not underestimate me," said Stefan. "She *knows* me." He gave me a look that let me know that my earlier dig about not knowing him had stung. "She just did not plan on you having the Alpha werewolf in your home to spoil her plans."

I'd been there—and I didn't think he would have done it.

Stefan sneered at me when he saw my face. "Don't waste your time on romantic notions about *me*. I am *vampire*, and I would have killed you."

"He's cute when he's mad," observed Warren dryly.

Stefan turned his back on us both.

"She's all by herself, and she doesn't even know it," he said in soft anguish.

He wasn't talking about me.

He'd been hurt a lot recently, and I thought he deserved a rest. So I turned to Warren, and asked, "Why aren't you upstairs at the meeting?"

Warren shrugged, his eyes veiled. "The boss will do better without me to rock the boat."

"Paul hates me more than he hates you," I told him smugly.

He threw his head back and laughed—which is what I'd intended. "Wanna bet? I kicked his ass from here to Seattle and back. He's not happy with me."

"You're a wolf. I'm a coyote—there's no comparison."

"Hey," said Warren in mock offense. "You're no threat to his masculinity."

"I'm polluting the pack," I told him. "You're just an aberration."

"That's because you called him a . . . Stefan?"

I looked around, but the vampire was gone. I hadn't gotten a chance to ask him about the crossed bones on my door.

"Shee-it," exclaimed Warren. "Shee-it."

"DID YOU CALL BRAN?" I ASKED ADAM THE NEXT EVE-ning, tugging down the short skirt of my favorite green-blue dress until it was as good a barrier between Adam's SUV's leather seats and my naked skin as it was going to be.

He hadn't told me where we were going on our date, but Jesse had called me as soon as he left and described what he was wearing—so I knew I'd need the big guns. Though we share a back fence, the distance by car is significantly longer, and I'd had time to skim into the correct dress before he pulled up at my door.

Adam does suits. He wears suits to work, to pack meetings, to political meetings. Since his hours are about the same as mine, that means six days a week. Still there was a difference between his usual work suits and the one he was wearing tonight. The first were made to announce that this was the man in charge. This one said, "And he's sexy, too." And he was.

"There's no need to call Bran," he told me irritably as he swung the big vehicle onto the highway. "Half the pack probably called Bran as soon as they got home. He'll call me when he's ready."

He was probably right. I hadn't asked, but his grim face when Warren and I emerged from the basement last night—after everyone had left except for Samuel—had told its own story.

Samuel had kissed me on the lips to irritate Adam and ruffled my hair, "There you are, Little Wolf. Still naturally talented at causing trouble, I see."

That was unfair. It had been Stefan and Adam who'd caused this. I informed Samuel of that, but only after he'd escorted me back home.

Adam called me once, earlier in the afternoon, to make sure I remembered he was taking me out. I'd promptly called Jesse with orders to let me know what her father was wearing. I owed her five bucks, but it was worth it to see Adam smiling when I hopped into his SUV.

But my mouth had soon taken care of that. His Explorer still had a heck of a dent on the fender from where one of the wolves had hit it—after being thrown by an angry fae. My fault. So I'd asked him if he had an estimate yet, and he'd growled at me. Then I'd asked about Bran.

So far our date was working out just spiffy.

I went back to playing with my skirt.

"Mercy," Adam said, his voice even more growly than it had been.

"What?" If I snapped at him, it was his own fault for getting grumpy at me first.

"If you don't stop playing with that dress, I'm going to rip it right off you, and we won't be heading for dinner."

I looked at him. He was watching the road, and both hands were on the wheel . . . but once I paid attention, I could see what I'd done to him. *Me*. With remnants of grease under my fingernails and stitches in my chin.

Maybe I hadn't screwed up the date as badly as all of that. I smoothed the skirt back down, successfully resisting the urge to pull it up farther only because I wasn't sure I could handle what might happen. I thought Adam was joking, but . . . I turned my head toward my side window and tried to keep the grin off my face.

He drove us to a restaurant that had just opened in the boom-town that was forming in West Pasco. Just a couple of years ago it had been barren desert, but now there were restaurants, a the-ater, a Lowe's and . . . a hugeyenormous (Jesse's word) giant-sized Wal-Mart.

"I hope you like Thai." He parked us out in the middle of west nowhere in the parking lot. Paranoia has odd manifestations. It gave me panic attacks and made him park where he could manage a quick getaway. Shared paranoia—could a happily-ever-after be far off for us?

I hopped out of the front seat and said in suitably resolute tones, "I'm sure they have hamburgers."

I shut the door on his appalled face. The locks clicked, and there he was, one arm on either side of me . . . grinning.

"You like Thai," he said. "Admit it."

I folded my arms and ignored the gibbering idiot who kept shrieking "he's got me trapped, trapped" in the back of my head. It helped that Adam up close is even better than half a car away. And Adam with a grin . . . well. He has a dimple, just one. That's all he needs.

"Jesse told you, didn't she?" I said grumpily. "Next time I see her, I'm going to expose her for the secret-sharing kid she is. See if I don't."

He laughed . . . and dropped his arms and backed away, proving he'd seen my erstwhile panic. I grabbed his arm to prove I wasn't scared and towed him around the Explorer toward the restaurant.

The food was excellent. As I pointed out to Adam, they did have hamburgers. Neither of us ordered them, though doubtless they would have been good, too. I could have been eating seaweed and dust, though, and I still would have enjoyed it.

We talked about cars—and how I thought his Explorer was a pile of junk and he thought I was stuck in the seventies in my preference for cars. I pointed out that my Rabbit was a respectable eighties model, as was my Vanagon—and the chances of his SUV being around in thirty years was nil. Especially if his wolves kept getting thrown at it.

We talked about movies and books. He liked biographies, of all things. The only biography I'd ever liked was *Carry On, Mr. Bowditch*, which I'd read in seventh grade. He didn't read fiction.

We got in an argument about Yeats. Not about his poetry, but about his obsession with the occult. Adam thought it was ridiculous . . . I thought it was funny that a werewolf would think it so and baited him until he caught me at it.

"Mercy," he said—and his phone rang.

I drank a sip of water and prepared to listen in to his conversation. But, as it turned out, it was very short.

"Hauptman," he answered shortly.

"You'd better get over here, wolf," said an unfamiliar voice and hung up.

He looked down at the number and frowned. I got up and walked around the table so I could look over his shoulder.

"It's someone from Uncle Mike's," I told him, having memorized the number.

Adam threw some money on the table and we trotted out the door. Grim-faced, he threaded the Explorer through the traffic at something more than the speed limit. We had just gotten on the interstate when something happened. . . . I felt a flash of rage and horror, and someone died. One of the pack.

I put my hand on Adam's leg, digging in with my nails at the roiling sorrow and rage that spun through the pack. He put his foot down and slid through the evening traffic like an eel. Neither of us said a word during the five minutes it took us to reach Uncle Mike's.

The parking lot was full of big SUVs and trucks, the kind most of the fae drive. Adam didn't bother parking, just drove right up until he was near the door and stopped. He didn't wait for me—but he didn't have to. I was right behind him when he brushed by the bouncer who guarded the door.

The bouncer didn't even protest.

Uncle Mike's smelled like beer, hot wings, and popcorn, which would have made it smell like every other bar in the Tri-Cities except that it also smelled like fae. I don't know that they organize themselves that way, but fae usually smell to me like the four elements that the old philosophers proposed: earth, air, fire, and water, with a healthy dose of magic.

None of those smells bothered me . . . only the blood.

Uncle Mike's commanding voice was backing people up and tightening the crowd until Adam and I were blocked in. That's when Adam lost it and began tossing people around.

Not really a safe thing to do at Uncle Mike's. Most of the fae I've met are no match for a werewolf . . . but there are ogres and other things that look just like everyone else until they get ticked off.

Even so, it wasn't until Adam began to change, ripping his charcoal suit, that I realized something more was happening than him losing his temper.

"Adam!" It was no use, my voice was lost in the noise of the crowd. I put a hand on his back so I didn't lose him, and I felt it.

Magic.

I jerked my hand back. It didn't feel like fae magic. I looked around for someone who was concentrating just a little too much on Adam but couldn't spot anyone over the crowd.

I did, however, see a little canvas bag hanging from the rafters just behind us. About the same place Adam started using physical force to move through the crowd. The ceilings in Uncle Mike's are about fourteen feet in the air. I wasn't going to reach that bag without a ladder—and I wasn't going to be able to find a ladder anytime soon.

A slender, almost effeminate man walked under the bag as I watched. He jerked to a halt, then threw back his head and roared. A sound so huge that it drowned out all of the noise in the building, shaking the rafters. His glamour, the illusion that made him look human, shattered, and I swear I could almost see a pile of sparkling dust spread out from him.

He was huge, an unearthly mass of gray and blue, still vaguely human-shaped, but his face looked like it had melted, leaving only vague bumps where his nose should have been. His mouth was pretty easy to spot—it would be hard to miss all those big teeth. Silvery eyes, too small for that huge face, glared out from under sparkly blue eyebrows. He shook himself, and the sparkly dust scattered again, melting as it touched warmer surfaces. He was shedding snow.

In the silence that followed, a small cranky voice said, "Freakin' snow elf." I couldn't see the speaker, but it sounded like it was coming from somewhere right next to the newly emerged monster.

He roared again and reached down, hauling a woman up by the hair. She was more angry than scared and pulled a weapon out of somewhere and cut her own hair, dropping down and out of my sight again. The thing—I'd never heard of a snow elf—shook the hair he held and threw it behind him.

I glanced back at Adam, but in the short moments since I'd last looked, he'd disappeared, leaving behind only a trail of bloody bodies, most of them still standing and ticked off. I looked at the snow elf and the bag above his head.

No one was watching me, not with a rampaging werewolf and an abominable snowman in the room. I stripped off the dress and bra, stepped out of my shoes and underwear as fast as I could. I'm not a werewolf; my coyote shape comes between one breath and the next, and brings exhilaration and not pain. The snow elf was still standing underneath the bag when I jumped up, landed on someone's shoulders, and looked for him.

The crowd was so tight it was like being at a Metallica concert, and I had a road of heads and shoulders right to the snow elf—who was ten feet tall at the very least and stuck up a whole person's worth over the rest of the people.

He saw me coming and grabbed for me, but I'm fast and he missed. Actually, he probably missed because he didn't know I was going to jump on his shoulder and launch myself at the little bag, rather than because of any speed or dexterity on my part. That damned mountain of a fae was fast, too.

The magic buzzed angrily at me as I snatched the bag in my jaws. I dangled for a moment before the string that held it broke. I fell and waited for the giant hands of the snow elf to crush me, but it was Uncle Mike himself who snatched me out of the air and tossed me toward the door.

As soon as I grabbed the bag, I knew I was right about it being some sort of vicious spell aimed at the wolves. I didn't know how Uncle Mike knew it, too, but he snarled, "Take that thing out of here," before he melted back into the crowd.

Like a Dr. Seuss poem, I scrambled under, around, and through before I got out the door. I'd have felt better if I hadn't known that someone I knew—because I knew most of Adam's pack at least by face—was dead. I'd have felt better if I had known Adam was all right. I'd have settled for just not having the towering mountain of enraged . . . snow elf following me at full speed.

I'd never met anyone who called himself an elf, so I supposed my view was skewed by Peter Jackson's version of Tolkien's fair folk. The thing following me like a freight train didn't fit my understanding of the word at all.

Later, if I survived, I might derive some amusement from the face of the bouncer, who suddenly realized what was coming at him—just before he broke and ran. I passed him as we both jumped the short step to the pavement outside the door. He ran with me a couple of steps before he figured out who the snow elf was chasing and took a sharp right.

The doorway slowed the monster down. He hit it with his shoulder, taking the whole entryway wall with him as he left the building. He threw the chunk of wall at me, but I hopped through the half-open doorway a second time, just before it hit the ground. I crossed the street at full speed and narrowly missed being hit by a semi on its way to the industrial district just past Uncle Mike's. Safe on the far side, I glanced behind me, then stopped.

The man the snow elf had been was on his knees at the edge of the parking lot, shaking his head as if he was slightly dazed. He looked up at me. The silvery eyes were the same.

"Are you all right?" he asked. "Sorry, so sorry. I haven't felt like that since . . . since my last battle. I didn't hurt you, did I?" His gaze caught on the chunks of wall and door that were left from when his missile had missed me.

The effects of the little bag were evidently limited by distance.

I dropped the bag on the ground and shook myself and gave him an "all's well" yip. I wasn't sure he got the message, but he didn't try to cross the road after me. I'd have changed back, but my clothes—my favorite dress, a pair of expensive (even at half-off) Italian sandals, and my underwear—were still in the bar somewhere. I'm not modest, but the snow elf and I didn't know each other well enough for me to want be naked in front of him.

He was dazedly trying to pick up the mess he'd made when people started leaving. One of Uncle Mike's people, easily distinguished from the patrons by the distinctive green doublet, stood on the edge of the parking lot and waved his hands at me in a pushing motion. I thought it was the bouncer who'd been at the door, but I'd have to have seen his face frozen in terror again to be certain of it.

I picked up the bag and backed away from the road a dozen yards, until my butt hit the side of an old warehouse fifty yards from the road.

Uncle Mike's parking lot gradually emptied, with Uncle Mike's minions directing traffic and helping the snow elf with his cleanup efforts. Adam's car sat in lonely splendor.

So did Mary Jo's Jeep. The one I'd given a free tune-up to when she'd taken her shift at guard-the-wimpy-coyote duty. I like Mary Jo. She's a firefighter, five-foot-three-and-a-half of solid muscle and solider nerve.

One of the pack was dead. In the sudden quiet of the night, I could feel the wave of mourning spreading through the pack as the others acknowledged the absence of one of their own. They knew who it was, but I wasn't familiar enough with the pack magic to be certain. I only had Mary Jo's car.

There were just six cars left in the patron's parking lot when Uncle Mike strode out of the hole that used to be a door. He clapped a hand on the snow elf's shoulder and patted him before hopping over a cement parking curb and crossing the street toward me. He had my dress in his hands.

I *changed* and grabbed the dress and pulled it on. No bra, no underwear, but at least I wasn't naked. I kicked the bag toward Uncle Mike. "What happened?"

He bent and picked up the bag. His face tightened, and he made a low, huffing sound . . . rather more like a lion or big cat of some kind than anything I'd ever heard out of him before.

"Cobweb," he said, "come throw this nasty bit of magic in the river for me, would you?"

Something small and bright, about the size of a lightning bug (there are none in the Tri-Cities) hovered over the bag for a moment, then it, and the bag, disappeared.

"It affected you, too?" I asked.

I don't know what kind of a fae Uncle Mike is. Something powerful enough to control a tavern full of drunken fae seven nights a week.

"No," he said. "Just that it was put in my territory, and I did not sense it."

He dusted off his hands, and his face regained its usual cheerful mien, but I'd seen beneath that facade a few times so his mask of affable tavern keeper didn't reassure me the way it once would have. You have to remember never to believe what you see with the fae.

"Smart coyote," he told me. "I didn't even check to see if there was a cause for their snarling, just assumed they were being nasty-tempered, the way werewolves are—and left it too late before I waded in."

"What happened?" I asked again, but when he didn't answer immediately, I gave him an impatient flick of my hand and ran bare-footed back across the street, through the parking lot, and into the bar.

Inside, with the missing section of wall behind me, it didn't look so bad: a big, empty tavern after a couple of football teams had gotten drunk and partied all night. Teams with really big players, I thought, looking at the beam that the snow elf had taken out with his head—elephants, maybe.

Adam, fully in human form again, sat with his back against the stage riser on the far side of the room, his arms folded over his chest. Somone had found him a pair of cutoffs to wear. Not like he was angry . . . just closed-up.

Next to him were two of his other wolves, Paul and one of Paul's cronies. Paul looked sick, and the other man, whose name escaped me, was curled around a very still form.

I couldn't see who it was, but I knew. Mary Jo's car in the parking lot told me. There was blood all over all of them. Adam's hands were covered, as was Paul's shirt. The other man was drenched in it.

The wolves weren't the only ones bleeding. There seemed to be a triage of sorts going on at the opposite end of the building. I recognized the woman who had cut her hair to free herself, but she seemed to be one of the aid-givers rather than a victim.

Adam looked up and saw me, his face very bleak.

There was glass on the floor, and my feet were bare—but it would have taken more than that to keep me from them.

Paul's friend was sobbing. "I didn't mean to. I didn't mean to. I'm so sorry." He was rocking the body he held, Mary Jo's body, as he apologized over and over again.

I couldn't get close to Adam without wading between Paul and his friend. I stopped while still out of reach. It didn't seem like a really good idea to give Paul an easy target just yet.

Uncle Mike had followed me in, but he'd gone to the other huddle of beings in that too-empty room first, and when he came over to us, he had the shorn woman in tow. Like me, he stopped before he intruded on their space.

"My apologies, Alpha," he said. "My guests are entitled to an evening of safety, and someone broke hospitality to bespell your wolves. Will you let us repair the damage if we can?" He waved at Mary Jo.

Adam's face changed from grim to intent in about half a breath. He stood up and took Mary Jo from the wolf who held her. "Paul," he said, when the man wouldn't let go.

Paul stirred and took his friend's hands, pulling them away. The man . . . Stan, I thought, though it might have been Sean, jerked once, then collapsed against Paul.

In the meantime, the woman was protesting in a rapid flow of Russian. I couldn't understand the words, but I heard her refusal clearly in her face and body language.

"Who are they going to tell?" Uncle Mike snapped. "They're werewolves. If they go to the press and reveal that there's a fae who can heal mortal wounds, we can go to the press and tell the interested humans just how much of the horrors of the werewolf have been carefully hidden from them."

She turned to look at the wolves, a snarl on her face—and then she just stopped when she saw me. Her pupils dilated until the whole of her eyes were black.

"You," she said. Then she laughed, a cackling sound that made the skin on the back of my neck crawl. "Of course it would be you."

For some reason the sight of me seemed to stop her protests. She walked to Mary Jo, who hung limply from Adam's curled arms. Like the snow elf had before her, the fae shed her glamour, but hers dripped from her head and down to her feet, where it puddled for a moment, as if it were made of liquid instead of magic.

She was tall, taller than Adam, taller than Uncle Mike, but her arms were reed-thin, and the fingers that touched Mary Jo were odd. It took me a moment to see that each one had an extra joint and a small pad on the underside, like a gecko's.

Her face . . . was ugly. As the glamour faded, her eyes shrank and her nose grew and hung over her narrow-lipped mouth like the gnarled limb of an old oak.

From her body, as the glamour cleared away, a soft violet light gathered and flowed upward from her feet to her shoulders, then down her arms to her hands. Her padded fingers turned Mary Jo's head and touched her under the chin where someone (probably Paul's repentant friend) had ripped out her throat.

The light never touched me . . . but I felt it anyway. Like the first light of the morning, or the spray of the salt sea on my face, it delighted my skin. I heard Adam draw in a sharp breath, but he didn't look away from Mary Jo. After a few minutes, Mary Jo's tank top started glowing white in the pale purple light of the fae's magic. The blood that had made it look dark in the dimmed lights of the bar was gone.

The fae jerked her hands away. "It is done," she told Adam. "I have healed her body, but you must give her pulse and breath. Only if she has not yet gone on will she return—I am no god to be giving life and death."

"CPR," translated Uncle Mike laconically.

Adam dropped to his knees, set Mary Jo on the ground, and tilted her head back and began.

"What about brain damage?" I asked.

The fae turned to me. "I healed her body. If they inspire her heart and lungs soon, there will be no damage to her."

Paul's friend was sitting at Adam's side, but Paul got up and opened his mouth.

"Don't," I said urgently.

His eyes flashed at being given an order by me. I should have just let Paul do it, but I was part of the pack now, willy-nilly—and that meant keeping the pack safe.

"You can't thank fae," I told him. "Unless you want to live the rest of your very long life in servitude to them."

"Spoilsport," said the fae woman.

"Mary Jo is precious to our pack," I told her, bowing my head. "Her loss would have left a wound for many months to come. Your healing is a rare and marvelous gift."

Mary Jo gasped, and Paul forgot he was angry with me. He wasn't anything special to her or she to him. She was sweet on a very nice wolf named Henry, and Paul was married to a human I'd never met. But Mary Jo was pack.

I would have turned to her, too, but the fae held my eyes. Her thin-lipped mouth curved into a cold smile. "This is the one, isn't it?"

"Yes," agreed Uncle Mike cautiously. He was a friend, usually. His caution told me two things. This fae might hurt me, and Uncle Mike, even in the center of his power, his tavern, didn't think he could stop her.

She looked me up and down with the air of an experienced cook at Saturday Market, examining tomatoes for blemishes. "I thought there would not be another coyote so rash as to climb the snow elf. You owe me nothing for this, Green Man."

I'd heard Uncle Mike called Green Man before. I still wasn't sure exactly what it meant.

And when the fae reached those long fingers out and touched me, I wasn't worried about much other than my own furry hide.

"I did it because of you, coyote. Do you know how much chaos you have caused? The Morrigan says that is your gift. Rash, quick, and lucky, just like Coyote himself. But that old Trickster dies in his adventures—but *you* won't be able to put yourself back together with the dawn."

I didn't say anything. I'd thought her to be just another of the Tri-Cities fae, denizens (mostly) of Fairyland, the fae reservation just outside of Walla Walla, built either to keep us safe from the fae, or the fae safe from the rest of us. Her healing Mary Jo had given me a clue—healing with magic is no common or weak gift among the fae.

Uncle Mike's caution told me she was scary powerful.

"We'll have more words at a later date, Green Man." She looked back at me. "Who are you, little coyote, to cause the Great Ones such consternation? You broke our laws, yet your defiance of our ruling has been greatly to our benefit. Siebold Adlebertsmiter is innocent and all the trouble was caused by humans. You must be punished—and rewarded."

She laughed as if I was pretty amusing. "Consider yourself rewarded."

The light that had continued to swirl around her feet uneasily stirred and darkened until it was a dark stone circle about three feet around and six inches thick. It solidified under her feet, lifting her half a foot in the air like Aladdin's carpet. The sides curved upward and formed a dish—the memory of an old story supplied the rest. Not a dish but a mortar. A giant mortar.

And she was gone. Not the way that Stefan could go, but just so swiftly my eyes couldn't follow her. I'd seen a fae fly through solid matter before, so it wasn't a surprise that she did so. Which was good, because I'd just had one terrible surprise, I didn't need any more.

The first rule about the fae is that you don't want to attract their attention—but they don't tell you what to do once you have.

"I thought Baba Yaga was a witch," I told Uncle Mike hollowly. Who else would be flying around in a giant mortar?

"Witches aren't immortal," he told me. "Of course she's not a witch."

Baba Yaga is featured in the stories of a dozen countries scattered around Eastern Europe. She's not the hero in most of them. She eats children.

I glanced over at Adam, but he was still focused on Mary Jo. She was shaking like someone on the verge of hypothermia, but seemed to be alive still.

"What about that bag," I asked. "What if someone picks it up from the river?"

"A few minutes of running water will remove any magic from a spell set in fabric," Uncle Mike told me.

"It was a trap for the wolves," I told him. I knew that because it had tasted like vampire. "No one else except for the mobile mountain was affected . . . Why him and none of the rest? And what in the world is a snow elf? I've never heard of one." As far as I'd ever known, "elf" was one of those generic terms coined by mundanes as a way to refer to the fae.

"The government," said Uncle Mike, after a moment to consider what he wanted to tell me (getting the fae to share information is harder than getting a drop of water from a stone), "requires us to register and tell them what kind of fae we are. So we chose something that appeals to us. For some it is an old title or name, for others . . . we make it up, just like the humans have made up names for us for centuries. My favorite is the infamous 'Jack-Be-Nimble.' I don't know what that is, but we have at least a dozen in our reservation."

I couldn't help but grin. Our government didn't know they had a tiger by the tail—and the tiger wasn't going to tell them anytime soon. "So he made up the snow elf bit?"

"Are you going to argue with him? As to why the bag aimed at the wolf worked—"

"I have another true form," said a soft, Norse-accented voice behind me. There weren't very many people who could sneak up on me—my coyote senses keep me pretty aware of my environment—but I sure hadn't heard him.

It was the snow elf, or whatever he was, of course. He was a couple of inches shorter than me—which he could have fixed as easily as Zee could have gotten rid of his bald spot. I supposed someone whose true form—at least one of them—was ten feet tall didn't mind being short.

He looked at me and bowed, one of those abrupt and stiff movements of head and neck that brings to mind martial artists. "I'm glad you are fast," he said.

I shook the hand he held out to me, which was cool and dry. "I'm glad I'm fast, too," I told him with honest sincerity.

He looked at Uncle Mike. "Do you know who set it? And if it was aimed at the werewolves or at me?"

Adam was listening to the conversation. I wasn't sure how I knew, because it looked like he was totally involved with his battered wolves. But there was something in the tension of his shoulders.

Uncle Mike shook his head. "I was too concerned with getting it away from you. Berserker wolves are bad enough, but a berserker snow elf loose in downtown Pasco is something I don't want to see."

I knew. The bag had smelled of vampire.

The snow elf knelt beside Mary Jo and touched her shoulder. Adam pulled her gently away, setting her in Paul's lap, and put himself between her and the snow elf.

"Mine," he said.

The elf raised his hands and smiled mildly, but there was a bite to his words. "No harm, Alpha. I meant no trouble. My days of roaming the mountains with a wolf pack at my beck and call are long over."

Adam nodded, keeping his eyes on the enemy. "That may be. But she is one of mine. And I am not one of yours."

"Enough," said Uncle Mike. "One fight a night is good enough. Go home, Ymir."

The kneeling elf looked at Uncle Mike, and the skin grew tight around his eyes for a moment before he smiled brightly. I noticed that his teeth were very white, if a little crooked. He stood up, using just the muscles of his thighs, like a martial artist. "It has been a long night." He made a slow turn that encompassed not just Uncle Mike, the wolves, and me, but everyone else in the room—who I just realized were all watching us . . . or maybe they were watching the snow elf. "Of course it is time to go. I'll see you all."

No one said anything until he was out of the building.

"Well," said Uncle Mike, sounding more Irish than usual. "Such a night."

———

MARY JO WAS MOVING BUT STILL DAZED WHEN WE GOT her outside. So Adam instructed Paul and his friend (whose name, as it happened, was Alec and not Sean or Stan at all) to take her to Adam's house. Paul packed Mary Jo in the back of her car with Alec and started to get in.

He looked at my feet. "You shouldn't be out here barefoot," he told the ground. Then he shut the car door, turned the key as he turned on the lights, and left.

"He meant thank you," said Adam. "I'll say it, too. I can think of a lot of things I'd rather do than try to defend Paul from Baba Yaga."

"I should have let her have him," I told Adam. "It would have made your life easier."

He grinned, then stretched his neck. "This could have been a very, very bad night."

I was looking over his shoulder at his SUV. "Would you settle for just a little bad? Your insurance doesn't have an exception for snow elves, right?"

It had looked all right at first, then I thought it just had a flat tire. But now I could see the right rear tire was bent up at a forty-five-degree angle.

Adam pulled out his cell phone. "That doesn't even register on my scale of bad tonight," he told me. He put his free arm around my shoulder, pulling me against him as his daughter answered the phone. He wasn't wearing a shirt.

"Hey, Jesse," he said. "It's been a wild night, and we need you to come pick us up at Uncle Mike's."

5

"SOME DATE," ADAM MURMURED. IT DIDN'T MATTER HOW quiet he was; we both knew that most of the pack was inside his house listening to us as we stood on his back porch.

"No one could ever accuse you of being boring," I said lightly.

He laughed with sober eyes. He'd scrubbed up in the bathroom at Uncle Mike's and changed as soon as we'd made it back to his house. But I could still smell the blood on him.

"You need to see to Mary Jo," I told him. "I need to go to bed." She would survive, I thought. But she'd survive better with me at home and not disrupting the pack, who was forcing her to fight to live.

He hugged me for not saying all of that out loud. He lifted me to my toes—clad in a pair of Jesse's flip-flops—and set me back down.

"You go scrub your feet clean first so none of those cuts get infected. I'll send Ben over to watch your house until Samuel is satisfied with Mary Jo's condition and goes home."

Adam watched from the porch as I walked home. I wasn't halfway there when Ben caught up with me. I invited him in, but he shook his head.

"I'll stay outside," he said. "The night air keeps my head clear."

I scrubbed my feet and dried them before I went to bed. I was asleep before my head hit the pillow. But I woke up while the dark still held sway, knowing that there was someone in my room. Though I listened closely, I couldn't hear anyone—so I was pretty sure it was Stefan.

I wasn't worried. The vampires, except Stefan, wouldn't have been able to cross the threshold of my home. Most anyone else would have woken Samuel.

The air told me nothing, which was odd—even Stefan had a scent. Restlessly, I rolled onto my side and right up against the walking stick, which had taken to sleeping with me every night. Mostly it gave me the creeps when it did that—walking sticks shouldn't be able to move about on their own. But tonight the warm wood under my hand felt reassuring. I closed my hand around it.

"There's no need for violence, Mercy."

I must have jumped because I was on my feet, stick in hand, before it registered just whose voice I was hearing.

"Bran?"

And suddenly I could smell him, mint and musk that told me werewolf combined with the certain sweet saltiness that was his own scent.

"Don't you have something more important to do?" I asked him, flipping on the light. "Like ruling the world or something?"

He didn't move from his spot on the floor, leaning against a wall, except to put his forearm over his eyes as light flooded the room. "I came here last weekend," he said. "But you were asleep, and I didn't let them wake you up."

I'd forgotten. In the hubbub of Baba Yaga, Mary Jo, the snow elf, and the vampires, I'd forgotten why he would have come to visit me personally. Suddenly I was suspicious of the arm he'd thrown over his eyes.

That Alphas are protective of their packs is an understatement—and Bran was the Marrok, the most Alpha wolf around. I might belong to Adam's pack just now, but Bran had raised me.

"I already talked it all over with Mom," I said defensively.

And Bran grinned hugely, his arm coming down to reveal hazel eyes, which looked almost green in the artificial light. "I bet you did. Are my Samuel and your Adam hovering over you and giving you a bad time?" His voice was full of (false) sympathy.

Bran is better than anyone I know, including the fae, at hiding what he is. He looked like a teenager—there was a rip in his jeans, just over the knee, and some ironic person had used a marker to draw an anarchy symbol just over his thigh. His hair was ruffled. He was perfectly capable of sitting around with an innocent smile on his face—and then ripping someone's head off.

"You're frowning at me," he said. "Is it such a puzzle that I'm here?"

I dropped to the middle of the floor. It is uncomfortable for me to be in the same room for very long with Bran if my head is higher than his. Part of it is habit, and part of it is the magic that makes Bran the leader of all the wolves.

"Did someone call you about Adam bringing me into the pack?" I asked.

This time Bran laughed, his shoulders shaking, and I saw how tired he was.

"I'm glad I amuse you," I told him grumpily.

Behind me the door opened, and Samuel said cheerily, "Is this a private party, or can anyone join?"

How cool was that? In one sentence, one word actually (party), Samuel told his father that we weren't going to talk about Tim or why I'd killed him, and that I was going to be okay. Samuel was good at things like that.

"Come in," I said. "How's Mary Jo?"

Samuel sighed. "Da, let me tell you now. If I am dead, and a fae offers to heal me—I'd prefer you tell her no." He looked at me. "I think she'll be fine, eventually. But she's not very happy right now. She's dazed and shocky to an extent I've never seen before in a wolf. At least she's not crying anymore. Adam finally forced her change, and that helped a lot. She's sleeping with Paul, Alec, Honey, and few others on the monstrosity of a couch Adam keeps in the TV room in the basement."

He gave his father a keen-eyed look, then sat on the floor beside me—and that was a message, too. He wasn't between Bran and me, not precisely. But he could have sat beside Bran. "So what brings you here?"

Bran smiled at him, having seen the message Samuel wanted him to. "You don't have to protect her from me," he said softly. "We've all seen she does a pretty good job of protecting herself."

With the wolves, there is always a lot more going on in a conversation than just the words. For instance, Bran had just told us that he'd seen the video, from the security camera, of me killing Tim . . . and of everything else, too. And that he'd approved of my actions.

It shouldn't have pleased me so much; I was no child. But Bran's opinion still meant a lot.

"And yes," he told me after a moment, "someone called me about Adam bringing you into the pack. Lots of someones. Let me tell you the answers to the questions I've been asked, and you can pass them on to Adam. No. I had no idea it was possible to bring someone who was not a werewolf into the pack. Especially you, upon whom magic can be unpredictable. No. Once done, only Adam or you can break those ties. If you want me to show you how, I will." He paused.

I shook my head . . . and then tempered it. "Not yet."

Bran gave me an amused look under his eyebrows. "Fine. Just ask. And no, I'm not mad. Adam is Alpha of his pack. I do not see how anyone has been harmed by this." Then he grinned, one of the rare smiles he had when he wasn't acting, just genuinely amused. "Except maybe Adam. At least he doesn't have a Porsche you can wrap around a tree."

"That was a long time ago," I said hotly. "I paid for that. And after you practically dared me to steal it, I don't see why you were so angry about it."

"Telling you not to take it out wasn't daring you, Mercy," Bran said patiently . . . but there was something in his voice.

Was he lying?

"Yes, it was," said Samuel. "And she's right—you knew it."

"So you didn't have any reason to be so mad I wrecked the car," I said, triumphantly.

Samuel laughed out loud. "You still haven't figured it out, have you, Mercy? He never *was* mad about the car. He was the first one at the scene of the accident. He thought you'd killed yourself. We all did. That was a pretty spectacular wreck."

I started to say something and found I couldn't. The first thing I'd seen after hitting the tree was the Marrok's snarling face. I'd never seen him that angry—and I'd done a lot, from time to time, to inspire his rage.

Samuel patted me on the back. "It's not often I see you absolutely speechless."

"So you had Charles teach me how to fix cars and how to drive them." Charles was Bran's oldest son. He hated to drive, and until that summer I'd thought he couldn't drive. I should have known better—Charles can do anything. And everything he did, he did very well. That's only one of the reasons that Charles intimidates me and everyone else.

"Kept you busy and out of trouble for a whole summer," said Bran smugly.

He was teasing . . . but serious as well. One of the oddest things about being grown-up was looking back at something you thought you knew and finding out the truth of it was completely different from what you had always believed.

It gave me courage to do what I did next.

"I need some advice," I told him.

"Sure," he said easily.

I took a deep breath and started with my killing Marsilia's best hope of returning to Italy, jumped to Stefan's appearance in my living room and the unexpected visit from my old college nemesis, and ended it all with the nearly fatal adventure at Uncle Mike's and the little bag that smelled like vampires and magic. I told him about Mary Jo and my fear that if I told Adam about the bag, it would cause a war.

"I'll stop by and see if I can help Mary Jo," Bran said after I'd finished. "I know a few tricks."

Samuel looked relieved. "Good."

"So," I told Bran, "it is *my* fault. I chose to go after Andre. But Marsilia's not attacking *me*."

"You expected a vampire to be straightforward?" asked Bran.

I supposed I had. "Amber gives me a reason to get out of town for a little while. Without me around, Marsilia might leave everyone else alone." And it would give me a chance to think through my response. A day or two to figure out something that wouldn't lead to more killing.

"And give Adam and me a chance to mount a proper response," Samuel growled.

I started to object . . . but they had the right to go on the offensive. The right to know that they were targets.

As long as Mary Jo survived, Adam wouldn't bring a war to Marsilia's doorstep. And if Mary Jo didn't survive . . . Perhaps Marsilia *was* crazy. I'd seen that kind of madness in the Marrok's pack, where the oldest wolves often came to die.

"If you leave, Marsilia might take that as a victory," said Bran. "I don't know her well enough to know if that will help you or hurt you in the end. I do think that getting out of here for a few days might not be a bad idea."

He didn't say Marsilia would quit targeting my friends, I noticed. I was pretty sure Uncle Mike would figure out that the vampires had used his place to target the wolves—and if I thought that, Marsilia surely would. She must be truly furious if she was willing to anger Uncle Mike and enrage Adam in order to get to me.

I was betting that if I left, she'd wait, because she wanted me to witness the pain I'd made her rain down upon my friends. But I wasn't sure. Still, it wouldn't hurt.

"The problem is . . . there's something a little off about Amber's offer. Or maybe just after Tim . . ." I swallowed. "I'm afraid to go."

Bran looked at me with keen yellow eyes, weighing something in his mind. "Fear is a good thing," he said at last. "It teaches you not to make the same mistake twice. You counter it with knowledge. What are you afraid of?"

"I don't know." Which wasn't the right answer.

"Gut check," Bran said. "What does your gut tell you?"

"I think that maybe it's the vampires again. Stefan lands in my lap to give me a good scare—and look, here's a way out. Out of the frying pan and into the fire."

Samuel was already shaking his head. "Marsilia isn't going to send you to Spokane to get you out of our protection before she takes care of you. Not that it isn't a good idea, but she'd send you to Seattle maybe, she has some allies there. But in Spokane, there's only one vampire, and he doesn't allow visitors. There are no packs, no fae, nothing but a few powerless creatures who manage to stay out of his sight."

I felt my eyes widen. Spokane is a city of nearly half a million people. "That's a lot of territory for a single vampire."

"Not for *that* single vampire," said Samuel at the same time Bran said, "Not for Blackwood."

"So," I said slowly. "What will this vampire do if I stay in Spokane for a few days?"

"How would he know?" Bran asked. "You smell like coyote. But a coyote smells a lot like a dog to someone who doesn't hunt in the forests—which I assure you, James Blackwood doesn't do—and most dog owners smell like their pets. I wouldn't want you to move to Spokane, but a couple of days or weeks won't put you in danger."

"So do you think it's a good idea if I go?"

Bran raised his hip and pulled his cell phone out of his back pocket.

"Don't you break them like that?" I asked. "I killed a couple of phones by sitting on them."

He just smiled and said into the phone, "Charles, I need you to find out about an Amber . . . ?" He looked at me and raised an eyebrow.

"Sorry to wake you, Charles. Chamberlain was her maiden name," I told Samuel's brother apologetically. "I don't know her married name." Charles would hear me as clearly as I heard him. Private phone calls around werewolves needed headsets, not a cell phone speaker.

"Amber Chamberlain," Charles repeated. "That should limit it to a hundred people or so."

"She lives in Spokane," I said. "I went to college with her."

"That helps," he told us. "I'll get back to you."

"Arm yourself with knowledge," said Bran when he hung up. "But I don't see why you shouldn't go."

"Take some insurance with you."

"It's Stefan," I shouted. Before I had the last word out of my mouth, Bran had Stefan up against the opposite wall from where he'd been sitting.

"Da." Samuel was on his feet as well, a hand on his father's shoulder. He didn't try to pry Bran's hands off Stefan's neck—that would have been stupid. "Da. It's all right. This is Stefan. Mercy's friend."

After a very long couple of seconds, Bran stepped back and dropped his hands from Stefan's throat. The vampire hadn't fought back, which was good.

Vampires are tough, maybe tougher than wolves because vampires are already dead. Stefan had been one of Marsilia's lieutenants, powerful in his own right. He'd been a mercenary in life . . . which had been in Renaissance Italy.

But Bran is Bran.

"That was stupid," said Samuel to Stefan. "What part of 'never sneak up on a werewolf' don't you understand?"

The Stefan I knew would have bowed gracefully, expressed his apologies with a hint of humor. This Stefan gave a stiff jerk of his neck. "I'm no use here. It's a good idea to get Mercy out of the line of fire—she's the weakest target. Send me to keep her safe in Spokane." He sounded almost eager . . . and I wondered what he'd been doing since he'd left Adam's. What was there for him to do? Maybe I wasn't the only one who was trying to find some action to take that wouldn't get me and everyone I cared about killed.

Still, I couldn't let him get away with calling me . . . "Weak?" I said.

Samuel turned on Stefan with a growl. "Stupid vampire. My father had her nearly talked into going, and you ruined it."

I laughed. I couldn't help it. I hoped going to Spokane would keep my friends safe, and they hoped me going to Spokane would keep *me* safe. Maybe we were both right.

Bran's phone rang, and we all listened to Charles tell us that Amber was married to Corban Wharton, a moderately successful corporate lawyer about ten years her senior. They had an eight-year-old son with some sort of disability, hinted at in various newspaper articles but not expressly stated. He rattled off an address or two, cell phone numbers and real phone numbers . . . and social security numbers and most recent tax reports, personal and business. For an old wolf, Charles knows how to make computers sit up and beg.

"Thank you," said Bran.

"I can go back to sleep now?" asked Charles. He didn't wait for an answer, just hung up his end of the connection.

I looked at Samuel. "It will make your life easier if I leave."

He nodded. "We can protect ourselves . . . but you are too vulnerable. And if you aren't here, if Marsilia doesn't know where you are, we can get her to the table for negotiations."

Bran looked at Stefan. "A vampire might draw too much attention in Spokane."

Stefan shrugged. "I'm not without resources. I was in this room for a quarter of an hour, and none of you noticed me. If I feed well, no one will know what I am."

"You always smell like vampire to me," I told him. Vampire and popcorn. The good buttery kind. No, I don't know why. I've never seen him eat the stuff—I don't know that vampires can.

He raised his hands. "No one without Mercy's nose, then. If I'm in the room with the Monster, then perhaps he'll notice. Otherwise, he'll never know I was there. I've done it before."

"The Monster?" Samuel asked.

"James Blackwood."

Vampires give titles to some of the more powerful ones. Stefan was the Soldier because he'd been a mercenary. Wulfe was the Wizard . . . and I knew he could do some magic. I resolved to stay away from any vampire that other vampires called the Monster.

"There is this, too," Stefan said. "I can jump from one location to another—and I can take Mercy with me."

"How far?" asked Bran with sudden intentness.

Stefan shrugged . . . and never quite straightened up, as if it was too much trouble. "Anywhere. But taking another person with me has a cost. I'll be useless for a day afterward." He looked at me. "I have the address." He'd have overheard Charles give it to the rest of us. "I can get there tonight and find a safe place nearby to spend the day."

Bran raised an eyebrow at me.

"I'll call Amber in the morning," I said. It felt like running away, but Bran seemed to think it was the right thing to do.

Stefan swept me a perfect bow and disappeared before he stood up.

"He used to hide his ability to do that," I told them. It worried me that he wasn't hiding it anymore. As if it didn't matter what people knew about him.

Samuel smiled at me. "You decided to go to Spokane because he needs to do something, didn't you? You were all set to stay until he started looking pathetic." I gave him a look, and he raised his hands in surrender. "I didn't say he didn't have a reason to look pathetic. You just need to remember that sad sack or not, he's still a vampire—and more than a match for you if he decides not to be friendly. You've cost him a lot, Mercy. He might not be your friend."

I hadn't thought about it that way. So I did, for maybe a tenth of a second. "If he was mad at me, he'd have killed me when he dropped in here starving. For that matter he could have come here anytime tonight and killed me. You need me gone—so quit trying to make trouble."

Samuel frowned at me. "I'm not trying to make trouble. But you have to remember he is a vampire, and vampires are not nice guys, no matter how chivalrous and gallant Stefan appears. I like him, too. But you are trying to forget what he is."

I thought about the two dead people whose only crime was that they had seen me when I staked Andre. "I know what he is," I said stubbornly.

"Vampire," said Bran. "Evil, yes." He grinned, and it made him look like he should be going to high school. "But I think his Mistress made a mistake when she chose to throw him away."

"She broke him," I said. And looking into Samuel's eyes, I whispered, "You stay safe, you and Adam. I'll keep Stefan busy looking for ghosts."

If I was really looking for ghosts, of course, it would be stupid to bring Stefan. Ghosts don't like vampires, and they won't come out when there are vampires around. Samuel knew that, and he grinned at me with serious eyes. "We'll be fine."

"Call me if you need me," said Bran—to both of us, I thought. "If I'm going to stop in to have a look at Mary Jo, I need to go now." He kissed me on my forehead, then did the same to Samuel (who had to bend down). I didn't know if he really knew who Mary Jo was, or just seemed to. But I'd never seen him meet a wolf he didn't know by name.

Speaking of which . . . "Hey, Bran?"

Halfway to the door, he turned back.

"What about that girl we sent to you? The one who was Changed so young and hadn't learned control. Is she all right?"

He smiled and looked a lot less tired. "Kara? She did fine last moon. Give her a few more months, and she'll be fully in control." Waving casually over his shoulder, he walked out into the dark.

"Get some rest," I called after him. He shut the front door behind him without answering.

We listened while Bran drove off—in a doubtlessly rented Mustang. Once he was gone, Samuel said, "You have a few hours. Why don't you get some more sleep? I think I'll hop the fence to Adam's and see what Da does for Mary Jo."

"Why didn't he just call?" I asked.

Samuel reached out and ruffled my hair. "He was checking up on you."

"Well," I said. "At least he didn't ask me if I was okay. I think I'd have had to do something to him if he had."

"Hey, Mercy," said Samuel with false solicitude, "are you okay?"

I punched him, connecting only because he hadn't expected it. "I am now," I told him, as he dropped to the ground and rolled—as if I'd really had some force behind my fist, which I hadn't.

———————

SPOKANE IS ABOUT 150 MILES NORTHEAST OF THE TRI-Cities, and you know you're getting close when you start seeing trees.

My cell phone rang, and I answered without pulling over. I usually obey the law, but I was late.

"Mercy?" It was Adam, and he wasn't happy with me. I guessed Samuel had told him about the vampires being responsible for the debacle at Uncle Mike's. I'd told him he could do it once I was safely out of town.

"Uh-huh." I pulled around an RV as we chugged up a small hill. It'd pass me on the downhill side, but I had to take my passing pleasures where I could—Vanagons are not speed demons. One of these days I was going to put a Subaru flat six in it and see what that would do. "Before you yell at me for not telling you about the vampires, you should know that I am risking a ticket by talking to you while I drive. Do you really want me to get a ticket for letting you yell at me?"

He gave a reluctant laugh, so I supposed he wasn't too upset. "You're still on the road? I thought you left this morning."

"Fixed a shift linkage in a Ford Focus at that rest stop near Connell," I told him. "Nice lady and her dog were stuck after having a clutch job done by her brother-in-law. He hadn't tightened down a few bolts, and one of them fell off. Took me an hour or so before we found someone who had a bolt and nut the right size." And I had the oil stains across my shoulders and the grit in my hair to prove it. In my Rabbit I kept a towel to put on the ground. I also kept a selection of useful car bits. It was going to be a while before my Rabbit was up and running.

"How is Mary Jo?"

"She's sleeping for real now."

"Bran helped?"

"Bran helped." I could hear the smile in his voice. "You be careful ghost hunting—and don't let Stefan bite you."

There was just a little edge to the last.

"Jealous?" I asked. Yep. The RV passed me on the downhill.

"Maybe a little," he said.

"Don't be. We'll be fine. Ghosts aren't as dangerous as crazy vampire ladies." I couldn't help the anxiety that crept into my voice.

"I'll be careful—and Mercy?"

"Uhm?"

"Consider yourself yelled at," he purred, then hung up.

I grinned at the phone and closed it.

AMBER'S DIRECTIONS TO HER HOUSE HAD BEEN CLEAR and easy to follow. The relief in her voice when I'd called that morning made me want to believe she really had a ghost problem and wasn't part of some secret vampire conspiracy to get me somewhere I'd be easier to kill. Despite Bran's assurances that it was unlikely Marsilia would ship me off to Spokane, I was still feeling . . . not paranoid, really. Cautious. I was feeling cautious.

Zee had agreed to work the shop while I was gone. I probably could have gotten him to work cheaper than usual because he was still feeling guilty about stuff that wasn't his fault. Cheaper would mean I could eat peanut butter instead of ramen noodles for the rest of the month, but I didn't think any of it was his fault.

He had talked to Uncle Mike about the crossed bones on my door. Definitely vampire work, he told me. The bones meant that I had broken faith with the vampires and was no longer under their protection—and anyone offering me aid of any kind was likely to find themselves on the wrong side of the vampires as well. The broad interpretation of that was horrifying. It meant that people like Tony and Sensei Johanson were at risk, too.

It meant that it was probably a good thing that I get out of town for a few days and figure out how to limit the number of victims Marsilia could claim.

Amber lived in a Victorian mansion complete with a pair of towers. The brick porch had been freshly tuck-pointed, the gingerbread work around the roof edge and the windows bore a new coat of paint. Even the roses looked ready for magazine display.

Frowning at the leaded glass glistening in the sun, I wondered when I'd last cleaned the windows in my house. Had I *ever* cleaned the windows? Samuel might have.

I was still thinking about it when the door opened. A startled boy gawked at me, and I realized I hadn't rung the doorbell.

"Hey," I said. "Is your mom home?"

He recovered quickly and gave me a shy look out of a pair of misty green eyes under long, thick eyelashes, and turned to ring the bell I hadn't.

"I'm Mercy," I told him, while we waited for Amber to emerge from the depths of the house. "Your mom and I went to school together."

His wary look deepened, and he didn't say anything. So I guessed she hadn't told him anything.

"Mercy, I was beginning to think you weren't coming." Amber sounded harassed and not at all grateful, and that was before she saw what I looked like—covered in old oil and parking-lot dirt.

Her son and I turned to look at her.

She still looked like a show dog, but her eyes were stressed. "Chad, this is my friend who is going to help us with the ghost." As she spoke, her hands flew in a graceful dance, and I remembered Charles had said her son had some sort of disability: he was deaf.

She turned her attention to me, but her hands still moved, letting her son know what she was saying. "This is my son, Chad." She took a deep breath. "Mercy, I'm sorry. My husband has a client coming over for dinner tonight. He didn't tell me until just a few minutes ago. It's a formal dinner . . ."

She looked at me, and her voice trailed off.

"What?" I said letting sharpness creep into my voice at the insult. "Don't I look like I'm up to a formal dinner? Sorry, the stitches in my chin don't come out for at least a week."

Suddenly she laughed. "You haven't changed a bit. If you didn't bring anything suitable, you can borrow something of mine. The guy who's coming is actually pretty well house-trained for a cutthroat businessman. I think you'll like him. I've got to do some inventorying and run to the grocery store." She tilted her head so her son could see her mouth. "Chad, would you take Mercy to the guest room?"

He gave me another wary look, but nodded. As he went back inside the house and started up the stairs, Amber told me, "I'd better warn you, my husband is pretty unhappy about the ghost. He thinks Chad and I are making it up. If you could manage not to mention it at dinner in front of his client, I'd appreciate it."

THERE WAS A BATHROOM ACROSS FROM THE ROOM I WAS
staying in. I took my suitcase and went in to scrub up. Before
I stripped off my grimy shirt, I closed my eyes and took a deep
breath.

Sometimes ghosts only appear to one sense or another. Sometimes I can only hear them—sometimes I can smell them. But the
bathroom smelled like soap and shampoo, water, and those stupid
blue tablets some people who didn't have pets put in their toilets.

I didn't see anything or hear anything either. But that didn't keep
the hair on the back of my neck from rising as I pulled off my shirt
and stuffed it into the plastic compartment in my suitcase. I scoured
my hands until they were mostly clean and brushed the dirt out of
my hair and rebraided it. And all the while I could feel someone
watching me.

Maybe it was only the power of suggestion. But I cleaned up as
fast as I could anyway. No ghostly writing appeared on the walls, no
one appeared in the mirror or moved stuff around.

I opened the bathroom door and found Amber waiting impa-
tiently right in front of the door. She didn't notice that she'd startled
me.

"I have to take Chad to softball practice, then do some shopping
for dinner tonight. Do you want to come?"

"Why not?" I said with a casual shrug. Staying in that house
alone didn't appeal to me—some ghost hunter I was. Nothing had
happened, and I was already jumpy.

I took shotgun. Chad frowned at me, but sat in back. I didn't
think I impressed him much. No one said anything until we dropped
Chad off. He didn't look happy about going. Amber proved that she
was tougher than me because she ignored the puppy-dog eyes and
abandoned Chad to his coach's indifferent care.

"So you decided not to become a history teacher," Amber said as she pulled away from the curb. Her voice was tight with nerves. The stress was coming from her end, I thought—but then she'd never been relaxing company.

"*Decided* isn't quite the word," I told her. "I took a job as a mechanic to support myself until a teaching position opened . . . and one day I realized that even if someone offered me a job, I'd rather turn a wrench." And then, because she'd given me the opening, "I thought you were going to be a vet."

"Yes, well, life happened." She paused. "Chad happened." That was too much honesty for her though, and she subsided into silence. In the grocery store, I wandered away while she was testing tomatoes—they all looked good to me. I bought a candy bar, just to see how much she'd changed.

Not that much. By the time she'd finished lecturing me on the evils of refined sugar, we were almost back to the house. She was feeling a lot more comfortable—and she finally told me more about her ghost.

"Corban doesn't believe we're haunted," she told me as she threaded her way through the city. She glanced at my face and away. "I haven't actually seen or heard anything either. I just told him I had, so he'd leave Chad alone." She took a deep breath and looked at me again. "He thinks Chad might do better at a boarding school—a private place for troubled kids that a friend of his recommended."

"He didn't look troubled to me," I said. "Aren't 'troubled' kids usually doing drugs or beating on the neighbor's kids?" Chad had looked like he'd rather have stayed home and read than go to play ball.

Amber gave a nervous half laugh. "Corban doesn't get along

very well with Chad. He doesn't understand him. It's the old Disney cliché of a quarterback dad and bookworm son."

"Does Corban know he's not Chad's father?"

She hit the brakes so hard that if I hadn't been belted in, I might have become better acquainted with her windshield. She sat there in the middle of the road for a moment, oblivious to the honking horns around us. I was glad we were in a stout Mercedes rather than the Miata she'd driven to my house.

"You forget," I said blandly. "I knew Harrison, too. We used to joke about his eyelashes, and I've never see eyes like his since. Not until today." Harrison had been her one true love for about three months until she dropped him for a premed student.

Amber started forward again and drove for a little until traffic settled down. "I'd forgotten you knew him." She sighed. "Funny. Yes, Corban knows he's not Chad's father, but Chad doesn't. It didn't used to matter, but I'm not so sure. Corban's been . . . different lately." She shook her head. "Still, he's the one who suggested I ask you to come over. He saw the article in the paper, and said, 'Isn't that the girl you said used to see ghosts? Why don't you have her come over and have a look-see?' "

I figured I'd been pushy enough, so I asked a question that was less intrusive. "What does the ghost do?"

"Moves things," she told me. "It rearranges Chad's room once or twice a week. Chad says he's seen the furniture moving around." She hesitated. "It breaks things, too. A couple of vases my husband's father brought over from China. The glass over my husband's diploma. Sometimes it takes things." She glanced at me again. "Car keys. Shoes. Some important papers of Cor's turned up in Chad's room, under his bed. Corban was pretty mad."

"At Chad?"

She nodded.

I hadn't even met him, and I didn't like her husband. Even if Chad was doing everything himself—and I had no evidence to the contrary—throwing him into reform school didn't sound like the way to make things better.

We picked up a morose Chad, who didn't seem inclined to converse, and she quit talking about the ghost.

AMBER WAS WORKING IN THE KITCHEN. I'D TRIED TO HELP, but she finally sent me to my room to stay out of her way. She didn't like the way I peeled apples. I'd brought a book from home—a very old book—with real fairy tales in it. It was borrowed and I'd have to return it soon, so I was reading as fast as I could.

I was taking notes on kelpies (thought extinct) when someone knocked at my door twice and then opened it.

Chad stood with a notebook and a pencil in hand.

"Hey," I said.

He turned the notebook around and I read, "How much is my dad paying you?"

"Nothing," I said.

His eyes narrowed, and he ripped away that page and showed me the next one. Evidently he'd thought about this for a while. "Why are you here? What do you want?"

I set my book aside and stared back at him. He was tough, but he wasn't Adam or Samuel: he blinked first.

"I have a vampire who wants to kill me," I told him. Which I shouldn't have, of course, but I wanted to see what would happen. Curiosity, Bran has told me more than once, might be as fatal for coyotes as it is for cats.

Chad crumpled the paper and mouthed a word. Evidently he hadn't expected that response.

I raised my eyebrow. "Sorry. You'll have to do better. I don't lip-read."

He scribbled furiously. "Lyer" said his paper.

I took his pencil, and wrote, "liar." Then I gave him back his notebook, and said, "You want to bet?"

He clutched his notebook to his chest and stalked off. I liked him. He reminded me of me.

Fifteen minutes later his mother barged in. "Red or purple?" she asked me, still sounding frantic. "Come with me."

Bewildered, I followed her down the hall and into the master bedroom suite, where she'd laid out two dresses. "I only have five minutes before I have to put the rolls in," she said. "Red or purple?"

The purple had considerably more fabric. "Purple," I said. "Do you have shoes I can borrow, too? Or do you want me to go barefoot?"

She gave me a wild-eyed look. "Shoes I have, but not nylons."

"Amber," I told her. "I will put on high heels for you. And I will wear a dress. But you aren't paying me enough to wear nylons. My legs are shaved and tan, that'll have to do."

"We can pay you. How much do you want?"

I looked but couldn't tell if she was joking or not. "No charge," I told her. "That way I can leave when things get scary."

She didn't laugh. I was pretty sure Amber used to have a sense of humor. Maybe.

"Look," I told her. "Take a deep breath. Find the shoes for me, and go put your rolls in the oven."

She did take a deep breath, and it seemed to help.

When I went back to my room, Chad was there again with his

notebook. He was staring at the walking stick on my bed. I hadn't brought it with me, but it had come anyway. I wished I could ask it what it wanted from me.

I picked it up and waited until he was looking at me so he could read my lips. "This is what I use to beat problem children with."

He clutched his notebook tighter, so I guessed his lipreading skills were up to par. I put the stick back on the bed. "What did you want?"

He turned his notebook around and showed me a newspaper article that had been cut out and was taped to a page of his notebook. "Alpha Werewolf's Girlfriend Kills Attacker" it said. There was a picture of me looking battered and dazed. I didn't remember anyone taking pictures, but there were large chunks of that night I was pretty shaky on.

"Yes," I said, like my stomach didn't suddenly hurt. "Old news."

He turned the page, and I saw he had another observation for me. "There R no vampyrs." I guessed spelling wasn't his strong suit. Even at ten, I'd been able to spell "are."

"Okay, thanks," I said. "Good to know. I guess I'll go home tomorrow."

He dropped his hands to his sides, the notebook swaying back and forth with irritation like a cat's tail. He knew sarcasm when he heard it, even if he was lip-reading it.

"Don't worry, kid," I told him more gently. "I'm not a part of the plot to send you off to kid-prison. If I don't see anything, it doesn't mean that there's nothing to see. And I'll tell your father so, too."

He blinked his eyes furiously, hugged his notebook again. He lifted his chin—a smaller, less-stubborn version of his mother's. And he left.

———————

AMBER TROTTED UP THE STAIRS DOUBLE TIME AND waved to me as she went past. I heard her knock, then open a door. "You need to clean up, too," she told her son. "You don't have to eat with us—there's a plate in the microwave—but I don't want you scuttling around trying to be unseen, either. You know how that irritates your father. So comb your hair, wash your hands and face."

I stripped off my clothes and pulled on the purple dress. It fit just fine—a little tight in the shoulders and snugger in the hips than I preferred, but when I looked at it in the full-length mirror, it looked just fine. Amber, Char, and I had always been able to trade clothes with each other.

The heels were higher than was comfortable, but as long as we were staying in the house, they should be all right. Char's feet had been smaller than Amber's and mine. I brushed out my hair again, then French-braided it. A touch of lipstick and eyeliner, and I was good to go.

I wished it was Adam I was about to eat with instead of Amber, her jerk of a husband, and some important client. It was enough to make me wish I had a plate in the microwave, too.

6

NEITHER OF THE TWO MEN WHO ENTERED THE HOUSE
was handsome. The shorter man was slightly balding, with plump
hands that had three thick gold rings on them. His suit was off-
the-rack, but the rack had been expensive. His eyes were pale, pale
blue, almost as pale as Samuel's wolf eyes. The resemblance made
me want to like him. He stood by almost shyly as the other man
hugged Amber.

"Hey, sweetie," Amber's husband said and, to my surprise, there
was honest warmth in his voice. "Thank you for fixing dinner for
us on such short notice."

Corban Wharton was striking rather than good-looking. His
nose was too long for his broad face. His eyes were dark and wide-
set—and smiling. There was something solid and reassuring about

him. He was the kind of person that you'd want beside you in a courtroom. When he looked at me, he frowned briefly, as if trying to place who I was.

"You must be Mercedes Thompson," he said, holding out his hand.

He had a good handshake, a politician's handshake—firm and dry.

"Call me Mercy," I said. "Everyone does."

He nodded. "Mercy, this is my friend and client Jim Blackwood. Jim—Mercy Thompson, my wife's friend who is visiting us this week."

Jim was talking to Amber and took just an instant to turn his attention back to Corban and me.

Jim Blackwood. James Blackwood. How many James Black-woods were there in Spokane, I wondered in dumb panic. Five or six? But I knew—even though the strong cologne he wore kept me from scenting vampire—I knew I wasn't going to be lucky.

He'd think I smelled like I had dogs, Bran had assured me. And even if he didn't, even if he knew what I was—I was just visiting. He couldn't take offense at that, right?

I knew better. Vampires could take offense at anything they liked.

"Mr. Blackwood," I greeted him, when he looked away from Amber. Keep it simple. I didn't know if vampires could sense lies like the wolves could, but I wasn't going to say, "It's very good to meet you," or something similar when I was wishing myself a hundred miles away.

I did my best to keep a social smile on my face while stupid thoughts began to pile up. How was he going to eat with us? Vampires didn't. Not that I'd ever seen. What were the chances of a vampire's showing up and it not being some plot of Marsilia's?

Blackwood hadn't sounded like a vampire who would do any-one's bidding.

"Call me Jim," he told me, just a hint of a British accent shading his voice. "I'm sorry to intrude on your visit, but we had some urgent business this afternoon, and Corban insisted on bringing me home."

His round face was merry, and his handshake was even more practiced than Corban's had been. If it weren't for that little talk I'd had with Bran, I'd never have known what he was.

"Shall we go eat now?" Amber suggested, calm and in control now that the preparations were finished. "It's ready and not going to get better if it sits around. I'm afraid I kept it simple."

Simple was pepper steak over rice with salads and fresh rolls followed by homemade apple pie. Somehow, the food disappeared from the vampire's plate. I never saw him eat or touch his plate—though I kept half an eye on it with morbid fascination. Maybe a little hope. If I'd seen even a single bite go in his mouth, then I'd have believed him to be just what he seemed.

I stayed quiet while the men talked business—mostly contract language and 401(k)s—and I was very happy to stay unnoticed. Amber slipped in a sentence here and there, just enough to keep the conversation going. I heard Chad sneak by the dining room and into the kitchen. After a while he left again.

"Very good meal as always," the vampire told Amber. "Beautiful, charming—and a fine cook. As I keep telling Corban, I *am* going to steal you one of these days." I felt a chill go down my spine—he wasn't lying—but Corban and Amber just laughed as if it were an old joke. Just then, he looked at me. "You've been awfully quiet tonight. Corban tells me you went to school with Amber and you're from Kennewick. What is it you do there?"

"I fix things," I mumbled to my plate.

"Things?" He sounded intrigued, just the opposite of what I'd hoped.

"Cars. Meet Mercedes the VW mechanic," said Amber with a touch of the sharpness that had been her trademark in the old days. "But I bet I can still get her going on the royal families of Europe or the name of Hitler's German shepherd." She smiled at James Blackwood, the Monster who kept his territory free of vampires or anything else that might challenge him. A coyote wouldn't be much of a challenge.

Amber chatted on . . . almost nervously. Maybe she thought I'd jump up and tell her husband's valuable client that they'd brought me over to catch a ghost in the act. She wouldn't be worried about it if she knew what he was. "You'd have thought with her background— she's half-Blackfoot . . . or is that Blackfeet? . . . Anyway, she never studied Native American history, just the European stuff."

"I don't like wallowing in tragedy," I told her, trying desperately to sound uninteresting. "And that's what Native American history is mostly. But now I just fix cars."

"Blondi," said Corban, "was the name of the dog."

"Someone told me she was named after the comic strip *Blondie*," I added. That supposition had led to many arguments among the Nazi trivia buffs I knew. I was hoping the conversation would devolve to Hitler. He was dead and could do no more harm—unlike the dead man in the room.

"You are Native American?" asked the vampire. Had he tried to catch my eyes?

I was very good at keeping my gaze from meeting other people's unless it was on purpose—a useful skill around the wolves. I looked at his jaw, and said, "Half. My father. I never knew him, though."

He shook his head. "I'm very sorry."

"Old news," I said. Deciding that if Hitler wasn't going to distract him from me, maybe business would. It always worked with my stepfather. "I take it Corban is keeping your company safely out of the courts?"

"He's very good at his job," said the vampire with a pleased and possessive smile. "With him beside me, Blackwood Industries will stay afloat for a few more months, eh?"

Corban gave a hearty, and heartfelt, laugh. "Oh, I think a few months at the least."

"To making money," said Amber, holding up her glass. "Lots of it."

I pretended to sip the wine with the rest of them and was pretty sure that my idea of making money was several orders of magnitude less than theirs.

———————

HE LEFT AT LAST. IT HADN'T BEEN AS HORRIBLE AS I'D feared. The Monster was charming and, I hoped, unaware that I was anything except a not-very-interesting VW mechanic. Except for that one moment, I'd mostly avoided notice.

Almost euphoric at my near escape, I didn't worry about ghosts at all while I changed. Then I went back downstairs to help Amber with the cleanup.

She must have been worried or something, too, because she was nearly as giddy as I was. We had an impromptu water fight in the kitchen that ended in a draw when her husband stuck his head in the doorway to see what the noise was all about, and nearly got a sponge in the face for his trouble.

Discretion suggested that having escaped detection once, I

should head home in the morning. But Amber was a little drunk, so I decided that conversation could wait until later. Dishes clean, clothes wet and soapy, I left Amber necking with her husband in the kitchen.

I opened the bedroom door to find Chad in the middle of my bed, his arms crossed over his chest. I could smell his fear from the doorway.

I closed the door behind me and took a good look around the room. "Ghost?" I mouthed.

He glanced around the room, too, then shook his head.

"Not here? In your room?"

He gave me a cautious nod.

"How about we go in your room, then."

Terror breathing out of every pore, he slipped off the bed and followed me to his room: brave kid. He opened his bedroom door cautiously—and then pushed it open, being very careful to keep his feet in the hallway.

"I assume you don't usually keep that bookcase facedown on the floor," I told him.

He gave me a dirty look, but he lost some of his fear.

I shrugged. "Hey, my boyfriend has a daughter"—*boyfriend* was such an inadequate word—"and I had a pair of little sisters. None of them keeps a clean room. I had to ask."

Except for the bookcase, it was hard to tell what part of the mess was a normal boy's habitat and how much the ghost had caused. But the bookcase, one of those half-sized things people put in kids' rooms, was easy to fix. I squeezed past Chad and into the room. The bookcase was even lighter than I'd thought.

When I started reshelving his books, he knelt beside me and helped. He read a little of everything—and not entirely limited to things I'd think a kid would read: *Jurassic Park*, *Interview with the Vampire*, and H. P. Lovecraft sat next to Harry Potter and *Naruto* manga numbers one through fifteen. We worked for about twenty minutes to put everything to rights, and by the time we finished, he wasn't scared anymore.

I could smell it, though. It was watching us.

I dusted my hands off and looked around. "You usually keep your room this neat, kid?"

He nodded solemnly.

I shook my head. "You need help. Just like your mom. My little sister kept fossilized lunches under her bed for the dust bunnies she raised there."

I picked up a game from the neat stack. "Want to play some Battleship?" I wasn't leaving him alone with that thing in there.

Chad armed himself with a notebook, and we went to war. Historically, war has often been used as a distraction for problems at home.

Both of us lay on our bellies on the floor facing each other and fired our missiles. Adam called, and I told him he'd have to wait— battle must take precedence over romance. He laughed, wished me good night and good luck, just like that old war correspondent.

Chad's two-point boat was devilishly well hidden, and he destroyed my navy while I hunted it fruitlessly.

"Argh!" I cried with feeling. "You sank my battleship!"

Chad's face lit with laughter, and someone knocked at the door. I supposed I hadn't needed to make so much noise since Chad couldn't hear me anyway.

"Come in," I said. Reading my lips, Chad looked suddenly horrified, and I reached over and patted his shoulder.

The door popped open, and I rolled halfway over and looked

back over my feet as if to see who it was. Most people would have needed to look, so I did, but I'd heard him coming—and Amber had never stalked angrily in her life. Stomp, yes. Stalk, no. Trust me—any predator knows the difference.

"Isn't it after bedtime?" Corban said. He was wearing a pair of sweats and an old Seattle Seahawks shirt. His hair was rumpled as if he'd been to bed. I supposed I'd woken him up.

"Nope," I told him. "We're playing games and waiting for the ghost to show up. Want to join us?"

"There isn't a ghost," he said to his son, out loud and in sign.

I'd started to like Corban over dinner, he had seemed like a decent guy. But he was being a bully now.

I rolled up until I was facing him. "Isn't there?"

He frowned at me. "There are no such things as ghosts. I am very happy you've come here to visit, but I don't approve of encouraging nonsense. If you tell them there isn't one here, they'll believe you. Chad has enough to deal with without everyone thinking he's crazy." He'd continued to sign, even though he was talking to me. I didn't know if he left out the bit where I was supposed to tell Chad and Amber there weren't any ghosts.

"He's a damn fine naval commander," I told Corban. "And I think he's too smart to make up ghosts."

He signed my reply, too. Then he said, "He just wants attention."

"He gets attention," I said. "He wants to stop being scared because someone he can't see or hear is making a mess in his room. I thought you were the one who suggested I come check it out. Why did you do that if you don't believe in ghosts?"

There was a loud bang as the car on the top of Chad's chest of drawers made a suicide run off its perch, zoomed three feet across the room to hit the bookcase, and fell onto the floor. I'd been watching it roll back and forth, just a little bit, out of the corner of my eye for the last fifteen minutes, so I didn't jump. Chad couldn't hear it, so he didn't jump. But Corban did.

I got up and picked the car up. "Can you do that again?" I asked, setting the car back on the top of the bookcase.

I knelt beside Chad and looked at him so he could see my mouth. "It just made that car fall off. We're all going to watch and see if it can do it again."

Silenced by the car's fall, Corban sat down next to Chad and put a hand on his shoulder—and we all watched the car turn slowly in place then fall off the back of the bookcase.

Then the bookcase fell facedown on the floor, right on top of Chad's plastic ocean fleet. I caught a glimpse of someone standing there, hands up, then nothing—and the sweet-salt smell of blood that I'd been smelling since I first entered the room faded away.

I stayed where I was while Corban checked the bookcase and the car for devices or strings or something. Finally, he looked back at Chad.

"Are you all right sleeping in here?"

"It's gone," I told them both, and Corban obliged me by signing it.

Chad nodded, and his hands flew. At the end of it, Corban grinned. "I guess that's true." He looked at me. "He told me the ghost hasn't killed him yet."

Corban hefted the bookcase upright again, and I looked down at the mess of books and game pieces.

I waited until Chad glanced my way. Then I pointed at his two-hole destroyer, plainly visible, surrounded by white, useless missile pegs. "So that's where you hid it, you little sneak."

He grinned. Not a full-fledged grin, but enough that I knew he'd be fine. Tough kid.

I left them to their manly nighttime rituals and went back to my room, all thoughts of going home tomorrow shelved. I wasn't going to abandon Chad to the ghost. I still had no idea how to get rid of it, but maybe I could help him live with it instead. He was already halfway there.

Corban knocked at my door a few minutes later, then cracked it open.

"I don't need to come in," he said. He stared at me grimly. "Tell me you didn't engineer that somehow. I checked for wires and magnets."

I raised my eyebrow at him. "I didn't engineer anything. Congratulations. Your house is haunted."

He frowned. "I'm pretty good at sniffing out lies."

"Good for you," I told him sincerely. "Now I'm tired, and I need to go to sleep."

He backed away from my doorway and started down the hall. But he hadn't gotten two steps before he turned back. "If it is a ghost, is Chad safe?"

I shrugged. Truthfully, the smell of blood bothered me. Ghosts, in my experience, tend to smell like themselves. Mrs. Hanna, who used to visit my shop sometimes—both when she was alive and after she died—smelled like her laundry soap, her favorite perfume, and the cats who shared her home with her. I didn't think the blood was a good sign.

Still, I gave him the truth as I knew it. "I've never been hurt by a ghost, and I only know of a few stories where someone was hurt, mostly only bruises. The Bell Witch supposedly killed a man named John Bell in Tennessee a couple of centuries ago—but it was probably something other than a ghost. And old John died of poison that the Witch was supposed to have put in his medicine, something more mundane hands could have done as well."

He stared at me, and I returned it.

"You date a werewolf," he said.

"That's right."

"And you say there are ghosts."

"And fae," I told him. "I work with one. After werewolves and fae, ghosts aren't such a leap now, are they?"

I shut my door and went to bed. After a few long minutes, he retreated to his bedroom.

I usually have a hard time sleeping in strange places, but it was very late (or really early), and I hadn't gotten a full night's sleep the night before either. I slept like a baby.

When I woke up the next morning there were two puncture marks, complete with a nifty purple bruise, on my neck. They were a lovely addition to the stitches in my chin. And my lamb necklace was gone.

I stared at the bite in the bathroom mirror and heard Samuel tell me that I shouldn't count upon Stefan still being my friend . . . and Stefan making it clear that he needed to feed in order to avoid detection. I knew there were consequences to being bitten, but I wasn't sure what they were.

Of course I'd met another vampire last night. For a moment I hoped it was him. That Stefan hadn't bitten me while I slept. Then I really thought about being bitten by James Blackwood, who scared the things that scared me. And I hoped it was Stefan.

Stefan would have needed an invitation into the house, though. Had I asked him in, and he'd somehow erased the memory? I hoped so. It seemed the lesser of two evils.

The bathroom door popped open—I'd just come in to brush my teeth, so it wasn't locked. Chad stared at my neck, then looked at me, eyes wide.

And I hoped it was Stefan, because I was going to stay here until I helped . . . somehow.

"No," I told Chad casually, "I wasn't lying about the vampires." I thought I wouldn't mention I'd received it last night if he didn't think of that himself. He didn't need to be worrying about vampires as well as ghosts.

"I shouldn't have told you about it," I said. "I'd appreciate it if you didn't tell your folks. The vampires like it better if no one knows they're around. And they take measures to ensure that is true."

He looked at me for a moment. Then he zipped an imaginary zipper across his lips, locked an invisible lock, and threw the key behind his back: some things are universal.

"Thank you." I put the cap on my toothbrush and packed up my bathroom kit. "Any more trouble last night?"

He shook his head and wiped a wrist across his forehead to wipe off imaginary sweat.

"Good. Do you get much activity from your ghost during the day?"

He shrugged, waited a moment, then nodded.

"So I'll talk to your mom and maybe go for a jog." No running in coyote form in the city, especially when my efforts to stay out of James Blackwood's way had already failed so spectacularly. But if I didn't run most days, I started to get cranky. "And then we can stake out your room for a while. Is there anywhere else the ghost visits?"

He nodded and mimed eating and cooking.

"Just the kitchen, or the dining room, too?"

He held up two fingers.

"Fine." I checked my watch. "Meet you here at eight sharp." I went back to my room, but I didn't catch Stefan's scent or anything out of the ordinary. Nor was there any sign of my necklace. Without it, I had no protection against vampires. Not that it had done me much good last night.

RUNNING IN THE CITY IS NOT MY FAVORITE THING. STILL, the sun was shining, making it unlikely that I'd run into a vampire for a while. I ran for about a half hour, then made a beeline for Amber's house.

Her car was gone from the driveway. She had things to do, she'd told me—a hair appointment, errands to run, and some shopping. I'd told her Chad and I would amuse ourselves on our own. Still, I'd expected her to wait for me to return. I wasn't sure I'd have left my ten-year-old son alone in a haunted house. However, he seemed unfazed when he met me at the bathroom door just as my watch read 8:00 A.M.

We explored the whole of the old house, starting with the bottom and working our way up. Not that it was necessary or important to explore, but I like old houses and I didn't have any better plan than waiting for the ghost to manifest. Come to think of it, I didn't have any better plan after it manifested. Banishing ghosts was not something I'd ever tried, and everything I'd read about it over the years (not much) seemed to indicate that doing it wrong was worse than not doing it at all.

The cellar had been redone at some point, but behind a smallish old-fashioned door, there was a room with a dirt floor filled with old wooden milk crates and junk stored down there by some long-ago person. Whatever its original purpose, it was now the perfect habitat for black widows.

"Wow." I pointed at the far corner of the ceiling with my borrowed flashlight. "Look at the size of that spider. I don't know that I've ever seen one that big."

Chad tapped me and I looked at his circle of light, centered on a broken ladder-back chair.

"Yep," I agreed. "That one's bigger. I think we'll just back out of here and look elsewhere—at least until we have a nice can of spider spray." I shut the door a little more firmly than I might have. I don't mind spiders, and a black widow is one of the beauties of its kind . . . but they bite if you get in their way. Just like vampires. I rubbed my neck to make sure the collar of my shirt and my hair were still covering my own bite. This afternoon I'd go shopping. I needed to pick up a scarf or high-necked shirt for better concealment before Amber or Corban saw it. Maybe I could find another lamb necklace.

The rest of the basement was surprisingly clean of junk, dust, and spiders. Maybe Amber hadn't been as intimidated by the widows as I'd been.

"We're not trying to find out who the ghost is," I told him. "Though we could do that if you wanted to, I suppose. I'm just looking around to see what I can see. If this turns out to be a trick someone is playing, I don't want to be taken in."

He slashed his hands down in a way that needed no translation, his eyes bright with anger.

"No. I don't think you're doing it." I told him firmly. "If that was faked last night, it was beyond any amateur fiddling. Maybe someone has a bone to pick with your dad and is using you to do it." I hesitated. "But I don't think it was faked." Why would someone plant the smell of fresh blood too faint for a human nose, for instance. Still, I felt obligated to be as certain as I could that no one was playing tricks.

He thought about that for a while, then gave me a solemn nod and pointed out things of interest. A small, empty room behind a very thick door that might have been a cold room. The old coal chute with a box of old blankets placed near the end. I stuck my head in the metal tunnel and sniffed, but only to confirm my suspicions: Chad had been sliding down the coal chute for fun.

His eyes peered worriedly out from under his too-long hair. It didn't look dangerous to me—it looked fun. More fun if no one else knew, I'd had a few places like that when I was his age. So I didn't say anything.

I showed him the old bare copper electrical wires, no longer in use but still present, and the quarry marks on the granite stone blocks used to wall in the basement. We checked out the basement ceiling below the kitchen and dining room. Since I didn't know exactly what had been happening in the kitchen and dining room, I didn't know what to look for. But it stood to reason that it would have been put in shortly before the haunting started—which was just a few months ago. Everything in that part of the basement looked as though it was older than I was.

The next two floors weren't nearly as interesting as the basement—no black widows. Someone had thoroughly modernized them and left not so much as a trace of an old servants' stairway or dumbwaiter. The woodwork was nice, but pine rather than hardwood—the craftsmanship good but not extraordinary. The house had been built by someone of the upper middle class, I judged, and not by one of the truly wealthy. My trailer had been built for the truly poor, so I was a good judge of such things.

The ghost hadn't been to Chad's room since last night—everything was neatly in place. As Corban had said, there were no signs of wires or strings or anything that could have made the car shoot across the room. I supposed it could have been done with magic—I didn't know a lot about magic. But I hadn't felt any, and I usually can tell if someone's using magic near me.

I looked at Chad. "Unless we find something really odd in the floor above your room, I'm pretty convinced this is the real deal."

In my room, my brush was on the floor, but I couldn't swear I hadn't left it there. Under Chad's gimlet eye, I made my bed and stuffed the clothes I'd scattered all over the floor into my suitcase.

"The real problem is," I told him as I tidied my mess and he sat on the bed, "that I don't know how to get the ghost to leave you alone. I can see it better than you, I think—you didn't see anything yesterday except the things moving around?"

He shook his head.

"I did. Nothing clear, but I could see it. But I don't know how to make it go away. It's not a repeater—a ghost that just repeats certain actions over and over. There's intelligence behind what it does—" I had to say it twice for him to get it all.

When he did, Chad's face twisted in a snarl, and he hissed.

I nodded. "It's angry. Maybe if we can figure out what it's angry about, we can—"

Something made a huge crashing noise. My reaction must have given it away because Chad stood up and touched my shoulder.

"Something downstairs," I told him.

We found it in the kitchen. The fridge hung open and the wall opposite it was dented and smeared with a wet and sticky substance that was probably orange juice. A container of it lay open on the floor along with half a dozen bottles of various condiments. The faucet was on full force. The sink was stoppered and rapidly filling with hot water.

While Chad turned the water off, I looked around the room. When Chad touched my arm, I shook my head. "I don't see it."

Heaving a sigh, I started cleanup. I seemed to be doing that a lot here. I scrubbed the wall, and Chad mopped the floor. There was nothing I could do about the dents in the wall—and looking at them, I thought maybe some of them were old.

Once everything was as good as it would get, I fixed sandwiches and chips for lunch. Thus fortified, we continued our explorations by going up to the attic.

There were actually two attics. The one above Chad's room was accessible by a narrow stairway hidden in a hall closet (maybe the last remnant of a servants' stair). I half expected dust and storage boxes, but the attic held only a modern office with a professional-looking computer set up on a cherry desk. There were skylights for an open, airy feeling to offset the walls of cherry barrister's book-cases weighed down by leather-bound legal tomes. The only whim-sical feature was a lacy pillow on the narrow window seat in front of the only window.

"You said there was another one?" I asked, standing on the stairs because entering the room seemed intrusive.

Chad led the way to the other side of the second floor and into his parent's bedroom. I wondered why the office had been personal-ized and charming while the bedroom suite, professionally decorated until it would have been as equally comfortable in a department store as it was in the old house, was impersonal and cold.

Inside the walk-in closet, there was a large rectangular door in the ceiling. We had to get a chair and pull it under the door before I could reach the latched hand pull, but the door turned out to be a folding staircase. Once we pulled the chair away, the stairs dropped all the way to the floor.

Flashlights in hand, we intrepid explorers climbed into the attic more suited to a house like this than the previous one had been. Structurally, it was the mirror image of the office minus the sky-lights and gorgeous view. Light battled through the coating of white paint that covered the only window, flickering on the motes of dust we had disturbed with our presence.

Four old steamer trunks were lined up against the wall next to a pedal sewing machine with SINGER scrawled in elaborate gold lettering over the scratched wooden side of the cabinet. There were more empty milk crates here, but in the attic, at least, someone had found a way to keep the spiders out. I didn't see any creepy-crawlies at all. Or even very much dust. Trust Amber to dust her attic.

The trunks were locked. But the look of disappointment on Chad's face had me digging out my pocketknife. A little wiggling, a little jiggling with the otherwise-useless toothpick, and the slimmest of the blades had the first trunk open before you could sing three verses of "Ninety-nine Bottles of Beer." I know because I hum when I pick locks—it's a bad habit. Since I have no desire to become a professional thief, though, I haven't bothered to try to break myself of it.

Yellowed linens with tatting around the edges and embroidered spring baskets, or flowers, or some other appropriately feminine imagery filled the first trunk, but the second was more interesting. House plans (which we took out), deeds, old diplomas for people whose names were unfamiliar to Chad, and a handful of newspaper articles dating back to the 1920s about people with the same last name as the people in the diplomas and deeds. Mostly death, birth, and marriage notices. None of the death notices were about people who had died violently or too young, I noticed.

While Chad was poring over the house plans he'd spread over the closed lid of the first trunk, I stopped to read about the life of Ermalinda Gaye Holfenster McGinnis Curtis Albright, intrigued by the excessive last name. She'd died at age seventy-four in 1939. Her father had been a captain on the wrong side of the Civil War, had taken his family west, finding his fortune in timber and railroads. Ermalinda had eight children, four of whom had survived her and had a huge number of children themselves. Twice a widow, she'd married a third man fifteen years before her death. He'd been— reading between the lines—far younger than she.

"You go, girl," I told her admiringly—and the stairway closed up and slammed shut so hard that the resultant vibration from the floor had Chad looking up from his plans. He wouldn't have heard the snick of the lock, though.

I dove for the door—too late, of course. When I put my nose to it, I didn't smell anyone. I couldn't think of any reason anyone would lock us in the attic, anyway. It wasn't as if we were going to perish up here . . . unless someone set the whole house on fire or something.

I pushed that helpful thought out of my head and decided it was probably our ghost. I'd read about ghosts who set houses on fire. Wasn't Hans Holzer's Borley Rectory supposedly burned down by its ghosts? But then I was pretty sure that Hans Holzer had been proved a fraud at some point . . .

"Well," I told Chad, "that tells us that our ghost is vindictive and intelligent, anyway." He looked pretty shook-up, clutching the plans in a way that would make any historian cringe at the way the fragile paper was wrinkling. "We might as well keep exploring, don't you think?"

When he still looked scared, I told him, "Your mother will be home sooner or later. When she comes upstairs, we can have her let us out." Then I had an idea. I slipped my phone out of my front pocket, but when I called the number I'd saved for Amber, I could hear the phone in her bedroom ring.

"Does your mom have a cell phone?" She did. He punched the number in, and I listened to her cell phone tell me she wasn't available. So I told her where we were and what had happened.

"When she gets the message, she'll come let us out," I told Chad when I was finished. "If she doesn't, we'll call your dad. Want to see what's in the last trunk?"

He wasn't happy about it, but he leaned on my shoulder while I finagled the last lock.

We both stared at the treasure revealed when the last trunk opened.

"Wow," I said. "I wonder if your parents know this is up here." I paused. "I wonder if this is worth anything?"

The last trunk was completely full of old records, mostly the thick black vinyl kind labeled 78 rpm. There was a method to the storage, I discovered. One pile was all children's entertainment—*The Story of Hiawatha*, various children's songs. And a treasure, *Snow White* complete with a storybook in the album cover that looked as though it had been made about the same time as the movie. Chad turned up his nose at *Snow White*, so I put it back in the correct pile.

My cell phone rang and I checked the number. "Not your mom," I told Chad. I flipped open the phone. "Hey, Adam. Did you ever listen to the Mello-Kings?"

There was a little pause, and Adam sang in a passable bass, "*Chip, chip, chip went the little bird* . . . and something, something, something went my heart. I assume there's a reason you asked?"

"Chad and I are going though a box of old records," I told him.

"Chad?" His voice was carefully neutral.

"Amber's ten-year-old son. I have in my own two hands a 1957 record by the Mello-Kings. I think it might be the newest one in here—nope. Chad just found a Beatles album . . . uhm, cover. It looks like the record is missing. So the Mello-Kings are probably the newest thing here."

"I see. No luck hunting ghosts?"

"Some." I looked ruefully at the closed door that was keeping us prisoner. "What about you? How're negotiations with the Mistress?"

"Warren and Darryl are to meet with a pair of her vampires tonight."

"Which ones?"

"Bernard and Wulfe."

"Tell them to be careful," I told him. "Wulfe is something more than just a vampire." I'd only met Bernard once, and he hadn't impressed me—or maybe I was just remembering Stefan's reaction to him.

"Go teach your granny to suck eggs," said Adam calmly. "Don't worry. Have you seen Stefan?"

I touched my fingers to my neck. How to answer that. *I don't know, he might have bitten me last night,* somehow didn't seem the right thing to say. "He has been making himself scarce so far. Maybe tonight he'll stop in to talk."

I heard the door open downstairs. "I need to go now, Amber's back."

"All right. I'll call you tonight." And he hung up.

Someone ran up the stairs and into the bedroom.

"Your mother's home," I told Chad, and began replacing the

records. They were heavy. I couldn't imagine what the whole trunk might weigh. Maybe they packed the trunk when it was already in the attic—or had eight strapping werewolves to carry it.

"It's locked," I told Amber, as she rattled the door. "I think there's some kind of a catch on your side."

She was breathing hard as she pulled the stairs down.

Her attention was all for Chad, and she didn't bother with speech as her hands danced.

"We're fine," I interrupted her. "You have some neat records here. Have you had them valued?"

She turned to stare at me, as if she'd forgotten I was there. Her pupils were . . . odd. Too large, I decided, even for the dim attic.

"The records? I think Corban found them when we bought this house. Yes, he checked them out. They're nothing special. Just old."

"Did you have a good time shopping?"

She looked at me blankly. "Shopping?"

"Amber, are you all right?"

She blinked, then smiled. It was so full of sweetness and light that it gave me cold chills. Amber was many things, but she wasn't sweet. There was something wrong with her.

"Yes. I bought a sweater and a couple of early Christmas presents." She waved it away. "How did you get stuck here?"

I shrugged, replacing the last records and pulling the trunk shut. "Unless you have someone breaking into your house to play nasty practical jokes, I'd say it was the ghost."

I stood up and started past her to the opened door. And I smelled vampire. Could Stefan be staying here? I paused to look around while Chad thundered down the attic stairs leaving his mother and me alone with the smell of vampire and fresh blood.

"What's wrong?" Amber said, taking a step forward.

She smelled of sweat, sex, and a vampire who was not Stefan.

"Was shopping all you were doing?" I asked.

"What? I had my hair done, paid a few bills—that's it. Are you all right?"

She wasn't lying. She didn't know she'd been a snack for a vampire. Today.

I looked at the daylight streaming through the windows and knew I desperately needed to talk to Stefan.

7

~~~

I WAITED UNTIL DARK, THEN QUIETLY SNUCK OUT THE back door and into the yard.

"Stefan?" I called, keeping it quiet so no one in the house would hear me.

It wasn't as stupid as all that to call for him. He'd come here to keep an eye on me. It made sense that he'd be nearby, somewhere. Watching.

I waited for a half an hour, though, and no Stefan. Finally, I went inside and found Amber watching TV.

"I'm going to bed," I told her.

Her neck, I noticed, was bared to the world without blemish— but there are other places a vampire can feed. My own neck sported a scarf, one of several I'd picked up that afternoon on a Goodwill shopping spree that Chad and I had taken. The only thing I'd found resembling a lamb had been a barrette with a cartoon sheep on it. Not something to invoke the protection of the Son of God.

"You look tired," she said with a yawn. "I know I'm exhausted." She muted the TV and faced me. "Corban told me about last night. Even if you can't do anything else, it means a lot to me that you've convinced him that Chad isn't just making things up and acting out."

I rubbed the vampire bite, safely hidden under bright red silk. Amber had a lot bigger problem than a ghost, but I had no idea how to help her with that one either.

"Good," I said. "I'll see you in the morning."

Once I was in my room, I couldn't force myself to go to sleep. I wondered if Corban knew what his client was and knew that the vampire was feeding from his wife, or if he was a dupe like Amber. I wondered at the oddity of Corban, who didn't believe in ghosts, suggesting Amber ask me to come and help them with theirs. But if the vampire had decided to bring me here . . . I had no idea why. Unless it was some secret conspiracy, a way for Marsilia to get rid of me, punish me for my sins without worrying about the wolves. But I didn't see Marsilia being anxious to owe a favor to any vampire—and a vampire who was so territorial that he allowed no other vampires at all was a poor candidate for cooperative problem solving.

Speaking of Blackwood . . . he'd called Amber to him in the day. I'd never heard of a vampire who was alive during the day, though admittedly my experience with vampires was limited. I wondered where Stefan was.

"Stefan?" I said, keeping my voice down. "Come out, come out, wherever you are." Maybe he couldn't get in because he hadn't been invited. "Stefan? Come in." But he still didn't answer.

My phone rang, and I couldn't help the silly butterflies in my stomach when I answered.

"Hey, Adam," I said.

"I thought you'd want to know that Warren and Darryl made it out of the vampire den alive."

I sucked in my breath. "You didn't actually agree to their meeting on Marsilia's grounds?"

He laughed. "No, it just sounded better than saying they made it out of Denny's alive. It might not be romantic, but it's open all night and set in the middle of a brightly lit parking lot with no dark places for skulking parties to ambush from."

"Did they accomplish anything?"

"Not exactly." He didn't sound worried. "Negotiations take time. This round was all posturing and threats. But Warren says he thinks Marsilia might be after something more than just your pretty little hide—a couple of hints Wulfe let drop. Marsilia knows I won't budge on you, but she might be willing to negotiate on something else. How are you doing?"

"The walking stick followed me here," I told him, because I knew it would make him laugh again.

He did. And the rough caress of his mirth made my bones melt. "Just don't buy any sheep while you're out, and you'll be safe."

The stick that followed me home and, in this case, to Spokane had originally had the power of making every sheep belonging to its caretaker bear twins. Like most fairy gifts, sooner or later it backfired on its human owner. I didn't know if it still worked that way, and I didn't know why it was following me around either, but I was getting sort of used to it.

"Any luck with your ghost?"

Now that we were safely out of the attic, I could tell him about it without him speeding all the way over to rescue me. If Blackwood had ignored me—mostly, anyway—he certainly wouldn't ignore the Alpha of the Columbia Basin Pack.

When I was finished, he asked, "Why'd it trap you in the attic?"

I shrugged and wriggled on the bed to get more comfortable. "I don't know. Probably the opportunity just presented itself. There are fae who cause mischief like this—hobs and brownies and the like. But this was a ghost. I saw it myself. What I haven't seen is any sign of Stefan. I'm a little worried about him."

"He's there to make sure Marsilia doesn't send anyone after you," said Adam.

"Right," I said. "So far, so good." I touched the sore spot on my neck. Could that be another explanation? Could it have been one of Marsilia's vampires?

But the sick feeling in my stomach told me that it wasn't. Not with Blackwood free to come and go in Amber's home. Not with Amber called, seduced, and fed from—*in daylight.*

"You don't get to be as old as Stefan is without being able to take care of yourself."

"You're right," I said, "but he's been cut adrift, and I'd be happier if he weren't making himself so scarce."

"He'd not be much help in a ghost hunt—don't ghosts avoid vampires?"

"Ghosts and cats, Bran says," I told him. "But my cat likes Stefan."

"Your cat likes anyone she can convince to pet her."

Something about the way he said it—a caress in his voice—made me suspicious. I listened carefully and heard it, a faint purr.

"She likes you, anyway," I said. "How'd she talk you into letting her into your house again?"

"She yowled at the back door." He sounded sheepish. I'd never seen or heard of a cat that would associate with werewolves or coyotes until Medea announced her presence at the door of my shop. Dogs will—and so will most livestock—but not cats. Medea loves anyone who will pet her . . . or has the potential to pet her. Not unlike some people I know.

"She's playing you and Samuel off each other," I informed him. "And you, my dear sir, have just succumbed to her wiles."

"My mother warned me about succumbing," he said meekly. "You'll have to save me from myself. When I have you to pet, I won't need her."

Faintly, through his phone, I heard the doorbell ring.

"It's pretty late for visitors," I said.

Adam started to laugh.

"What?"

"It's Samuel. He just asked Jesse if we've seen your cat."

I sighed. "Men are so easy. You'd better go confess your sins."

When I disconnected, I stared into the dark wishing I were home. If I were sleeping with Adam next to me, no stupid vampire would be chewing on my neck. Finally, I got up, turned on the light, and brought out the fairy book to read. After a few pages, I quit worrying about vampires, pulled the comforter closer around my shoulders—Amber must like her AC down at werewolf levels—and lost myself in the story of the Roaring Bull of Bagbury and other fae who haunt bridges.

I woke up shivering sometime later, clutching the fairy staff, which I'd last seen leaning against the wall next to the door. The wood under my fingers was hot—a contrast to the rest of the room. The cold was so intense my nose was numb and my breath fogged.

A moment after I woke up, a high-pitched, atonal wail rang through the walls of the house, abruptly cutting off.

I dumped my covers on the floor. The rare old book met the same fate—but I was too worried about Chad to stop and rescue it. I ran out of my bedroom and took the requisite four steps to the boy's room.

The door wouldn't open.

The knob turned, so it wasn't locked. I put my shoulder against the door, but it didn't budge. I tried to use the walking stick, which was still warmer than it should have been, as a crowbar, to force the door open, but it didn't work. There was nowhere to get a good place to pry.

"Let me," whispered Stefan just behind me.

"Where have you been?" I said, relief making me sharp. With the vampire here, the ghost would go.

"Hunting," he said, putting his shoulder to the door. "You looked like you had everything under control."

"Yeah," I said. "Well, appearances can be deceiving."

"I see that."

I heard the wood begin to break as it gave reluctantly for the first few inches. Then it jerked away from the vampire and flung itself against the wall with a spiteful bang, leaving Stefan to stumble into the bedroom.

If my room had been cold, Chad's was frigid. Frost layered everything in the room like unearthly lace. Chad lay still as the dead in the center of his bed—he wasn't breathing, but his eyes were open and scared.

Both Stefan and I ran for the bed.

The ghost wasn't gone though, and Stefan didn't scare it away. We couldn't get Chad out of the bed. The comforter was frozen to him and to the bed, and it wouldn't release him. I dropped the walking stick on the floor and grabbed the comforter with both hands and pulled. It quivered under my hold like a living thing, damp from the frost that melted from contact with my skin.

Stefan reached both hands just under Chad's chin and ripped the comforter in half. Quick as a striking snake he had Chad up and off the bed.

I collected the staff and followed them out of the room and into the hall, wishing I'd updated my CPR skills since high school.

But, safely out of the room, Chad started sucking in air like a vacuum.

"You need a priest," Stefan told me.

I ignored him in favor of Chad. "You okay?"

The boy gathered himself together. His body might be thin, but his spirit was pure tungsten. He nodded, and Stefan set him down on his feet, steadying him a little when Chad swayed.

"I've never seen anything like that," I admitted. I could see inside Chad's room to the water that ran down the rapidly clearing window. I looked at Stefan. "I thought ghosts avoided you."

He was staring into the room, too. "So did I. I . . ." He looked at me and stopped speaking. He tilted my chin up and looked at my neck, at both sides of my neck. And I realized that I'd been bitten a second time. "Who's been chewing on you, *cara mia*?"

Chad looked at Stefan, then hissed and used his fingers to make a pair of vampire fangs.

"Yes, I know," Stefan told him—signing it, too. "Vampire." Who knew? Stefan could sign; somehow it didn't seem like a vampire kind of thing to do.

Chad had a few more things to say. When he was finished, Stefan shook his head.

"That vampire isn't here; she wouldn't leave the Tri-Cities. This is a different one." He looked at me, angling his face so Chad couldn't see what he said. "How do you do it?" he asked conversationally. "How do you go to a city of half a million and attract the only vampire here? What did you do, run into him while jogging at night?"

I ignored the panic in my stomach caused by being bitten twice by some jerk I'd only met once. Calling him a jerk made him less scary. Or it should have. But James Blackwood had bitten me twice while I slept through it . . . or worse, he'd made me forget it.

"Just lucky, I guess," I said. I didn't want to talk about it with Chad right here. He'd be a lot safer if he didn't know James Blackwood was a vampire.

Chad made a few more hand motions.

"Sorry," said Stefan. "I'm Stefan, Mercy's friend."

Chad frowned.

"He's one of the good guys," I told him. He gave me a "fine, but what's he doing in my house in the middle of the night" look. I pretended not to know what it meant. And I didn't speak ASL, so he was out there, too. Not fair, I supposed, but I didn't want to lie to him—and I really didn't want to tell him the whole truth.

"They need to get away from here," said Stefan. "And I'm taking you back to the Tri-Cities." He looked like he was going to say something else, but glanced at Chad and shook his head. Probably something more about Blackwood.

"Let me put some clothes on," I said. "I think better when I'm not running around in a T-shirt and underwear."

I dressed in the bathroom—getting a good look at the second bite while I did so. Then I covered them both up with my new used silk-embroidered red scarf.

Go back home? What would that accomplish? For that matter what had I accomplished here?

I'd come to help Amber and get out of Marsilia's sight for a little bit. That had succeeded—or at least not hampered Adam's negotiating. I didn't know that I'd helped Amber at all . . . not yet.

I stared at my pale, sleep-starved face and wondered how I was going to do that. Blackwood had them in his care.

I shivered. Though there was nothing I could pinpoint, no cold spot, no smell, no sound—I could feel something watching me. "Leave the boy alone," I told my unseen watcher.

And every hair on my head tingled with sensation.

I waited for it to attack or show itself. But nothing else happened, just that momentary connection, which faded more slowly than it had come.

Stefan knocked. "Everything all right?"

"Fine," I said. Something had happened, but I had no idea what. I was tired and scared and angry. So I brushed my teeth and opened the bathroom door.

Stefan and Chad were leaning on opposite sides of the hallway, discussing something that had their hands moving a mile a minute.

"Stefan."

He threw up his hands and appealed to me. "How can he think *Dragon Ball Z* is better than *Scooby-Doo*? This generation has no appreciation for the classics."

I stood on tiptoe and kissed his cheek. Keeping my mouth turned away from Chad, I said, "You're a nice man."

Stefan patted my head.

I checked Chad's bedroom, but it looked as if nothing had happened, and not even a trace of dampness from the frost remained.

Only the two pieces of comforter on either side of Chad's bed gave any hint of trouble.

"There are a couple of vampires that can do stuff like this," Stefan said, waving his hand at Chad's room. "Move things without touching them, kill people without being in the room. But I've never heard of a *ghost* with this much power. They tend to be pathetic things trying to pretend they are alive."

I didn't smell vampire, only blood—fading as the frost had faded. I had seen the ghost—not clearly, but it had been there. Still, I turned so Chad couldn't read my lips. "Do you think Blackwood is playing ghost?"

Stefan shook his head. "No, it's not the Monster. Wrong heritage. There was an Indian vampire in New York—" He looked at me and grinned. He pressed a finger to his forehead. "Indian with a dot, not a feather. Anyway, he and his get all could have done something like what we saw tonight . . . except for the cold. But only the vampires he made directly could do it—and he only made Indian women into vampires. They were all killed a century or more ago, and I think Blackwood predated him anyway."

Chad had been watching Stefan's mouth with every evidence of fascination. He made a few gestures, and Stefan signed back, saying, "They're dead. No. Someone else killed them. Yes, I'm sure it was someone else." He glanced at me. "Want to explain to the kid that I'm more a Spike than a Buffy? A villain, not a superhero?"

I batted my eyelashes at him. "You're my hero."

He jerked several steps back from me as if I'd hit him. It made me wonder what Marsilia had said to him while she'd tortured him.

"Stefan?"

He turned back to us with a hiss and an expression that made Chad back into me. "I'm a vampire, Mercy."

I wasn't going to let him get away with the morose, self-hating vampire act. He deserved better than that. "Yeah, we got that. It's the fangs that give it away—translate that for Chad, please." I waited while he did so, his hands jerky with anger or something related to it. Chad relaxed against me.

Stefan continued signing, and said, almost defiantly, "I'm no one's hero, Mercy."

I turned my face until I was looking directly at Chad. "Do you think that means I won't get to see him in spandex?"

Chad mouthed the last word with a puzzled look.

Stefan sighed. He touched Chad's shoulder, and when the boy looked up, he finger-spelled *spandex* slowly. Chad made a yuck face.

"Hey," I told them, "watching good-looking men run around in tight-fitting costumes is high on my list of things I'd like to do before I die."

Stefan gave in and laughed. "It won't be me," he told me. "So what do we do next, Haunt Huntress?"

"That's a pretty lame superhero name," I told him.

"Scooby-Doo is already taken," he said with dignity. "*Anything* else sounds lame in comparison."

"Seriously," I said, "I think we'd better go find his parents." Who hopefully were sleeping peacefully despite Chad's cry and doors banging into walls, not to mention all the talking we'd been doing. Now that I thought of it, it was a bad sign they weren't out here fussing.

"We? You want me to come, too?" Stefan raised an eyebrow.

I wasn't going to tell Chad to lie to his parents. And if something had happened to Amber and her husband, I wanted Stefan with me. Their room was on the opposite side of the house from Chad's and mine, their door was thick—and they didn't have nifty hearing like

Stefan and I did. Maybe they were sleeping. I clutched my walking stick.

"Yeah. Come with us, Stefan. But, Chad?" I made sure he could see my face. "You don't want to tell your folks Stefan is a vampire, okay? For the same reasons I told you before. Vampires don't like people knowing about them."

Chad stiffened and glanced at Stefan and away.

"Hey. No, not Stefan," I said. "He doesn't mind. But others will." And his father probably wouldn't believe him about that either—and maybe he'd tell Blackwood about it. Blackwood, I was pretty sure, wouldn't be happy if Chad knew about vampires.

So we trekked to Amber's room and opened the door. It was dark inside, and I could see two still figures in the bed. For a moment I froze, then realized I could hear them breathing. On the bedside table next to Corban was an empty glass that had held brandy—I could smell it now that I was through panicking. And on Amber's side was a prescription bottle.

Chad slid past me and scrambled over their footboard and into bed beside them. With his parents here, he was no longer required to be brave. Cold feet did what all the noise had failed to do, and Corban sat up.

"Chad . . ." He saw us. "Mercy? Who's that with you, and what are you doing in my bedroom?"

"Corban?" Amber rolled over. She sounded a little dopey but woke up just fine when she noticed Chad and then us. "Mercy? What happened?"

I told them, leaving out Stefan's vampire status. I didn't, actually, mention him at all except as part of "we." They didn't care. Once they heard Chad hadn't been breathing, they weren't worried about Stefan at all.

"I've never seen anything like it," I admitted to them both. "I'm out of my league. I think you need to get Chad out of here and into a hotel tonight."

Corban had listened to everything with a poker face. He got out of bed and grabbed a robe in almost the same motion. I heard him walk down the hall, but he didn't go into Chad's room. Just stood outside it for a moment and returned. I knew what he saw—nothing but a ripped-up comforter—and was glad he'd been there for the little toy-car demonstration.

He stood in the doorway of his bedroom and looked at us. "First, we pack for a couple of days. Second, we find a hotel. Third, I talk to my cousin's brother-in-law, who is a Jesuit priest."

"I'm headed home," I told him before he could tell me to go away and never come back. I needed to help them do something about Blackwood, who was snacking on Amber, but I didn't know what. And from the sounds of it, no one had ever been able to do something about this vampire. "There's nothing I can do for you, and I have a business to run."

"Thank you for coming," Amber said. She got out of bed and hugged me. And I knew what she was most grateful for was convincing her husband that Chad hadn't been lying. I thought that was the least of her worries.

Over her shoulder, Corban stared at me as if he suspected I'd somehow caused everything. I wondered about that, too. *Something* had made their ghost much worse, and I was the obvious place to look for a reason.

I left them to their preparations, packed my own bags, and hugged Amber again before I left.

She still smelled like vampire—but then so did Stefan and I.

STEFAN WAITED UNTIL WE WERE MOSTLY OUT OF SPO-
kane, driving past the airport, before he said anything. "Do you
need me to drive?"

"Nope," I answered. I might be tired, but I didn't like anyone
else to drive my Vanagon. As soon as Zee and I put the Rabbit back
together, the van was going back in the garage. Besides . . . "I don't
think I'll be sleeping again anytime in the next millennium. How did
he bite me twice without my knowing it?"

"Some vampires can do that," Stefan said in the same sort of soothing voice a doctor uses to tell you that you have a terminal illness. "It's
not among my gifts—or any of our seethe except perhaps Wulfe."

"He bit me twice. That's worse than just once, right?" Silence
followed my question.

Something wiggled in my front pocket. I twitched, then realized
what had happened. I pulled my vibrating cell phone out without
looking at the number. "Yes?" Maybe I sounded abrupt, but I was
scared and Stefan hadn't answered me.

There was a little silence, and Adam said, "What's wrong? Your
fear woke me up."

I blinked really fast, wishing I was home already. Home with
Adam instead of driving in the dark with a vampire.

"I'm sorry it bothered you."

"A benefit of the pack bond," Adam told me. Then, because he
knew me, he said, "I'm Alpha, so I get things first. No one else in the
pack felt it. What scared you?"

"The ghost," I told him, then let out my breath in a gusty sigh.
"And the vampire."

He coaxed the whole story out of me. Then he sighed. "Only you could go to Spokane and get bitten by the one vampire in the whole city." He didn't fool me. For all the amusement in his voice, I could hear the anger, too.

But if he was pretending, I could pretend. "That's pretty much what Stefan said. I don't think it's fair. How was I to know that Amber's husband's best client was the vampire?"

Adam gave me a rueful laugh. "The real question is why didn't we suspect that's what would happen. But you are safe now?"

"Yes."

"Then it'll wait until you get here."

He hung up without saying good-bye.

"So," I said, "tell me what Blackwood can do to me now that he's fed off me twice."

"I don't know," Stefan told me. Then he sighed. "If I have exchanged blood with someone twice, I can always find him, no matter where he goes. I could call him to me—and if he is near, I could force him to come to me. But that is with a true blood exchange—yours to me, mine to you. Eventually . . . it is possible to force a master-slave relationship upon those you exchange blood with. A precaution, I suppose, because a newly turned vampire can get nasty. A simple feeding is less risky. But your reactions are not always the usual. There could be no ill effects to you at all."

I thought of Amber, who had been feeding the vampire for who knows how long, and her husband, who could be in the same condition, and felt sick. "Out of the frying pan and into the fire," I said. "Damn it." *Okay. Think positive.* If I hadn't gone to Spokane at all, the vampire would still have had Amber and her husband, only no one would have known. "If I was unconscious, could he have forced a blood exchange?"

He sighed and slumped in his seat. "You don't remember him biting. That doesn't mean you were unconscious."

I wasn't expecting it. I hadn't had one since leaving the Tri-Cities. But I managed to pull over, hop out of the van, and make it to the barrow pit at the side of the road before throwing up. It wasn't sickness . . . it was sheer, stark terror. The panic attack to end all panic attacks. My heart hurt, my head hurt, and I couldn't stop crying.

And then it stopped. Warmth ran through me and around me: pack. Adam. So much for not bothering Adam's wolves, who were already unhappy about me, with my troubles. Stefan wiped my face off with a Kleenex and dropped it to the ground before picking me up and carrying me back to the car. He didn't put me in the driver's seat.

"I can drive," I told him, but there was no force in my voice. Pack magic had broken the panic attack, but I could still feel them all waiting and ready.

Ready to rescue me again.

He ignored my feeble protest and put the old van in gear.

"Is there any reason why he'd have simply fed from me and not done a blood exchange?" I asked, more out of a morbid desire to know everything rather than any real hope.

"With a blood exchange, you can call upon him as well," Stefan said reluctantly.

"How many? Just one exchange?"

He shrugged. "It varies from person to person. With your idiosyncratic reaction to vampire magic, it could take a hundred or only one."

"When you say I could call him. Does that mean he'd have to come to me?"

"A vampire's relationship to those he feeds upon is not an equal one, Mercy," he snapped. "No. He could hear you. That is all. If you have blood exchanges with all of your *food*"—he bit out the word—"the voices in your head can drive you mad. So we only do it with our own flocks. There are some benefits. The sheep becomes stronger, immune to pain for a brief time—as you know from your own experiences. A vampire gains a servant and eventually a slave who will willingly feed him and take care of his needs during the day."

"I'm sorry," I told him. "I didn't mean to make you angry. I just have to know what I'm up against."

He reached over and patted my knee. "I understand. I'm sorry." The next words came slower. "It is shaming to me, to be what I am. The man I was would never have accepted life at the expense of so many. But I am not he, not any longer."

He passed a semi (we were going uphill). "If he was just feeding from you because you were convenient, then he probably didn't do an exchange . . . except . . ."

"Except what?"

"I don't think that he could have blocked your memory so well if it wasn't a real exchange. A human, yes. But you are strong-willed." He shrugged. "Most Master vampires feed off their get—other vampires. Blackwood will tolerate no other vampires in his territory, and I don't know that he has any get himself. Maybe he makes up the difference by exchanging blood whenever he feeds."

I mulled over what he'd told me, then dozed a little. I woke with a start as we took the exit onto Highway 395 at Ritzville. Only a little over seventy miles until we got home.

"He won't be able to coerce you if you find another vampire to tie yourself to," Stefan said.

I looked at him, but he was staring intently at the road—as if we were threading through the mountains of Montana instead of gliding down an empty stretch of mostly flat and straight pavement.

"Are you offering?"

He nodded. "I am perilously short of food. The exchange will feed me better, and I won't have to hunt again for a few nights."

I thought for a minute. Not that I was going to do it, but there was more to his offer—with vampires, I was learning, there usually was. With Stefan that didn't necessarily mean that he was hiding some benefit to him.

"And you'll gain yourself an enemy," I guessed. "James Blackwood holds Spokane, all by himself, against all the supernatural peoples, not just vampires. That means he's obsessively possessive—and tough. He won't be happy with you for keeping me from him."

He shrugged. "He probably can't call you all the way from Spokane when you are in the Tri-Cities. He probably wouldn't even try, if he exchanges blood every time he feeds. But if you are tied to me, that would be certain." He spoke slowly. "We already have had one blood exchange. And I can make sure it won't be horrible."

If Blackwood called me to him, if he took me as one of his sheep, Adam would bring the pack in to rescue me. Mary Jo had almost paid the ultimate price for my problems already. As long as I stayed in the Tri-Cities, he might not even realize that the reason he couldn't call me was Stefan.

"Adam is my mate," I told him. I didn't know if I should tell him that Adam had made me one of the pack. "Can Blackwood get Adam through me?"

Stefan shook his head. "I can't either. It's been tried. Our old Master . . . Marsilia's maker, liked wolves and experimented. The ties of the blood operate on a different level from the werewolf pack. He took an Alpha's mate, she was a werewolf also, to his menagerie hoping to control the Alpha and his whole pack through her, and it failed."

"Marsilia likes werewolf to dine upon," I said. I'd seen it for myself.

"From what I've seen, I'd say that feeding upon them seems to be addictive," he glanced at me. "I've never done it myself. Not until the other night. I don't intend to do it again."

I was either about to make the stupidest decision of my life or the smartest.

"Is it permanent?" I asked. "This bond between the two of us?"

He gave me a sharp look. Started to say something, but stopped before the words left his mouth.

Finally, he said, "I've told you things tonight that other vampires don't know. Forbidden things. If I were Marsilia's get truly, or if she had not broken my ties with the seethe, I could not have told you that much."

He tapped the palm of his hands on the steering wheel and a giant RV towing a Honda Accord passed us. "These things drive like anemic school buses," he said. "Odd that it should be so much fun."

I waited. If the answer had been yes, the bond is permanent, he wouldn't be so indecisive. If it wasn't permanent, once Blackwood was eliminated, it could be removed. A temporary bond with Stefan wasn't as scary as, say, the more permanent bond between Adam and me.

"Marsilia can break the bonds between Master and sheep," he said. "She can either take them herself, or simply dissolve them."

"That's not very helpful," I told him. "I have the distinct impression that she'd just as soon kill us both as see us."

"There is that," he said softly. "Yes. But I think, from a few things he's let drop, that Wulfe can do it, too." His voice grew very cold and un-Stefan-like. "And Wulfe owes me in such a way that even if Marsilia has declared me enemy to the seethe, he could not turn down my request." He relaxed and shook his head. "But as soon as the bond between us was ended, you'd be vulnerable to Blackwood again."

I didn't find Wulfe much of a step up from Marsilia. But then, I didn't have a choice, did I? I'd abandoned Amber until I could regroup, but I couldn't leave Amber to die at Blackwood's whim.

I wondered if Zee still felt guilty enough, because I got hurt trying to help him, to allow me use of his fae-spelled knife and the amulet I'd used to hunt vampires. Maybe even another magically virtuous stake.

I'd never seriously considered killing Marsilia as a way to save myself. First, I'd been to the seethe. Second, she had too many minions who would kill me back.

So why did I think I could kill Blackwood?

I knew, *I knew*, that the James Blackwood I'd met was not the real face of the vampire. But I *had* met him, and he wasn't too scary. He didn't have minions. And he was using Amber without her knowledge or permission, turning her into his slave: a woman who left her child alone in a house with a ghost and an almost stranger. I couldn't help Amber with her ghost . . . maybe I'd even made it worse. But I could help her with the vampire.

"All right," I said. "I'd rather have to"—I nearly choked on the next word—"obey you than listen to him."

He watched me for a heartbeat. "All right," he agreed.

———

HE PULLED OVER AT A REST AREA. THERE WAS A ROW OF semis parked for the night, but the lot for cars was empty. He unbuckled and walked between the front seats to the back. I followed him slowly.

He sat on the bench seat in the back and patted the seat beside him. When I hesitated, he said, "You don't have to do this. I'm not going to force you."

If I didn't have Stefan to interfere, Blackwood probably could make me do whatever he wanted. I'd have no way to help Amber.

Of course, if Marsilia killed me first, I wouldn't have to worry about any of it.

"Am I putting Adam and his pack in more danger?" I asked.

Stefan did me the courtesy of considering it, though I could smell his eagerness: he smelled like a wolf hot on the trail of something tasty. If I ran, I wondered, would he be compelled to chase me the way a werewolf would have?

I stared at him and reminded myself that I'd known him a long time. He'd never made any move he thought would harm me. This was Stefan, not some nameless hunter.

"I don't see how," he told me. "Adam won't like it, I'm sure. Witness his reaction when I called you by accident. But he's a practical man. He knows all about desperate choices."

I sat down beside him, all too conscious of the cool temperature of his body, cooler, I thought than usual. I was glad to know that this would help him, too. I was really, really tired of causing all my friends nothing but grief.

He brushed my hair away from my neck, and I caught his hand.

"What about the wrist?" The last time he'd bitten my wrist.

He shook his head. "It's more painful. Too many nerves near the surface." He looked at me. "Do you trust me?"

"I wouldn't be doing this if I didn't."

"Okay. I'm going to restrain you a little because if you jerk while I'm still at your neck, you might make me cut through the wrong thing and you could bleed to death." He didn't pressure me, just sat on the plush bench seat as if he could stay there the rest of my life.

"How?" I said.

"I'll have you fold your arms over your stomach, and I'll hold them there."

I did a panic check, but Tim had never restrained me that way. I tried not to think about how he'd held me down and was only moderately successful.

"Go up to the front of the van," Stefan said. "The keys are in the ignition. You'll have to drive yourself home because I can't stay here. I have to hunt now. I'll—"

I wrapped my arms around myself and leaned against him. "Okay, do it."

His arm came slowly around my shoulders and over my right arm. When I stayed put, he put his hand over my arms in such a way that I couldn't free myself.

"All right?" He asked calmly, as if need hadn't turned his eyes jewel-bright, like Christmas lights in the dark van.

"All right," I said.

His teeth must have been razor-sharp because I didn't feel them slice through skin, only the cool dampness of his mouth. Only when he began to draw blood did it start to hurt.

Who feeds at my table?

The roar in my head made me panic as Stefan's bite had not. But I held very still, like a mouse when it first notices the cat. If you don't move, it might not attack.

The steady draw of Stefan's mouth faltered for an instant. Then he resumed feeding, patting my knee with his free hand. It shouldn't have comforted me, but it did. He'd heard the scary monster, too, and he wasn't running.

After a while, the ache deepened into pain—and the now-wordless roar of anger echoing in my head grew muffled. I started to feel cold, as if it wasn't just blood he was taking, but all the warmth in my body. Then his mouth moved, and he laved the wounds with his tongue.

"If you looked into a mirror," he whispered, "you would not see my marks. He wanted you to see what he'd done."

I shivered helplessly, and he lifted me to his lap. He was warm, hot to my cold skin. He lifted me a little and pulled a folding knife out of his pocket. He used the knife and sliced down his wrist like you're supposed to if you want to do suicide right.

"I thought the wrist was too painful," I managed through my sluggish thoughts and vibrating jaw.

"For *you*," he said. "Drink, Mercy. And shut up." A faint smile crossed his face, then he leaned his head back so I couldn't see his expression anymore.

Maybe it should have bothered me more. Maybe if this had been a normal night, it would have. But useless squeamishness was beyond me. I've hunted as a coyote for most of my life, and she never stopped to cook her food. The taste of blood was nothing new or horrible to me, not when it was Stefan's blood—and he wasn't dying or in pain or anything.

I put my lips against his wrist and closed my mouth over the cut. Stefan made a noise—it didn't sound like pain. He put his free hand on my head lightly and then lifted it off as if he didn't want to coerce me even that much. This was my choice freely made.

His blood didn't taste like rabbit or mouse. It was more bitter—and somehow sweeter at the same time. Mostly it was hot, sizzling hot, and I was cold. I drank as the cut under my tongue slowly closed.

And I remembered this taste. Like eating at McDonald's twice in a day and ordering the same meal. I had a momentary flash of memory, just Blackwood's voice in my ears.

I didn't remember what he'd said or what he'd done, but brief memory of the sound had me curled up on the bench seat, my forehead on Stefan's thigh while I cried. Stefan pulled his wrist away and used his other hand to pet my head lightly.

"Mercy," he said gently. "He won't do that again. Not now. You are mine. He can't fog your mind or force you to do anything."

With my voice muffled by the fabric of his jeans, I said, "Does this mean you can read my mind?"

He laughed a little. "Only while you drink. That isn't my gift. Your secrets are safe." His laugh washed away Blackwood's voice.

I lifted up my head. "I'm glad I don't remember more of what he did," I told Stefan. But I thought that my desire to see Blackwood's body burn like Andre's might have a more personal reason than just what he was doing to Amber.

"How are you feeling?" he asked.

I took a breath and evaluated myself. "Awesome. Like I could run from here to the Tri-Cities faster than the van could take us."

He laughed. "I don't think that's true . . . unless we get a flat tire."

He stood up and he looked better than I'd seen him since . . . since before he'd landed on the floor of my living room looking like something that had been buried a hundred years. I got up and had to sit down again.

"Balance," he said. "It's a little like being drunk. That'll fade fast, but I'd better drive us home."

I should have felt terrible. Some small voice was yammering that I should have checked with my Alpha before doing anything this . . . permanent.

But I felt fine, better than fine—and it wasn't just the vampire's blood. I felt truly in control of my life for the first time since Tim's assault. Which was pretty funny under the circumstances.

But *I'd* made the decision to put myself in Stefan's power.

"Stefan?" I watched the reflectors on the side of the road pass by.

"Hmm."

"Did anyone talk to you about the thing someone painted on the door of my shop?" I'd kept forgetting to ask him about it—though subsequent events had made it more obvious that it had been some sort of threat from Marsilia.

"No one said anything to me," he said. "But I saw it myself." Headlights reflected red in his eyes. Like the flash of a camera, only scarier. It made me smile.

"Marsilia had it done?"

"Almost certainly."

I could have left it there. But we had time to kill, and I had Bran's voice in my head saying, *Information is important, Mercy. Get all the facts you can.*

"What exactly does it mean?"

"It's the mark of a traitor," he said. "It means that one of our own has betrayed us, and she and all who belong to her are fair marks. A declaration of war."

It was no more than I had expected. "There's some sort of magic in it," I told him. "What does it do?"

"Keeps you from painting over it for long," he said. "And if it stays there long, you'll start attracting nasties who have no affiliation to the vampire."

"Terrific."

"You could always replace the door."

"Yeah," I told him glumly. Maybe the insurance company would replace it when I explained that the bones couldn't be painted over, but I didn't get my hopes up.

We drove for a while in silence, and I worried through the past few days, trying to see if there was something I'd missed or something I should have done differently.

"Hey, Stefan? How come I couldn't smell Blackwood after he bit me? Tonight I was a little distracted, but yesterday, with the first bite, I checked."

"He would have known what you are after he tasted you." Stefan stretched, and the van swayed a little with his movement. "I don't know whether he was trying to fool you into thinking him human, or if he always cleans up after himself in that way. There were things in the Old Country that hunted us by scent—not just werewolves— or by things that were left behind, hair, saliva, or blood. Many of the older vampires always remove any trace of themselves from their lairs and from their hunting grounds."

I'd almost forgotten they could do that.

The change in the sound of the car's engine as he slowed for city traffic woke me up.

"Do you want to go to your home or Adam's?" he asked.

Good question. Even though I was pretty sure Adam would understand what I'd done, I wasn't exactly looking forward to discussing matters with him. And I was too tired to work my way through exactly what I wanted to leave out—and how I was going to kill Blackwood. I really wanted to talk to Zee before I talked to Adam, and I wanted to get a good long sleep before I did either.

"Mine."

I'd gone back to dozing when the van slowed abruptly. I looked up and saw why: there was someone standing in the middle of the road, looking down as if she'd lost something. She wasn't paying any attention at all to us.

"Do you know her?" We were on my road, just a few properties from our house, so Stefan's question was reasonable.

"No."

He stopped about a dozen yards away, and she finally looked up. The purr of the van's engine subsided, and Stefan glanced behind him, then opened the door and got out.

Trouble.

I stripped off my clothes, popped open my door, and shifted as I hopped out. A coyote may not be big, but it has fangs and surprisingly effective claws. I slipped under the van's side and out under the front bumper, where Stefan was leaning, his arms crossed casually across his chest.

The girl was no longer alone. Three vampires stood beside her. The first two I'd seen before, though I didn't know their names. The third was Estelle.

In Marsilia's seethe there had once been five vampires who had reached some sort of power plateau so that they did not depend upon the Mistress of the seethe for survival: Stefan; Andre, whom I'd killed; Wulfe, the übercreepy wizard in a boy's body; Bernard, who reminded me of a merchant out of a Dickens novel; and Estelle, the Mary Poppins of the undead. I'd never seen her when she wasn't dressed like an Edwardian governess, and tonight was no exception.

As if he'd been waiting for me to appear at his side, Stefan glanced down at me, then said, "Estelle, how nice to see you."

"I'd *heard* she hadn't destroyed you," Estelle said in her prim

English voice. "She tortured you, starved you, banished you—then sent you to kill your little coyote bitch."

Stefan spread his hands out as if to showcase his own living . . . undead flesh. "It is as you heard it." There was a musical cadence to his voice, and he sounded more Italian than usual.

"Yet here you are, you and the bitch both."

I growled at her, and I heard Stefan's smile in his reply. "I don't think she likes being called a bitch."

"Marsilia is mad. She's been mad since she awoke twelve years ago, and she hasn't gotten better with time." Estelle's voice softened, and she stepped forward. "If she weren't mad, she would never have tortured you—her favorite."

She obviously waited for Stefan's reply, which didn't come. "I have a proposition for you," she told him. "Join with me, and we will put Marsilia out of her misery—you know that she'd have urged you to do just that if she were aware of what she's become. She will see us all destroyed in her obsession with returning to Italy. This is our home—our seethe bows to no other. Italy holds nothing for us."

"No," Stefan said. "I will not move against the Mistress."

"She is your Mistress no more," Estelle hissed. She strode forward until I was pressed against Stefan's leg. "She tortured you—I saw what she did. You, who love her—she starved you and flayed the skin from you. How can you support her now?"

Stefan didn't reply.

And I knew, with absolute certainty, that I was right to trust him to protect me and not turn me into his mindless slave. Stefan didn't turn on those he loved. No matter what.

Estelle threw up her hands. "Idiot. Fool. She will go down, either by my hand or by Bernard's. And you know that the seethe will do better in my hands than in that fool Bernard's. I have contacts. I can make us grow and thrive until not even the courts of Italy will rival what we build."

Stefan quit leaning against the van. He spat on the ground with deliberate slowness.

She tensed, furious at the insult, and he smiled grimly. "Do it," he said—and, with a flick of his wrist and the magic of a *Highlander* episode, he held a sword in one hand. It was efficient-looking rather than beautiful: deadly.

"Soldier, you'll regret this," Estelle said.

"I regret many things," he replied, his voice sharpening with a cold, roiling anger. "Letting you walk off tonight might be another one. Maybe I shouldn't do it."

"Soldier," she said. "Remember who it was who betrayed you. You know how to reach me—don't wait until it is too late."

The vampires left with preternatural speed, their human bait running after them. Stefan waited, sword in hand, while a car purred to life and one of the seethe's black Mercedes lit up. It roared past us and disappeared into the night.

He looked around, then asked me, "Do you smell anything, Mercy?"

I tested the air, but, except for Stefan, the vampires were gone . . . or upwind. I shook my head and trotted back to the van. Stefan, gentleman that he had once been, stayed outside until I was dressed.

"That was interesting," I said, as he got in and put the van in gear.

"She's a fool."

"Marsilia?"

Stefan shook his head. "Estelle. She's no match for Marsilia. Bernard . . . he's tougher and stronger even if he's younger. Together, they might manage something, but it'll be without me."

"It didn't sound like they were working together," I said.

"They'll work together until they've achieved their goals, then fight it out. But they are fools if they think they'll even get that far. They've forgotten, or have never known, what Marsilia can be."

———————

HE PULLED UP IN THE DRIVEWAY, AND WE BOTH GOT OUT of the van.

"If you need me, if you hear Blackwood call you again—just think of my name as you wish me at your side, and I'll come." He looked grim. I hoped it was the encounter with Estelle and not worry for me.

"Thank you."

He brushed a thumb over my cheek. "Wait for a while before you thank me. You might change your mind."

I patted his arm. "Decision's made."

He gave me a shallow bow and disappeared.

"That is just so cool," I told the empty air, and, suddenly so tired I could hardly keep my eyes open, I went inside and tucked myself into bed.

8

~~~

ADAM WAS SITTING ON THE FOOT OF MY BED WHEN I woke up the next . . . afternoon. He was leaning against the wall reading a well-worn copy of *The Book of Five Rings*. It was resting on Medea's back, and she was purring, wiggling her stub tail— which she uses more like a dog than a cat.

"Aren't you supposed to be at work?" I asked.

He turned a page, and said in an absent voice, "My boss is flexible."

"Doesn't dock your pay for shirking," I mused. "How can I get a boss like yours?"

He grinned. "Mercy, even when Zee *was* your boss, he wasn't. I have no idea how you would ever find anyone you'd listen to . . .

unless you wanted to." He marked his place and set the book beside him. "I'm sorry your foray into exorcism didn't go well."

I considered it. "It depends upon your outlook, I suppose. I learned a few things . . . like did you know that Stefan knew sign language? Why do you suppose a vampire would need to learn to sign? That ghosts aren't always harmless. I always thought the only way a ghost could kill was if it scared someone to death."

He waited, curling his fingers over the lump my toes made in the covers. His other hand was rubbing Medea's head, just behind her ears. Adam knows how to *listen* better than most people. So I told him what I hadn't told him before.

"I think it might have been my fault."

"What do you mean?"

"Until I came, it wasn't doing much . . . just standard poltergeist stuff. Moving things around. Frightening, all right, but not dangerous. Then I show up, and things change. Chad almost gets killed. Ghosts just don't do that—even Stefan said so. I think I did something to make it worse."

He tightened his hold on my toes. "Has that ever happened to you before?"

I shook my head.

"Then maybe you're claiming too much credit. Maybe it would have happened anyway, and if you hadn't been there with Stefan, the boy would have died."

I wasn't sure he was right, but confessing my fear made me feel better, anyway.

"How is Mary Jo?" I asked.

He sighed. "She's still a little . . . off, but Samuel's sure now that she'll be fine in a few more days." He relaxed and smiled at me a little. "She's ready to go out and take on the whole seethe all by herself. She also told Ben that if he'd keep his mouth shut, she'd love to get naked with him. We've decided we'll know that she's back to herself when she quits flirting with him."

I couldn't help but laugh. Mary Jo was as liberated as a woman could get—being a werewolf had not altered that a bit. Ben was a misogynist of the highest (or lowest, depending upon your viewpoint) order with the added bonus of a foul mouth. The two of them were like flame and dynamite.

"No more troubles with the vampires?" I asked.

"None."

"But negotiations didn't accomplish much," I said.

He nodded comfortably. "Don't worry so, Mercy. We can take care of ourselves."

Maybe it was the way he said it . . .

"So what did you do?"

"We have a couple of guests staying with us now. Neither of them seems to have Stefan's ability to disappear at will."

"And you'll keep them until . . ."

"Until we have an apology for the events at Uncle Mike's and reparations paid to Mary Jo. And an agreement not to try something like that again."

"Do you think you'll get it?"

"Bran called her to deliver our request. I'm certain we'll get it."

Some tightness eased in my chest. The one thing that Marsilia did care about was the seethe. If Bran got involved in a battle, Marsilia's seethe was dead. The vampires in the Tri-Cities simply didn't have the numbers that the Marrok could bring into play—and Marsilia knew it.

"So she'll have to concentrate on me," I said.

He smiled. "The agreement is that she will not attack the pack unless one of us newly and directly attacks her."

"She doesn't know I'm pack," I said.

"After we get that apology and promise from her in writing, I'll take great pleasure in informing her of that."

I sat up and rolled forward until I was up on all fours and my face was an inch from his. I kissed him lightly. He kept his hands on the cat.

"I like the way you operate, mister," I said. "Can I interest you in the pancakes I'm going to make after I shower?"

He tilted his head and gave me a deeper kiss, though he left his hands where they'd been. When he moved away, neither of us was breathing steadily.

"Now you can tell me why you smell like Stefan," he said—almost gently.

I raised my arm and sniffed. I *did* smell like Stefan, more than riding home in a van would have accounted for.

"Weird."

"Why do you smell like the vampire, Mercy?"

"Because we exchanged blood," I told him—and then explained what Stefan had told me about vampire bites on the way from Spokane. I couldn't remember which part was supposed to be secret and which parts weren't—but it didn't matter. I wasn't going to keep anything from Adam, not when he'd made me part of his pack.

Stefan was certain that neither he nor Blackwood would have been able to affect the wolves through me. But I didn't know enough about pack magic to be certain—and I didn't think he did either. The only thing I did know was that Adam would agree with what I had done, though I knew he wouldn't be ecstatic about it.

By the time I'd finished, he'd dumped Medea on the floor (for which he'd have to atone if he wanted to touch her again today) in favor of pacing the room. He kept going a few rounds. He stopped when he was across the room and gave me an unhappy look.

"Stefan is better than Blackwood."

"That's what I thought."

"Why didn't you tell me about Blackwood after the first bite?" he asked. He sounded . . . hurt.

I didn't know.

He gave a short, unamused laugh. "I'm trying. I really am. But you have to bend a little, too, Mercy. Why didn't you tell me what was going on until you were on your way back here? When it was too late to do anything about it."

"I should have."

He looked at me with dark, wounded eyes. So I tried to do better.

"I'm not used to leaning on people, Adam." I started slowly, but the words came faster as I continued. "And . . . I've cost you so much lately. I thought—a vampire bite. Ick. Scary . . . But it didn't seem too harmful. Like a giant mosquito or . . . the ghost. Frightening but not harmful. I've been bitten before, you remember, and nothing bad happened. If I'd told you—you'd have made me come home. And there was Chad—you'd like him—this ten-year-old kid with more courage than most grown-ups, who was being terrorized by a ghost. I thought I could help. And I could stay out of Marsilia's hair so she would *listen* to you. It wasn't until Stefan was so worried—and that was right before we came home, after the second bite—that I realized that there was something more dangerous about them."

I shrugged helplessly, blinking back tears that I would *not* let fall. "I'm *sorry*. It was stupid. I'm stupid. I can't move without making everything worse." I turned my face away.

"No," he said. The bed sagged as he sat down next to me. "It's all right." He bumped my shoulder deliberately with his. "You aren't stupid. You're right. I'd have made you come home if I'd had to collect you myself with ropes and a gag. And your boy Chad would have died."

I leaned a little against his shoulder, and he leaned a little back.

"You never used to get into trouble like this"—amusement threaded through his voice—"except for a few memorable occasions. Maybe it's like that fae woman, the one at Uncle Mike's, said." He didn't say Baba Yaga's name. I didn't blame him. "Maybe you've absorbed a little of Coyote, and chaos follows you." He touched my neck lightly. "That vampire is going to be sorry for this."

"Stefan?"

He laughed, and this time he meant it. "Him, too, probably. But I won't have to do anything about that. No. I was speaking of Blackwood."

Adam stuck around until I'd showered, and he ate the pancakes I made afterward. Samuel came in while we were eating. He looked tired and smelled like antiseptic and blood. Without a word, he poured the last of the batter in the pan.

When Samuel looked like that, it meant he'd had a bad day. Someone had died or been crippled, and he hadn't been able to fix it.

He took his cooked pancakes and sat down at the table beside Adam. After dousing his meal in maple syrup, he stopped moving. Just looked at the pool of liquid sugar as if it held the secrets of the universe.

He shook his head. "I guess my eyes were bigger than my appetite." He dumped the food in the garbage disposal and ran it like he'd enjoy stuffing a person down it.

"So what is it this time?" I asked. "'Johnny fell down and broke his arm' or 'my wife ran into a door'?"

"Baby Ally got bitten by their pit bull," he growled, flipping the switch so the disposal quieted. In an artifically high-pitched voice, he said, "'But Iggy's so good. Sure he's bitten me a couple of times. But he's always adored Ally. He watches her while I shower.'" He walked off a little steam, then said, in his own voice, "You know, it's not the pit bulls. It's the people who own them. The kind of people who want a pit bull are the very last people who should have a dog. Or a child. Who leaves a two-year-old alone with a dog that's already killed a puppy? So now the dog dies, the girl gets reconstructive surgery and will probably still have scars—and her idiot mother, who caused it all, goes unpunished."

"Her mom will probably feel bad for the rest of her life," I ventured. "It's not jail time, but she'll be punished."

Samuel gave me a look under his brows. "She's too busy making sure everyone knows it wasn't her fault. By the time she's through, people will be sympathizing with her."

"Same thing happened with German shepherds a couple of decades ago," said Adam. "Then Dobermans and Rottweilers. And the ones who suffer are the kids and the dogs. You aren't going to change human nature, Samuel. Someone who's seen as much of it as you have should know when to quit fighting."

Samuel turned to say something, got a good look at my neck, and froze.

"I know," I said. "Only I could go to Spokane and get the only vampire in the whole city to bite me on the first day I was there."

He didn't laugh. "Two bites means he owns you, Mercy."

I shook my head. "No. Two blood exchanges means he owns me.

So I had Stefan bite me again, and now Stefan owns me instead of the Boogeyman of Spokane."

He leaned a hip against the counter, folded his arms over his chest, and looked at Adam. "You approved this?" He sounded incredulous.

"Since when did Mercy ask my approval . . . or anyone's approval before she did something? But I'd have told her to go ahead if she asked me. Stefan is a step above Blackwood."

Samuel frowned at him. "She's now second in your pack. That gives Stefan your pack as well as Mercy."

"No," I told him. "Stefan says not. Says it's been tried before and didn't work."

"A vampire's sheep does as it is told." Samuel's voice grew deep and rough with worry, so I didn't take offense at being called a sheep. Though I would have under other circumstances, even if it were true. "When he tells you to call the wolves, you'll have no choice. And if the vampire, whose slave you are, tells a different story—I know which one I'd doubt. 'Old vampires lie better than they tell the truth.'" The last was a werewolf aphorism. And it was true that a lying vampire could be difficult to detect. They had no pulse, and they didn't sweat. But lies still have a feel to them.

I shrugged, trying to look as if Samuel wasn't worrying me. "You can ask Stefan how it works tonight if you want."

"If she calls the pack, she has to use my power to do it," Adam said. "She can't do that if I don't let her."

I tried not to show the relief I felt. "Good. Don't let me call the pack for a while, all right?"

"A while?" said Samuel. "Did Stefan tell you he could let you go after a little while? Maybe when Blackwood loses interest? A vampire never loses its sheep except to death."

He was scared for me. I could see that. It didn't stop me from snapping at him anyway. "*Look*. I was out of options." I didn't tell them that Wulfe could sever the bond between Stefan and me. It had been told to me in confidence, and I really did try not to blurt out everything anyone told me in secret. Except, maybe, to Adam.

He closed his eyes and looked sick. "Yes. I know."

"A vampire can't take an Alpha wolf as a sheep," said Adam. "Maybe we can work from that to free Mercy when it seems useful. What we don't want to do is go off half-cocked and get rid of Stefan so the"—he gave me an ironic lift of his eyebrow—"Boogeyman of Spokane takes over again. I'm with Mercy. If you have to listen to a vampire, Stefan's not the worst choice."

"Why can't a vampire take over an Alpha?" I asked.

It was Samuel who answered me. "I'd almost forgotten that. It's the way the pack works, Mercy. If a vampire isn't strong enough to take every wolf in the pack, all at once, he can't take the Alpha. It doesn't mean it can't happen—there are a couple of vampires in the Old Country . . . no, most of them are gone, I think. Anyway there are none here who could do it."

"What about Blackwood?" I asked.

Samuel shrugged unhappily. "I've never met Blackwood, and I'm not sure Da has either. I'll ask."

"Do that," said Adam. "In the meantime, that makes Stefan an even better choice. He's not going to be taking over. I think I'm mostly bothered by the close ties between Blackwood and your friend Amber."

I'd lost my appetite. After scraping my plate clean, I put it in the dishwasher. Me, too. Killing Blackwood was the only solution to it I could see. I started to put my glass in the dishwasher but changed my mind and refilled it with cranberry juice. Its bite suited my mood.

"Mercy?" Adam had obviously asked me something I hadn't heard.

I looked at him, and he asked me again. "Blackwood has a relationship with both Amber and her husband?"

"That's right," I told him. "Her husband is his lawyer, and Blackwood is feeding on Amber and . . ." It seemed like something that I should hide. But I'd smelled the sex on her. "Anyway I don't think that she knows anything. She thought she'd been out shopping." Her husband? I didn't want him to be part of it. "I'm pretty sure he doesn't know his client is preying on Amber. But I don't know how much else he knows."

"When did the hauntings start?" Samuel looked grim. "How long have they been having trouble with a ghost?"

I had to think about it. "Not long. A few months."

"About the time that demon-ridden vampire showed up," said Adam.

"So?" I said. That one had never made the papers.

Adam turned to Samuel, his movement such that anyone watching would know that he was a predator. "What do you know about Blackwood?"

Adam's voice and posture were just a little too agressive for an Alpha standing in Samuel's kitchen. Another day, another time, Samuel would have let it go. But he'd had a bad day . . . and I thought that the vampires hadn't helped. He snarled and snapped a hand out to shove Adam back.

Adam caught it and knocked it away as he came to his feet.

Bad, I thought, carefully not moving. This was very bad. Power, rank with musk and pack, vibrated through the house, making the air thick.

Both of them were on edge. They were dominants—tyrants if

I'd have allowed it. But their strongest, most urgent need was to protect.

And I'd been recently harmed while under their protection. Once with Tim and a second time with Blackwood—and to a lesser extent with Stefan. It left them both dangerously aggressive.

Being a werewolf wasn't like being a human with a hot temper—it was a balance: a human soul against a predator's instinctive drives. Push it too hard, and it was the animal in control—and the wolf didn't care who it hurt.

Samuel was the more dominant, but he wasn't an Alpha. If it came to a fight, neither of them would fare well. In a few breaths, the pause before battle would stretch too long, and someone would die.

I grabbed my full glass of juice and tossed it on them, putting out a forest fire with a thimbleful of cranberry juice. They were standing almost nose to nose, so I got them both. The rage in their eyes as they turned to me would have caused a lesser person to run. I knew better.

I ate a bite of pancake from Adam's plate that attached itself like glue to the back of my throat. I reached across the table and took Samuel's coffee cup and rinsed the sticky knot down my throat.

You can't pretend not to be scared by werewolves. They know. But you can meet their eyes, if you're tough enough. And if they let you.

Adam's eyes closed, and he took a couple of steps until his back rested against the wall. Samuel nodded at me—but I saw more than he'd have wanted me to. He was better than he'd been, but he wasn't the happy wolf I'd grown up knowing. Maybe he hadn't been as easygoing as I'd once thought—but he'd been better than this.

"Sorry," he told Adam. "Bad day at the office."

Adam nodded, but didn't open his eyes. "I shouldn't have pushed."

Samuel took a towel out of a drawer and wet it down in the sink. He cleaned cranberry juice off his face and rubbed his hair with it—which made it stick straight up in the air. If you couldn't see his eyes, you might have thought he was just a kid.

He grabbed a second towel and soaked it, too. Then said, "Heads up," and threw it at Adam. Who caught it in one hand without looking. It might have been more impressive if one wet end hadn't slapped him in the face.

"Thanks," he said . . . dryly, while water slid down his face after the cranberry juice. I ate another piece of pancake.

By the time Adam cleaned up, his eyes were clear and dark and I'd finished all of his pancakes and used Samuel's towel to mop up the mess on the floor. I thought Samuel would have done it—but not in front of Adam. Besides, I'd made the mess.

"So," he said to Samuel without looking directly at him. "Do you know anything about Blackwood other than that he's a nasty piece of work and to stay out of Spokane?"

"No," Samuel said. "I don't think my father does either." He waved a hand. "Oh, I'll ask. He'll have data—how much he's worth, what his business interests are. Where he stays and the names of all the people he's been bribing to keep everyone from suspecting what he is. But he doesn't know Blackwood. I'd say it is safe to say that he's big and bad—otherwise, he wouldn't have held Spokane for the past sixty years."

"He is active during the day," I said. "When he took Amber, it was daytime."

Both of them stared at me, and, mindful of their recent dominance issues, I dropped my eyes.

"What do you think?" asked Adam, his voice still a little hoarser than normal. He had a hotter temper than Samuel at the best of times. "Does he know what Mercy is?"

"He had his minion call her into his territory, and he staked his claim on her—I'd say that would make it a big affirmative." Samuel growled.

"Now wait a minute," I said. "What would a vampire want with me?"

Samuel raised his eyebrows. "Marsilia wants to kill you. Stefan wants to"—he put on a Romanian accent for the next three words—"suck your blood. And Blackwood apparently wanted you for the same reason."

"You think he set this whole thing up just to get me to Spokane?" I asked incredulously. "First of all, there was a ghost. I saw it myself. Not silly vampire tricks or any other kind of tricks. This was a ghost. Ghosts don't like vampires." Although this one had stuck around for longer than I'd expected. "Second, why me?"

"I don't know about the ghost," Samuel said. "But the second question has a multitude of possible answers."

"The first one that occurs to me"—Adam was still keeping his eyes down—"is Marsilia. Suppose she knew immediately what had happened to Andre. She knows she can't go after you, so she trades favors with Blackwood. He turns Amber into his go-to girl, and when the opportunity presents itself, he sends her to get you—just as Marsilia dumps Stefan in the middle of your living room. And once you didn't die—Amber comes and summons you to Spokane. A few wolves get hurt—"

"Mary Jo almost died," I said. "And it could have been worse." I thought of the snow elf, and said, "A *lot* worse."

"Would Marsilia have cared? Worried about your friends here—and informed that the crossed bones on the door of your shop means that all of your friends are at risk—you take the rope Blackwood has thrown you. And you follow his bait all the way to Spokane."

Samuel shook his head. "It doesn't quite track," he said. "Vampires don't cooperate the way the wolves do. Blackwood doesn't have the reputation of doing anyone favors."

"Hey, my pretty," said Adam in a deadpan imitation of a Disney witch, "would you like a taste of something sweet? All you have to do is lure Mercy to Spokane."

"No," I said. "It works on the surface, but not when you really look. I can ask, but I'd bet the relationship between Amber's husband and Blackwood goes back years, not months. So he knew them first. If Marsilia just called him and gave him my name, it would be unlikely that he'd know that Amber knew me—we haven't spoken since I got out of college."

I'd had my paranoid moments because of the timing of Amber's request. But there was simply no way Marsilia had sent Amber, and the likelihood of further Byzantine plots went down from there.

I drew a breath. "I expect that Blackwood thought I was human, at least until he bit me the first time. Bran says I smell like a coyote— doglike unless you know coyotes—but not magic. Stefan told me Blackwood would know I wasn't human after he tasted me."

Both of the werewolves were watching me now.

"Bad luck does just happen," I told them.

"Blackwood doesn't seem to be the kind of person to do favors for another vampire." Samuel's voice sounded almost cheery.

He didn't. Vampires were evil, territorial, and . . . I thought of something.

"What if he's making a play to add the Tri-Cities to his territory," I asked. "Say he read about the attack on me—and saw that I was Adam's girlfriend. Maybe he has connections and got to see the video of Adam tearing into Tim's body, so he knows our relationship isn't casual. Maybe Corban sees him read the article and mentions that his wife knew me, and the vampire sees an opportunity to make the Tri-Cities werewolves cooperate with him in preparation to move in on Marsilia. Maybe he doesn't know he can't use me to take over the pack. Maybe he would have used me as a hostage. The ghost is happenstance. Just a convenient reason to convince Amber to invite me over."

"Marsilia's just lost her two right-hand men," said Samuel. "Andre and Stefan. She's vulnerable now."

"She has three other powerful vampires," I told him. "But Bernard and Estelle don't seem pleased with Marsilia lately." I told them about the confrontation the night before. "There's Wulfe, I guess, but he's . . ." I shrugged. "I wouldn't want to have to depend upon Wulfe for loyalty—he's not the type."

"Vampires are predators," Adam said. "Same as us. If Blackwood smells weakness, I suppose it makes sense that he'd try for more territory."

"I like it," Samuel said. "Blackwood isn't a team player. This fits. It doesn't mean it's right, but it fits."

Adam stretched the tension out of his neck, and I heard vertebrae pop. He gave me a little smile. "Tonight I call Marsilia and tell her what we just talked about. It's not set in stone, but it's plausible. I bet we'll find Marsilia more cooperative." He looked at Samuel. "If you're home, I'd better go to work. I'll have Jesse come here when school's out, too—if you don't mind. Aurielle's booked, Honey has work to do, and Mary Jo is . . . not up to snuff."

After Adam left, Samuel went to bed. If anything started happening, he'd be up fast enough—but it told me that Samuel, at least, didn't think there'd be an attack in the daytime.

Neither of them even so much as mentioned the cranberry juice I'd thrown on them.

———————

A FEW HOURS LATER, A CAR DROVE UP AND JESSE GOT out. She waved at the receding car, then bounced into the house in a wave of optimism, black-and-blue-striped hair, and—

I put a hand over my nose. "What is that perfume you're wearing?"

She laughed. "Sorry, I'll go wash up. Natalie had a new bottle and insisted on spraying everyone with it."

I waved her to my bedroom with the hand that wasn't plugging my nose. "Go use mine. Samuel's trying to sleep next to the main bath." And when she just stood there. "Hurry, for Pete's sake. That stuff is rank."

She sniffed her arm. "Not to my nose. It smells like roses."

"There are no roses," I told her, "that smell like formaldehyde."

She grinned at me, then bounced off to my bathroom to scrub up.

"So," she said when she returned, "since we're both under house arrest until the vamps settle down, and since I was an ace student today and got my homework done at school—how about you and I make some brownies?"

We made brownies, and she helped me change the oil in my van. It was getting dark by the time we set up my air compressor to blow out the water in my very small underground sprinkler system for the winter when Samuel appeared at the door bleary-eyed and growly, a brownie in one hand.

He made some grumbles about twittering girls who made too much noise. I looked up at the darkening sky and thought the late-

193

ness of the hour had more to do with his rising than the roar of my air compressor.

He made Jesse laugh with his snarls. He made a pretense of being offended and turned to me. "Are you finished?"

He could see I was rolling up cords and hose, so I rolled my eyes at him.

"Disrespect," he told Jesse, shaking his head sadly. "That's all I get. Maybe if I take you out and feed you, she'll start treating me with the respect I deserve."

But he grabbed the compressor before I could start rolling it to the pole barn.

"Where are you taking us?" Jesse said.

"Mexican," he said positively.

She groaned and suggested a Russian café that had just opened nearby. The two of them argued restaurants all the way to the pole barn and back and into the car.

In the end, we went out for pizza, a place on Columbia with a playground, noise, and great food. Adam was waiting, watching the little TV in my kitchen, when we got back. He looked tired.

"Boss run you ragged?" I asked sympathetically, handing him a brownie.

He looked at it. "Did you make this, or did Jesse?"

Her indignant "Dad" got her an unrepentant grin. "Just kidding," he said as he ate.

"I've been staying up nights," he told me. "Between the vampires and the Washington bigwigs, I'm going to have to start taking naps like a two-year-old."

"Trouble?" asked Samuel carefully.

He meant, trouble over me—or rather over that nifty video I'd never seen of Adam in a half-wolf form, ripping up Tim the Rapist's dead body.

Adam shook his head. "Not really. Mostly just the same old, same old."

"Have you called Marsilia?" I asked.

"What?" Jesse had been getting a glass of milk for her dad, and she set it down a little too hard.

"Mercy," growled Adam.

"Part of the reason you're here is that your dad has a pair of vampires in his holding cell," I informed her. "We're in negotiation with Marsilia so she'll quit trying to kill everyone."

"I only get told half of what goes on," said Jesse.

Adam covered his eyes in a mock-exasperated fashion, and Samuel laughed. "Hey, old man. This is the tip of the iceberg. Mercy's going to be leading you around with a ring in your nose." But there was something in his eyes that wasn't amusement.

I didn't think anyone else noticed or heard the odd note of unhappiness in his voice. Samuel didn't want me, not really. He didn't want to be an Alpha . . . but he wanted what Adam had, Jesse as much as me, I thought—a family: kids, a wife, a white picket fence or whatever the equivalent had been when he was a kid.

He wanted a home, and his last home had died with his last human mate long before I was born. He glanced at me just then, and I didn't know what was in my face, but it stopped him. Just stopped all the expression, and for a moment he looked amazingly like his half brother, Charles—one of the scariest people I've ever met. Charles can just *look* at raging werewolves and have them whimpering in the corner.

But it was only for an instant. He patted me on my head and said something funny to Jesse.

"So," I said. "Did you call Marsilia, Adam?"

He watched Samuel, but said, "Yes, ma'am. I got Estelle. She's supposed to give Marsilia my message and have her call me back."

"She's playing one-upmanship games," observed Samuel.

"Let her," Adam said. "Doesn't mean I need to do the same."

"Because you have the edge," I said with satisfaction. "You have a bigger threat."

"What?" asked Jesse.

"The Big Bad Boogeyman vampire of Spokane," I said, sitting on the table. "He's coming to get her."

It wasn't a sure thing, but it didn't have to be as long as we could convince Marsilia of it. If I had been Marsilia, I would've been worried about Blackwood.

ADAM AND JESSE WENT HOME. SAMUEL WENT TO BED, and so did I. When my cell phone rang, I was in the middle of a dream about garbage cans and frogs—don't ask, and I won't tell.

"Mercy," Adam purred.

I looked down at my feet, where Medea slept. She blinked her big green-gold eyes at me and purred again.

"Adam."

"I called to tell you that I finally got in touch with Marsilia herself."

I sat up, suddenly not sleepy at all. "And?"

"I told her about Blackwood. She listened all the way through, thanked me for my concern, and hung up."

"She's hardly going to panic over the phone and swear to be forever friends," I said, and he laughed.

"No, I don't think so. But I thought I'd do my bit for goodwill and let her two baby vamps go."

"Besides, now that Jesse knows they're there, you're not going to be able to keep her away."

"Thanks for that."

"Anytime. Hostage-holding is for the bad guys."

He laughed again, this time faintly bitterly. "You obviously haven't seen the good guys in action."

"No," I told him. "Maybe you were just mistaken on who the good guys were."

There was a long pause, and he said in a soft, midnight voice, "Maybe you're right."

"You're the good guy," I explained to him. "So you have to cope with all the good-guy rules. Fortunately, you have an exceptionally talented and incredibly gifted sidekick . . ."

"Who turns into a coyote," he said, a smile in his voice.

"So you don't have to worry about the bad guys very much."

And we settled into some serious, heart-accelerating flirting. Over the phone, passion brought on no panic attack.

I hung up eventually. We both had to get up in the morning, but the call left me restless and not sleepy in the slightest. After a few minutes I got up and took a good look at the stitches in my face. They were tiny and neat, individually tied and set so when my face altered, they wouldn't pull. Trust a werewolf to give me stitches so I could shift with them.

I stripped out of my clothes and opened my bedroom door. And as a coyote, I popped out of the newly installed dog door and dashed out into the night.

I covered several miles before heading out to the river and my favorite running ground. It wasn't until I stopped to get a drink from the river that I smelled vampire—and not *my* vampire. I stood in the shallows of the river and lapped at the water as if I hadn't sensed a thing.

But it didn't matter because this vampire had no desire to remain unseen. If I hadn't smelled him, the distinctive sound of a shotgun shell jacked into place was quite an announcement of intentions. He must have followed me from home. Or maybe his sense of smell was werewolf good. At any rate, he knew who I was.

Bernard stood on the bank, the gun held with obvious familiarity with the barrel pointed at yours truly. Vampire with shotgun—it seemed a little like Jaws with a chain saw, too much of a good thing.

I'd have preferred a chain saw in this case. I hate shotguns. I have scars on my butt from a close-range hit, but that wasn't the only time I'd been shot—just the worst. Montana ranchers don't like coyotes. Even coyotes who are just passing through and would never attack a lamb or chase a chicken. No matter how much fun chasing chickens is . . .

I wagged my tail at the vampire.

"Marsilia was so certain he'd kill you," Bernard told me. He always sounded to me like one of the Kennedys, his *a*'s broad and flat. "But I see that he fooled her. She's not as smart as she thinks—and that will be her downfall. I need you to call your Master so I can talk to him."

It took me a moment to remember who the Master he was referring to was. And then I didn't know how to do it. I had so many new ties, and I didn't know how to use any of them. What if I tried to call Stefan and ended up with Adam here?

I took too long. Bernard pulled the trigger. I think he meant to miss me—unless he was a really bad shot. But several of those stupid pellets hit, and I yipped sharply. He had the next shell in the gun before I finished complaining.

"Call him," Bernard said.

Fine. It couldn't be that difficult, or Stefan would have told me more about how to do that. I hoped.

Stefan? I thought as hard as I could. *Stefan!*

If I'd thought he'd be in any danger, I'd never have tried it, but I was pretty sure that Bernard, like Estelle, was going to try to recruit Stefan for his side in the civil war Marsilia had brewing in her seethe. He wouldn't try anything right away, and after the way Stefan had dealt with Estelle, I wasn't worried about Bernard as long as the element of surprise wasn't a factor.

Bernard was wearing jeans, running shoes, and a semicasual button-front shirt—and he still looked like a nineteenth-century businessman. Even though his shoes had a glow-in-the-dark swoosh on them, he wasn't someone who would blend in with the crowd.

"I'm sorry you're so stubborn," he said. But before he could get the gun up for a final, painful-if-not-fatal shot, Stefan appeared from . . . somewhere and jerked the gun out of his hands. He swung it by the barrel into a rock, then handed the not-so-useful remains back to Bernard.

I waded out of the water and shook off over both of them—but neither reacted.

"What do you want?" asked Stefan coolly. I padded over to him and sat at his feet. He looked down at me and before Bernard could answer his first question, he said, "I smell blood. Did he hurt you?"

I opened my mouth and gave him a laughing look. I knew from experience that the couple of birdshot in my backside weren't deep, probably not even deep enough that they would need to be dug out—fur has many advantages. I wasn't all that happy about it, but Stefan didn't have a wolf's understanding about body language. So I told him I was fine in a way he couldn't mistake—and my rump hurt when I wagged my tail.

He gave me a look that might, under other circumstances, have been doubtful. "Fine," he said, then looked over at Bernard, who was twirling the broken shotgun.

"Oh," said Bernard. "Is it my turn? You're through coddling your pretty new slave? Marsilia was certain that you were so fond of your last flock that you wouldn't have the stomach to replace them soon."

Stefan was very still. So angry he had even stopped breathing.

Bernard braced the shotgun on the ground and gripped it one-handed, butt up—leaning on it as if it were one of those short canes that Fred Astaire used to dance with.

"You should have heard them screaming your name," he said. "Oh, I forgot, you did."

He braced himself for an attack that never came. Instead, Stefan folded his arms and relaxed. He even started breathing again, for which I was grateful.

Have you ever sat around while someone held their breath? For a while it doesn't bother you, but eventually you start holding your breath with them, willing them to breathe. It's one of those automatic reflexes. Fortunately, the only vampire I associate with much likes to talk—so he breathes.

I sat at his side, trying to look harmless and cheerful—but looking around for more vampires. There was one in the trees; she'd let herself be silhouetted briefly against the sky. There was no way to communicate what I'd seen to Stefan as there would have been with Adam. He'd have read the tilt of my head and the paw on his foot.

Bernard's verbal attack hadn't had quite the effect he'd expected . . . or at least been ready for. But that didn't seem to faze him. He smiled, showing his fangs. "She had only you left," he told Stefan. "Wulfe's been ours for months, and so was Andre. But he was afraid of you, so he wouldn't let us *do* anything." There was a world of frustration in the last two words, and he jerked up the gun, threw it casually over his shoulder, and began pacing.

For the first time, he looked to me like what he was. Somehow, before, he'd always looked like an extra from a Dickens movie— someone full of pomp and circumstance and nothing more. Now, in motion, he looked like a predator, the Edwardian facade nothing but a thin skin to hide what was beneath.

Estelle had always unnerved me, but I discovered I hadn't been afraid of Bernard until just then.

Stefan stayed silent while Bernard ranted. "He was worse than Marsilia, in the end. He brought that thing . . . that uncontrollable abomination among us." He paused and stared at me. I dropped my eyes immediately, but I could feel his attention burning into my skin. "It is good your sheep killed it, though Marsilia couldn't see it. It would have brought upon us our doom—and she did us the second favor by killing Andre."

He stopped speaking for a moment, but his eyes were still on me, digging through fur to see *me*. It was uncomfortable and scary.

"*We* would let her live—and if Marsilia has her way, she is dead—just like your last flock." Bernard waited for that to sink in. "Marsilia has minions who work in the day . . . Hell. With the crossed bones on your coyote's business proclaiming her a traitor to all of us, how long do you think she'll survive? Goblins, harriers, the carrion feeders—there are a lot of Marsilia's allies who hunt in the day."

"She is the Alpha's mate. The wolves will keep her safe when I cannot."

Bernard laughed. "There are some of them who would kill her faster than Marsilia ever would. A coyote? Please." His voice softened. "You know she will die. If Marsilia wanted to kill her for slaying Andre, how do you think she'll feel now that you've taken the coyote for your own? She doesn't want you, but our Mistress has ever been jealous. And you protected this one for years when you should have told us all that there was a walker living among us. You took chances for her—what would have happened if another vampire had noticed what she was? Marsilia knows you care for her, more than you ever did the sheep you fed off. Eventually, Mercedes will die, and it will be your fault."

Stefan flinched at that. I didn't need to look at his face to see it, because I felt him jerk against me.

"You need Marsilia to die, or Mercy will," Bernard said. "Whom do you love, Soldier? The one who saved you or the one who abandoned you? Whom do you serve?"

He waited, and so did I.

"She was a fool to let you go alive," Bernard murmured. "There were two others she trusted with the place she sleeps. Andre is dead. But you know, don't you? And you rise a full hour before she does. You can keep this from being a bloody battle with many casualties. Who will die? Lily, our gifted musician, almost certainly. Estelle hates her, you know—she is talented and beautiful when Estelle is neither. And Marsilia loves her dearly. Lily will die." Then he smiled. "I'd kill her myself, but I know that you care for her, too. You could *protect* her from Estelle, Stefan."

And he went on naming names. Lesser vampires, I thought, but people Stefan cared for.

When he finished, he looked at Stefan's stubborn face and shook his head in exasperation. "Stefan, for *God's* sake. What are you doing? You belong nowhere. She doesn't want you. She couldn't be more plain if she had killed you outright. Estelle is foolish. She thinks she can rule when Marsilia is gone. But I know better. Neither of us is strong enough to hold the seethe unless we could work together—but we will not. There are no ties between us, no love, and that is the only way two nearly equal vampires can work together for long. But you could. I would serve you as faithfully as you have served all these years. We need you if we are to survive." He had begun pacing again. "Marsilia will see us all dead. You know that. She is crazy—only a crazy woman could put her trust in Wulfe. She'll have the humans hunting us again, not just this seethe but all of our kind. And we will not survive. *Please*, Stefan."

Stefan went down on one knee and wrapped his arm around my shoulders. He bowed his head and whispered to me. "I am sorry." Then he stood up. "I am an old soldier," he told Bernard. "I serve only one, even though she has forsaken me." He stretched out his hand, and this time I felt him pull something from me as his sword appeared in his hand. "Would you try me here?" he asked.

Bernard made a frustrated noise, then threw up his hands in a theatrical gesture. "No. No. Please, Stefan. Just stay out of it when the fight begins."

And he turned and ran. It wasn't like the way Stefan could disappear, but it would have pushed me to keep with him—and I'm fast. It was fast enough that he probably didn't hear Stefan say, "No."

He stood beside me and watched Bernard until the vampire was out of sight. And he waited a little more. I watched the female slip out of the trees and found another one as he left his cover. That one Stefan raised a hand to and got a salute in return.

"It will be a bloodbath," he told me. "And he is right. I could stop it. But I won't."

I wondered suddenly why Marsilia had let him live. If he knew where she slept, and no one else did, if he rose before her and could take himself wherever he chose, then he was a threat to her. She surely knew that if Bernard did.

Stefan sat on a likely boulder and linked his hands over a knee. "I meant to come to you when darkness fell," he told me. "There are things I need to tell you about this link between us—" He gave me a shadow of his usual smile. "Nothing dire."

He looked out at the water. "But I thought I'd clean up my front porch a little first. The newspapers have been piling up because no one is living there now." I had the sinking feeling I knew where this was going. "I was thinking I'd have to call and have the newspaper stopped—and then I read the newspaper. About the man you killed. So I went to Zee and got the full story."

He looked at me. "I'm sorry," he said.

I stood up deliberately and shook as if my fur was wet.

He smiled again, just a quirk of his lips. "I'm glad you killed him. Wish I'd been there to watch."

I thought of where he'd been, tortured by Marsilia, and wished I could watch him kill her as well.

I sighed and walked over to him, then put my chin on his knee. We both watched the water flow under the sliver of moon. There were houses nearby, but where we sat it was only us and the river.

9

I LEFT STEFAN FINALLY. I NEEDED TO GET UP EARLY TO get back to work, and it might be nice to have some sleep. When I glanced back over my shoulder for a last, concerned look, he was gone. I hoped he hadn't gone back to his house—that didn't seem like the smartest place for him to hang out—but he would do as he pleased. He was like me in that way.

The lights were on at home, and I redoubled my pace as soon as I saw them. I dove through the dog door and found Warren pacing in the living room. Medea sat on the back of the couch and watched him with an annoyed look on her face.

"Mercy," Warren said with relief. "Get changed; get dressed. We're attending a peace powwow with the vampires, and you were *specifically* requested."

I ran into my room and shifted back to human. What with one thing and another, I had a roomful of dirty clothes and nothing more. "We're talking peace-treaty time?" I asked throwing dirty pants over my shoulder.

"We hope so," Warren said, following me into the room. "Who shot you?"

"Vampire, no biggie," I said. "He wasn't aiming to kill. I don't even think any of the shot stuck."

"Nope, but you won't be happy about sitting down tonight."

"I'm never happy sitting down when there are vampires around—Stefan usually excepted. What did Marsilia say?"

"She didn't call us, and we couldn't get a lot of sense out of the vampire who did. She read a note, then giggled a lot."

"Lily?" I looked at Warren.

"That's what Samuel said." He pulled a shirt off his shoulder, where I must have thrown it, and dropped it on the floor.

"She called him, too?"

He shrugged. "Yes. Marsilia wanted him there, too. No, I don't know what it's about, and neither does Adam. However, it's unlikely that she's going to annihilate us once we get there. Adam sent me here to bring you when you got back. I think he wanted you dressed, though."

"Smart aleck," I told him, hopping into my jeans. I found a decent bra and put that on. I finally found a clean shirt folded in the shirt drawer. I wondered who'd but it there.

It's not that I'm not neat. In my garage, every tool is exactly where it belongs at the end of the day. Sometimes there's a little friction when Zee has been in there because he and I have a different idea of where some of the tools should be.

Someday, when time presents itself, I'll clean my room. Having a roommate forces me to keep the rest of the house reasonably clean. But no one cares about my room, and that puts it pretty far down on my list of to-dos. It's below, for instance, keeping solvent, saving Amber from Blackwood, and attending the meeting with Marsilia. I'll almost certainly get to it before I get around to planting a garden, though.

I pulled on the clean shirt. It was dark blue and emblazoned with BOSCH GENUINE GERMAN AUTO PARTS. Not the shirt I'd have picked out to pay a formal call on the Vampire Queen, but I supposed she'd have to take it or leave it. At least it didn't have any oil stains.

Warren picked up a handful of jeans and unburied my shoes. "Now all you need is socks, and we can go."

His cell phone rang, and he tossed the shoes at me and answered. "Yes, boss. She's here and almost dressed."

Adam's voice was a little muffled, and he was talking very quietly—but I still heard him. He sounded a little wistful.

"Almost, eh?"

Warren grinned. "Yep. Sorry, boss."

"Mercy, get a wiggle on," Adam said in a louder voice. "Marsilia's holding things up until you're here—since you were a material part of the recent unrest."

He hung up.

"I'm wiggling. I'm wiggling," I muttered, pulling on socks and shoes. I wished I'd had a chance to replace my necklace.

"Your socks don't match."

I marched out the door. "Thank you. Since when did you become a fashionista?"

"Since you decided to wear a green sock and a white sock," he said, following me. "We can take my truck."

"I have another pair just like it, too," I said. "Somewhere." Except I thought I'd thrown out the mate to the green sock last week.

THE WROUGHT-IRON GATES AROUND THE SEETHE WERE open, but the driveway was clogged with cars, so we parked off the gravel driveway. The Spanish-style adobe compound was lit with orangish lantern-style lights that flickered almost like the real thing.

I didn't know the vampire at the door, and, very unvampirelike, he simply opened the door, and said, "Down the hall to the stairway at the end and downstairs to the bottom."

I hadn't remembered there being a stairway at the end of the hall when I'd been here before. Probably because the huge, full-length-and-then-some painting of a Spanish villa had been in front of it instead of leaning against a side wall.

Although we'd entered on the ground floor, the stairway we were on took us down two full flights. I can see in the dark almost as well as a cat, and the stairwell was dark for me—a human would be almost helpless. As we descended, the smell of vampire clogged my nose.

There was a small anteroom with a single vampire—another one I didn't recognize. I didn't actually know more than a handful of Marsilia's vampires by sight. This one had silvery gray hair and a very young-looking face, and was dressed in a traditional black funeral suit. He'd been seated behind a very small table, but as we came down the last three steps, he stood up.

He ignored Warren entirely, and said, "You are Mercedes Thompson." He wasn't quite asking a question, but his statement was far from certain. He also had an accent of some sort, but I couldn't place it.

"Yes," said Warren shortly.

The vampire opened the door and swept us a short bow.

The room we entered was huge for a house—more a small gymnasium than a room. There were stands of seats—bleachers really, on either side of the long side of the room. Bleachers filled with silent watchers. I hadn't realized that there were so many vampires in the whole of the Tri-Cities, then I saw that a lot of the people were human—the sheep, I thought, like me.

And in the very center of the room was the huge oak chair festooned with carvings and accented with dull brass. I couldn't see them, but I knew the brass thorns on the arms of the chair were sharp and dark with old blood . . . some of it was mine.

That chair was one of the treasures of the seethe, vampire magic and old magic combined. The vampires used it to determine the truth of whatever poor being had the brass thorns stuck in its hands. It's gruesomely appropriate that a lot of vampire magic has to do with blood.

The presence of the chair raised my suspicions that this wasn't to be a negotiation for peace between the vampires and the werewolves. The last time I'd seen that chair, it had been at a trial. It made me nervous, and I wished I knew exactly what the words were that had been used to invite us here.

It was easy to pick out the werewolves—they were standing in front of two rows of empty seats: Adam, Samuel, Darryl and his mate, Aurielle, Mary Jo, Paul, and Alec. I wondered which ones Marsilia had specified and which were Adam's choice.

Darryl was the first to notice us because the door was almost as silent as the crowd of vampires. His eyes swept over me from head to toe and for a moment he looked appalled. Then he glanced around the crowd—all the vampires and their menageries were dressed up in their finest, be that ball gown or double-breasted suit. I thought I saw at least one Union army jacket. He looked at my T-shirt, then relaxed and gave me a subtle smile.

It seemed he decided it was okay I hadn't dressed up to meet the enemy. Adam had been talking rather intently with Samuel (about the upcoming football game, I later found out—we don't discuss important matters in front of the bad guys) but looked at his second, then looked up as we walked over to him.

"Mercy," he said, his voice ringing in the room as if it were empty. "Thank goodness. Maybe now we can get some business done."

"Maybe," Marsilia said.

She was right behind us. I knew she hadn't been there a moment ago because Warren jumped when I did. Warren was more wary than I was—no one snuck up on him. Ever. The side effect of being hunted by his own kind for most of his century-and-a-half-long life.

He turned, shoving me behind him, and snarled at her—something he wouldn't have normally done. All the vampires in the room rose to their feet, and their anticipation of blood was palpable.

Marsilia laughed, a beautiful, ringing laugh that stopped a second before I expected it to, making it more unsettling than her sudden appearance. Her sudden, businesslike appearance. The only other times I'd seen her, she'd worn clothing designed to attract attention to her beauty. This time she wore a business suit. The only concession to femininity was the narrow skirt instead of pants and the rich wine color of the wool.

"Sit," she said—as if she were talking to a poodle—and the roomful of vampires sat. She never looked away from me.

"How kind of you to make an appearance," she said, her abyss-dark eyes cold with power.

Only Warren's warmth allowed me to answer her with anything

approaching calm. "How kind of *you* to issue your invitations in advance, so I could be on time," I said. Perhaps not wisely—but, hey, she already hated me. I could smell it.

She stared at me a moment. "It makes a joke," she said.

"*It* is rude," I returned, taking a step to the side. If I got her mad enough to attack me, I didn't want Warren to take the hit.

It was only when I stepped around him that I realized I was meeting her gaze. Stupid. Even Samuel wasn't proof against the power of her eyes. But I couldn't look down, not with Adam's power rising to choke me. I wasn't just a coyote here, I was the Alpha of the Columbia Basin Pack's mate—because he said so, and because I said so.

If I looked down, I was acknowledging her superiority, and I wouldn't do that. So I met her eyes, and she chose to allow me to do so.

She lowered her eyelids, not so far as to lose our informal staring contest, but to veil her expression. "I think," she said in a voice so soft that only Warren and I heard her, "I think that had we met at a different place and time, I could have liked you." She smiled, her fangs showing. "Or killed you."

"Enough games," she said, louder. "Call him for me."

I froze. *That's* why she wanted me. She wanted Stefan back. For a moment all I could see was the blackened dead thing that she'd dropped in my living room. I remembered how long it had taken me to realize who it was.

She'd done that to him—and now she wanted him back. Not if I could help it.

Adam hadn't moved from where he'd been standing, telling the room he trusted me to take care of myself. I wasn't sure he really thought so—I knew I didn't—but he needed me to stand on my own two feet. "Call whom?" he asked.

She smiled at him without looking away from me. "Didn't you know? Your mate belongs to Stefan."

He laughed, an oddly happy sound in this dirge-shadowed room. It was a good excuse to turn my back on Marsilia and quit playing the stare game. Turning my back meant that I didn't lose—only that the contest was over.

I tried not to let the sick fear I felt show on my face. I tried to be what Adam—and Stefan—needed me to be.

"Like a coyote, Mercy is adaptable," Adam told Marsilia. "She belongs to whom she decides. She belongs everywhere she wants to, for just as long as she wants to." He made it sound like a good thing. Then he said, "I thought this was about preventing war."

"It is," said Marsilia. "Call Stefan."

I lifted my chin and glanced at her over my shoulder. "Stefan is my friend," I told her. "I won't bring him to his execution."

"Admirable," she told me briskly. "But your concern is misplaced. I can promise that he won't be hurt physically by me or by mine tonight."

I slanted a glance at Warren, and he nodded. Vampires might be hard to read, but he was better at sensing lies than I was, and his nose agreed with mine: she was being truthful.

"Or hold him here," I said.

The smell of her hatred had died away, and I couldn't tell anything about how she felt. "Or hold him here," she agreed. "Witness!"

"Witnessed," said the vampires. All of them. All at exactly the same time. Like puppets, only creepier.

She waited. Finally, she said, "I mean him no harm."

I thought of earlier tonight, when he'd turned down Bernard even though I was pretty sure he agreed with Bernard's assessment of her continued rule of the seethe. In the end, he loved her more than he loved his seethe, his menagerie of sheep, or his own life.

"You harm him by your continued existence," I told her, as quietly as I could. And she flinched.

I thought about that flinch . . . and about the way she'd let him live even though he, of all her vampires, had reason to see her dead—and had the means to do so. Maybe Stefan wasn't the only one who loved.

It hadn't kept her from torturing him, though.

I closed my eyes, trusting Warren, trusting Adam to keep me safe. I only wished I could keep Stefan safe. But I knew what he would want me to do.

Stefan, I called, just as I had earlier—because I knew he would want me to. Surely he knew where I was calling from and would come ready to protect himself.

Nothing happened. No Stefan.

I looked toward Marsilia and shrugged. "I called," I told her. "But he doesn't have to come when I call."

It didn't seem to bother her. She just nodded—a surprisingly businesslike gesture from a woman who would have looked more at home in a Renaissance gown of silk and jewels than she did in her modern suit.

"Then I call this meeting to order," she said, strolling to the old thronelike chair in the center of the room. "First, I would call Bernard to the chair."

He came, reluctant and stiff. I recognized the pattern of his movement—he looked like a wolf called against his will. I knew he wasn't of her making, but she had power over him just the same. He was still wearing the clothes I'd last seen him in. The harsh overhead fluorescent lights glinted off the small balding spot on the top of his head.

He sat unwillingly.

"Here, *caro*, let me help." Marsilia took each hand and impaled it on the upthrust brass thorns. He fought. I could see it in the grimness of his face and the tenseness of his muscles. I couldn't see that it cost Marsilia anything at all to keep him under her control.

"You've been naughty, no?" she asked. "Disloyal."

"I have not been disloyal to the seethe," he gritted out.

"Truth," said a boy's voice.

The Wizard himself. I hadn't seen him—though I'd looked. His light gold hair had been trimmed close to his skull. He had a vague smile on his face as he strolled down from the top of the bleachers across from us. He used the bleacher seats as stairs.

He looked like a young high school student. He'd died before his features had had a chance to grow into maturity. He looked soft and young.

Marsilia smiled when she saw him. He hopped over the last three seats and landed lightly on the hardwood floor. She was shorter than he was, but the kiss he gave her made my stomach hurt. I knew he was hundreds of years old, but it didn't matter—because he looked like a kid.

He stepped back and reached out a finger and ran it over Bernard's hand and down to the chair arm. When he picked it up it dripped blood. He licked it off slowly, letting a few drops roll down the palm of his hand, over his wrist, until it stained the light green sleeves of his dress shirt.

I wondered who he was performing for. Surely the vampires wouldn't be bothered by his licking blood—and I was sort of right but mostly wrong. *Bothered* might not be the word, but there was a generalized motion from the stands as vampires leaned forward and some of them even licked their lips.

Ugh.

"You have betrayed me, haven't you, Bernard?" Marsilia was still looking at Wulfe, and he held out his hand. She took it and traced the drying blood, letting her mouth linger over his wrist while Bernard quivered, trying not to answer the question.

"I have not betrayed the seethe," Bernard said again. And though she grilled him for ten minutes or more, that was all he would say.

Stefan appeared beside me. His eyes were on the sleeve of his white dress shirt as he casually fixed a cuff link, then he pulled the sleeve of his subtly pin-striped gray suit over it with a just-right tug. He looked at me, and Marsilia looked at him.

She waved her hand at Bernard. "Get up—Wulfe, put him somewhere obvious, would you?"

Shaking and stumbling, Bernard rose, his hands dripping on the pale floor all the way to the stands, where Wulfe cleared out space on the bottom tier of seats for them both. He began cleaning Bernard's hands, like a cat licking ice cream.

Stefan didn't say anything, just ran his eyes over me in a quick survey. Then he looked at Adam, who nodded regally back, though he smiled a little, and I realized that he and Stefan were wearing the same thing, except that Adam wore a dark blue shirt.

Mary Jo saw the resemblance and grinned. She turned to say something to Paul, I thought, when a surprised look came over her face, and she just dropped. Alec caught her before she hit the floor as if this wasn't the first time she'd done something like that. Leftovers from the close brush with death, I hoped, not something the vampires were doing.

Stefan left me for Mary Jo. He touched her throat, ignoring Alec's silent snarl.

"Relax," Stefan told the wolf. "She will take no harm from me."

"She's been doing that a lot," Adam told him. That he didn't step between his vulnerable pack member and the vampire was an unsubtle message.

"She's waking up," Stefan said just before her eyes fluttered open.

And only after Mary Jo was clearly awaken did Stefan look at Marsilia.

"Come to the chair, Soldier," she told him.

He stared at her for so long that I wondered if he would do it. He might love her, but he didn't like her very much at the moment—and, I hoped, didn't trust her either.

But he patted Mary Jo's knee and walked out to where Marsilia waited for him.

"Wait," she told him before he sat down. She looked at the stands across from us, where the vampires and their food sat. "Do you want me to question Estelle, first? Would that make you happier?"

I couldn't tell who she was speaking to.

"Fine," she said. "Bring Estelle here."

A door I hadn't noticed opened on the far side of the room and Lily, the gifted pianist and quite insane vampire who never left the seethe and Marsilia's protection, came in carrying Estelle like a new groom carried his bride over the threshold. Lily was even dressed in a frothy white mass of lace that could have been a wedding dress to Estelle's dark suit. Though I'd never seen a bride with blood all over her face and down her gown. If I were a vampire, I think I'd only wear black or dark brown—to hide the stains.

Estelle hung limp in Lily's arms, and her neck looked like a pack of hyenas had been chewing on her.

"Lily," Marsilia chided. "Haven't I told you about playing with your food?"

Lily's sapphire eyes glittered with a hungry iridescence visible even in the overly brightly lit room. "Sorry," she said. She skipped a couple of steps. "Sorry, 'Stel." She smiled whitely at Stefan, then she plopped Estelle's limp form on the chair, like a doll. She moved Estelle's head so it wasn't flopped to the side, then straightened her skirt. "Is that good?"

"Fine. Now be a good girl and go sit next to Wulfe, please."

Lily had been in her thirties, I thought, when she was killed, but her mind had stopped developing far earlier. She smiled brightly and skipped over to Wulfe and bounced down to the seat beside him. He patted her knee, and she put her head on his shoulder.

As with Bernard, Marsilia stuck Estelle's hands on the thorns. The limp vampire came to shrieking, screaming life as soon as her second hand was pierced.

Marsilia allowed it for a minute, then said, "Stop," in a voice that fired like a .22. It popped but didn't thunder.

Estelle froze midscream.

"Did you betray me?" Marsilia asked.

Estelle jerked. Shook her head frantically. "No. No. No. Never."

Marsilia looked at Wulfe. He shook his head. "If you control her enough to keep her on the chair, Mistress, she can't answer with truth."

"And if I don't, all she does is scream." She looked into the bleachers. "As I told you. You can try it yourself if you choose? No?" She pulled Estelle's hands off the chair. "Go sit by Wulfe, Estelle."

A Hispanic man came to his feet on one of the seats behind me. He had a tear tattooed just below one eye and he, like Wulfe, hopped down to the floor via the seats, though without Wulfe's grace. It was more as if he fell slowly down the bleachers, landing on hands and knees on the unforgiving floor.

"Estelle, Estelle," he moaned, brushing by me. He was human, one of her sheep, I thought.

Marsilia raised an eyebrow, and a vampire followed Estelle's human at three or four times his speed. He caught up to him before the man had made it halfway across the floor. The vampire had the appearance of a very elderly man. He looked as though he'd died of old age before being made a vampire, though there was nothing old or shaky in the hold he kept on the struggling man.

"What would you have me do, Mistress?" the old man said.

"I would have had you not allow him to interrupt us here," Marsilia said. I glanced at Warren, who frowned. She was lying then. I'd thought so. This was part of the script. After a thoughtful moment Marsilia said, "Kill him."

There was a *snap*, and the man dropped to the ground—and every vampire in the place who had been breathing stopped. Estelle fell to the ground, four or five feet from Wulfe. I glanced away and unexpectedly caught Marsilia staring at me. She wanted me dead; I could see it in the hungry look she had. But she had more pressing business just now.

Marsilia gestured at the chair in invitation to Stefan. "Please, accept my apologies for the delay."

Stefan stared at her. If there was an emotion on his face, I couldn't read it.

He'd taken a step forward, and she stopped him once again. "No. Wait. I have a better idea."

She looked at me. "Mercedes Thompson. Come let us partake of your truth. Witness for us the things you have seen and heard."

I folded my arms, not in outright refusal—but I didn't go waltzing over either. This was Marsilia's show, but I wouldn't let her have the upper hand completely. Warren's hand closed over my shoulder—a show of support, I thought. Or maybe he was trying to warn me.

"You will do as I say because you want me to stop hurting your friends," she purred. "The wolves are more worthy targets . . . but there is that delicious policeman—Tony, isn't it? And the boy who works for you. He has such a big family, doesn't he? Children are so fragile." She looked at Estelle's man, dead almost at her feet.

Stefan stared at her, then looked at me. And once I saw his eyes, I knew the emotion he was trying to hold back . . . rage.

"You sure?" I asked him.

He nodded. "Come."

I wasn't happy about doing it, but she was right. I wanted my friends safe.

I sat on the chair and scooted forward until my arms wouldn't be stretched out trying to reach the sharp brass. I slammed both hands down and tried not to wince as the thorns bit deep—or gasp as magic pulsed in my ears.

"Yum," said Wulfe—and I nearly jerked my hands away again. Could he taste me through the thorns, or was he just trying to harass me?

"I sent Stefan to you," Marsilia said. "Will you tell our audience what he looked like?"

I looked at Stefan, and he nodded. So I described the wizened thing that had fallen to my floor as closely as I could remember it, working to keep my voice impersonal rather than angry or . . . anything else inappropriate.

"Truth," said Wulfe when I finished.

"Why was he in that state?" Marsilia asked.

Stefan nodded so I answered her. "Because he tried to save my life by covering up my involvement in Andre's . . . death? Destruction? What *do* you call it when a vampire is killed permanently?"

The skin on her face thinned until I could see the bones beneath.

And she was even more beautiful, more terrible in her rage. "Dead," she said.

"Truth," said Wulfe. "Stefan tried to cover up your involvement in Andre's death." He looked around. "I helped cover it up, too. It seemed the thing to do at the time . . . though I later repented and confessed."

"There are crossed bones on the door of your home," Marsilia said.

"My shop," I answered. "And yes."

"Did you know," she said, "that no vampire except Stefan can go into your shop? It is your home as much as that ratty trailer in Finley is."

Why had she told me that? Stefan was watching her, too.

"Tell our audience the *why* of the bones."

"Betrayal," I said. "Or so I am told. You asked me to kill one monster, and I chose to kill two."

"Truth," said Wulfe.

"When did Stefan know you were a walker, Mercedes Thompson?"

"The first time I met him," I told her. "Almost ten years ago."

"Truth," said Wulfe.

She looked toward the bleachers again and addressed someone there. "Remember that." She turned to stare at me, then glanced at Stefan as she asked me, "Why did you kill Andre?"

"Because he knew how to build sorcerers—demon-possessed. He'd done it once, and you and he planned on doing it again. People died for his games—and more people would die for yours, both of yours."

"Truth," said Wulfe.

"What care we how many people die?" asked Marsilia, waving

at the dead man and speaking to everyone here. "They are short-lived, and they are food."

She's meant it rhetorically, but I answered her anyway.

"They are many, and they could destroy your seethe in a day if they knew it existed. It would take them a month to wipe all of you out of existence in this country. And if you were creating monsters like that *thing* Andre brought into existence, I would help them." I leaned forward as I spoke. My hands throbbed in time with my heartbeat, and I found that the rhythm of my words followed the pain.

"Truth," said Wulfe in a satisfied tone.

Marsilia put her mouth near my ear. "That was for my soldier," she murmured in tones that reached no farther than my ears. "Tell him that."

She lowered her mouth until it hovered over my neck, but I didn't flinch.

"I do think I would have liked you, Mercedes," she said. "If you weren't what you are, and I wasn't what I am. You are Stefan's sheep?"

"We exchanged blood twice," I said.

"Truth," said Wulfe, sounding amused.

"You belong to him."

"You would think so," I agreed.

She let out a huff of exasperation. "You make this simple thing difficult."

"*You* make it difficult. I understand what you are asking, though, and the answer is yes."

"Truth."

"Why did Stefan make you his?"

I didn't want to tell her. I didn't want her to know I had any connection to Blackwood whatsoever—though probably Adam had already told her. So I attacked.

"Because you murdered his menagerie. The people he cared about," I said hotly.

"Truth," Stefan ground out.

"Truth," agreed Wulfe softly.

Marsilia, her face angled toward me, looked obscurely satisfied. "I have what I need of you, Ms. Thompson. You may vacate the chair."

I pulled my hands off the chair and tried not to wince—or relax—as the uncomfortable pulse of magic left me. Before I could get up, Stefan's hand was under my arm, lifting me to my feet.

His back was to Marsilia, and all his attention seemed to be on me—though I had the feeling that all of his being was focused on his former Mistress. He took one of my hands in both of his and raised it to his mouth, licking it clean with gentle thoroughness. If we hadn't been in public, I'd have told him what I thought of that. I thought he caught a little of it in my face because the corners of his mouth turned up.

Marsilia's eyes flashed red.

"You overstep yourself." It was Adam, but it didn't sound like him.

I turned and saw him stride over the floor of the room without making a noise. If Marsilia's face had been frightening, it was nothing compared to his.

Stefan, undeterred, had picked up my other hand and treated it the same way—though he was a little more brisk about it. I didn't jerk it away because I wasn't sure he'd let me—and the struggle would light Adam's fuse for sure.

"I heal her hands," Stefan said, releasing me and stepping back. "As is my privilege."

Adam stopped next to me. He picked up my hands—which did look better—and gave Stefan a short, sharp nod. He tucked my hand around his upper arm, then returned with me to the wolves.

I could feel in the pounding of his heart, in the tightness of his arm, that he was on the edge of losing it. So I dropped my head against his arm to muffle my voice. Then I said, "That was all aimed at Marsilia."

"When we get home," said Adam, not bothering to speak quietly, "you will allow me to enlighten you about how something can accomplish more than one purpose at the same time."

Marsilia waited until we were seated with the rest of the wolves before she continued her program for the evening.

"And now for you," she said to Stefan. "I hope you have not reconsidered your cooperation."

In answer, Stefan sat in the thronelike chair, raised both hands over the sharp thorns, and slammed them down with such force that I could hear the chair groan from where I stood.

"What do you wish to know?" he asked.

"Your feeder told us that I killed your former menagerie," she said. "How do you know it to be true?"

He lifted his chin. "I felt each of them die, by your hand. One a day until they were no more."

"Truth," agreed Wulfe in a tone I hadn't heard from him before. It made me look. He sat with Estelle collapsed at his feet, Lily leaning against one side, and Bernard sitting stiffly on the other. Wulfe's face was somber and . . . sad.

"You are no longer of this seethe."

"I am no longer of this seethe," Stefan agreed coolly.

"Truth," said Wulfe.

"You were never mine, really," she told him. "You had always your free will."

"Always," he agreed.

"And you used that to hide Mercy from me. From justice."

"I hid her from you because I judged her no risk to you or the seethe."

"Truth," murmured Wulfe.

"You hid her because you liked her."

"Yes," agreed Stefan. "And because there would be no justice in her death. She had not killed one of us—and would not, except that you set that task to her." For the first time since he sat in the chair, he looked directly at her. "You asked her to kill the monster you could not find—and she did it. Twice."

"Truth."

"She killed *Andre*!" Marsilia's voice rose to a roar, and power echoed in it and through the room we were in. The lights dimmed a little, then regained their former wattage.

Stefan smiled sourly at her. "Because there was no choice. *We* left her no choice—you, I, and Andre."

"Truth."

"You chose her over *me*," Marsilia said, and her power lit the air with strangeness. I took a step closer to Adam and shivered.

"You *knew* she hunted Andre, *knew* she'd killed him—and you hid what she did from me. You forced me to torture you and destroy your power base. You must answer to me." Her voice thundered, vibrating the floor and rattling the walls. The suspended lights drifted back and forth, making shadows play.

"Not anymore," said Stefan. "I do not belong to you."

"Truth," snapped Wulfe, suddenly coming to his feet. "That is fair truth—you felt it yourself."

Across from us, high in the bleachers, a vampire stood up. He had soft features, wide-spaced eyes, and an upturned nose that should have made him look something other than vampire. Like Wulfe and Estelle's human, he strode down the seats. But there was no bounce to his step or hesitation. His path might as well have been straight and paved for all it impeded him. He landed on the floor and walked to Wulfe.

He wore a tuxedo and a pair of dark-metal gauntlets. Hinged metal on the top and chain link below. He flexed his fingers and blood dripped from the gloves to the floor.

No one made any move to clean it up.

He turned, and in a light, breathy voice, he said, "Accepted. He is no man of yours, Marsilia."

I had no idea who he was, but Stefan did. He froze where he sat, all of his being focused on the vampire in the bloody gauntlets. Stefan's face was blank, as if the whole world had tilted from its axis.

Marsilia smiled. "Tell me. Did Bernard approach you to betray me?"

"Yes," Stefan said, without expression.

"Did Estelle do the same?"

He took a deep breath, blinked a couple of times, and relaxed in the chair. "Bernard seemed to have the seethe's best interest at heart," he said.

"Truth," Wulfe said.

"But Estelle, when she asked me to join her against you, Estelle just wanted power."

"Truth."

Estelle shrieked and tried to get to her feet, but she couldn't move away from Wulfe.

"And what did you tell them?" she asked.

"I told them I wouldn't make a move against you." Stefan sounded utterly weary, but somehow his words carried over the noise Estelle was making.

"Truth," declared Wulfe.

Marsilia looked at the gauntlet-wearing vampire, who sighed and bent to Estelle. He petted her hair a couple of times until she quieted. We all heard the crack when her neck broke. He took his time separating her head from her body. I looked away and swallowed hard.

"Bernard," Marsilia said, "we believe it would be good if you return to your maker until you learn the habit of loyalty."

Bernard stood up. "It was all a trick," he said, his voice incredulous. "All a trick. You killed Stefan's people—knowing he loved them. You tortured him. All to catch Estelle and me in our little rebellion . . . a rebellion born from the heart of your own Andre."

Marsilia said, "Yes. Don't forget that I set up his little favorite, Mercedes, to be the lever I needed to move the world. If she hadn't killed Andre, if he hadn't helped her cover it up, then I could not have sent him out from the seethe. Then I could not have used him to witness against you and Estelle. Had you been of my making, disposing of you would have been much easier and cost me less."

Bernard looked at Stefan, who was sitting as if it would hurt to move, his head slightly bent.

"Stefan, of all of us, was loyal to the death. So you tortured him, killed his people, threw him out—because you *knew* that he'd refuse us. That his loyalty was such that despite what you had done to him, he'd still remain yours."

"I counted on it," she said. "By his refusal, your rebellion is robbed of its legitimacy." She looked at the man who'd killed Estelle. "You, of course, had *no* idea that your children would behave so."

He gave her a small smile, one predator to another, "I'm not on the chair." He pulled off the gauntlets and tossed them into Wulfe's lap. "Not even by such a slim connection." His hands were bloodied, but I couldn't tell if it was from one wound or many. "I've heard your truths, and can only hope you'll find them as galling as I."

"Come, Bernard," he said. "It is time for us to leave."

Bernard rose without protest, shock and dismay in every line of his body. He followed his maker to the doorway, but turned back before leaving the room entirely. "God save me," he said looking at Marsilia, "from such loyalty. You have ruined him for your whim. You are not worthy of his gift—as I told him."

"God won't save any of us," said Stefan in a low voice. "We are all of us damned."

He and Bernard stared at each other across the room. Then the younger vampire bowed and followed his maker out the door. Stefan pulled his hands free and stood up.

"Stefan—" said Marsilia, sweet-voiced. But before she finished the last syllable, he was gone.

10

MARSILIA FROZE FOR A MOMENT, STARING AT THE PLACE Stefan had been. Then she looked at me, a look of such malevolence I had to work not to step back even though there was half of a very large room between us.

She closed her eyes and brought her features back under control. "Wulfe," she asked, "do you have it?"

"I do, Mistress," the vampire said. He stood up and drifted over to her, pulling an envelope out of his back pocket.

Marsilia looked at it, bit her lip, then said in a low voice, "Give it to her."

Wulfe altered his path so he came more directly to us. He handed me the envelope that was none the worse for the time it had spent in his pocket. It was heavy paper, the kind that wedding invitations or graduation announcements are engraved on. Stefan's name was gracefully lettered across the front. It was sealed with red wax that smelled like vampire and blood.

"You will give this to Stefan," Marsilia said. "Tell him there is information here. Not apologies or excuses."

I took the envelope and felt a strong desire to crumple it and drop it on the floor.

"Bernard is right," I said. "You used Stefan. Hurt him, *broke* him, in order to play your little game. You don't deserve him."

Marsilia ignored me. "Hauptman," she said with calm courtesy, "I thank you for your warning about Blackwood. In return for this, I accede to your truce. The signed documents will be sent to your house."

She took a deep breath and turned from Adam to me. "It is the judgement of this night that the action you took against us . . . killing Andre . . . has not resulted in damage to the seethe. That you had no intention of moving against the seethe was borne out by your truth-tested testimony." She sucked in a breath. "It is my judgement that the seethe suffered no harm, and you are not an ally turned traitor. No further punishment will be taken against you—and the crossed bones will be removed . . ." She glanced down at her wrist.

"I can do it tonight," said Wulfe in gentle tones.

She nodded. "Removed before dawn." She hesitated, then said in a quiet voice, as if the words were pulled from her throat, "This is for Stefan. If it were up to me, your blood and bones would nourish my garden, walker. Take care not to push me again."

She turned on her heel and left out the same door Bernard had taken.

Wulfe looked at Adam. "Allow me to escort you out of the seethe so that no harm comes to you."

Adam lowered his eyelids. "Are you implying I cannot protect my own?"

Wulfe dropped his eyes and bowed low. "But of course not. Merely suggesting that my presence might save you the trouble. And save us the mess to clean up afterward."

"Fine."

Adam led the way. I let the other wolves pass me and tried not to be hurt when Mary Jo and Aurielle deliberately avoided looking at me. I didn't know what cause . . . or rather which cause was bothering them—coyote, vampire prey, or causing Marsilia to target the pack. It didn't matter, really—there was nothing I could do about any of it.

Warren, Samuel, and Darryl waited until the others were gone, then Warren gave me a little smile and went ahead. Darryl paused, and I looked at him. I outranked him, which put me at the end of the pack, to protect us from attack from behind. Then he smiled, a warm expression I couldn't say I'd ever seen on his face, not directed at me anyway. And he went ahead.

"Oh no, you don't," said Samuel, amused. "I'm outside the pack, and so I can tag along with you."

"I really need a good night's sleep," I told him as I fell into step beside him.

"I guess that's what comes from fraternizing with vampires." He put a hand over my shoulder. A cold hand.

I'd been so busy sweating with fear I'd become accustomed to both the feeling and the smell. I hadn't noticed that Samuel was scared, too.

The last time he'd come here, Lily had taken him for a snack— and Marsilia had done worse, robbing him of his will until he was hers.

For me it would have been terrifying. I couldn't imagine what it would feel like to a werewolf who lived only because he controlled his wolf. All the time.

I reached up and put my hand over his. "Let's get out of here," I said. And all the way through the room, I was conscious of the two still bodies on the floor, and of the vampires and their menageries, who sat silently on the bleachers, obedient to orders I couldn't hear. They watched us leave with their predatory eyes, and I felt them on my back all the way to the door.

Just like the ghost in the bathroom at Amber's house.

———

I SAT SHOTGUN IN THE SUBURBAN ADAM HAD DRIVEN over. I didn't know if it was a rental or a new vehicle—which is what it smelled like. Paul, Darryl, and Aurielle filled the first backseat. Samuel drove his own car, a nifty new Mercedes in bing cherry red.

Mary Jo, who had been heading toward Adam's vehicle until she saw me, abruptly changed directions and got into Warren's old truck. Alec, trailing her around like a lost puppy, followed.

"And I thought *Bran* could be Byzantine," I said finally, trying to relax in the safety of the leather upholstery as Adam drove through the gates.

"I didn't catch it all," said Darryl. He must have been tired because his voice was even deeper than usual, buzzing my ears so I had to listen closely to catch all of his words. "For some reason she had to convince Stefan that he was out of the seethe. Then, when her traitors approached him, he had to refuse their offers before he could witness that they'd made them?"

"That's what it sounded like to me," said Adam. "And only

with his witness and their maker's consent could she deal with her traitors."

"Makes sense," offered Paul almost shyly. "The way the seethe works, if he belonged to her—his witness is hers. If those two were imposed on her, she couldn't have them killed at her word. She'd need outside verification."

I wondered if I'd been set up. I thought of Wulfe's oh-so-convenient aid when I'd killed Andre. He'd known I was looking for Andre—I'd stumbled upon his resting place before I found Andre's. I'd thought he kept it from the Mistress for his own reasons . . . but maybe he hadn't. Maybe Marsilia had planned it.

My head hurt.

"Maybe we were suspecting the wrong vampire of trying to take over Marsilia's seethe," Adam said.

I thought about the vampire who had been Bernard's maker and had stood to watch this . . . trial.

I didn't want to be sympathetic; I wanted to hate Marsilia cleanly for what she had done to Stefan. But I'd become passing familiar with evil and all its shades, and that vampire, Bernard's maker, set off every alarm that I had. Not that all vampires weren't evil . . . I wished suddenly that I could say except for Stefan. But I couldn't. I'd met his menagerie, the ones Marsilia had killed—and I knew that for most of them, except for the very few who became vampire, Stefan would be their death. Still, the other vampire had hit pretty high on my coyote's "get me out of here" scale. There had been something in his face . . .

"Makes me glad I'm a werewolf," said Darryl. "All I have to worry about is when Warren will lose his self-control and challenge me."

"Warren's self-control is very good," said Adam. "I wouldn't wait dinner on his losing it."

"Better Warren as second than a coyote in the pack," said Auri-elle tightly.

The atmosphere in the car changed.

Adam's voice was soft, "Do you think so?"

"'Rielle," Darryl warned.

"I think so." Her voice brooked no argument. She was a high school teacher, Darryl's mate, which made her . . . not precisely third in the pack—that was Warren. But second and a half, just below Darryl. If she had been a man, I didn't think she would have ranked much lower.

"Unlike vampires, wolves tend to be straightforward critters," I murmured, trying not to feel hurt. Rejection, for a coyote raised by wolves, was nothing new. I'd spent most of my adulthood running from it.

I wouldn't have thought that exhaustion and hurt was a recipe for epiphany, but there it was. I'd left my mother and Portland before she could tell me to go. I'd lived alone, stood on my own two feet, because I didn't want to learn to lean on anyone else.

I'd seen my resistance to Adam as a fight for survival, for the right to control my own actions instead of a life spent following orders . . . because I wanted to obey. The duty that Stefan clung to with awful stubbornness was the life I'd rejected.

What I hadn't seen was that I had been unwilling to put myself in a place where I could be rejected again. My mother had given me to Bran when I was a baby. A gift he returned when I became . . . inconvenient. At sixteen, I'd moved back in with my mother, who was married to a man I'd never met and had two daughters who hadn't known of my existence until Bran had called my mother to tell her he was sending me home. They had been all that was loving and gracious—but I was a hard person to lie to.

"Mercy?"

"Just a minute," I told Adam, "I'm in the middle of a revelation."

No wonder I hadn't just rolled over at Adam's feet like any sensible person would when courted by a sexy, lovable, reliable man who loved me. If Adam ever rejected me . . . I felt a low growl rise in my throat.

"You heard her," said Darryl, amused. "We'll have to wait for her revelation. We have a prophet for our Alpha's mate."

I waved at him irritably. Then looked up at Adam, whose eyes were, quite properly, on the road.

"Do you love me?" I asked him, pulse pounding in my ears.

He gave me a curious look. He was wolf, he knew intensity when he heard it. "Yes. Absolutely."

"You'd better," I told him, "or you'll regret it."

I looked over my shoulder at Aurielle, holding the full force of my will close to me. Adam was mine.

Mine.

And I would take up all the burdens he could give me, even as he did the same with mine. It would be an equal sharing. That meant he protected me from the vampires . . . and I protected him from what problems I could.

I stared at Aurielle, met the predator in her eyes with the one in mine. And after only a few minutes, she dropped her eyes. "Suck it up and deal with it," I told her, and I put my head on Adam's shoulder and fell asleep.

IT WAS, SADLY, NOT VERY LONG BEFORE ADAM STOPPED the car. I stayed where I was, half-awake, while Darryl, Aurielle, and Paul got out of the car. We stayed where we were until I heard Darryl's Subaru fire up, and Adam started for home.

"Mercy?"

"Mmm."

"I'd like to take you home with me."

I sat up, rubbed my eyes, and sighed. "Once I go horizontal, I'm going to be out like a light," I told him. "It's been days"—I tried to remember, but I was too tired—"several at least since I had a good night's sleep." The sun, I noticed, was brightening in the sky.

"That's all right," he said. "I'd just . . ."

"Yeah, me too." But I shivered a little. It was all very well and good to get hot and heavy over the phone, but this was real. I stayed awake all the way to his house.

AN ALPHA'S HOME IS SELDOM EMPTY—AND WITH THE recent troubles, Adam was keeping a guard there, too. When we came in, we were greeted by Ben, who gave us an offhand salute and trotted back downstairs, where there were a number of guest bedrooms.

Adam escorted me up the stairs with a hand on the small of my back. I was sick-to-my-stomach nervous and found myself taking in deep breaths to remind myself that this was Adam . . . and all we were going to do was sleep.

Repairs were in progress on the hall bathroom. The door was back up, and mostly the hall wall next to it just needed taping, texturing, and painting. But the white carpet at the top of the stairs was still stained with brown spots of old blood—mine. I'd forgotten about that. Should I offer to have his carpet cleaned? Could blood be cleaned out of a white carpet? And what kind of stupid person puts white carpet in a house frequented by werewolves?

235

Bolstered by indignation, I took a step into his bedroom and froze. He glanced at my face and pulled a T-shirt out of a drawer and threw it at me. "Why don't you use the bathroom first," he said. "There's a spare toothbrush in the top right-hand drawer."

The bathroom felt safer. I folded my dirty clothes and left them in a small pile on the floor before pulling on his T-shirt. He wasn't much taller than me, but his shoulders were broad, and the sleeves hung down past my elbows. I washed my face around the stitches in my chin, brushed my teeth, then just stood there for a few minutes, gathering courage.

When I opened the door, Adam brushed by and closed the bathroom behind him—pushing me gently into his room to face the bed with its turned-down comforter.

There should be only so much terror you can feel in a night. I should have met my limit and then some. And the fear of something that wasn't going to happen—Adam would never hurt me—shouldn't have been enough to register.

Still, it took every bit of courage I had to crawl into his bed. Once I was there, though, in one of those odd little psychological twists everyone has, the scent of him in the sheets made me feel better. My stomach settled down. I yawned a few times and fell asleep to the sound of Adam's electric razor.

I awoke surrounded by Adam, his scent, his warmth, his breath. I waited for the panic attack that didn't come. Then I relaxed, soaking it up. By the light sneaking in around the heavy blinds, it was late afternoon. I could hear people moving around the house. His sprinklers were on, valiant defenders of his lawn in the never-ending battle against the sun.

Outside, it was probably in the seventies, but his house—like mine since Samuel moved in—had a chill edge to the air that made the warmth surrounding me that much better. Werewolves don't like the heat.

Adam was awake, too.

"So," I said . . . half-embarrassed, half-aroused, and, just to round things out, half-scared, too. "Are you up for a trial run?"

"A trial run?" he asked, his voice all rumbly with sleep. The sound of it helped a lot with the halves I was feeling—virtually eliminating embarrassed, reducing scared, and pushing aroused up a few notches.

"Well, yes." I couldn't see his face, but I didn't need to. I could feel his willingness to participate in my trial pressed against my backside. "Thing is, I've had different things happen with these stupid panic attacks. If I stop breathing, you could just ignore it. Eventually I start breathing again, or I pass out. But if I throw up . . ." I let him draw his own conclusions.

"Quite a mood breaker," he observed, his face on the back of my neck as he wrapped an arm more fully around me on top of the covers.

I tapped his arm with my finger, and warned, only half in jest, "Don't laugh at me."

"I wouldn't dream of it. I've heard stories about what happens to people who laugh at you. I like my coffee without salt, please. Tell you what," he said, his voice dropping even lower. "Why don't we just play for a bit—and see how far it gets? I promise not to be"—amusement fought with other things in his voice—"dismayed if you throw up."

And then he slid down in the bed.

When I flinched, he stopped and asked me about it. I found I couldn't say anything. There are things you don't tell someone you're still trying to impress. There are other things you don't want to remember either. Panic tightened my throat.

"Shh," he said. "Shh." And he kissed me there, where he'd caused me to shy. It was a gentle, caring touch—almost passionless, and moved on to somewhere less . . . tainted.

But he was a good hunter. Adam isn't patient by nature, but his training was very thorough. He worked his way back to the first bad spot and tried again.

I still flinched . . . but I told him a little. And like the wolf he was, he laved the wound in my soul, bandaging it with his care—and moved on to the next. He explored thoroughly, found each mental wound—and a few I didn't know I had—and replaced them with other . . . better things. And when passion began to grow too wild, too fast . . .

"So," he murmured, "are you ticklish here?"

Yep. Who'd have known it? I looked at my inner elbow as if I'd never seen it before.

He laughed, bounced over a little, and made a raspberry noise with his mouth on my belly. My knees jerked up in reflex, and I bopped him on the head with my elbow.

"Are you all right?" I pulled away from him and sat up—all desire to laugh gone. Trust me to clobber Adam while we're making out. Stupid, clumsy idiot, me.

He took one look at my face, put both arms over his head, and rolled on his back, moaning in agony.

"Hey," I said. And when he didn't stop, I poked him in the side—I knew some of his ticklish spots, too. "Stop that. I didn't hit you that hard." He'd been taking lessons from Samuel.

He opened one eye. "How would you know?"

"You have a hard head," I informed him. "If I didn't damage my elbow, I didn't hurt your head."

"Come here," he said opening his arms wide, eyes glittering with laughter . . . and heat.

I crawled over on top of him. We both closed our eyes for a bit while I made myself comfortable. He ran his hands over my back.

"I love this," he told me, a little breathless and yellow-eyed.

"Love what?" I turned my head and put my ear on his chest so I could hear the pounding of his heart.

"Touching you . . ." He deliberately ran a hand over my bare butt. "Do you know how long I've wanted to do this?"

He dug in with his fingers. Tension from the night before had left me tight, and it felt good. I went limp, and if I could have purred, I would have.

"Someone looking at us might think we're asleep," I told him.

"You think so? Only if they don't notice my pulse rate . . . or yours."

He hit just the right spot, and I moaned.

"Just like Medea," he murmured. "All I have to do is put my hands on you. You can be spitting mad . . . and then you lean against me and go all soft and still." He put his mouth against my ear. "That's how I know you want me as much as I want you." His arms were tight around me, and I knew that I wasn't the only one with wounds.

"I don't purr as well as Medea," I told him.

"Are you sure about that?"

And he proceeded to show me what he meant. If I didn't ever reach Medea's volume, I came close. By the time he got down to business, there was no room in the inferno he'd made of me for fear or memory.

There was only Adam.

———

THE NEXT TIME I WOKE UP, I WAS SMILING. I WAS ALONE in the bed, but that didn't matter because I could hear Adam downstairs—he was talking to Jesse. Either they were making lunch—I checked the window shades—dinner, or someone was getting chopped into small bits.

Soon I'd start worrying. But for now . . . the vampires weren't going to kill everyone I knew. They weren't even going to kill *me*. The sun was up. And matters between Adam and me were right and tight.

Mostly. We had a lot of things to talk about. For instance, did he want me to move in? For a night, it was wonderful. But his house wasn't exactly private; any of his pack could be here on any given day.

I liked my home, scruffy as it was. I liked having my own territory. And . . . what about Samuel? I frowned. He was still . . . not whole, and for some reason bunking at my house was helping. With me he could have a pack, but not be Alpha and responsible for everyone. I wasn't sure it would work out so well for him if I moved in with Adam—and I knew it wouldn't work out if he moved over here, too.

See, worrying already.

I took a deep breath and let it go. Tomorrow I would worry about Samuel, about Stefan, and about Amber, whose ghost was the least of her problems. I was just going to enjoy today. For the whole day I was going to be happy and carefree.

I slid out of bed and realized I was stark naked. Which was only to be expected. But there was no sign of underwear on the floor or in the bedding. I was head and shoulders under the bed when Adam said, from the doorway, "I spy with my little eye something that begins with the letter *A*."

"I'll spy your little eye and squish it," I threatened, but, since the bed hid me, there was a grin on my face. I'm not body shy—not growing up among werewolves. I can fake it so people don't get the wrong idea . . . but with Adam it would be the right one. I wiggled the something in question, and he patted it. "I've been smelling whatever you've been cooking"—something with lemon and chicken—"it's making me hungry. But I can't find my underwear."

"You could go without," he suggested, sitting on the bed just to the right of me.

"Hah," I said. "Not on your life, buster. Jesse and who knows who else are down there. I'm not running around without underwear."

"Who would know?" he asked.

"I would know," I told him, pulling my head out from under the bed only to see that he had my bright blue panties dangling from a finger.

"They were under the pillow," he said with an innocent smile.

I snatched them and put them on. Then I hopped up and went to the bathroom, where the rest of my clothes were. I dressed, took a step toward the bathroom, and had a flashback.

I'd been here, unworthy, soiled . . . stained. I couldn't face them, couldn't look into their faces because they all knew . . .

"Shh, shh," Adam crooned in my ear. "That's over. It's over and done with."

He held me, sitting on the bathroom floor with me on his lap, while I shook and the flashback faded.

When I could breathe normally again, I sat up with an attempt at dignity. "Sorry," I said.

I'd thought that last night would have taken care of the flashbacks, the panic attacks—I was cured, right?

I reached up and grabbed a hand towel and wiped my wet face—and found that it just kept getting wet. I'd been so sure everything would be back to normal now.

"It takes longer than a week to get over something like that," Adam told me, as if he could read my mind. "But I can help, if you'll let me."

I looked at him, and he ran a thumb under my eyes. "You'll have to open up, though, and let the pack in."

He smiled, a sad smile. "You've been blocking pretty ferociously since sometime on the trip back from Spokane. If I were to guess, I expect it was when you let Stefan bite you."

I had no idea what he was talking about, and I guessed it showed.

"Not on purpose?" he said.

Somehow, I'd slid off his lap and was leaning against the opposite wall. "Not that I know."

"You had a panic attack on the way home," he told me.

I nodded and remembered the warmth of the pack that had pulled me out of it. Remarkable, awesome—and buried under the rest of the events of the past two nights.

His lids lowered. "That's better . . . a bit better." He looked up from the floor and focused on me, yellow highlights dancing in his irises. He reached out and touched me just under my ear.

It was a light touch, just barely skin to skin. It should have been casual.

He laughed a little, sounding just a bit giddy. "Just like Medea, Mercy," he said, dropping his hand and drawing a breath that sounded just a little ragged. "Let me try this again." He held out his hand.

When I put mine in it, he closed his eyes and . . . I felt a trickle of life, warmth, and health dribbling from his hand to mine. It felt like a hug on a summer's day, laughter, and sweet honey.

I spread out into it through him, sliding into something I just knew were warm depths that would surround me with—

But the pack didn't want me. And the minute the thought crossed my mind, the trickle dried up—and Adam jerked his hand back with a hiss of pain that brought me up to my knees. I reached out to touch him, then pulled my hand back so I didn't hurt him again.

"Adam?"

"Stubborn," he said with an appraising look. "I got bits and pieces from you, though. We don't love you, so you won't take anything from us?" The question in his voice was self-addressed, as if he weren't quite sure of his analysis.

I sat back down on my heels, caught by the accuracy of his reading.

"Instincts drive the wolf . . . coyote, too, I imagine," he told me after a moment. He looked relaxed, one knee up and the other stretched out just to the side of me. "Truth is without flourishes or manners and runs with a logic all its own. You can't let the pack give without giving in return, and if we don't want your gift . . ."

I didn't say anything. I didn't understand how the pack worked, but the last part was right. After a bit, he said, "It's inconvenient sometimes to be a part of the pack. When the pack magic is in full swing—like now with the moon close to her zenith—there's no hiding everything from each other all the time like we do as humans. Some things, yes, but we can't chose which ones stay safely secret. Paul knows I'm still angry with him over his attack on Warren, and it makes him cringe—which just makes me angrier because it's not remorse for trying to attack Warren when he was hurt but fear of my anger."

I stared at him.

"It's not all bad," he told me. "It's knowing who they are, what's important to them, what makes them different. What strengths they each contribute to the pack."

He hesitated. "I'm not sure how much you'll get. If I want to, at full moon in wolf form, I can read everyone almost always—that's part of being Alpha. It allows me to use the individuals to build a pack. Most of the pack get bits and pieces, mostly things that concern them or big things." He gave me a little smile. "I didn't know that bringing you into the pack would work at all, you know. I couldn't have done it with a human mate, but you are always an unknown." He looked at me intently. "You knew Mary Jo had been hurt."

I shook my head. "No. I knew someone had been hurt—but I didn't know it was Mary Jo until I saw her."

"Okay," he said, encouraged by my answer. "It shouldn't be bad for you then. Unless you need them, or they need you, the pack will just be . . . a shield at your back, warmth in the storm. Our mate bond—when it settles down—will probably add a little oddity to it."

"What do you mean 'when it settles down'?" I asked him.

He shrugged. "Hard to explain." He gave me an amused look. "When I was learning how to be a wolf, I asked my teacher what mating felt like. He told me it was different for different couples— and being Alpha adds a twist to it as well."

"So you don't know?" Because that wasn't an answer—and Adam didn't evade questions. He answered or told you he wasn't going to.

"I do now," he said. "Our bond"—he made a gesture with his hand indicating something in the small space in the bathroom that lay between us—"feels to me like a bridge, like the suspension bridge over the Columbia. It has foundations and the cables and all that it needs to be a bridge, but it doesn't span the river yet." He looked at my face and grinned. "I know it sounds stupid, but you asked.

Anyway, if all you felt when Mary Jo was dying was that someone was hurt, that you caught the few who don't welcome you as part of our pack is my fault. You felt them through me. On your own, you won't even be aware of it unless certain conditions are met. Things like proximity, how open you are to the pack, and if the moon is full." He grinned. "Or how grumpy you are with them."

"So if I don't feel it, it shouldn't matter if they don't want me?"

He gave me a neutral look. "Of course it matters—but it won't be shoved down your throat every minute of the day. Mostly, I expect you'll know the ones who don't want a coyote in the pack. As Warren knows the wolves who hate what he is more than what he does." Briefly, sorrow lit his eyes for Warren's trials, but he kept speaking. "Just as Darryl knows the wolves who resent being given orders by a black man made uppity by a good education." He smiled, just a little. "You aren't alone, most people are prejudiced about something. But you know, after a while the edges wear down. You know who hated Darryl the most when he joined us, way back when we were still in New Mexico?"

I raised my eyebrows in inquiry.

"Aurielle. She thought he was an arrogant, self-important snob."

"Which he is," I observed. "But he's also smart, quick, and given to small kindnesses when no one is watching."

"So," he nodded. "We are none of us perfect, and as pack, we learn to take these imperfections and make them only a small part of who we are. Let us bring you truly into our shelter, Mercedes. And the wolves who resent you will deal with it as you will deal with the ones you don't like, for whatever reason. I think, with the healing you have already done on your own, the pack can help stop your panic attacks."

"Ben's rude," I said, considering it.

"See, you already know most of us," Adam said. "And Ben adores you. He doesn't quite know how to deal with it yet. He's not used to liking anyone . . . and liking a *woman* . . ."

"Ish," I said, deadpan.

"Let's try again," he suggested, and put out his hand.

This time when I touched him, all I felt was skin and calluses, no warmth, no magic.

He tilted his head and evaluated me sternly. "It's hard to argue with instinct, even with reason and logic, isn't it? May I knock?"

"What?"

"May I see if I can touch you first? Maybe that'll allow you to open to the pack."

It sounded harmless enough. Warily, I nodded . . . and I felt him, felt his spirit or *something*, touch me. It wasn't like when I'd called Stefan. That had been as intimate as talking was—not very much. Adam's touch reminded me more of the presence I felt sometimes in church—but this was unmistakably Adam and not God.

And because it was Adam, I let him in, accepting him into my secret heart. Something settled into place with a rightness that rang in my soul. Then the floodgates opened.

THE NEXT TIME I WAS CONSCIOUS OF ANYTHING REAL, I was back in Adam's lap but on his bedroom floor instead of in the bathroom. A number of the pack surrounded us and stood with their hands linked. My head hurt like the one and only time I'd gotten truly drunk, only much worse.

"We're going to have to work on your filtering skills, Mercy," said Adam, his voice sounding a little rough.

As if that was a signal, the pack broke apart and became individuals again—though I hadn't been aware they were anything else until it was gone. Something stopped, and my head didn't hurt so much. Uncomfortable at being on the floor when everyone else was on their feet, I rolled forward and tried to use my hands to get leverage so I could stand.

"Not so fast," Samuel murmured. He hadn't been one of the circle, I'd have noticed him, but he pushed his way through to the front of the line. He gave me a hand and pulled until I was on my feet.

"I'm sorry," I told Adam, knowing something bad had happened, but I couldn't quite focus on what it had been.

"Nothing to be sorry for, Mercy," Samuel assured me with a little edge to his voice. "Adam is old enough to know better than to draw his mate into the pack at the same time as he seals your mate bond. Sort of like someone teaching a baby to swim in the ocean. During a tsunami."

Adam hadn't gotten up when I did, and when I looked at him, his face was grayish underneath his tan. He had his eyes closed, and he was sitting as if moving would be very painful. "Not your fault, Mercy. I asked you to open up to me."

"What happened?" I asked him.

Adam opened his eyes, and they were as yellow as I'd ever seen them. "Full-throttle overload," he said. "Someone probably should call Darryl and Warren and make sure they're all right. They stepped in without notice and helped tuck you back into your own skin."

"I don't remember," I said warily.

"Good," said Samuel. "Fortunately for us all, the mind has a way of protecting itself."

"You went from fully closed to fully open," Adam said. "And when you opened yourself up to me, the mate bond settled in, too.

Before I realized what happened you . . ." He waved his hands. "Sort of spread out through the pack bonds."

"Like Napoleon trying to take over Russia," said Samuel "There just wasn't enough of you to go around."

I remembered a bit then. I'd been swimming, drowning in memories and thoughts that weren't mine. They'd flowed over me, around me, and through me like a river of ice—stripping me raw as the shards passed by. It had been cold and dark; I couldn't breathe. I'd heard Adam calling my name . . .

"Aurielle answered," reported Ben from the hallway. "She says Darryl is fine. Warren's not picking up, so I called his boy toy's cell. Boy will check up and call me back."

"I bet you didn't call him a boy toy to his face," I said.

"You can effing believe I did," answered Ben with injured dignity. "You should have heard what he called me."

Kyle, Warren's human boyfriend, who in his day job was a barracuda divorce lawyer, had a tongue that could be as razor-sharp as his mind. I'd bet money on the outcome of any verbal skirmish between Kyle and Ben, and it wouldn't be on Ben.

"Is Dad all right?" asked Jesse. The wolves moved aside almost sheepishly to let her through—and I realized they must have kept her away while the matter was still in doubt. Judging by Adam's eyes, he held on to control by a gnat's hair—so keeping his vulnerable human daughter away had been a good idea. But I knew Jesse—I wouldn't have wanted to have been the one keeping her back.

Adam got hastily to his feet and almost didn't lean on Mary Jo—who'd put her hand out when he swayed.

"I'm just fine," he told his daughter, and gave her a quick hug.

"Jesse's the one who called Samuel," Mary Jo told him. "We didn't even think of it. He told us what to do."

"Jesse's the bomb," I said with conviction. She gave me a shaky grin.

"The trick," Samuel said to me, "is to join with the pack and with Adam—without losing yourself in them. It's instinctive for the werewolves, but I expect you're going to have to work on it."

IN THE END, I WENT HOME FOR DINNER, SLIPPING OUT ALmost unnoticed in the gathering that followed our close call. I needed some time alone. Adam saw me leave, but made no move to stop me—he knew I'd be back.

There was a bowl of tuna fish, pickles, and mayo in the fridge, so I made a sandwich and fed what was left to the cat. As she ate with delicate haste, I called Kyle's cell phone.

"Uhmm?"

The sound was so relaxed, I pulled the phone away from my ears to make sure it was *Kyle's* phone I'd gotten. But there it was on the little screen—KYLE'S CELL.

"Kyle? I was calling to see how Warren was."

"Sorry, Mercy," Kyle laughed, and I heard water splash. "We're in the hot tub. He's fine. How are you? Ben said you were all right."

"Fine. Warren?"

"Was passed out in the hallway, where he'd evidently been headed to the kitchen with an empty glass."

"Wasn't empty when I was carrying it," Warren's warm Southern-touched voice sounded amused.

"Ah," said Kyle, "I didn't notice much besides Warren. But he woke up in a few minutes—"

"Cold water in your face does that," observed Warren, amused.

"But he was stiff and sore—thus the hot tub."

"Tell him I'm sorry," I told Kyle.

"Nothin' to be sorry for," said Warren. "Pack magic can be tricky sometimes. That's what Adam, Darryl, and I are for, sweetheart. I don't feel you in the pack anymore. Problems?"

"Probably not," I told him. "Samuel says I just burned out the circuit for a while. It should come back on line soon."

"Apparently it wasn't necessary that I pass anything on," said Kyle dryly.

A car pulled into the driveway—a Mercedes, I thought. But I didn't recognize the individual car. "Give Warren a hug from me, instead," I said. "And enjoy the hot tub."

I hung up before Kyle could say something outrageous in response and went to the door to see who was there.

Corban, Amber's husband was just coming up the steps. He looked disconcerted when I opened the door before he knocked. He also looked upset, his tie askew, his cheeks unshaven.

"Corban?" I said. I couldn't imagine why he was here when a phone was so much easier. "What's wrong?"

He recovered from his momentary hesitation and all but hopped up the last step. He put out a hand, and I noticed he was wearing leather driving gloves—and holding something odd-looking. That's all I had time to notice before he hit me with the Taser.

Tasers are becoming commonplace among police departments, though I'd never actually seen one in the flesh before. Somewhere on YouTube there is a cameraphone video showing what happened to a student who broke some rule or other in a university library. He was Tasered, then Tasered again because he wouldn't get up when they told him to.

It hurt. It hurt like . . . I didn't know what. I dropped to the ground and lay there frozen while Corban frisked me. He went through my pockets, dropping my cell phone to the porch. He grabbed my shoulders and knees and tried to jerk lift me.

I'm a lot heavier than I look—muscle will do that—and he was no werewolf, just a desperate man whispering, "I'm sorry. I'm sorry."

I'd make sure he was sorry, I thought through the haze of pain. "I don't get mad I get even" was more of a credo than a cliché to me.

The people I'd seen Tasered were only knocked out of commission for a few seconds. Even the kid in the library had been able to make noise. I was absolutely helpless, and I didn't know why.

I tried touching the pack or Adam for help. I found where the connection should have been, but the Taser had nothing on the pain when I tried to force contact. My head hurt so badly it felt like my ears should be bleeding.

It was still daylight, so calling Stefan wasn't going to be much help.

The second time, he got me up and took me to his car. His trunk popped with a beep, and he dumped me in it. My head bounced off the floor a couple of times. When I got out of this, Amber was going to be a widow.

Scrabbling fingers pulled my hands together behind my back, and I recognized the signature sound of a zip tie. He used another on my ankles. Prying my mouth open, he stuffed it with a sock that tasted of fabric softener and smelled faintly of Amber, then he wrapped what felt like an Ace bandage around that.

"It's Chad," he told me, eyes wild. "He has Chad."

I caught a glimpse of the fresh bite mark in his neck just before he shut the trunk.

11

~~~

IT MUST HAVE BEEN AT LEAST FIFTEEN MINUTES BEFORE
the effects wore off, and I began to function again. The first conclusion I came to was that whatever he'd hit me with had been no
normal Taser. No way in Hell. Ill and shaking, I huddled in the vibrating trunk and tried to come up with a plan.

I couldn't shift yet, but before we reached Spokane I'd be able
to. And the zip ties weren't tight enough to hold the coyote. The car
was newer, and I could see the tab that would release the trunk. So
I wasn't trapped.

The realization did a lot to stop my panic. No matter what, I
wouldn't have to face Blackwood.

I relaxed into the floor of the trunk and tried to figure out why the vampire wanted me badly enough to ruin his lawyer to get me. It might be that he didn't value Corban—but I'd gotten the feeling that their association was of long standing. *Was* he trying to take over the Tri-Cities as well as Spokane? Take me down and hold me hostage to force the wolves to act against Marsilia?

It had seemed like a possibility . . . had it been just yesterday? But with the warfare between wolf and vampire at an end in the Tri-Cities, kidnapping me to influence Adam seemed like a stupid move to make just now. And a vampire who was stupid didn't successfully hold a city against all comers. There was a chance, just barely, that he hadn't heard what happened. It was that chance that meant I couldn't dismiss the theory outright.

And Marsilia was down three of her most powerful vampires. If he wanted to move against her, now was the time to strike at her. Kidnapping me wasn't a strike—it was, at best, an end run. Especially now that Marsilia had declared a truce with the wolves. Kidnapping me, I judged, would do nothing except send Adam to Marsilia with an offer of alliance.

See? It was stupid to take me—if his purpose was to take over Marsilia's territory.

Since Blackwood couldn't be that dumb, and I found myself indisputably lying in Corban's trunk, I was inclined to think we had been wrong about Blackwood's intentions.

So what *did* he want with me?

It could be as simple as pride. He'd claimed me as food—maybe as he claimed anyone who came to Amber's house. Then Stefan came along and took me from him.

The theory had the benefit of conforming to the KISS principle— Keep It Simple, Stupid. It meant that Blackwood didn't have anything to do with Chad's ghost. It supposed that it was sheer dumb bad luck that I had gone blithely into his hunting ground when I went to Amber's to look for a ghost.

Vampires are arrogant and territorial. It was not only possible but probable that having fed from me, he would believe I belonged to him. If he was possessive enough—and his holding the city for himself presupposed that Blackwood was very possessive—it was entirely reasonable that he would send a minion to fetch me.

It was a neat, simple solution, and it didn't depend upon my being anything special. Ego, Bran liked to say, got in the way of truth more often than anything else.

Trouble was, it still didn't *quite* fit.

Being alone in the trunk with nothing better to do gave me time to analyze the whole thing. From the beginning, Amber's first approach had bothered me. Upon reflection, it struck me as even more wrong. The Amber with whom I'd had a water fight, who gave dinner parties for her husband's clients, would be neither so thoughtless or gauche as to approach me to help her with a ghost because she'd read about my rape—the rape of a near stranger, really, after all these years—in the newspaper.

I hadn't seen her in a long time. But, in retrospect, there had been an awkwardness in her manner that was unlike either the woman she'd been or the one she'd grown to be. It might have been explained by the odd situation, but I thought it more probable that she'd been sent.

Which left the question, why did Blackwood want me?

What could he have known about me before he required me to travel to Amber's?

The newspapers announced that I was dating a werewolf. Amber knew I saw ghosts. I sucked in a deep breath—she also knew I'd been raised with a foster family in Montana until I was sixteen. It wasn't something I'd kept hidden—just the part about my foster family being werewolves, except that time when I was drunk.

But among the werewolves, the knowledge of the walker, the coyote shapeshifter, who'd been raised by Bran, was well-known. So say that he didn't know anything about me until the newspaper articles. Say Amber looked at the newspaper, and said, "Goodness—I know her. I wonder if she might not be useful helping us deal with our ghost. She said she could see ghosts."

Blackwood said to himself, "Hmm. A girl whose boyfriend is the Alpha of the Tri-Cities. A girl with an affinity for ghosts." And being much older than me, he might have known more about walkers than I did. So he put two and two together and got, "Hey, I wonder if she might not be that walker who was raised by Bran a few years ago." So he asked Amber if I was from Montana. And she told him I was raised by a foster family there.

Maybe he wanted something from a walker. Here I had an uncomfortable moment remembering Stefan telling me about the Master of Milan, who was addicted to the blood of werewolves. But Stefan had taken blood from *me* and hadn't seemed to be much affected by it. Anyway, suppose Blackwood wanted a walker and so he sent Amber to find me and persuade me to come to Spokane.

I didn't like it as well as the KISS theory. But that was mostly because it meant that he wouldn't quit hunting me just because I'd escaped from this car. It meant that he'd just keep coming until he got what he wanted—or he was killed.

It fit what I knew. Walkers are rare. If there are other walkers around, I've never met one. So if he figured out what I was, and he wanted one, it would be logical for him to come after me. The question it left me was, What did he want with a walker?

The tingling in my arms and legs had faded and left only a dogged ache behind. It was time to escape . . . and then I really thought about what Corban had said: "He has Chad."

Corban had kidnapped me because Blackwood had Chad. I wondered what Blackwood would do if Corban came back, and I'd escaped him.

Maybe he'd just send him out again. But I remembered Marsilia's indifference when she'd ordered Estelle's man killed . . . when she'd killed all of Stefan's people. She was hurt that he was still angry with her after he'd figured out what she had done. Maybe she had no understanding of Stefan's attachment to his people . . . because humans were food.

Maybe Blackwood would simply kill Chad.

I couldn't take that chance.

Abruptly, the sharp edge of terror made itself at home in my innards because I really was trapped. I couldn't escape, not when it could mean that Chad would die.

Dry-mouthed, I tried to sort out my tools. There was the fairy staff, of course. It wasn't there at the moment, but eventually it would come to me. It was accounted by the fae to be a powerful artifact—if only vampires were afraid of sheep.

I couldn't find the pack or Adam. Samuel had said that the connections would reset. He hadn't given me a timeline—and I hadn't been anxious to repeat the experience, so I hadn't asked. Adam said that distance made the connection thinner.

I remembered that Samuel had once run all the way to Texas to escape his father . . . and it had worked. But Spokane was a lot closer to the Tri-Cities than Texas was to Montana. So maybe if I stalled Blackwood long enough, I could call the whole pack in to save me—again.

After dark, and it would soon be after dark, there was Stefan. I could call to him, and he'd come to me, just as he had when Marsilia had asked me to do it—but I'd have to do it before Blackwood forced me to exchange blood with him again. I assumed that what had worked to break Blackwood's hold would work in the reverse.

And, as with calling in the pack, I would only be calling him in to die. If he didn't judge himself to be a match for Blackwood—and he hadn't—I could only accept his opinion. He knew more about Blackwood than I did.

If I left, I left a boy I liked to die at the hands of a monster. If I stayed . . . I would be putting myself in the hands of a monster. The Monster.

Maybe he didn't intend to kill me. I could make myself believe that easily. Less easy to dismiss was the already demonstrated desire of his to make me his puppet.

I could always leave. I *shifted* and told myself that it was because I didn't want to face Blackwood while I was tied up and helpless. As coyote I wiggled out of the bonds and gag, then I shifted back, got dressed, and fingered the release tab on the trunk's lock.

So I rode in the trunk of Corban's car all the way to Spokane. When the car slowed and left the smooth growl of the interstate for the stop and go of city traffic, I straightened my clothes. My fingers touched a stick . . . the silver-and-wood staff was tucked under my cheek. I stroked it because it made me feel better.

"You'd better hide yourself, my pretty," I murmured in a fake pirate accent. "Or you'll be put in his treasure room and never let see the light of day."

Something under my ear chimed, we took a hard corner, and I lost track of where the staff was. I hoped it had listened to me and left. It wouldn't be much help against a vampire, and I didn't want it to come to harm while it was in my care.

"Now you're talking to inanimate objects," I said out loud. "And believing they are listening to you. Get a grip, Mercy."

The car slowed to a crawl, then stopped. I heard the clang of chain and metal on pavement, then the car moved slowly forward. It sounded like Blackwood's gates were a little more upscale than Marsilia's. Did vampires worry about things like that?

I rolled up, crossed my legs, and bent over until my chin rested on my heels. When Corban opened the trunk, I simply sat up. It must have looked as though I'd been doing it all along. I hoped that it would draw his attention away from the contents of the trunk, so he wouldn't notice the staff. If it was still in there at all.

"Blackwood has Chad?" I asked him.

His mouth opened, but no sound came out.

"Look," I said, climbing out of the trunk with less grace than I'd planned. Damned Taser or stun gun or whatever it had been. "We don't have much time. I need to know what the situation is. You said he had Chad. Exactly what did he tell you to do? Did he tell you why he wanted me?"

"He has Chad," Corban said. He closed his eyes, and his face flushed red—like a weight lifter after a great effort. His voice came slowly. "I get you when you are alone. No one around. Not your roommate. Not your boyfriend. He would tell me when. I bring you back. My son lives."

"What does he *want* me for?" I asked, while still absorbing that Blackwood had known when I was alone. I couldn't believe someone could have been following me—even if I hadn't detected them, there was still Adam and Samuel.

He shook his head. "Don't know." He reached out and grabbed my wrist. "I have to take you now."

"Fine," I said, and my heart rate doubled. *Even now,* I thought with a quick glance at the gate and the ten-foot stone walls. *Even now I could break away and run.* But there was Chad.

"Mercy," he said, forcing his voice. "One more thing. He *wanted* me to tell you about Chad. So you would come."

Just because you knew it was a trap didn't mean you could stay out if the bait was good enough. With a ragged sigh, I decided that one deaf boy with the courage to face down a ghost should inspire me to a tenth of his courage.

My course laid out, I took a good look at the geography of Blackwood's trap for me. It was dark, but I can see in the dark.

Blackwood's house was smaller than Adam's, smaller even than Amber's, though it was meticulously crafted out of warm-colored stone. The grounds encompassed maybe five or six acres of what had once been a garden of roses. But it had been a few years since any gardener had touched these.

He would have another house, I thought. One suitably grand with a professional garden and lawn service that kept it beautiful. There he would receive his business guests.

This place, with its neglected and overgrown gardens, was his home. What did it tell me about him? Other than that he liked quality over size and preferred privacy to beauty or order.

The walls surrounding the grounds were older than the house, made of quarried stone and hand laid without mortar. The gate was wrought iron and ornate. His house wasn't really small—it just looked undersized for the presentation it was given. Doubtless the house it had replaced had been huge and better suited to the property, if not to the vampire.

Corban paused in front of the door. "Run if you can," he said. "It isn't right . . . not your problem."

"Blackwood has made it my problem," I told him. I walked in

front of him and pushed open the door. "Hey, honey, I'm home," I announced in my best fifties-movie-starlet voice. Kyle, I felt, would have approved of the voice, but not the wardrobe. My shirt was going on a day and a half, the jeans . . . I didn't remember how long I'd been wearing the jeans. Not *much* longer than the shirt.

The entryway was empty. But not for long.

"Mercedes Thompson, my dear," said the vampire. "Welcome to my home at long last." He glanced at Corban. "You have served. Go rest, my dear guest."

Corban hesitated. "Chad?"

The vampire had been looking at me like I was something that delighted him . . . maybe he needed some breakfast. Corban's interruption caused a flash of irritation to sweep briefly across his face. "Have you not completed the mission I gave you? What harm could the boy come to if that is true? Now go rest."

I let all thoughts of Corban drift from me. His fate, his son's fate . . . Amber's fate were beyond my control right now. I could afford only to concentrate on the here and now.

It was a trick Bran had taught to us all on our first hunt. Not to worry about what had been or what would be, just the now. Not what a human might feel knowing she'd killed a rabbit that had never done her any harm. That she'd killed it with teeth and claws, and eaten it raw with relish . . . including parts her human side would rather have not known were inside a soft and fuzzy bunny.

So I forgot about the bunny, about what the results of tonight might be, and focused on the here and now. I forced back the panic that wanted to stop my breath and thought, *Here and now.*

The vampire had given up his business suit. Like most of the vampires I'd met, he was more comfortable in clothing of other eras. Werewolves learn to go with the times so they don't fall into the temptation of living in the past.

I can place women's fashions of the past hundred years within about ten years, and before that to the nearest century. Men's clothing not so much, especially when they are not formal clothes. The button fly on his cotton pants told me it was before zippers were used much. His shirt was dark brown with a tunic neck that would allow it to be pulled over his head, so there were no buttons on it.

Know your prey, Bran had told us. *Observe.*

"James Blackwood," I said. "You know, when Corban introduced us, I couldn't believe my ears."

He smiled, pleased. "I scared you." But then he frowned. "You are not frightened now."

Rabbit, I thought hard. And made the mistake of meeting his eyes the way I had that little bunny's so long ago—as I had Aurielle's last night. But neither Aurielle nor the bunny had been a vampire.

I WOKE UP TUCKED INTO A TWIN-SIZED BED, AND, NO MATTER how hard I tried, I couldn't see beyond that moment when he'd met my eyes. The room was mostly dark, with no sign of a window to be seen. The only light came from a night-light plugged into a wall socket next to a door.

I threw back the covers and saw that he'd stripped me to my panties. Shuddering, I dropped to my knees . . . remembering . . . remembering other things.

"Tim is dead," I said, and the sound came out in a growl worthy of Adam. And once I'd heard it and knew it for a fact, I realized I didn't smell of sex the way that Amber had. I did, however, smell of blood. I reached up to my neck and found the first set of bite marks, the second, and a new third just a centimeter to the left of the second.

Stefan's had healed.

I shook a little in relief that it wasn't worse, then a little more in anger that didn't quite hide how frightened I was. But relief and anger wouldn't leave me helpless in the middle of a panic attack.

The door was locked, and he had left me with nothing to pick it with. The light switch worked, but it didn't show me anything I hadn't seen. A plastic bin that held only my jeans and T-shirt. There was a quarter and the letter for Stefan in my pants pockets, but he'd taken the pair of screws I'd collected while trying to fix the woman's clutch at the rest stop on the way to Amber's house.

The bed was a stack of foam mattress pads that would yield nothing I could make into weapon or tool.

"His prey never escapes," whispered a voice in my ear.

I froze where I knelt beside the bed. There was no one else in the room with me.

"I should know," it . . . he said. "I've watched them try."

I turned slowly around but saw nothing . . . but the smell of blood was growing stronger.

"Was it you at the boy's house?" I asked.

"Poor boy," said the voice sadly, but it was more solid now. "Poor boy with the yellow car. I wish I had a yellow car . . ."

Ghosts are odd things. The trick would be getting all the information I could without driving it away by asking something that conflicted with its understanding of the world. This one seemed pretty cognizant for a ghost.

"Do you follow Blackwood's orders?" I asked.

I saw him. Just for an instant. A young man above sixteen but not yet twenty wearing a red flannel shirt and button-up canvas pants.

"I'm not the only one who must do as he tells," the voice said, though the apparition just stared at me without moving its lips.

And he was gone before I could ask him where Chad and Corban were . . . or if Amber was here. I should have asked Corban. All that my nose told me was that the air-filtration system he had on his HVAC system was excellent, and the filter had been dosed lightly with cinnamon oil. I wondered if that had been done on my account, or if he just liked cinnamon.

The things in the room—plastic bin and bed, pillow and bedding, were brand-new. So were the paint and the carpet.

I pulled on my shirt and pants, regretting the underwire bra he'd taken. I could maybe have managed something with the underwire. I've jimmied my share of car door locks and a few house locks along the way as well. The shoes I didn't mind so much.

Someone knocked tentatively at the door. I hadn't heard anyone walking. Maybe it was the ghost.

The scrape of a lock and the door opened. Amber opened the door, and said, "Silly, Mercy. Why did you lock yourself in?" Her voice was as light as her smile, but something wild lurked behind her eyes. Something very close to a wolf.

Vampire? I wondered. I'd met one of Stefan's menagerie who was well on his way to vampirehood. Or maybe it was just the part of Amber who knew what was going on.

"I didn't," I told her. "Blackwood did." She smelled funny, but the cinnamon kept me from pinpointing it.

"Silly," she said again. "Why would he do that?" Her hair looked as if she hadn't combed it since the last time I'd seen her, and her striped shirt was buttoned one button off.

"I don't know," I told her.

But she had changed subjects already. "I have dinner ready. You're supposed to join us for dinner."

"Us?"

She laughed, but there was no smile in her eyes, just a trapped beast growing wild with frustration. "Why Corban, Chad, and Jim, of course."

She turned to lead the way, and I noticed she was limping badly.

"Are you hurt?" I asked her.

"No, why do you ask?"

"Never mind," I said gently, because I'd noticed something else. "Don't worry about it."

She wasn't breathing.

Here and now, I counseled myself. No fear, no rage. Just observation: know your enemy. Rot. That's what I'd been smelling: that first hint that a steak's been in the fridge too long.

She was dead and walking, but she wasn't a ghost. The word that occurred to me was *zombie.*

Vampires, Stefan had once told me, have different talents. He and Marsilia could vanish and reappear somewhere else. There were vampires who could move things without touching them.

This one had power over the dead. Ghosts who obeyed him. *No one escapes,* he'd told me. Not even in death.

I followed Amber up a long flight of stairs to the main floor of the house. We arrived in a broad swath of space that was both dining room, kitchen, and living room. It was daylight . . . morning from the position of the sun—maybe ten o'clock or so. But it was dinner that was set at the table. A roast—pork, my nose belatedly told me—sat splendidly adorned with roasted carrots and potatoes. A pitcher of ice water, a bottle of wine, and a loaf of sliced homemade bread.

The table was big enough to seat eight, but there were only five chairs. Corban and Chad were sitting next to each other, with their backs to us on the only side set with two places. The remaining three chairs were obviously of the same set, but one, the one opposite Corban and Chad, had a padded backrest and arms.

I sat down next to Chad.

"But, Mercy, that's my place," Amber said.

I looked at the boy's tear-stained face and Corban's blank one . . . He, at least, was still breathing. "Hey, you know I like kids," I told her. "You get him all the time."

Blackwood still hadn't arrived. "Does Jim speak ASL?" I asked Amber.

Her face went blank. "I can't answer any questions about Jim. You'll have to ask him." She blinked a couple of times, then she smiled at someone just behind me.

"No, I don't," said Blackwood.

"You don't speak ASL?" I looked over my shoulder—not incidentally letting Chad see my lips. "Me either. It was one of those things I always meant to learn."

"Indeed." I'd amused him, it seems.

He sat down in the armchair and gestured to Amber to take the other.

"She's dead," I told him. "You broke her."

He went very still. "She serves me still."

"Does she? Looks more like a puppet. I bet she's more work and trouble dead than she was alive." *Poor Amber.* But I couldn't let him see my grief. Focus on this room and survival. "So why do you keep her around when she's broken?" Without allowing him time to answer, I bowed my head and said a quiet prayer over the food . . . and asked for help and wisdom while I was at it. I didn't get an answer, but I had the feeling someone might be listening—and I hoped it wasn't just the ghost.

THE VAMPIRE WAS STARING AT ME WHEN I FINISHED.

"Bad manners, I know," I said, taking a slice of bread and buttering it. It smelled good, so I put it down on the plate in front of Chad with a thumbs-up sign. "But Chad can't pray out loud for the rest of us. Amber is dead, and Corban . . ." I tilted my head to look at Chad's father, who hadn't moved since I'd come into the room except for the gentle rise and fall of his chest. "Corban's not in any shape to pray, and you're a vampire. God's not going to listen to anything you have to say."

I took a second slice of bread and buttered it.

Unexpectedly, the vampire threw back his head and laughed, his fangs sharp and . . . pointy. I tried not to think of them in my neck.

It wasn't nearly as creepy as Amber laughing right along with him. A cold hand touched the back of my neck and was gone—but not before someone whispered, "Careful," in my ear. I hated it when ghosts snuck up on me.

Chad grabbed my knee, his eyes widening. Had he seen the ghost? I shook my head at him while Blackwood wiped his dry eyes with his napkin.

"You have always been something of a scamp, haven't you?" Blackwood said. "Tell me, did Tag ever discover who it was that stole all of his shoelaces?"

His words slipped inside me like a knife, and I did my best not to react.

Tag was a wolf in Bran's pack. He'd never left Montana, and only he and I knew about the shoelace incident. He'd found me hiding from Bran's wrath—I don't remember what I'd done—and when I wouldn't come on my own he'd taken off his bootlaces and made a collar and leash out of them for coyote me. Then he'd dragged me through Bran's house to the study.

He knew who'd stolen his shoelaces all right. And until I left for Portland, I'd given him shoelaces every holiday—and he'd laugh.

No way any of Bran's wolves were spying for the vampires.

I hid my thoughts with a couple of mouthfuls of bread. When I could swallow, I said, "Great bread, Amber. Did you make it yourself?" Nothing I could say about the shoelaces struck me as useful. So I changed the subject to food. Amber could always be counted upon to talk about nutrition. Death wouldn't change that.

"Yes," she told me. "All whole grains. Jim has taken me for his cook and housekeeper. If only I hadn't ruined it for him." Yeah, poor *Jim*. Amber had forced him to kill her—so he wouldn't get a new cook.

"Hush," Blackwood said.

I turned my head so I sort of faced Blackwood. "Yeah," I said. "That won't work anymore. Even a human nose is going to smell rotting flesh in a few days. Not what you want in a cook. Not that you need a cook." I took another bite of bread.

"So how long have you been watching me?" I asked.

"I'd despaired of ever finding another walker," he told me. "Imagine my joy when I heard that the Marrok had taken one under his wing."

"Yeah, well," I said, "it wouldn't have worked very well for you if I'd stayed." Ghosts, I thought. He'd used ghosts to watch me.

"I'm not worried about werewolves," said Blackwood. "Did Corban or Amber tell you what my business is?"

"Nope. Your name never crossed their lips once you were gone."

It was the truth, but I saw his mouth tighten. He didn't like that. Didn't like his pets not paying attention to him. It was the first sign of weakness I'd seen. I wasn't sure if it would be useful or not. But I'd take what I could get.

Know your enemy.

"I deal with . . . specialty ammunition," he said, looking at me through narrowed eyes. "Most of it top secret government stuff. I have, for instance, been very successful with a variety of ammunition designed for killing werewolves. I have, among other things, a silver version of the old Black Talon. Silver is a lousy metal for bullets; it doesn't expand well. Instead of mushrooming, this one opens up like a flower." He spread his hand so it looked like a starfish.

"And then there are those very interesting tranquilizer darts of Gerry Wallace's design. Now that was a surprise. I'd never have thought of DMSO as a delivery system for the silver—or a tranquilizer gun as a delivery system. But then, his father was a vet. This is why tools may be useful."

"You knew Gerry Wallace?" I asked, because I couldn't help it. I took another bite as if my stomach weren't clenched, so he wouldn't think that the answer mattered too much.

"He came to me first," Blackwood said. "But it didn't suit me to do as he asked . . . the Marrok is a bit larger target than I wanted to take on." He smiled apologetically. "I am essentially a lazy creature, so my maker used to say. I sent Gerry on his way with an idea about building a superweapon against werewolves in some convoluted scheme sure to fail and no memory of coming to me at all. Imagine my surprise when the boy actually came up with something interesting." He smiled gently at me.

"You need to watch Bran closer," I told him. I grabbed a pitcher of water and poured it. "He's more subtle, and it makes that omniscient thing work better for him. If you tell everyone everything you know, they don't wonder about things you don't tell them. Bran . . ." I shrugged. "You just *know* he knows what you're thinking."

"Amber," said the vampire. "Make sure your husband and the boy who is not his son eat their dinner, would you?"

"Of course."

Chad's cold hand on my knee squeezed very tight. "You say that like it's a revelation," I told Blackwood. "You need to work on your verbal ammunition, too. Corban has always known that Chad's not his biological son. That doesn't matter to him at all. Chad's still his son."

The stem of the water glass the vampire was holding broke. He set the pieces very carefully on his empty plate. "You aren't afraid enough of me," he said very carefully. "Perhaps it is time to instruct you further."

"Fine," I said. "Thank you for the meal, Amber. Take care of yourselves, Corban and Chad."

I stood up and lifted an inquiring eyebrow.

He thought it was stupidity that I wasn't afraid of him. But if you shiver in fear in a pack of werewolves, that's *really* stupid. If you're scared enough, even a wolf with good control starts having problems. If his control isn't strong—well, let's just say that I learned to be very good at burying my fear.

Pushing Blackwood wasn't stupid either. If he'd killed me the first time—well, at least it would have been a quick death. But the longer he let it go on, the more I knew he needed me. I couldn't imagine for what—but he needed me for something.

My bad luck he was taking it on as a challenge. I wondered what he thought would scare me more than Amber before I caught a good tight hold on my thoughts. There was no future, just the vampire and me standing by the table.

"Come," he said, and led the way back down the stairway.

"How is it that you can walk in the daylight?" I asked him. "I've never heard of a vampire who could run around during the day."

"You are what you eat," he said obscurely. "My maker used to say that. *Mann ist was mann ißt.* She wouldn't let me feed off drunkards or people who consumed tobacco." He laughed, and I wouldn't let myself think of it as sinister. "Amber reminds me a bit of her . . . so concerned with nutrition. Neither of them was wrong. But my maker didn't understand the full implications of what she said." He laughed again. "Until I consumed her."

The door to the room I'd awoken in was open. He stopped and turned off the light as we passed. "Mustn't waste electricity."

And then he opened another door to a much bigger room. A room of cages. It smelled like sewage, disease, and death. Most of the cages were empty. But there was a man curled naked in the floor of one of the cages.

"You see, Mercedes," he said, "you aren't the first rare creature to be my guest. This is an oakman. I've had him for . . . How long have you belonged to me, Donnell Greenleaf?"

The fae stirred and raised his face off the cement floor. Once he must have been a formidable figure. Oakmen, I remembered from the old book I'd borrowed, were not tall, no more than four feet, but they were stout "as a good oaken table." This one was little more than skin and bones.

In a voice as dry as high summer in the Tri-Cities, he said, "Fourscore years and a dozen and one. Two seasons more and eighteen days."

"Oakmen," said Blackwood smugly, "like the oaks they are named after, eat only the sunlight."

You are what you eat indeed.

"I've never tried to see if I could live on light," he said. "But he keeps me from burning, don't you, Donnell Greenleaf?"

"It is my honor to bear that burden," said the fae in a hopeless voice, his face to the floor.

"So you kidnapped me so you could turn into a coyote?" I asked incredulously.

The vampire just smiled and escorted me to a largish cage, with a bed. There was also a bucket from which the odor of sewage was emanating. It smelled like Corban, Chad, and Amber.

"I can keep you alive for a long time," the vampire said. He grabbed me by the back of my neck and shoved my face against the cage while he stood behind me. "Maybe even all of your natural life. What? No smart comment?"

He didn't see the faint figure that stood before me with her finger over her pursed mouth. She looked as if she'd been somewhere between sixty and a hundred years old when she'd died—like Santa's wife, she was all rounded and sweet. *Quiet,* that finger said. Or maybe, just—*Don't let on you can see me.*

Blackwood didn't see her, even though he had been using the other ghost as an errand boy. I wondered what it meant. She smelled like blood, too.

He put me in the cage next to the one that he had been keeping Chad and Corban in. Presumably he didn't need to confine Amber anymore. "This could have been so much more pleasant for you," he said.

The woman and her hushing finger were gone, so I gave my tongue free rein. "Tell that to Amber."

He smiled, showing fangs. "She enjoyed it. I'll give you one last chance. Be cooperative, and I'll let you stay in the other room."

Maybe I could get out through the roof of the other room. But somehow I didn't think so. The cage in the Marrok's house looks just like all the rest of the bedrooms. The bars are set behind the drywall.

I leaned against the far side of my cage, the one that backed up to the cement outer wall. "Tell me why you can't just order me around? Make me cooperate?" Like Corban.

He shrugged. "You figure it out." He locked the door with a key and used the same key to open the oakman's door.

The fae whimpered as he was dragged out of the cage. "I can't feed from you every day, Mercy," Blackwood said. "Not if I want to keep you around. The last walker I had died fifty years ago—but I kept him for sixty-three years. I take care of what is mine."

Yeah, I bet Amber would agree with that one.

Blackwood knelt on the floor where the oakman lay curled in a fetal position. The fae was staring at me with large black eyes. He didn't fight when Blackwood—with a look meant for me—grabbed his leg and bit down on the artery in the fae's groin to feed.

"The oak said," the fae said in English-accented Welsh, "Mercy would free me in the Harvest season."

I stared at him, and he smiled before the vampire did something painful to him and he closed his eyes to endure. If he'd understood Welsh, I was sure he'd have done something more extreme. How the oakman knew *I'd* understand him, I didn't know.

There are two ways to free a prisoner—escape is the first. I had the feeling that the oakman was looking for the second.

When he finished, the oakman was barely conscious, and Blackwood looked a dozen years younger. Vampires weren't supposed to do that—but I didn't know any vampires who fed from fae either. He picked up the oakman with no visible effort and tossed him over his shoulder. "Let's get you a little sun, shall we?" Blackwood sounded cheery.

The door to the room closed behind him, and a woman's trembly voice said, "It's because you're too much for him right now, dear. He did try to make you his servant . . . but your ties to the wolves and to that other vampire—and how *did* you manage that, clever girl?—have blocked him. It won't be forever. Eventually, he'll exchange enough blood for you to be his—but not for a few months yet."

Mrs. Claus ghost stood in the cage with her back to me, looking at the door that had closed behind Blackwood.

"What does he want from me?" I asked her.

She turned and smiled at me. "Why, *me*, dear."

She had fangs.

"You're a vampire," I said.

"I was," she agreed. "It isn't the usual thing, I admit. Though that young man you met earlier is one as well. We're tied to James. Both his. John was the only vampire James ever made—and I blush to admit that James is my fault."

"Your fault?"

"He was always so kind, so attentive. A nice young man, I thought. Then one night one of my other children showed me the murdhuacha James had captured—one of the merrow folk, dear." That faint accent was Cockney or Irish, I thought, but so faint I couldn't be sure.

"Well," she said, sounding exasperated. "We just don't do that, dear. First off—the fae aren't a people to toy with. Secondly, whatever we exchange blood with could become vampire. When they're magical folk, the results can be unpleasant." She shook her head. "Well, when I confronted him . . ." She looked down at herself ruefully. "He killed me. I haunted him, followed him from home all the way to here—which wasn't the smartest idea I've ever had. When he took that other man, the one who was like you—well, *then* he saw me. And found he still had use for this old woman."

I had no idea why she was telling me so much—unless she was lonely. I almost felt sorry for her.

Then she licked her lips, and said, "I *could* help you."

Vampires are evil. It was almost as if the Marrok himself were whispering in my ear.

I raised an eyebrow.

"If you feed me, I'll tell you what to do." She smiled, her fangs carefully concealed. "Just a drop or two, love. I'm only a ghost—it wouldn't take much."

12

~~~

"I COULD JUST TAKE IT FROM YOU WHILE YOU SLEEP, dear," the ghost said. "I was only trying to make it a gift. If you give it as a gift, I can help you." She looked like the sort of woman you'd hire to watch your children, I thought. Sweet and loving, a little complacent.

"You won't," I growled. And I felt a little pop of something. Something I'd done.

Her eyes widened and she backtracked. "Of course not, dearie. Of course not—if you don't want me to."

She'd tried to cover it up. But I'd done something. I'd felt it once before, in the bathroom at Amber's house when I'd told the ghost to leave Chad alone. Magic. It wasn't the magic the fae used, or the witches, but it was magic. I could smell it.

"Tell me," I said, trying to put some push behind it, imitating the authority that Adam wore closer than any of his well-tailored shirts. "How did Blackwood manage the haunting at Amber's house. Was it you?"

Her lips tightened in frustration, and her eyes lit up like the vampire she had been. But she answered me. "No. It was the boy, James's little experiment."

Outside of the cages and out of reach was a table stacked with cardboard boxes. A pile of five-gallon buckets—six or eight of them—was on one corner. They fell over with a crash and rolled to the drain in the center of the room.

"That's what you were," she called in a vicious tone that sounded wrong coming out of that grandmotherly face. "He made you vampire and played with you until he was bored. Then he killed you and kept playing until your body rotted away."

Like Blackwood had done to Amber, I thought, except he hadn't managed to make her into a vampire before he'd turned her into a zombie. *Here and now,* I told myself. *Don't waste energy on what you can't change just now.*

The buckets quit rolling and the whole room was silent—except for my own breathing.

She shook herself briskly. "Never fall in love," she told me. "It makes you weak."

I couldn't tell if she was talking about herself or the dead boy or even Blackwood. But I had other things I was more interested in. If I could just get her to answer my questions.

"Tell me," I said, "exactly why Blackwood wants me."

"You *are* rude, dear. Didn't that old wolf teach you any manners?"

"Tell me," I said, "how Blackwood thinks to use me."

She hissed, showing her fangs.

I met her gaze, dominating her as if she were a wolf. "Tell me."

She looked away, drew herself up, and smoothed her skirts as if she were nervous instead of angry, but I knew better.

"He is what he eats," she said finally, when I didn't back down. "He told you so. I'd never heard of it before—how should I have known what he was doing? I thought he was feeding from it because of the taste. But he supped its power down as he drank its blood. Just as he will yours. So that he can use me as he wants to."

And she was gone.

I stared after her. Blackwood was feeding from me, and he'd gain . . . what? I drew in a breath. *No.* The ability to do just what I had been doing—controlling a ghost.

If she'd stuck around, I'd have asked her a dozen more questions. But she wasn't the only ghost around here.

"Hey," I said softly. "She's gone now. You can come out."

He smelled a little differently than she did, though mostly they both smelled like stale blood. It was a subtle difference, but I could discern it when I tried. His scent had lingered as I'd questioned the old woman, which was how I'd known he hadn't left.

He had been the one in Amber's house. The one who'd almost killed Chad.

He faded in gradually, sitting on the open cement floor with his back toward me. He was more solid this time, and I could see that his shirt had been hand-sewn, though it wasn't particularly well-done. He wasn't from this century or the twentieth—probably sometime in the eighteen hundreds.

He pulled a bucket free of the pile and rolled it across the floor, away from us both, until it hit the oakman's empty cage. He gave me a quick, sullen look over his shoulder. Then, staring at the remaining buckets, he said, "Are you going to make me tell you things?"

"It was rude," I admitted, without really answering. If he knew something that would help me get Chad, Corban, and me out of there in one piece, I'd do anything I needed to. "I don't mind being rude to someone who wants to hurt me, though. Do you know why she wants blood?"

"With blood, freely given, she can kill people with a touch," he said. "It doesn't work if she steals it—though she might do that just for spite." He waved a hand, and a box tipped on its side, spilling packing peanuts on the tabletop. Five or six of them whirled up like a miniature tornado. He lost interest, and they fell to the ground.

"With her touch?" I asked.

"Mortal, witch, fae, or vampire: she can kill any of them. They called her Grandmother Death when she was alive." He looked at me again. I couldn't read the expression on his face. "When she was a *vampire*, I mean. Even the other vampires were scared of her. That's how he figured out what he could do."

"Blackwood?"

The ghost scooted around to face me, his hand going through the bucket he'd just been playing with. "He told me. Once, just after it had been his turn to drink from her—she was Mistress of his seethe—he killed a vampire with his touch." Lesser vampires fed from the Master or Mistress who ruled the seethe, and were fed from in return. As they grew more powerful, they quit needing to feed from the one who ruled the seethe. "He said he was angry and touched this woman, and she just crumbled into dust. Just like his Mistress could do. But a couple of days later, he couldn't do it. It wasn't his turn to feed from her for a couple more weeks, so he hired a fae-blooded prostitute—I forget what kind she was—and drained her dry. The fae's powers lasted longer for him. He experimented and figured out that the longer he let them live while he fed, the longer he could use what he'd gained from them."

"Can he still do that?" I asked intently. "Kill with a touch?" No wonder no one challenged him for territory.

He shook his head. "No. And she's dead, so he can't borrow her talents anymore. She can still kill if he feeds her blood. But he can't use her now like he used to before that old Indian man died. It's not that she minds the killing, but she doesn't like to do what he wants. Especially *exactly* what he wants and no more. He uses her for business, and business"—he licked his lips as if trying to remember the exact words Blackwood had used—"business is best conducted with precision." He smiled, his eyes wide and innocent. They were blue. "She prefers bloodbaths, and she's not above setting up the killing ground to point to James as the killer. She did that once, before he'd realized he wasn't still controlling her. He was very unhappy."

"Blackwood had a walker," I said, putting it together. "And he fed from him so he could control her—the lady who was just here."

"Her name is Catherine. I'm John." The boy looked at a bucket, and it moved. "He was nice, Carson Twelve Spoons. He talked to me sometimes and told me stories. He told me that I shouldn't have given myself to James, that I shouldn't be James's toy. That I should let myself go to the Great Spirit. That he would have been able to help me once."

He smiled at me, and this time I caught a hint of malice. "He was a bad Indian. When he was a boy, not much older than me, he killed a man to take his horse and wallet. It made him not able to do the things he should have been able to do. *He* couldn't tell me what to do."

The malice freed me from the distracting pity I'd been feeling. And I saw what I'd missed the first time I'd looked him in the eye.

And I knew the reason that this ghost was different from any I'd seen before.

Ghosts are remnants of people who have died, what's left after the soul goes on. They are mostly collections of memories given form. If they can interact, respond to outside stimuli, they tend to be fragments of the people they had been: obsessive fragments—like the ghosts of dogs who guard their masters' old graves or the ghost I'd once seen who was looking for her puppy.

Immediately after they die, though, sometimes they are different. I've seen it a couple of times at funerals, or in the house of someone who's just passed away. Sometimes the newly dead keep watch over the living, as if to make sure that all is well with them. Those are more than remnants of the people they'd been—I can see the difference. I've always thought those are their souls.

That was what I'd seen in Amber's dead eyes. My stomach clenched. When you die, it should be a release. It wasn't fair, wasn't right, that Blackwood had somehow discovered a way to hold them past death.

"Did Blackwood tell you to kill Chad?" I asked.

His fists clenched. "He has *everything*. Everything. Books and toys." His voice rose as he spoke. "He has a yellow car. Look at me. *Look at me!*" He was on his feet. He stared at me with wild eyes, but when he spoke again, he whispered. "He has everything, and I'm dead. Dead. Dead." He disappeared abruptly, but the buckets scattered. One of them flew up and hit the bars of my cage and broke into chunks of tough orange plastic. A shard hit me and cut my arm.

I wasn't sure if that was supposed to be a yes or a no.

Alone, I sat down on the bed and leaned against the cold cement wall. John the Ghost knew more about walkers than I did. I wondered if he'd told the truth: there was a moral code I had to follow to keep my abilities—which now seemed to include some sort of ability to control ghosts. Though, with my indifferent success at it, I suspected it was something that you had to practice to get right.

I tried to figure out how that talent might help me get all of us prisoners out of there safely. I was still fretting when I heard people coming down the stairs: visitors.

I stood up to welcome them.

The visitors were fellow prisoners. And a zombie.

Amber was chattering away about Chad's next softball game as she led Corban, still obviously under thrall to the vampire, and Chad, who was following because there was nothing else for him to do. He had a bruise on the side of his face that he hadn't had when I left him in the dining room.

"Now you get a good night's sleep," she told them. "Jim's going to bed, too, as soon as he gets that fae locked back up where he belongs. We don't want you to be tired when it's time to get up and be doing." She held the door open as if it were something other than a cage—did she think it was a hotel room?

Watching the zombie was like watching one of those tapes where they take bits that someone actually said and piece them together to make it sound like they were talking about something else entirely. Sound bites of things Amber would have said came out of the dead woman's mouth with little or no relation to what she was doing.

Corban stumbled in and stopped in the middle of the cage. Chad ran past his mother's animated corpse and stopped, wide-eyed and shaking next to the bed. He was only ten, no matter how much courage he had.

If he survived this, he'd be in therapy for years. Assuming he could find a therapist who'd believe him. *Your mother was a what?*

Have some Thorazine . . . Or whatever the newest drug of choice was for the mentally ill.

"Oops," said Amber, manically cheerful. "I almost forgot." She looked around and shook her head sadly. "Did you do this, Mercy? Char always said that you both suited each other because you were slobs at heart." As she was talking, she gathered up the buckets—though she didn't bother cleaning up the broken one—and stacked most of them where they had been. She took one and put it inside Chad and Corban's cage before removing the used one in the corner. "I'll just take this up and clean it, shall I?"

She locked the door.

"Amber," I said, putting force in my voice. "Give me the key." She was dead, right? Did she have to listen to me, too?

She hesitated. I saw her do it. Then she gave me a bright smile. "Naughty, Mercy. Naughty. You'll be punished for that when I tell Jim."

She took the bucket and whistled when she shut the door. I could hear her whistling all the way up the stairs. I needed more practice, or maybe there was some trick to it.

I bowed my head and waited for Blackwood to bring the oakman back with my arms crossed over my middle and my head turned away from Chad. I ignored it when he rattled the cage to catch my attention. When Blackwood came in, I didn't want him to find me holding Chad's hand or talking to him or anything.

I didn't think there was a rat's chance in a cattery that Blackwood would let Chad live after everything he'd seen. But I didn't intend to give the vampire any more reason to hurt him. And if I lowered my guard, I'd have a hard time keeping the fear at bay.

After a time, the oakman stumbled in the door in front of Blackwood. He didn't look much better than he had when Blackwood had finished with him. The fae looked a little above four feet tall, though he'd be taller if he were standing straight. His arms and legs were oddly proportioned in subtle ways: legs short and arms overlong. His neck was too short for his broad-foreheaded, strong-jawed head.

He walked right into his cell without struggling, as if he had fought too many times and suffered defeat. Blackwood locked him in. Then, looking at me, the vampire tossed his key in the air and snatched it back before it hit the ground. "I won't be sending Amber down with keys anymore."

I didn't say anything, and he laughed. "Pout all you want, Mercy. It won't change anything."

Pout? I looked away. I'd show him pout.

He started for the door.

I swallowed my rage and managed to not let it choke me. "So how did you do it?"

Vague questions are harder to ignore than specific ones. They inspire curiosity and make your victim respond even if he wouldn't have talked to you at all otherwise.

"Do what?" he asked.

"Catherine and John," I said. "They aren't like normal ghosts."

He smiled, pleased I'd noticed. "I'd like to claim some sort of supernatural powers," he told me, then laughed because he found himself so funny. He wiped imaginary tears of mirth from his eyes. "But really it is their choice. Catherine is determined to somehow avenge herself upon me. She blames me for ending her reign of terror. John . . . John loves me. He'll never leave me."

"Did you tell him to kill Chad?" I asked coolly, as if the answer were mere curiosity.

"Ah, now, that is the question." He shrugged. "That's why I need you. No. He ruined my game. If he'd done as I'd told him, you'd have brought yourself here and given yourself to me to spare your friends. He made them run. It took me half the day to find them. They didn't want to come with me—and . . . Well, you saw my poor Amber."

I didn't want to know. Didn't want to ask the next question. But I needed to know what he'd done to Amber. "What did you eat that let you make zombies?"

"Oh, she's not a zombie," he told me. "I've seen zombies three centuries old that look almost as fresh as a day-old corpse. They're passed down in their families like the treasures they are. I'm afraid I'll have to get rid of Amber's body in a week or so unless I put her in the freezer. But witches need knowledge as well as power—and they're more trouble to keep than they are worth. No. This is something I learned from Carson—I trust Catherine or John told you about Carson. Interesting that one murder left him unable to do anything with his powers, when I—who you'll have to trust when I tell you that I've done much, much worse than a mere larcenous homicide—had no trouble using what I took from him. Perhaps his trouble was psychosomatic, do you think?"

"You told me how you keep Catherine and John," I said. "How are you keeping Amber?"

He smiled at Chad, who was standing as far from his father as he could get. He looked fragile and scared. "She stayed to protect her son." He looked back at me. "Any more questions?"

"Not right now."

"Fine—oh, and I've seen to it that John won't be coming back to visit you anytime soon. And Catherine, I think, is best kept away, too." He closed the door gently behind him. The stairs creaked under his feet as he left.

When he was gone, I said, "Oakman, do you know when the sun goes down?"

The fae, once more sprawled on the cement floor of his cage, turned his head to me. "Yes."

"Will you tell me?"

There was a long pause. "I will tell you."

Corban stumbled forward a step and swayed a little, blinking rapidly. Blackwood had released him.

He took a deep, shaky breath, then turned urgently to Chad and began signing.

"I don't know how much Chad caught of what's going on . . . too much. Too much. But ignorance might get him killed."

It took me a second to realize he was talking to me—his whole body was focused on his son. When he was finished, Chad—who still was keeping a lot of space between them—began to sign back.

While watching his son's hands, Corban asked me, "How much do you know about vampires? Do we have any chance of getting out of here?"

"Mercy will grant me freedom this Harvest season," said the oakman hoarsely. In English this time.

"I will if I can," I told him. "But I don't know that it'll happen."

"The oak told me," he said, as if that should make it as real as if it had already happened. "It is not a terribly old tree, but it was very angry with the vampire, so it stretched itself. I hope it has not . . . doneitselfpermanentharm." His words tumbled over each other and lost consonants. He turned his head away from me and sighed wearily.

"Are oaks so trustworthy?" I asked.

"Used to be," he told me. "Once."

When he didn't say anything more, I told Corban the most important part of what I knew about the monster who held us. "You can kill a vampire with a wooden stake through the heart, or by cutting off his head, drowning him in holy water—which is impractical unless you have a swimming pool and a priest who will bless it—direct sunlight, or fire. I'm told it's better if you combine a couple of methods."

"What about garlic?"

I shook my head. "Nope. Though a vampire I know told me that given a victim who smells like garlic and one that doesn't, most of them will pick the one who doesn't. Not that we have access to garlic or wooden stakes."

"I know about the sunlight—who doesn't? But it doesn't seem to affect Blackwood."

I nodded toward the oakman. "Apparently he is able to steal some of the abilities of those he drinks from." No way was I going to talk about blood exchanges with Chad watching. "The oakmen like this gentleman here feed from sunlight—so Blackwood gained an immunity to the sun."

"And blood," said the oakman. "In the old days we were given blood sacrifices to keep the trees happy." He sighed. "Feeding me blood is how he keeps me alive when this cold-iron cell would kill me."

Ninety-three years he'd been a prisoner of Blackwood's. The thought chilled any optimism that had survived the ride here from the Tri-Cities. The oakman wasn't mated to a werewolf, though—or bound to a vampire.

"Have you ever killed one?" the oakman asked.

I nodded. "One with help and another one who was hampered because it was daytime and he was sleeping."

I didn't think that was the answer he'd been expecting.

"I see. Do you think you can kill this one?"

I turned around pointedly, looking at the bars. "I don't seem to be doing so well at that. No stake, no swimming pool of holy water, no fire—" And now that I'd said that, I noticed that there was very little that was even flammable here. Chad's bedding, our clothes . . . and that was it.

"You can put me down as something else that won't be of any use," Corban said, bitterly. "I couldn't even stop myself from kidnapping you."

"That Taser was one of Blackwood's developments?"

"Not a Taser—Taser's a brand name. Blackwood sells his stun gun to . . . certain government agencies who want to question prisoners without showing any harm. It's a lot hotter than anything Taser makes. Not legal for the civilian market but—" He sounded proud of it—proud and slick, as if presenting the product at a sales meeting. He stopped himself, and said simply, "I'm sorry."

"Not your fault," I told him. I looked at Chad, who still seemed thoroughly spooked. "Hey, why don't you translate for me a minute."

"Okay." Corban looked at his son, too. "Let me tell him what I'm doing." He wiggled his hands, then said, "Go."

"Blackwood's a vampire," I told Chad. "What that means is that your father can't do anything but follow Blackwood's orders—it's part of what a vampire does. I'm a little protected for the same reason I can see ghosts and talk to them. That's the only reason he hasn't done the same thing to me . . . yet. You'll know when your father's being controlled, though. Blackwood doesn't like your dad signing to you—he can't read sign. So if your dad's not signing to you, that's one thing to look for. And your dad fights his control, and you can see that in his shoulders—"

I broke off because Chad began gesturing wildly, his fingers exaggerating all the movements. His equivalent of yelling, I supposed.

Corban didn't translate what Chad said, but he signed very slowly so he wouldn't be misunderstood and spoke his words out loud when he answered. "Of course I'm your father. I held you in my arms the day you were born and sat vigil in the hospital when you almost died the next day. You are mine. I've earned the right to be your dad. Blackwood wants you alone and afraid. He's a bully and feeds on misery as much as blood. Don't let him win."

Chad's bottom jaw went first, but before I saw tears, his face was hidden against Corban.

It wasn't the best time for Amber to come in.

"It's hot upstairs," she announced. "I'm to sleep down here with you."

"Do you have the key?" I asked. Not that I expected Blackwood to have forgotten. Mostly I just wanted to keep her attention and let Chad, who hadn't noticed her, have his moment with his dad.

She laughed. "No, silly. Jim was not very happy with you—I'm not going to help you escape. I'll just sleep out here. It'll be quite comfortable. Just like camping out."

"Come here," I said. I didn't know that it would work. I didn't know anything.

But she came. I didn't know if she was compelled, or just following my request.

"What do you need?" She stopped within an easy arm's reach.

I put my arm through the bars and held out my hand. She looked at it a moment, but took it.

"Amber," I said solemnly, looking into her eyes. "Chad will be safe. I promise."

She nodded earnestly. "I'll take care of him."

"No." I swallowed and then put authority in my voice. "You're dead, Amber." Her expression didn't change. I narrowed my eyes at her in my best Adam imitation. *"Believe me."*

First her face lit up with that horrible fake smile, and she started to say something. She looked down at my hand, then over to Corban and Chad—who hadn't noticed her yet.

"You're dead," I told her, again.

She collapsed where she stood. It wasn't graceful or gentle. Her head bounced off the floor with a hollow sound.

"Can he take her again?" asked Corban urgently.

I knelt and closed her eyes. "No," I told him with more conviction than I felt. Who knew what Blackwood could do? But her husband needed to believe it was over for her. At any rate, it wouldn't be Amber who walked around in her body. Amber was gone.

"Thank you," he told me, with tears in his eyes. He wiped his face and tapped Chad on the shoulder.

"Hey, kid," he said, and he stepped away so Chad could see Amber's body. They talked for a long time then. Corban played it tough and gave his son the gift of the belief in the superman qualities of fathers for at least one more day.

We slept, all of us, as far from Amber's body as we could get. They pushed the bed up close to my cell and the two of them slept on that and I slept on the floor next to them. Chad reached though the bars and kept a hand on my shoulder. The cell floor could have been a bed of nails, and I would still have slept.

"MERCY?"

The voice was unfamiliar—but so was the cement under my cheek. I stirred and regretted it immediately. Everything hurt.

"Mercy, it is dark, and Blackwood will be here soon."

I sat up and looked across the room at the oakman. "Good evening." I didn't use his name. Some of the fae can be funny about names, and the way Blackwood had overused it made me think that the oakman was one of those. I couldn't thank him, and I searched for a way to acknowledge his honoring my request, but I didn't find one.

"I'm going to try something," I said finally. I closed my eyes and called to Stefan. When I felt I'd done as good a job at that as I could, I opened my eyes and rubbed my aching neck.

"What are you trying to do?" Corban asked.

"I can't tell you," I said. "I'm very sorry. But Blackwood can't know—and I'm not sure it worked." But I thought so. I never had been able to feel Stefan like I did Adam. If Blackwood hadn't managed to take me over . . . yet . . . that should mean Stefan could still hear me. I hoped.

I tried touching Adam, too. But I couldn't feel anything from him or the pack. It was probably just as well. Blackwood had said he was ready for werewolves, and I believed him.

Blackwood didn't come down. We all tried not to notice Amber, and I was grateful for the coolness of the basement. The ghosts didn't show up either. We talked about vampires until I'd told them everything I knew in general—only leaving out the names.

Stefan also did not come.

After hours of tedium and a few minutes of embarrassment when someone had to use the buckets left for us, I finally tried to sleep again. I dreamed of sheep. Lots of sheep.

SOMEWHERE IN THE MIDDLE OF THE NEXT DAY I REGRET-ted that I had not eaten the food Amber had prepared. But I was more thirsty than anything. The fairy staff showed up once, and I told it to go away and be safe, speaking softly so no one would notice. When I glanced back at the corner it had been in, it was gone again.

Chad taught me and the oakman how to swear in ASL and worked with us until we were pretty good at finger spelling. It left my hands aching, but kept him occupied.

We knew that Blackwood was paying attention to us again when Corban stopped in the middle of a sentence. After a few minutes he turned his head, and Blackwood opened the door.

The vampire looked at me without favor. "And where do you suppose I'm going to find another cook for you?" He took the body away and returned a few hours later with apples and oranges and bottled water—tossing them carelessly through the bars.

His hands smelled of Amber, rot, and earth. I supposed he'd buried her somewhere.

He took Corban away. When Chad's father returned, he was stumblingly weak and had another bite mark on his neck.

"My friend is better at that than you are," I said in a snotty voice because Blackwood had paused, with the cage door open, to look at Chad. "He doesn't leave huge bruises behind."

The vampire slammed the door, locked it, and stowed the key in his pants pocket. "Whenever you open your mouth," he said, "I marvel that the Marrok didn't wring your neck years ago." He smiled a little. "Fine. Since you are the cause of my hunger, you may feed it."

The cause of his hunger . . . when I sent Amber away from her dead body, it must have hurt him. Good. Now all I had to do was get him to make a lot more zombies or whatever he wanted to call them. Then I could destroy them, too. I might weaken him enough that we could take him. Of course, the nearest available people to become zombies were us.

He opened my cage door, and I had to think really hard about the present not to panic. I fought him. I didn't think he'd expected it.

Years of karate had honed my reflexes, and I was faster than a human would have been. But I was weak—an apple a day might keep the doctor away, but it's not, by itself, the best diet for optimum performance. After a time that was too short for my ego to be happy, he had me pinned.

He left me aware this time when he bit my neck. It hurt the whole time, either a further punishment or Stefan's bites were giving him trouble—I didn't know enough to tell. When he tried to feed me in return, I fought as hard as I could and finally he grabbed my jaw and forced his gaze on me.

I woke up on the far side of the cage, and Blackwood was gone. Chad was making noise, trying to get my attention. I rose to hands and knees. When it was quite clear that I wasn't going to get up farther than that, I sat up instead of standing. Chad stopped making those sad, desperate sounds. I made the sign he'd taught me for the "f-word" and finger-spelled, very slowly with clumsy fingers. "That's it. No more Ms. Nice Girl. Next time I scalp him."

It made him smile a very little. Corban was sitting in the middle of their cage looking at a mark in the cement.

"Well, oakman," I said, tiredly. "Is it daylight or darkness?"

Before he answered me, Stefan was there in my cage. I blinked stupidly at him. I'd given up on him, but I hadn't realized it until he was there. I reached out and touched his arm lightly to make sure he was real.

He patted my hand and gave a quick look up as if he could

see through the ceiling to the floor above. "He knows I'm here. Mercy—"

"You have to take Chad," I told him urgently

"Chad?" Stefan followed my gaze and stiffened. He started to shake his head.

"Blackwood killed his mother—but left her a zombie to do his chores until I killed her for real." I told him. "Chad has to be taken to safety."

He stared at the boy, who was staring back. "If I take him, I can't come back for a couple of nights. I'll be unconscious, and no one knows where you are but me—and Marsilia." He bit her name out as if he still weren't happy with her. "And she wouldn't lift a finger to help you."

"I can survive a couple of nights," I told him with conviction.

Stefan clenched his hands. "If I do it," he told me fiercely, "if I do this and you survive—you will forgive me for the others."

"Yes," I said. "Get Chad out of here."

He was gone, then reappeared standing next to Chad. He started to use ASL to say something—but we both heard Blackwood race down the stairs.

"To Adam or Samuel," I said urgently.

"Yes," Stefan told me. "Stay alive."

He waited until I nodded, then he disappeared with Chad.

———

BLACKWOOD WAS MUCH MORE UNHAPPY ABOUT STE-fan's presence in his house than he was with Chad's escape. He ranted and raved, and if he hit me again, I was worried I might not be able to keep my promise to Stefan.

Apparently he came to the same conclusion. He stood looking

down at me. "There are ways to keep other vampires out of my home. But they are taxing, and I expect that your friend Corban won't survive my thirst." He bent forward. "Ah, now you are frightened. Good." He inhaled like a wine taster with a particularly fine vintage.

He left.

I curled up on the floor and hugged my misery to me—along with the fairy staff. The oakman stirred.

"Mercy, what is it that you have?"

I raised one hand and waved it feebly in the air so he could see it. It didn't hurt as much as I thought it should.

There was a little pause, and the Oakman said, reverently, "How did that come to be here?"

"It's not my fault," I told him. It took me a moment to sit up . . . and I realized that Blackwood had been much more in control of himself than he appeared because nothing was broken. There wasn't much of me that wasn't bruised—but not broken was good.

"What do you mean?" the oakman asked.

"I tried to give it back," I explained, "but it keeps showing up. I told it that this wasn't a good place for it, but it leaves for a while, then comes back."

"By your leave," he said formally, "may I see it?"

"Sure," I said, and tried to throw it to him. I should have been able to do it. The distance between our cages was less than ten feet, but the . . . bruises made it more difficult than normal.

It landed on the floor halfway between us. But as I stared at it in dismay, it rolled back toward me, not stopping until it was against the cage bars.

The third time I threw it, the oakman caught it out of the air.

"Ah, Lugh, you did such fine work," he crooned, petting the

thing. He rested a cheek against it. "It follows you because it owes you service, Mercy." He smiled, awakening lines and wrinkles in the dark-wood-colored face and brightening his black eyes to purple. "And because it likes you."

I started to say something to him, but a surge of magic interrupted me.

The oakman's smile drained away. "Brownie magic," he told me. "He seeks to lock the other vampire out. The brownie was His before me, and she found her release just this past spring. His use of her power is still nearly complete." He looked over at Corban. "The magic he works *will* leave him hungry."

I had one thing I could do—and it meant abandoning my word to Stefan. But I couldn't let Blackwood kill Corban without making any attempt to defend him.

I stripped out of my clothes and *shifted*. The bars in my cage were set close together. But, I hoped, not too close.

Coyotes are narrow side to side. Very narrow. Anything I can get my head through, I can get everything else through, too. When I stood on the other side of my cage, I shook my fur straight and watched the door open.

Blackwood wasn't watching for me, he was looking at Corban. So I got in the first strike.

Speed is the one physical power I have. I'm as fast as most werewolves—and from what I've seen, most vampires, too.

I should have been weakened and a little slow because of the damage Blackwood had dealt me—and the lack of real food and because I'd been feeding the vampire. Except that exchanging blood with a vampire can have other effects. I'd forgotten that. It made me strong.

I wished, fiercely, that I weighed a couple of hundred pounds instead of just over thirty. Wished for longer fangs and sharper claws—because all I could do was surface damage he healed almost as soon as I inflicted it.

He grabbed me in both hands and threw me at the cement wall. It seemed as though I flew in slow motion. There was time to twist and hit on my feet instead of my side as he'd intended. There was power to vault off unhurt and hit the ground, already running back to attack.

This time, though, I didn't have surprise on my side. If I'd been running from him, he couldn't have caught me. But up close, the advantage of superior speed lost out to the disadvantage of my size. I hurt him once, digging my fangs into his shoulder, but I was looking for a kill—and there was just no way a coyote, no matter how fast or strong, could kill a vampire.

I dodged back, looking for an opening . . . and he fell face-first on the cement floor. Standing like a victory flag, stuck deep into Blackwood's back, was the walking stick.

"Fair spearman was I once," the oakman said. "And Lugh was better still. Nothing he built but what couldn't become a spear when needed."

Panting, I stared at him, then down at Blackwood. Who wiggled.

I shifted back to human because I could deal with doors better that way. Then I ran for the kitchen where, hopefully, there would be a knife big enough to go through bone.

The wooden block beside the sink yielded both a butcher knife and a large French chef's knife. I grabbed one in each hand and ran down the stairs.

The door was shut and the knob wouldn't turn. "Let me in," I ordered in a voice I hardly recognized as mine.

"No. No," said John's voice. "You can't kill him. I'll be *alone*."

But the door opened, and that was all I cared about.

I didn't see John, but Catherine was kneeling beside Blackwood. She spared a glare for me, but she was paying more attention to the dying (I fervently hoped) vampire.

"Let me drink, dear," she crooned to him. "Let me drink, and I'll take care of her for you."

He looked at me as he tried to get his arms underneath him. "Drink," he said. Then he smiled at me.

With a crow of triumph she bent her head.

She was still drinking when the butcher knife swooshed through her insubstantial head and cut cleanly through Blackwood's neck. An axe would have been better, but with his strength still lingering in my arms, the butcher knife got the job done. A second cut took his head completely off.

His head touched my toes, and I edged them away. A knife in either hand, I had no chance to feel triumphant or sick at what I'd done. Not with a very solid Catherine smiling her grandmotherly smile only six feet from me.

She smiled, her mouth red with Blackwood's blood. "Die," she said, and reached out—

Last year Sensei spent six months on sai forms. The knives weren't so well-balanced for fighting, but they worked. It was a butcher's job I made of it—and I managed it only by clinging fiercely to the here and now. The floors, the walls, and I were all drenched in blood. And she wasn't dead . . . or rather she was dead already. The knives kept her off me, but none of the wounds seemed to affect her at all.

"Throw me the stick," said the oakman softly.

I dropped the French chef's knife and grabbed the staff with my free hand. It slid out of Blackwood's back as if it didn't want to be there. For a moment I thought that the end was a sharp point, but my attention was focused on Catherine and I couldn't be sure.

I tossed it to the Oakman and drove Catherine away from Corban's cage. He'd collapsed when I'd cut off Blackwood's head in a motion not unlike Amber's zombie. I hoped he wasn't dead—but there wasn't anything I could do about it if he was.

Out of the corner of my eye, I saw the oakman lick the blood-covered stick with a tongue at least eight inches long. "Death blood is best," he told me. And then he flung the stick at the outside wall, and said a word . . .

The blast knocked me off my feet and onto Blackwood's corpse. Something hit me in the back of the head.

I STARED AT THE POOL OF SUNLIGHT THAT COVERED MY hand. It took me a moment to realize that whatever had hit me must have knocked me out. Under my hand was a thick pile of ash, and I jerked away. Buried in the ash was a key. It was a pretty key, one of those ornate skeleton keys. It took all my willpower to put my hand back into what had been Blackwood and pick it up. I hurt from head to heels, but the bruises the vampire had inflicted after Chad escaped were mostly gone. And the others were fading as I watched.

I didn't want to think about that too much.

The oakman had a hand stretched though the bars, but he hadn't been able to touch the sunlight streaming into the basement from the hole he'd blasted in the wall with my walking stick. His eyes were closed.

I opened the cage, but he didn't move. I had to drag him out. I didn't pay attention to whether or not he was breathing. Or I tried very hard not to. So what if he wasn't, I thought. Fae are very hard to kill.

"Mercy?" It was Corban.

I stared at him a moment, trying to figure out what to do next.

"Could you unlock my door?" His voice was soft and gentle. The sort of voice you'd use on a madwoman.

I looked down at myself and realized that I was naked and covered with blood from head to toe. The butcher knife was still in my left hand. My hand had cramped around it, and I had to work to drop it on the floor.

The key unlocked Corban's door, too.

"Chad's with some friends of mine," I told him. My voice slurred a bit, and I recognized that I was a little shocky. The realization helped me a little, and my voice was clearer when I told him, "The kinds of friends who might be able to protect a boy from a vampire run amok."

"Thank you," he said. "You were unconscious a long time. How are you feeling?"

I gave him a tired smile. "My head hurts."

"Let's get you cleaned up."

He led me up the stairs. I didn't think that I should have grabbed my clothes until I stood alone in a huge, gold-and-black bathroom. I turned the shower on.

"John," I said. I didn't bother looking for him because I could feel him. "You will never harm anyone again." I felt the push of magic that told me whatever it was I could do to ghosts had worked on him. So I added, "And get out of this bathroom," for good measure.

I scrubbed myself raw and wrapped myself in a towel big enough for three of me. When I came out, Corban was pacing in the hall in front of the bathroom.

"Who do you call about something like this?" he asked. "It doesn't look good. Blackwood is missing; Amber is dead—probably buried in the backyard. I'm a lawyer, and if I were my own client, I'd advise myself to avoid trial, plead guilty, and do reduced time if I could get it."

He was scared.

It finally occurred to me that we'd survived. Blackwood and his sweet grandmotherly vampire ghost were gone. Or at least I hoped she was gone. There wasn't a second pile of ashes in the basement.

"Did you notice the other vampire?" I asked him.

He gave me a blank look. "Other vampire?"

"Never mind," I told him. "I expect the sunlight killed her."

I got up and found a phone on a small table in the corner of the living room. I dialed Adam's cell phone.

"Hey," I said. It sounded like I'd been smoking cigars all night.

"Mercy?" And I knew I was safe.

I sat on the floor. "Hey." I said again.

"Chad told us where you are," he told me. "We're about twenty minutes away."

"Chad told you?" Stefan would still be unconscious, I'd known. It just hadn't occurred to me that Chad could tell them where we were. Stupid me. All he'd have needed was a piece of paper.

"Chad's all right?" asked Corban urgently.

"Fine," I told him. "And he's leading the cavalry here."

"It sounds like we're not needed," said Adam.

I needed him.

"Blackwood is dead," I told Adam.

"I thought so, since you are calling me," Adam said.

"If it weren't for the oakman, it might have been bad," I told him. "And I think the oakman is dead."

"All honor to him, then," said Samuel's voice. "To die killing one of the dark-bound evils is not a bad thing, Mercy. Chad asks after his father."

I wiped my face and gathered my thoughts. "Tell Chad he's fine. We're both fine." I watched bruises fade from my legs. "Could you . . . could you stop at a convenience store and buy a yellow toy car for me? Bring it with you when you come?"

There was a little pause. "A yellow toy car?" asked Adam.

"That's right." I remembered something else. "Adam, Corban's worried that the police will think he's killed Amber—and probably Blackwood, though there won't be any body."

"Trust me," said Adam. "We'll fix it for everyone."

"All right," I told him. "Thank you." And then I thought a little more. "The vampires will want Chad and Corban gone. They know too much."

"You and Stefan and the pack are the only ones who know that," said Adam. "The pack doesn't care, and Stefan won't betray them."

"Hey," I told him lightly—pressing the handset into my face until it almost hurt. "I love you."

"I'll be there."

―――――――

I LEFT CORBAN SITTING IN THE LIVING ROOM AND WALKED reluctantly down the stairs. I didn't want to know for sure that the oakman was dead. I didn't want to confront Catherine if she was still about . . . and I thought she would have killed me if she could have. But I also didn't want to be naked when Adam came.

The oakman was gone. I decided that it must be a good thing. The fae didn't—as far as I knew—turn into dust and blow away when they died. So if he wasn't here, that meant he'd left.

"Thank you," I whispered because he wasn't there to hear me. Then I put my clothes on and ran up the stairs to wait for rescue with Corban.

When Adam came, he had the yellow car I'd asked him for. It was a one-sixteenth scale model of a VW bug. He watched as I took it out of the package and followed me down the stairs and set it on the bed in the small room where I'd first woken up.

"It's for you," I said.

No one answered me.

"Are you going to tell me what that was about?" Adam asked as we went back upstairs.

"Sometime," I told him. "When we're telling ghost stories around a campfire, and I want to scare you."

He smiled, and his arm tightened around my shoulders. "Let's go home."

I closed my hand on the lamb necklace I'd found on the table next to the phone, as if someone had left it for me to find.

13

~~~

THE FOLLOWING SATURDAY, WE PAINTED THE GARAGE.
True to his word, Wulfe had removed the crossed bones. The least
he could have done was repaint the door, but he'd managed to remove the bones and leave the graffiti that had covered them alone.
I thought he'd done it just to bug me.

Gabriel's sisters had voted for pink as the new color and were
very disappointed when I insisted on white. So I told them they
could paint the door pink.

It's a garage. What can it hurt?

"It's a garage," I told Adam, who was looking at the Day-Glo
pink door. "What can it hurt?"

He laughed and shook his head. "It makes me squint, even in
the dark, Mercy. Hey, I know what I can get you for your next

birthday," he said. "A set of open-end wrenches in pink or purple. Leopard print, maybe."

"You have me confused with my mother," I said with dignity. "The door was painted with cheap spray paint—as no reputable paint company had anything this gaudy in their color palette. Give it a couple weeks, and it'll turn this sickly orangish pink color. Then I can hire them to paint it brown or green."

"Police have searched Blackwood's house," Adam told me. "They haven't found any sign of Blackwood or Amber. Officially, they believe Amber might have run off with Blackwood." He sighed. "I know that it tarnishes Amber unfairly, but it was the best story we could come up with and still leave her husband in the clear."

"The people who matter know," I told him. Amber didn't have any immediate family she cared for. In a few months, I was tentatively planning a trip to Mesa, Arizona, where Char was living. I'd tell her, because Char was the only other person Amber would care about. "No one is going to get into trouble about this, are they?"

"The people who matter know," he answered with a faint smile. "Unofficially, Blackwood scared the bejeebers out of a lot of people who are glad to see him gone. No one will take it further."

"Good." I touched the bright white wall next to the door. It looked better. I hoped that it wouldn't scare away customers. People are funny. My customers look at my run-down-appearing garage and know they are saving the money I don't put into face-lifts.

Tim's cousin Courtney had paid for all of the paint and labor in return for my dropping the charges against her. I figured she had been hurt enough.

"I heard you and Zee worked out something on the garage."

I nodded. "I have to repay him immediately—he said so, and he is fae so it must be done. He's going to loan me the money to do it at the same interest rate as the original loan."

He grinned and opened the pink door so I could precede him inside. "So you're paying him the same amount as before?"

"Uncle Mike came up with it, and it made Zee happy." Amused him was more like it. All the fae have a strange sense of humor.

Stefan was sitting on my stool by the cash register. He'd spent two nights unmoving in Adam's basement, then disappeared without a word to either Adam or me.

"Hey, Stefan," I said.

"I came to tell you that we no longer share a bond," he told me stiffly. "Blackwood broke it."

"When?" I asked. "He didn't have time. You answered my call— and it wasn't very long after that when Blackwood died."

"I imagine when he fed from you again," Stefan said. "Because when Adam called me to tell me you'd disappeared, I couldn't find you at all."

"Then how did you manage to find me?" I asked.

"Marsilia."

I looked at his face, but I couldn't read how much it had cost him to ask for her help. Or what she'd demanded in return.

"You didn't tell me," Adam said. "I'd have gone with you."

The vampire smiled grimly. "Then she would have told me nothing."

"She knew where Blackwood denned?" Adam asked.

"That's what I hoped." Stefan picked up a pen and played with it. I must have used it last because his fingers acquired a little black grease for his trouble. "But no. What she did know was that Mercy had a message for me with a blood-and-wax seal. Her blood. She could track the message. Since it was just outside of Spokane, we were both pretty sure Mercy still had it with her."

That reminded me. I pulled the battered missive out of my back pocket. It hadn't gone through the wash with my jeans—but only because Samuel had a habit of checking pockets before he did laundry. Something about nuts and bolts in the dryer being irritatingly noisy— I thought that was directed at me, but I could have been paranoid.

Stefan took the letter like I was handing him a bottle of nitro-glycerine. He opened it and read. When he was through, he balled it up in a fist and stared at the counter.

"She says," he told us in a low, controlled voice, "that my people are safe. She and Wulfe took them and convinced me that they had died—so I would believe it. It was necessary that I believe they were dead, that Marsilia no longer wanted me in the seethe. She has them safe." He paused. "She wants me to come home."

"What are you going to do?" Adam asked.

I was pretty sure I knew. But I hoped that he made her work like hell for it. She might not have killed his people, but she'd hurt them—Stefan had felt it.

"I'm going to take the matter under advisement," he said. But he straightened out the note and read it again.

"Hey, Stefan," I said.

He looked up.

"You're pretty terrific, you know? I appreciate all the chances you took for me."

He smiled, folded the letter carefully. "Yeah, well you're pretty terrific yourself. If you ever want to be dinner again sometime . . ." He popped out of the office without saying good-bye.

"Better collect your purse," said Adam. "We don't want to be late."

Adam was taking me to Richland, where the local light opera company was performing *The Pirates of Penzance*. Gilbert and Sullivan, pirates and no vampires, he'd promised me.

It was a great production. I laughed until I was hoarse and came out humming the final number. "Yes," I told him. "I think the guy playing the Pirate King was awesome."

He stopped where he was.

"What?" I asked, frowning at the big smile on his face.

"I didn't say I liked the Pirate King," he told me.

"Oh." I closed my eyes—and there he was. A warm, edgy presence right on the edge of my perception. When I opened my eyes, he was standing right in front of me. "Cool," I told him. "You're back."

He kissed me leisurely. When he was finished, I was more than ready to head home. Fast.

"You make me laugh," he told me seriously.

I WENT BACK TO MY HOUSE TO SLEEP. SAMUEL WAS working until the early-morning hours, and I wanted to be there when he got home.

I stopped before I went in because something was different. I took a deep breath but didn't smell any vampires lurking at my door. But there was an oak tree next to my bedroom window.

It hadn't been there when I'd left this morning to go paint. But there it was, with a trunk nearly two inches around and branches that were a couple of feet taller than my trailer. There was no sign of freshly turned earth, just the tree. Its leaves were starting to change color for the autumn.

"You're welcome," I said. When I started back to go into the house, I tripped over the walking stick. "Hey. You're back."

I set it on my bed while I showered, and it was still there when I got out. I put on one of Adam's flannel shirts because the fall nights were pretty nippy and my roommate didn't want to turn up the heat. And because it smelled like Adam.

When the doorbell rang, I pulled on a pair of shorts and left the stick where it was.

Marsilia stood on the porch. She was wearing low-rise jeans and a low-cut black sweater.

"My letter was opened tonight," she told me.

I folded my arms over my chest and did not invite her in. "That's right, I gave it to Stefan."

She tapped a foot. "Did he read it?"

"You didn't actually kill his people," I told her in a bored voice. "You just hurt them and ripped his ties from them so he'd think they died."

"You disapprove?" She raised an eyebrow. "Any other Master would have killed them—it would have been easier. If he had been himself, he'd have known what we'd done." She smiled at me. "Oh, I see. You were worried about his sheep. Better hurt a little and alive—wouldn't you say?"

"Why are you here?" I asked her.

Her face went blank, and I thought she might not answer. "Because the letter was read, and Stefan did not come."

"You tortured him," I said hotly. "You almost forced him to do something he'd never willingly do—"

"I wish he'd killed you," she told me sincerely. "Except that would have hurt him. I know Stefan. I know his control. You were never in any danger."

"He doesn't believe that," I told her. "Now you throw him a bone. 'Look, Stefan, we didn't really kill your people. We tortured you, hurt you, abandoned you—but it was all in a good cause. We meant Andre to die, and let you twist in guilt for months because it served our purpose.' And you wonder why he didn't come back to you."

"He understands," she said.

"I do." Stefan's hands came down upon my shoulders, and he pulled me a few inches back from the threshold of the door. "I understand the why and the how."

She stared at him . . . and for a moment I could see how old, how tired she was. "For the good of the seethe," she told him.

He put his chin on the top of my head. "I know." He wrapped both arms around me just above my chest and pulled me against him. "I'll come back. But not right now." He sighed into my hair. "Tomorrow. I'll get my people from you then." And he was gone.

Marsilia looked at me. "He's a soldier," she told me. "He knows about sacrificing himself for the good of the whole. That's what soldiers do. It's not the torture he can't forgive me for. Nor deceiving him about his people. It's because I put you in harm's way he is so angry." Then she said, very calmly, "If I could kill you, I would."

And she disappeared, just like Stefan had.

"Right back atcha," I told the space where she had been.

We Treasure Your Comments!

Rate 1-10	Comments
10	Auesame!! 4th book in series. Keeps together very well. Fun, exciting and enthralling. Cant wait to Read whats next. Kelly L Roch NY.
10	Very Good. Love this series. But I Read them too fast!! Hopefully She will continue this series for a while! Rachael P.
10	Very Good Read!. Dawen W.
10+	I like her wrighting SO much I Started the seiries SO I had all backgroun